# REBECCA DEAN

# The Golden Prince

HARPER

*Harper*
An imprint of HarperCollins*Publishers*
77–85 Fulham Palace Road,
Hammersmith, London W6 8JB

www.harpercollins.co.uk

A Paperback Original 2010
1

A catalogue record for this book
is available from the British Library

ISBN: 978 0 00 731572 7

Set in Sabon by Palimpsest Book Production Limited,
Falkirk, Stirlingshire

Printed and bound in Great Britain by Clays Ltd, St Ives plc

**Mixed Sources**
Product group from well-managed
forests and other controlled sources
www.fsc.org  Cert no. SW-COC-001806
© 1996 Forest Stewardship Council

FSC is a non-profit international organisation established
to promote the responsible management of the world's forests.
Products carrying the FSC label are independently certified
to assure consumers that they come from forests that are managed
to meet the social, economic and ecological needs
of present and future generations.

Find out more about HarperCollins and the environment at
**www.harpercollins.co.uk/green**

*This book is dedicated with love to my grandson,*
*Jacob George Grumbridge*

Thanks are due to Claire Bord, my editor when I first began writing *The Golden Prince*, and to Sarah Ritherdon who has been my editor for the greater part of the way and who has been enormously helpful and supportive. Thanks are also due to the rest of the team at HarperCollins, in particular to Victoria Hughes-Williams and to my two copy editors, Clare Parkinson and Richenda Todd. My agent, Sheila Crowley, has been constantly encouraging and I am deeply grateful for her pep talks and friendship. Of many excellent biographies of Edward, Frances Donaldson's *Edward VIII* and Philip Ziegler's *King Edward VIII* were of most help in illuminating the character of Edward when a young man, as was Edward's autobiography, *A King's Story*.

# ONE

**May 1911**

A slightly built, blond young man stood beneath Dartmouth Naval College's flamboyantly splendid portico. With his hands deep in his pockets he stared glumly across a broad terrace to where twin flights of steps led down to manicured gardens and beyond the gardens to a steeply sloping, tree-studded hillside.

At the foot of the hill lay the river Dart, thick with college boats of all shapes and sizes. More than anything in the world he wished that, like many of the other cadets in his group, he were aboard one of them. Although he hated the academic side of his training, he loved being out of doors and active. Spending time aboard a sailing cutter, with the wind of the estuary blowing against his face, was the only thing that made life at Dartmouth bearable.

His cadet captain strolled from the shaded recesses of the grand entrance hall and drew to a halt alongside him. 'Off on a weekend's leave?' he asked affably.

David nodded, making an effort to look happier about it than he felt.

His captain hesitated slightly, as if about to say more.

Then, thinking better of it, he merely nodded and, with one hand hooked in the pocket of his naval uniform, he strolled on his way.

David watched him, his eyes bleak. He knew very well that his captain had been about to offer his usual goodbye to cadets going home on leave: 'Give my best to your parents.' Given David's unique circumstances, this would have been an utterly inappropriate familiarity.

Besides, he simply had too many names. Seven, to be exact. Edward, after both his grandfather and an uncle who had died as a young man. Albert, after his great-grandfather. Christian, after one of his godfathers. George after his father, or was it because George was the patron saint of England? He wasn't quite sure. Certainly Andrew was after the patron saint of Scotland, Patrick after the patron saint of Ireland and David after the patron saint of Wales. With that little lot to choose from it was no wonder people paused before addressing him.

Within his family circle he was known as David, and David was how he always thought of himself. If he'd had any close friends, it was the name he would have liked them to use – only he didn't have any close friends.

'It wouldn't be wise,' his father had said grimly, hands clasped behind his back, legs astride. 'Not in your position. That's why you're at Dartmouth and not Eton or Harrow. When you leave Dartmouth your former classmates will be pursuing careers at sea and you will rarely, if ever, see them. That wouldn't be the case at Eton or Harrow. Any friend-ships formed there would run the danger of continuing after your education and would become a burden to you. You don't want that, David, do you?'

'No, sir,' he'd replied dutifully, thinking there was nothing he'd like better than to have a couple of lifelong friends.

As if he had read his thoughts, his father's protuberant blue eyes had narrowed.

'If that is all, sir . . .?' David had said, eager to be free now that the familiar knot of fear was forming in the pit of his stomach; eager to be on the other side of the library door once again.

Beneath his trim beard and waxed moustache his father's mouth had tightened, but the expected explosion of temper hadn't come. He had merely made a sound in his throat that could have meant anything and given a curt nod of dismissal.

As his cadet captain disappeared from view, David gave a heavy sigh, knowing all too well that in a few hours' time there would be a similar interview at the castle and that this time his father's ferocious temper might very well not be held in check.

He stepped from beneath the portico and began walking along the terrace fronting the college. Weekends at home were definitely not weekends he looked forward to, but they did have one redeeming feature. They enabled him to prac- tise his driving. Slightly cheered, he rounded the building and strolled across the broad gravelled drive to his Austro- Daimler.

As expected, Captain Piers Cullen was seated behind the wheel.

'No, Captain Cullen,' he said pleasantly. 'I'm doing the driving, at least until we're in sight of Windsor. Crank-start her up for me, there's a good chap.'

Reluctantly, Piers Cullen stepped out of the open-topped car and, with even deeper reluctance, began cranking the engine.

David put on motoring goggles and a pair of driving gauntlets. The car had been a birthday present from his German first cousin once removed, Willy, and was the best present he could ever remember receiving. It had, of course, annoyed his father, who believed it had been chosen purely for that purpose. 'Damn Willy's impudent cheek!' he had said

3

explosively. 'He's only sent it because the model is named Prinz Heinrich!'

David hadn't cared that the car had been named after Willy's younger brother. It went faster than he'd ever hoped a car could go and though his father had been led to believe that on public roads Captain Cullen acted as his chauffeur, in reality David drove it at every opportunity he got.

As he drove out of Dartmouth and into the rolling green countryside he saw with pleasure that Devon was looking its best. Even though it was nearly the end of May primroses still massed on the grassy verges of the country lanes and bluebells carpeted the floor of every wooded valley they passed.

He neared the market town of Totnes, wondering just what the weekend ahead held. His father would probably want to engage in what was commonly referred to as a 'small shoot' and, as far as exercise was concerned, that would be it. For someone like David, whose sense of well-being depended on a lot of physical activity, it wasn't going to be enough.

He thought again of the inevitable interview in the library and grimaced. His marks during the year had been nowhere near what his father expected of him, though God knows he had tried hard enough and had even come top out of fifty-nine in German and English. In history he had come second and in French third. It was maths – any form of maths – that let him down. 'Forty-eighth in geometry and forty-fifth in trigonometry?' he could just hear his father bellowing. 'Forty-*eighth* and forty-*fifth*?'

'Steady on the speed, sir,' Piers warned when they were out in open country again. 'That last corner was taken very wide . . .'

David made a non-committal sound not very different from the one his father often made. Cullen was a humourless killjoy and having him alongside for a two-hundred-mile journey was tiresome, if unavoidable.

His low spirits fell further as they crossed the county border into Dorset. His younger brother, Bertie, wouldn't be home as Bertie's leave from Dartmouth came much nearer the end of term. As Harry, Georgie and John were too young to count, this meant there would only be his fourteen-year-old sister Mary for company and finding something fun they could do together wouldn't be easy. Though his younger brothers' nursery could be raided for board games, his father always insisted such games be played with no uproarious laughter, which, to David, defeated their point; and they wouldn't be able to play cards, because there wouldn't be a pack to be found.

As Dorset merged into the airy uplands of Hampshire the loneliness he always fought to keep at bay swept over him with such force he could hardly breathe. He had no one he could truly call a friend. Piers Cullen was a dour Scotsman whose companionship he wouldn't voluntarily seek. As far as Dartmouth was concerned, his father had never had to worry about friendships, for the boys he would have liked to make friends with kept their distance and the others toadied up to him – and he hated toadies.

He was so deep in thought he didn't see the blind bend ahead until it was too late for him to slow down. As Piers Cullen gave a shout of alarm, he took it far too wide and far too fast.

Too late he saw what was in front of him. Too late he saw that short of a miracle, there was going to be an accident of tragic proportions.

He slammed his foot on the brake. Slewed the wheel to the left. Then, with a girl's screams, Cullen's desperate *'Jesus God!'* and horrendous barking ringing in his ears, he plummeted into a future beyond all his imaginings.

# TWO

Wearing a straw boater with a scarlet ribbon around its shallow crown, a high-necked white blouse and an ankle-length navy skirt, Rose Houghton ran down the last few steps of the sturdy oak staircase and headed in the direction of Snowberry's kitchen.

Built as an extension to the main building, the kitchen incorporated sixteenth-century posts and beams from the timber-framed house that had originally stood on the site. It was a gigantic room lit by long bands of windows and the marble-topped pastry table where Millie, Snowberry's cook, was busy rolling dough was at the very far end of it.

Rose was accustomed to walking long distances at Snowberry, and to having dogs at her heels. As her high-button boots rang out on the stone-flagged floor a chocolate-brown Labrador sprang up from where he had been lying beneath the table and bounded to greet her.

'Yes, I'm going into the village, Homer, and yes, you can come with me.' She fondled his ears, saying to Millie, 'Has Grandpa told you that when he comes back from the dentist he's bringing Lord Jethney with him? That means meringues for pudding tonight. Perhaps you could top them with stewed apples and cream like last time?'

'Perhaps I could, and perhaps I couldn't,' Millie said, not troubling to look up from what she was doing. 'And if you're taking that silly dog out from under my feet, take Fizz and Florin as well. This is a kitchen, not a kennels.'

The cocker spaniels in question were already at Rose's feet, tails wagging in eager anticipation.

'The reason the dogs are always in here is because you're always giving them titbits.'

She spoke with loving affection. Millie had been at Snowberry since before Rose was born, having entered Lord May's service when his only child, Rose's father, had married. She had baked Rose's christening cake and the christening cakes for all three of Rose's younger sisters. She had prepared the funeral meats when Rose's father had died at the shockingly young age of thirty-six and two years later, on Rose's mother's remarriage to a French nobleman, she had baked the wedding cake.

'Though I wouldn't have done,' she'd often said afterwards, 'not if I'd known she was going to leave the children behind her when she went off to live in France.'

She was the only person indignant at the arrangement. Lord May had been delighted that his four granddaughters were to remain beneath his roof. Nine-year-old Rose, seven-year-old Iris and five-year-old Marigold hadn't had the slightest desire to leave Snowberry – not once it had been explained to them that their army of much-loved pets wouldn't be allowed to accompany them if they did so. As for three-year-old Lily: she'd been too young to have any opinion.

None of them had missed their mother as much as Millie had thought they would – or should. Their day-to-day care had always been in the hands of nannies and nursery maids and when their father died their mother had sought comfort by plunging into a hectic London social life. From then on she became only a visitor to Snowberry. That she now lived in Paris, instead of London, made very little difference to her daughters, who thought of her more as a much-loved aunt than a mother.

With the dogs close behind her Rose left Millie to her pastry-making and walked out of the kitchen and out of the house. From the distant tennis court she could hear Marigold shouting, 'The ball was *out*, Lily. You can't continue being umpire if you don't umpire properly!'

What Lily's response was, she couldn't hear. Nor could she hear if Iris was also protesting. One thing, however, was certain. No matter how much fuss Marigold and Iris made, Lily would remain sweet-tempered.

Fizz and Florin, easily diverted, raced off to see what the fuss was about. Rose walked around the corner of the house to the stables where, as well as three horses and a pony, bicycles and (when not in use) her grandfather's stately Talbot motor car were kept.

She had two letters to post for her grandfather, letters that she had written for him earlier that morning.

'Because of my failing eyesight you're going to have to deal with all my correspondence, Rose,' he had said to her when she had returned to Snowberry after three years at St Hilda's, Oxford. 'Also, as I can no longer do as much as I used to, I'm going to need your help in managing the estate.'

It had been a bolt from the blue. One she had been totally unprepared for.

While at St Hilda's she had joined the Women's Social and Political Union, putting her organizational skills to very good use. Now what she wanted most in the world was to live an independent life in London, forge a career for herself and, until that aim was achieved, meet regularly with her suffragette friends and work alongside Mrs Emmeline Pankhurst and her daughter, Christabel at the WSPU head office.

8

That she wasn't going to be able to was a fierce disappointment. It was one she had overcome. She loved her grandfather far too much to ever let him down.

As she wheeled the bicycle out of the stables she reflected how supportive he had been when she had said she wanted to try for a place at St Hilda's. For a man born the year before Victoria became queen, he was wonderfully progressive in his thinking when it came to the education of women.

It had been her ultra-chic, elegant and soignée mother who had still been living in the dark ages.

'Oxford? *Absolument impossible!*' she had said in near hysterics, so appalled that she had forgotten for a moment she was on a visit to England and wasn't at home in France. 'Oxford is for plain middle-class girls who have no hope of marrying well!'

Rose had been torn between exasperation and amusement. 'Actually, Mama, Oxford is for anyone who has brains and wants to use them.'

Her mother had thrown up her hands in an extravagant gesture of despair, thankful that her other daughters showed no signs of becoming bluestockings and that her two French stepdaughters were far easier to understand.

Wryly amused at how constantly and inadvertently she disappointed her mother, Rose cycled down Snowberry's long driveway and, with Homer gamely keeping up with her, sped out on to the country road that lay beyond its high wrought-iron gates. As a child she had looked striking – her sea-green eyes and thickly waving auburn hair had seen to that – but she had never been chocolate-box pretty. And chocolate-box prettiness was what her mother had expected in a daughter. She had also expected her to be demure and captivatingly shy.

On both counts Rose had failed abysmally.

It had been the final straw for her mother that as a young woman she had preferred to spend three years at St Hilda's

9

rather than as a sensational adornment of London and Parisian high society. In her most recent letter her mother had written:

Though at least I have the satisfaction of knowing you will be in London and attending all the celebratory parties and balls when King George is crowned, as will Iris and Marigold. It's such a pity that Lily hasn't yet been presented at court and so isn't eligible for invitations. As for your grandfather, as he so rarely takes his seat in the House of Lords, it's a miracle the Earl Marshal even remembered to add him to the abbey guest list. I'd give trillions to have been invited as well, but not a chance now I'm married to a French marquess. C'est une grande pitié.

The stone wall that ran along the side of the narrow road, marking the limit of the Snowberry estate, had given way to a thick hedge of hawthorn and beech rife with wild honeysuckle. Ahead of her was a blind bend and Rose could hear the sound of a motor car approaching it from the opposite direction.

'On to the verge, Homer!' she shouted. Keeping him safely to the inside of the bicycle she swerved as near to the verge as possible in order to be well out of the way of whatever was coming.

No amount of swerving would have been enough.

The car careered round the bend, taking it so wide she thought it was going to hit her head-on.

She wrenched the handlebars violently to the left, screaming at Homer to get out of the way.

In equal horror the driver of the car spun his wheel, slewing across the road away from her, clipping her back wheel as he did so.

The result was catastrophic.

As the bicycle went into a spin she was thrown with great force over its handlebars. For a split second she was aware of the screech of tyres and of demented barking. Then she hit the ground, slamming into a ditch beneath the hedgerow.

The impact was so savage every atom of breath was knocked from her body. Pain seared through her and she fought against being sucked into a whirling black vortex, terrified that if she lost consciousness, she might never regain it.

As she lost the battle the last thing she was aware of was someone running towards her, and a voice hoarse with fear shouting, '*Oh, God! Oh, Christ, Cullen! I think she's dead!*'

# THREE

'We need a doctor. If you stay with her, sir, I'll drive for help.'

The voice was different to the first one. Terse and authoritative and with a definite Scottish burr.

Rose tried to get her brain to function. If there was talk only now of a doctor and an ambulance then she must have been just fleetingly unconscious. Which must mean that she wasn't critically hurt.

Somewhere near to her Homer was whining piteously. He needed reassuring that she was all right, but she hadn't, as yet, reassured herself. She tried to open her eyes but her eyelids wouldn't obey the commands she was sending them. Coarse grass was prickling her cheek. She could smell foxgloves and hedge-parsley.

'But what if she dies while I'm on my own with her?' There was a half-sob in the voice of the person she could sense was down on one knee at her side, but whether his distress was on her account, or his own, she couldn't tell. Nor, because she was so angry, did she very much care.

Gingerly she flexed her legs, discovering with relief that neither of them was broken.

'Don't go just yet, Cullen!' Though the now familiar voice was still unsteady, there was vast relief in it. 'She's moving!'

Rose's eyelids obeyed the command she had been giving them for so long. They fluttered open and the first thing she saw was dry mud and, beyond it, tangled weeds.

That she had landed in a ditch increased her anger to boiling point. She struggled into a sitting position and then, in a manner very different to the tearful one her anxious audience had been expecting, said furiously to the tight-lipped man in army uniform who was looking down at her, 'Just what the *hell* did you think you were doing driving so fast around a blind bend? You could have killed Homer! You could have killed me!'

Outrage at being spoken to in such a way – and especially by a woman – flared through his eyes. 'Are you all right?' he demanded curtly. 'No broken bones?'

His manner showed he no longer felt he was addressing a well-brought-up young lady. Rose didn't care. She wasn't in the habit of swearing like a stable boy, but there were times when she thought it a perfectly reasonable reaction and this was one of them.

The young man who had been kneeling white-faced beside her helped her to her feet, saying apologetically, 'Actually, I was the one who was driving . . .'

Rose wasn't listening. She was too busy making a fuss of Homer and too conscious of how dishevelled she looked. Her straw boater was nowhere in sight. Her hair was coming loose from its pins. There was mud on her high-throated, lace-trimmed blouse – and possibly on her face as well – and there were grass stains on her skirt.

She had never been so angry in her life.

'I'm so sorry,' the fey-looking young man said again. 'All my fault. I'm afraid your bicycle is unridable. I'll pay for the repairs of course . . .'

Rose steadied her breathing, removed a stem of hedge-parsley from her hair and glared at him. He seemed to be no older than Lily and with his golden hair and fiercely blue eyes would have looked more at home in a choirboy's surplice than in what appeared to be a naval uniform. Also, though she was certain she'd never previously met him, he looked oddly familiar,

'Are you telling me that *you* were driving?' she said as witheringly as she would have done to a younger brother.

He flushed. 'Yes, I'm afraid I was and—'

'Then in taking that corner as you did, you behaved very, very stupidly.'

The older man sucked in his breath. 'This has gone quite far enough! You simply cannot speak in such a way to—'

'I can speak common sense to anyone I please.' Rose, now fully recovered from her shock, brushed a stray fallen leaf from her skirt and eyed him coolly. It was men like him who were refusing to give women the vote and keeping them subservient and she hadn't the slightest intention of letting him intimidate her. 'I don't care who your young friend is,' she said in the crisp, no-nonsense way that had served her so well at St Hilda's and as a member of the WSPU. 'He could be Prince Edward or the Aga Khan for all I care. He took that corner in a way that could have ended in someone's death and I want to make quite sure he realizes it and never does such a thing again.'

The young man flushed an even deeper red and said, sounding terribly apologetic about it, 'Actually, I am Prince Edward.'

It was a ridiculous statement and Rose ignored it.

'If you have a pen and paper on you,' she said, speaking to the older man, 'I would like to give you my name and address so that you can reimburse me for the damage done to my bicycle.'

14

He didn't deign to speak to her. Instead he said to his golden-haired companion, 'This has gone quite far enough, sir. I propose that I make a financial settlement now, to avoid any further unpleasantness, and that we continue on our way as speedily as possible.'

Rose did a double take. Sir? She wondered if the younger man outranked him. She squinted for a glimpse of gold braid on the naval-looking uniform and couldn't see any: even if there had been some, she didn't think rank would still count when they were members of different sections of the armed services.

Slowly she became aware of a sickening sensation building within her that had nothing to do with how bruised she was.

That silkily straight blond hair. Those stunningly blue eyes. The handsome face so delicately boned it stopped just short of effeminacy. No wonder she thought she had seen him before. Because he took no part in public life as yet, there had been few published photographs of the heir to the throne, but she knew now with ghastly certainty she was in his presence – and that she had just sworn in front of him and told him he had behaved very, very stupidly.

She was so appalled that for the first time in her life she didn't know what to do. Should she curtsey? After all that had happened and in the grass-stained state she was now in, to do so would be ridiculous. She should certainly apologize for swearing in front of him and not addressing him as 'sir'. Telling him he had behaved stupidly had been unfortunate, but as it had also been true she didn't feel she should apologize for that. Doing so would be hypocritical and compromise her principles.

As she struggled with her dilemma he rescued her by saying with concern, 'You've grazed your face badly and it's bleeding, Miss . . .?'

'Houghton, Rose Houghton,' she said, adding hastily, 'sir'.

The older man clicked his tongue with impatience while Prince Edward clumsily handed her a spotlessly white handkerchief.

She accepted it gratefully.

'I shall now give Miss Houghton a lift to wherever it is she wishes to be taken, Captain Cullen,' the Prince said, and for the first time Rose realized that his accent was quite odd. Very plummy, but with a slight trace of cockney in it. She wondered where on earth the cockney had been picked up. She also realized that Captain Cullen was absolutely aghast at the prospect of her being given a lift anywhere.

Seemingly unaware of his equerry's fierce disapproval the Prince returned his attention to her. 'Where is it you would like to be taken, Miss Houghton?'

'Home, sir,' she said, having no desire to continue on to the village when she needed to wash, apply something soothing to her grazed face and change into clean clothes.

'Then if you would give me directions, we'll be on our way.'

'That is very kind of you, sir. Snowberry is half a mile on the right-hand side in the direction you were heading.'

She stepped towards her bicycle. It had fallen in the middle of the road but someone, presumably Captain Cullen, had lifted it out of the road and on to the grass verge. The rear wheel was buckled, the spokes dented. She lifted the flap of her saddlebag and took out the two letters she had been on her way to post. At the sight of King George V's head on the stamps – and at the thought that his son and heir was about to give her a lift – amusement put paid to any lingering remnants of anger. It intensified as a thunderous-faced Captain Cullen yanked the bicycle upright.

'This won't do, sir. It's colossally irregular,' he said, so tight-lipped that Rose thought it a miracle he could speak

16

at all. 'If news of this escapade gets back to Windsor it would be catastrophic. I would lose my position and His Majesty's trust in you would be greatly damaged.'

'It's only a half-mile drive,' the Prince said with exquisite patience as Homer, anxious for Rose's safety, tried to clamber into the motor car with her. 'No harm can come of it.' He turned to Rose, giving her a shy, sweet smile. 'D'you think your dog would like to get in the jump-seat, Miss Houghton? It will be rather fun for him, don't you think?'

From the expression in his voice, Rose suspected that, now he knew she wasn't seriously hurt, he was finding this deviation from the routine of his life rather fun as well. She bundled Homer into the jump-seat and a minute later they were passing Captain Cullen who, the bicycle hoisted on one shoulder, was walking up the road, fury and indignation evident in every line of his body.

'Don't forget the name of the cottage!' the Prince called out helpfully to him. 'It's Snowberry! I'll wait for you there!'

Giggles fizzed in Rose's throat. Whatever Snowberry was, it wasn't a cottage. She just hoped Captain Cullen wouldn't find the walk up its long drive too fatiguing.

The Prince, his lesson learned, was now driving with meticulous care. The noise of the engine and the sound of the wind streaming past their ears made talking difficult – and this was, she assumed, why the Prince had lapsed into silence. Then she wondered if the silence between them was caused by his shyness. He was, after all, very young. Sixteen or seventeen. She couldn't remember which. Her instinct was to try to put him at his ease, but she knew it wasn't done to speak to the heir to the throne without being spoken to first. Remembering how grossly she had already breached this particular piece of royal etiquette – and in what an appalling way – she decided that any further breaches couldn't possibly matter.

'I'm very appreciative, sir,' she said as they neared Snowberry's gates. 'We turn in here.'

He swung the wheel to the right and coasted into Snowberry's grandiose drive, saying, 'I take it, then, that Snowberry isn't your average country cottage, Miss Houghton?'

Her mouth tugged into a smile. 'No, sir. It's a William and Mary house, built in sixteen eighty-nine on the foundations of an Elizabethan manor house. My grandfather is Lord May. Snowberry is his family home. I've lived here with my three younger sisters ever since the death of my father sixteen years ago.'

'And your mother?' he asked.

'My mother remarried. She and her husband, the marquis de Villoutrey, live in Paris.'

They cruised round the last curve of the drive and Snowberry lay in all its mellow beauty before them. With its huge buttressed chimneystacks, soaring chimneys, gables and diamond-leaded windows, it was achingly beautiful.

Rose felt her throat tighten. Though she longed to spend time in London, being politically active as a suffragette, she loved her home deeply and didn't believe there was another house as perfect in the whole of England.

The Prince brought the Daimler to a noisy halt. 'What a cracking house, Miss Houghton,' he said as, from behind him, Homer rested a friendly paw on his shoulder.

Coming from a young man whose various homes included Windsor Castle, Buckingham Palace, Balmoral and Sandringham, the compliment gave Rose great pleasure.

Under normal circumstances she would have waited until her driver had opened the passenger door before stepping out of the car, but the situation was so bizarre – how could she expect a prince to open her car door for her? – that she opened it herself, stepping down from the running-board in such a hurry she nearly fell.

Regaining her balance, she said, flustered, 'Thank you very much for bringing me home, sir.'

He, too, had now stepped from the car and she wondered what she was to do with him until Captain Cullen arrived.

The correct thing, of course, was to invite him inside and offer him some refreshment. Orange juice, or perhaps tea. But how could she sit in the drawing room sipping orange juice or tea with her future king when her hair was dishevelled, the graze on her face needed attention and there were grass stains on her skirt?

He said in his habitually hesitant manner, 'Does Snowberry have an orangery, Miss Houghton?'

She shot him a blazing smile, aware that her problem was solved. 'Yes, sir. Would you like to see it?'

He nodded, and as they began walking he said, 'Kensington Palace has a splendid orangery. There aren't only orange trees in it; there are lemon trees and fifteen-foot-high tangerine trees.'

'We have lemons and tangerines and a few years ago we began growing Persian limes.'

'Persian limes?' He looked fascinated.

Rose suppressed a smile. It was like being with a very likeable nephew. If over the last forty minutes or so royal protocol had gone to the winds, he showed no signs of minding. In fact she had a sneaking suspicion that he was trying to prolong the experience.

She was just about to tell him that one of the advantages of Persian limes was that they had no seeds when they rounded the corner of the house to be greeted by the sight of Lily, her waist-length dark hair held away from her face by tortoiseshell combs, sprinting towards them over the vast lawn as fast as her skirt would allow.

'We heard the motor car, Rose!' she shouted. 'Who is our visitor? Would he like to make a double at tennis?'

Rose clamped her mouth tight shut, knowing that to yell that their visitor was His Royal Highness Prince Edward would be even worse than remaining silent until Lily was near enough for a dignified introduction to take place.

Her hopes that Lily would also now stay silent were shot to pieces. 'It's jolly hot, isn't it?' she called out to the Prince cheerily as she drew nearer. 'There's a jug of lemonade down by the tennis court.'

There was a happy smile of welcome on her face, until she registered how dishevelled Rose was and saw the graze on her face. Her smile vanished instantly. 'Rose! You're hurt! What's happened?'

'I came off my bicycle,' Rose said as Lily raced up to her, 'and, Lily, before you say anything further, I must explain who—'

'But you must go and bathe it, Rose!' Lily was too concerned about Rose's injury to care about introductions. 'It looks dreadful! It might turn septic and leave a scar!'

It was a possibility Rose hadn't thought of.

As he saw her flinch, David's horror at having caused the accident returned and, dragging his attention away from the most angelic face he had ever seen, he blurted, 'Is there a family doctor who can get here quickly, Miss Houghton? If not, as soon as Cullen arrives I'll have him go for one.'

'Cullen?' Lily was bewildered.

He looked towards her again. In the May sunshine her turbulent hair shone blue-black. Her eyes were wide-set, thick-lashed, and the most extraordinary shade of violet. Unlike her sister, who was five foot six or five foot seven, she was small-boned and so petite that just looking at her robbed him of breath.

'My equerry,' he said, bewildering her even further. He flushed a deep scarlet. 'It was my idiotic driving that caused your sister to fall from her bicycle. The bicycle got pretty mangled and Captain Cullen is carrying it back. He'll be here in ten minutes or so.'

'So Rose's accident was *your* fault!'

There was so much reproach in her voice that he was mortified beyond speech.

Rose was equally mortified, but for a very different reason. Five years ago, when she was eighteen, she had been presented at court and knew from first-hand experience just how rigid royal etiquette was. One didn't speak until one was spoken to. In a private situation any prince with the title of 'Royal Highness' was addressed as 'sir', but in asking a direct question, 'Your Royal Highness' had to be used.

Prince Edward's mention of his equerry had meant nothing to Lily and it was obvious that she still had no idea with whom she was speaking. It was also obvious that Prince Edward had never been spoken to by a non-family member as he'd been spoken to first by herself and now by Lily, and Rose wasn't at all surprised at his stupefied silence.

Taking a deep breath, she said in a firm voice and with heavy emphasis on his title, 'Your Royal Highness, allow me to introduce my youngest sister, Miss Lily Houghton.'

Lily blinked.

The graze was still leaking blood and Rose pressed the handkerchief with the royal crest hard against her cheekbone, saying tautly, 'This isn't a tease, Lily.'

To her despair Lily still didn't drop into a curtsey but, completely baffled, remained motionless.

Rose flashed a glance towards the Prince and saw that he was looking discomfited.

Her embarrassment was so intense she found herself wishing Captain Cullen would arrive. Instead it was Iris who put an end to the impasse.

Curious as to who their visitor was and what was keeping Lily, she'd walked from the tennis court to join them and as

21

she came within speaking distance, she said, alarmed, 'What's happened, Rose? Why is your cheek bleeding? Did you come off your bicycle on the gravel?'

'Rose came off her bicycle on the road,' Lily said before Rose could answer. 'Prince Edward knocked her off it in his motor car.'

'*Who* knocked her off it?'

'His Royal Highness Prince Edward,' Rose said, wondering how much worse things could get and wishing a pit would open at her feet and swallow her up. She took a deep steadying breath. 'Your Royal Highness, allow me to present my sister, Miss Iris Houghton.' Her fierce hope that Iris's reaction would be a vast improvement on Lily's was fulfilled. Iris's eyes flew to David's and a second later, recognizing him instantly in a way her sisters had not, she sank into a very accomplished curtsey.

The result was that David looked even more discomfited. 'The graze on your sister's face needs attending to, Miss Houghton,' he said, struggling to keep his eyes on her and not on Lily. 'A doctor needs to be called.'

'Yes, sir.' Then Iris, practical to her fingertips, turned to Rose. 'Let me look at the damage, Rose.'

Rose took the handkerchief away and though Lily sucked in her breath, Iris said, 'It's really not so bad, Rose. All it needs is to be bathed and Vaselined.'

David's relief was vast. 'Then could that be taken care of immediately? Please don't mind me. I'll wait here until Captain Cullen arrives.'

'You would be more comfortable down by the tennis court having a glass of lemonade,' Lily said, blithely uncaring that she shouldn't be speaking to him with such easy familiarity. 'Marigold would love to meet you, too. It doesn't seem fair that we've met you and she hasn't.'

This time it was Rose's turn to suck in her breath.

Iris looked as if she was about to pass out.

David flushed an even deeper red, saying with shy awkwardness, 'I would like that enormously, Miss Houghton.'

Lily flashed him a sunny smile. 'Please call me Lily. Everyone calls me Lily.'

David paused, about to do something he had never done before in his life: suggest that the Houghton sisters drop all royal protocol and call him by the name only his family used. It would cause an awful row if his father was to hear about it, but he never would. The friendships he was now making – and he was certain that he was, for the first time in his life, on the brink of making real friendships – were ones his father would never know about.

'Please call me David,' he said, shooting Lily an engaging smile. 'I'd like all of you to call me David.'

Her answering smile had his heart doing somersaults.

'Would you like to make up a four for tennis?' she asked as she led him across the lawn in the direction of the tennis court, while Rose and Iris hurried into the house. 'Rose won't want to play, not with her face smarting as it must be doing, but she can umpire. I've been umpiring for Iris and Marigold and I'm sick to death of it. A doubles game would be great fun.'

As two spaniels bounded to meet them David felt as if he had entered an entirely different world; it was a world aeons removed from the stiff rigidity of his royal home life or his life at naval college, where, if anyone tried to befriend him, they only did so because of who he was.

The Houghton girls' naturalness with him was something he had never previously experienced. True, Rose had done her best to behave correctly once she knew his identity, but there had been nothing toadying in the way she had done so. She filled him with colossal admiration – and awe. The way she had reacted after her brief moment of unconsciousness had been incredible. He'd never known anyone lay into Piers Cullen in the way she had done. She had been just as forthrightly blunt where he, David, was concerned. She had called his action in taking the corner so wide and at such speed very stupid. Which it had been. Even once she realized who he was, she hadn't apologized. It was exactly the way a member of his family – one of his young German aunts, for instance – might have treated him. It had given him a glimmer of what it must be like to be an ordinary person – and the desire to be an ordinary person, and not someone different and set apart, was something he had longed to experience ever since he could remember.

If Rose seemed like a young, but intimidating aunt, Iris reminded him of his sister, Mary. Where Lily was as beautiful as a Raphael Madonna and Rose was breathtakingly striking, Iris, with her hazel eyes, brown hair coiled in a no-nonsense knot, was a plain Jane. Her build, sturdy rather than slender, was also reminiscent of his sister's, as was her down-to-earth practicality; in the same situation, Mary would also have asked to see the damage done to Rose's face before calling a doctor. When he thought of the embarrassing questions that might have been asked if a doctor had been called, he was very grateful for her undramatic common sense.

Then there was Lily – and Lily was the most magical creature he had ever met.

As they neared the end of the formal lawn, the magical creature said chattily, 'I do hope you are going to stay long enough to meet Grandfather. He's in Winchester this afternoon, at the dentist's. He never likes leaving Snowberry and as he especially doesn't like leaving it in order to go somewhere horrid your being here when he comes home will cheer him enormously.'

Whenever she spoke to him he flushed. He simply couldn't

help it. She also left him tongue-tied, because although he'd never stammered – Bertie was the stammerer in the family – he was fearful that with her he might be just about to start.

The lawn petered out into a belt of rough grass and wild flowers. Beyond it lay a small lake and between scattered trees he could see a boathouse and a diving-board.

They didn't continue on towards it. 'The tennis court is over here, on the left.' She indicated a gateway set in a magnificent six-foot-high yew hedge. 'Marigold is going to die with delight when I introduce her to you.' Her smile deepened. 'Marigold, unlike Rose, really loves all the excitement that goes with royal events, though even Rose is making an exception where the coronation next month is concerned. I can't quite believe that King George is your father. It's odd, isn't it?'

'Very,' he said with feeling.

'Iris doesn't often get excited by anything,' Lily continued, not registering the inflection in his voice, 'though she is excited at the thought of being in London for the coronation procession and at the thought of all the coronation parties and balls she's been invited to. *I* would be excited as well if I was going to all the parties and balls, but I haven't been presented at court yet, so I won't be going. Grandfather has asked me if I will wait until next year. He hated all the disruption when Rose, Iris and Marigold had their seasons. I'll probably be lucky to get presented at all.'

For David it was a most bizarre conversation, not just because of its subject matter but because he'd never before had a casual chat with any girl other than his sisters and cousins. Once, when he was eight or nine, he'd had dancing lessons with well-born children who were not blood-related, but the experiment had not lasted long and he remembered very little of it.

25

Other than that, because he had never been sent away to school but had been educated at home by a private tutor, there had been no social interaction with anyone outside his family until he had gone to naval college at the age of thirteen. There his socializing had been limited strictly to boys and, because of the barrier of his royal status, there had been no end-of-term invitations to private homes. Even if someone had had the temerity to issue such an invitation, he wouldn't have been allowed to accept it.

Though Lily and her sisters couldn't possibly realize it, this occasion at Snowberry was his very first experience of a home outside his royal family circle. If he wanted to enjoy it again – and he did – then he would somehow have to square such visits with Piers Cullen whose role as his equerry included keeping his father closely informed of all his activities

'Marigold!' Lily called out as they stepped through the gateway. 'You are never going to believe this! Stop practising serving and come and be introduced to His Royal Highness Prince Edward!'

Totally inexperienced as he was when it came to girls, David knew the instant he laid eyes on Marigold that not only was he way out of his depth; but Piers Cullen – and every other man he knew – would be out of their depth also.

Marigold was, in the crude slang he'd picked up at naval college, hot stuff. It was nothing to do with the way she looked, though a superb figure, cat-green almond eyes and orange-tawny hair with a flower decorating it would, he supposed, take a girl far, even when her nose was too big and her mouth too wide. The sexiness was in her blatant self-confidence and in the knowing expression in her eyes; it was an expression that certainly shouldn't have been visible in a girl not much older than Lily.

Immediately Piers Cullen saw Marigold he would label

her as being 'fast', and David knew that the result of that would be finding himself en route to Windsor in double-quick time.

One way of stalling such an outcome would be if Cullen were to find him in the middle of a game of tennis. Iris's racquet lay on a canvas chair at the side of the court. He picked it up and spun it in his hand, saying in his tentative manner, 'How about we have a knock-up until Rose and Iris join us?'

Lily's flawless face lit up with pleasure.

'The two of us against the one of you?' Marigold arched an eyebrow.

'Why not?'

This time David's smile was no longer shy. This time, with his new-found friends, his smile had a confidence that transformed him from a gauche boy into a young man of spellbinding charm.

# FOUR

With barely contained fury Piers Cullen watched the Austro-Daimler disappear up the hill in a cloud of exhaust fumes. Of all the annoyances he'd had to endure as an equerry, the present fiasco was the worst. But this, he reminded himself as he shifted the bicycle so that it would sit a little more comfortably on his shoulder, wasn't an annoyance. It was an outrage.

The worst of it wasn't the indignity he was suffering, though it was one he would never forget or forgive. The worst of it was the prospect of the King getting to hear of his son's escapade. King George's temper, over even the most minor of misdemeanours, was ferocious – and his eldest son disappearing with an unknown girl and no other companion was not a misdemeanour. It was a catastrophe of epic proportions, for Rose Houghton would be able to accuse Prince Edward of any impropriety she chose.

The mere thought brought beads of sweat to his forehead. The reason no well-brought-up young woman was allowed to be alone with a young man without a chaperone being present wasn't simply to safeguard the girl's reputation. It was to safeguard the young man's reputation as well. Or at least this was so where the heir to the throne was concerned.

Once again he shifted the bicycle into another position on his shoulder. The Prince certainly wouldn't instigate any unseemly behaviour. He wasn't seventeen for another three weeks and in Piers's estimation he was young for his age rather than precocious. He judged the Houghton girl, however, to be several years older, possibly twenty-three or twenty-four, and she was no shy shrinking violet. When he thought of the way she had sworn when speaking to him, rage surged through him in a hot engulfing tide. A young woman like that would be capable of any kind of wild allegation if she thought it would be to her profit.

As if that scenario weren't horrendous enough, there was another, even worse possibility. What if there were another accident? This time a fatal one?

If the heir to the throne were to be killed when he, Piers, should have been with him and wasn't, then he might as well simply slit his throat. He tried to imagine Prince Edward's younger brother, Prince Albert, succeeding to the throne in Edward's stead, but found the idea farcical. Bertie was highly nervous and had a speech impediment too severe for any kind of public speaking.

A horse pulling a cart full of animal feed came clopping up behind him and he stepped a little closer to the verge.

'Halloa there, soldier!' the carter called out as he came alongside him. 'Would you like a lift a littleways?'

The undignified address was too much for him to take. 'I'm a royal equerry, you country bumpkin!' he roared. 'I wouldn't be seen dead on your filthy cart!'

'Youm be a nutter!' came the aggrieved response. 'And I wouldn't 'ave youm on my cart, not for all the tea in China!'

As the cart trundled past him, Piers continued to fume. Where the devil was the blasted cottage he was looking for? He couldn't see sight or sign of a house of any description, only fields on one side of the road and, on the other, the kind of wall that signified the boundary of private parkland, with the parkland itself hidden from view by a belt of trees.

The bicycle wasn't unduly heavy to carry, but it was awkward as well as being demeaning and he fought the temptation to toss it into the nearest field. Damn that Houghton girl. If it hadn't been for her, he and Prince Edward would have been back at Windsor by now. He liked Windsor. He liked being an equerry. He liked the status it gave him.

When Lord Esher, on behalf of King George, had interviewed him for the position he had emphasized how difficult the selection process had been. 'Several people have been mentioned to His Majesty as being suitable for the post, but, having known your father as I have for so many years, and taking into account your excellent army record, I think you are well fitted for the position,' he had said in his ponderous manner. 'You will always have to take into account Prince Edward's youth. You will have to be always watchful, without seeming so. Instructive, without being boring. Most of all you will have to retain the high moral standards that have made you eligible for this position.'

High moral standards were no difficulty for him. Both his father and his grandfather had been Church of Scotland ministers – his father a highly distinguished one – and he was a puritan by both upbringing and inclination. Though he had opted for the army as a career, rather than the Church, he had never joined in the camaraderie of army life. He was a loner. A loner who didn't smoke, didn't drink, didn't often seek female company – and when he did he always behaved with immaculate correctness. All were virtues of which King George highly approved.

He had now reached the top of the long sloping hill and there was still no cottage in sight. There was, though, an imposing gateway and scrolled in the wrought-iron work was the name of the house: 'SNOWBERRY'.

He stared at it, his mouth tight, his nostrils pinched and white, knowing Rose Houghton must have thought his looking for a run-of-the-mill cottage a great joke.

Gritting his teeth he embarked on the long walk up Snowberry's elm-tree lined driveway. By the time the parkland came to an end and the gardens began, much as he hated being so, he was impressed.

Wisteria and honeysuckle flowered against mellow stone walls. Bees hovered over huge banks of lavender. Early roses gave off a heady, sweet scent. The house looked as if it had always been there, hidden from the narrow country road in splendour that was timeless. He wasn't much of a historian, but he judged it to be mid-seventeenth century, possibly even older. It was the sort of house that never changed hands, but was passed down in the same family from one generation to another. Rose Houghton may have been everything he hated in a woman, but if Snowberry was her home, she was also extremely fortunate.

Dropping the bicycle to the ground he strode past the carelessly parked Austro-Daimler and rapped hard on the door.

An elderly butler opened it to him.

'Captain Cullen,' he said to him abruptly. 'Equerry to His Royal Highness Prince Edward.'

'Is that so, sir?' The butler gave a puzzled frown. 'Is his lordship expecting you?'

'His Royal Highness is expecting me!' Piers snapped, wondering if the old fool was senile.

'That may be so, sir, but this is the home of the Earl of May. His lordship is not at home and there is presently no guest at Snowberry, royal or otherwise—'

'Actually there is, William.'

Piers looked beyond the butler to where Rose Houghton, accompanied by another young woman of similar age, was crossing the hall to take charge of the situation.

31

'Lily has taken Prince Edward down to the tennis court so that Marigold may meet him,' she said as she reached the open doorway. 'I should have told you, William, but there were unusual circumstances.' The bruising fast coming up on her face, and the raw graze, indicated just how unusual the circumstances had been.

Turning to Piers she said with cool politeness, 'Please come in, Captain Cullen.'

Piers, who wanted only to march down to the tennis court in order to retrieve Prince Edward from Lily and Marigold – whoever they might be – stepped into an enormous stone-flagged hall.

'It's quicker to walk through the house to the rear than to walk around it,' Rose said, and he saw that she had changed into a spotlessly clean lace blouse and dove-grey skirt and that her thick knot of waving chestnut hair had been brushed and repinned. 'May I first introduce you to my sister? Captain Cullen, Iris. Iris, Captain Cullen. Captain Cullen is Prince Edward's equerry and has kindly brought my damaged bicycle home for me.'

Piers gave an abrupt nod in the direction of a pleasant-faced young woman with intelligent brown eyes. Then to Rose he said equally abruptly, 'The tennis court, Lady Rose, if you please.'

'Aah!' Rose tilted her head to one side. 'I see that William has caused confusion. The Earl of May is my grandfather. My father was the late Viscount Houghton.'

Once again she had caught him out in a wrong assumption and he shot her a look of pure malevolence. 'Then to the tennis court, *Miss* Houghton,' he said through gritted teeth.

She led the way through a house that was flooded with sunshine and as lyrically lovely on the inside as it was on the outside. Lovingly polished William and Mary furniture emanated a pleasing scent of beeswax polish and on every surface there was a vase or a bowl of flowers. In the drawing room winged armchairs decorated with needlepoint panels cohabited happily with Edwardian sofas. On one of the many cushions a Burmese cat was curled, contentedly asleep. On a rosewood card table a jigsaw was waiting to be finished. On another table ivory chess pieces had been left enticingly in mid play. It was a family room; a room to linger in.

He wasn't allowed to.

'The tennis court is quite a walk,' Rose said as they exited the house via French doors. 'My grandfather wanted it sited as far away from the house as possible so that it wouldn't spoil the view.'

Piers didn't blame him.

A vast lawn studded with specimen trees led down to a small lake. Beyond the lake the vista dissolved into woods and, beyond the woods, into gentle hills.

Homer loped to meet them, greeting him as if he was an old friend. Piers wasn't a dog person and if Homer had hoped for a friendly pat he was left disappointed. Piers saw Rose Houghton's full-lipped mouth tighten and didn't care. All he wanted was to put the day back on course and that meant having Prince Edward at the wheel of his Austro-Daimler heading once more for Windsor Castle.

As two spaniels bounded up from the lower end of the lawn to join Homer's welcome party he glanced down at his watch. It was ten to three. It wasn't late enough for alarm to be caused at Windsor. There had been no set time for their departure from Dartmouth and there was no set time for their arrival. A longer interruption to their journey would, though, begin to cause concern. If a telephone call were made to the naval college and the approximate time of their departure given, he would have a lot of explaining to do.

At the thought of giving such an explanation to King

33

George a nerve pulsed at the corner of his jaw. The fiasco that the afternoon had turned into had gone on long enough. Whether Prince Edward liked it or whether he didn't, he was going to have to put this little adventure behind him and get on with the tedious rigidity of his royal life.

He could hear a tennis ball being thwacked across a net and voices and laughter.

A terrible fear seized hold of him. Surely Prince Edward couldn't be playing tennis with two young women he had met in so casual and careless a way?

Rose Houghton led him through a gateway cut into a high yew hedge and his fear was confirmed.

Two girls, one with dark hair tumbling in ringlets down her back, the other wearing a flower in upswept fiery hair, were with the Prince, knocking a tennis ball backwards and forwards across the net.

As if that wasn't shocking enough, Edward had discarded his collarless round-necked naval jacket.

Never before had Piers seen Prince Edward in shirtsleeves and waistcoat and he doubted if anyone else – other than his valet – had either, for King George's insistence on correct dress for members of his family at all times and for every occasion was written in stone. When Edward was in the presence of his father he was expected to wear a morning coat. At dinner he wore a tailcoat with a white tie. If he were to play a game of tennis at Windsor or Sandringham with one of his brothers he, and they, would be dressed accordingly in buckskin shoes, knickerbockers, a shirt with a stiff collar and an appropriate tie fastened with a gold pin. Any deviation was totally unthinkable. Or had been until now.

'Your friend is here,' the sensuous-looking girl with the flower in her hair called out richly to Edward as she hit a cross-court volley. 'So are Rose and Iris. Have we to start a game of doubles?'

David let the ball bounce, caught it in his hand and turned to face Piers.

'The girls want a game of mixed doubles,' he said pleasantly. 'As there are six of us – and as we thought that under the circumstances Rose would be happier not playing but umpiring – if you want to make up a foursome I'm sure Iris, Marigold or Lily would act as ball boy.'

Piers sucked in his breath, grateful only that it hadn't been suggested that *he* should act as ball boy.

'I'm afraid a game of doubles isn't going to be possible, sir,' he said, wondering for how much longer he could keep his temper under control. 'Our journey to Windsor has already been delayed by well over an hour. Any longer and questions will be asked.' He picked up Edward's jacket from where Edward had dropped it on the umpire's chair. 'If we leave directly, sir, we will run into no problems.'

The sensuous-looking girl gave a heavy sigh of disappointment, saying as she walked towards the net, 'Oh, David, do the two of you really have to do a bunk?'

Piers's jaw dropped. He was so shocked he felt physically dizzy. Then he felt violently sick. Not because of the vulgar slang she had used, but because no one, *no one*, ever referred to the Prince by the name used within his family.

His fellow naval cadets – those in his year group – had, he knew, been given permission to drop his title and call him Edward. One boy, Lord Spencer's son, even called him Eddy. No one else took such liberties. Piers had been in Edward's service for nearly twelve months, ever since Edward's grandfather, King Edward VII, had died, and he had never been invited to call him anything other than Edward – and then only when no one else was present.

Yet now he had invited these four girls – four girls he knew nothing whatever about – to call him David. Hard on the heels of Piers's shock came fierce, roaring jealousy. Then hard on the heels of his jealousy came a resentment so burning he knew it would never leave him.

Through his raging emotion he saw the smaller girl of the two, the one whose hair was a torrent of smoke-dark ringlets, approaching him.

'Dear Captain Cullen,' she said in the loveliest voice he had ever heard and as if she had known him for years, 'do please delay your journey long enough for us all to play at least one set of doubles with you and David. It will be such fun.'

The sweetness of the expression on her face smote his heart. Her smile was so winsome that his knees felt weak. Her black-lashed eyes were a colour he had never thought humanly possible.

When she handed him her racquet, he took it. It would have been unthinkable for him to have done anything else.

Her smile widened and he saw that she had the tiniest, prettiest dimples imaginable.

'If you and Marigold play against David and Iris, Rose will umpire and I will be ball boy.'

'Yes,' he said stupidly, knowing he was the victim of something he had thought didn't exist except in men's imaginations. A *coup de foudre*. He, Piers Cullen, a man who had never committed a rash act in his life, had in one life-changing second fallen unreasonably, instantaneously, head over heels in love.

# FIVE

Two hours later, when the Austro-Daimler roared away down the drive with David at the wheel, Rose said drily, 'Snowberry can't have seen many afternoons as extraordinary as this one.'

'Oh, I don't know.' Marigold's voice was languid. 'Didn't Queen Anne stay overnight in 1710?'

'She didn't play tennis and she didn't invite her host and hostess to call her by her first name.'

'David isn't his first name.' Iris was pedantic as always. 'It's actually his last name.'

'Whatever, it was *extraordinary*.' With the car now out of sight Rose turned to go into the house. 'As was his asking if he could visit Snowberry again.'

'But surely that was just politeness?' As they stepped into the vast entrance hall Iris began to look worried. 'I mean, from his point of view, coming here again in such a casual manner wouldn't be the done thing at all, would it?'

'I shouldn't think so. He did seem to enjoy himself though, didn't he?'

Marigold, who had played an extremely strenuous game of tennis, undid the top buttons of her blouse, blotting the

37

sweat from full, lush breasts with a handkerchief. 'Whether he did or didn't, my deb friends in London are going to be green-eyed with jealousy when I tell them he dropped in for a game of tennis.'

Rose came to a halt in the middle of the hall. 'Because of the circumstances – the way he came to be here – I don't want you to say a word to anyone, Marigold.'

'Heavens, no.' Iris's pale skin turned a shade paler. 'If it became public knowledge that Prince Edward had been responsible for a road accident in which Rose had been knocked from her bicycle it could cause all kinds of trouble for him. You know what people are like. It would get exaggerated and before you know where you are the story going the rounds would be that he'd nearly killed her.'

Rose refrained from saying that as far as she was concerned, he very nearly had. Instead she said, 'We'll tell Grandfather, of course. And Rory.' Rory Sinclair was their second cousin, the grandson of their grandfather's only sister, Sibyl, Lady Harland. 'Other than that we'll keep it to ourselves. I'm sure that's what David would want. Also, if we keep it to ourselves, there's far more chance of his coming here again. And I'd be happy if he did, because I liked him.'

Marigold weighed up what was most advantageous to herself: enjoying brief envy because Prince Edward had paid an isolated visit to Snowberry, or saying nothing about his visit in the hope that he would become a regular visitor. The latter was rather long odds, but she liked taking a risk.

'OK,' she said agreeably. 'I'll go along with keeping this afternoon a secret. What time d'you think Grandfather and Lord Jethney will be here?'

Rose shot her a sharp glance. Though Lord Jethney was their grandfather's close friend, he was only in his forties. One of the youngest ministers in the Government, he was also married with two sons. Of late, Marigold had been showing far too much interest in him.

'Who knows?' she said coolly, thanking her lucky stars that Jethney hadn't arrived while the heir to the throne was playing a vigorous game of mixed doubles in his shirtsleeves.

Marigold returned Rose's speculative gaze with amusement, well aware that her elder sister knew that young men bored her and that she preferred older men, men like Theo Jethney, who possessed both sophistication and power.

'I'm going upstairs to bathe and change,' she said, uncaring that Rose's suspicions had been aroused. 'Let's just hope', she added as a parting shot, 'that if David does visit again, he does so without Captain Cullen. He didn't like you one little bit, Rose.'

Rose, well aware of the antipathy between herself and Captain Cullen, gave a dismissive shrug. She had more important things to worry about than an army officer who took himself so seriously he couldn't even crack a polite smile. As Lily said wistfully that she wished their grandfather had been at home while David had been with them, she wondered if it was about time she took Iris into her confidence where her worries about Marigold were concerned.

'I think David will visit us again,' Lily said, 'because he told me that this afternoon was the happiest afternoon he's ever had. Which is sad, isn't it? Because all we did was play tennis and drink lemonade.'

Rose was in agreement that it was sad, but didn't want to talk about their afternoon with Prince Edward any longer. What she wanted was to talk with Iris about Marigold while Lily was safely out of earshot.

'It's time the rabbits were fed,' she said, knowing that now she had been reminded, Lily wouldn't waste a second in rushing off to feed them. 'Iris, I'd like you to look at this graze again, please. It feels as if there is still dirt in it.' As Lily hurried off to the large grassy pen where her pet rabbits were corralled, Rose led the way up the stairs to the room she and Iris shared.

Once there, she flung herself down on her bed and said, 'Don't bother about my face, Iris. It feels fine. I want to talk to you about Marigold.'

'Marigold?' Iris seated herself on a Victorian button-backed chair near to one of the windows.

'Unless I'm very much mistaken she's making a set for Theo Jethney.'

Iris's eyebrows rose nearly into her hair. 'You can't mean it. He's old enough to be her father.'

'Marigold likes older men.'

'An older man to a girl of nineteen is someone who is twenty-seven or twenty-eight. Lord Jethney is in his forties!'

Rose chewed the corner of her lip. The trouble with Iris was that she wasn't intuitive; she never had a sixth sense about things. She didn't believe anyone capable of a dishonourable action – and especially not someone she loved. Rose, who had intuition in abundance, could have written the script for Iris's next reaction.

'Besides,' Iris said flatly, 'Theo Jethney is a married man.'

The tone of her voice made it clear that that settled the matter completely.

Rose shifted position on the bed, propping herself up on one arm. 'This may come as a shock to you, Iris, but sometimes single young women aren't too fussed about whether a man is married or not.'

'Respectable well-brought-up single young women are!' There were spots of angry colour in Iris's cheeks. 'Honestly, Rose! Your experiences with some of the young women in the WSPU is showing!'

Rose felt an answering spurt of anger and suppressed it. Now was no time to be having a row with Iris over her membership of the WSPU. What she needed, in the situation she foresaw with Marigold, was Iris's understanding and support. The remark was, however, one she wasn't going to let pass.

'If you would come to a WSPU meeting you would see how wrong your assumptions are about those members who are working-class. But it's Marigold's morals I'm worried about, not anyone else's.'

She sat up, swinging her legs to the floor. 'The trouble is, Marigold simply doesn't care about the consequences of any of her actions. If she wants something, she sees no reason why she shouldn't have it. Coupled with her sexiness it makes for dangerous situations.'

'Marigold can't help having red hair and being bosomy and sexy. She just *is*. That's why her debutante friends nick-named her Nell Gwynne.'

Rose, realizing Iris thought the nickname had been given for no other reason than Marigold's looks, regarded her with something close to despair. The temptation to point out that as the mistress of Charles II, Nell had been a young woman of notoriously easy virtue, and that that was the reason behind the nickname, was strong, but she resisted it.

She'd gone as far as was necessary in persuading Iris that she needed her support when she spoke to Marigold about Lord Jethney, without forcing Iris to face the fact that Marigold's friends had nicknamed her after one of the most famous and popular whores in English history.

'If Marigold *is* flirting with Lord Jethney, and if you think there is a chance he may be tempted to take advantage of it, wouldn't it be best to speak to Grandfather so that he can have a friendly word with him? If Grandfather said some-thing on the lines of "Marigold has developed a crush on you, Jethney. Let her down kindly, old chap," it would mean Lord Jethney knew an eye was being kept on the two of

41

them and then nothing further would come of things, would it? You must also speak to Marigold. You must tell her that she's not only putting her reputation at risk, she's putting Grandfather's friendship with Lord Jethney in jeopardy as well.'

Rose nodded, rising to her feet, wondering why it was that when she'd got the outcome she'd hoped for – which was Iris's support – she felt so depressed and irritated. Was it because Iris had, as always, left it to her to take care of things? Ever since their mother had remarried and gone to live in France she had been the one who kept everyone in order, ensuring that family life ran smoothly. If there was a problem, it was to her that it was brought. Everything, it seemed, was down to her and always had been.

Before she went to Oxford she had never minded, but Oxford had changed her and she wanted more out of life now than simply being a mother, as well as a sister, to her younger siblings.

'I'm going to take the dogs for a walk,' she said, aware that the situation couldn't change while her grandfather was so dependent on her – or that it couldn't change until one of her sisters stepped into her shoes where Snowberry was concerned. And as Lily was still too young, and Marigold entirely too selfish, that left Iris.

Iris was ideally suited to the role, because all she wanted out of life was to marry Toby Mulholland, the only son of Viscount Mulholland, whose family home, Sissbury Castle, was a mere ten miles from Snowberry. The two of them had been inseparable since childhood and though she couldn't for the life of her understand what Iris saw in Toby – who was pleasant, but vacuous – Iris adored him.

Rose walked down the broad staircase into the entrance hall, her thoughts still on Iris. Sometime in the not-too-distant future Iris would be mistress of Sissbury and as Sissbury's estate was even larger than Snowberry's, it made sense that Iris should become familiar with estate account books and estate correspondence.

With Fizz and Florin at her heels she left the house, heading towards the belt of woodland closest to the house. If Iris could be persuaded to take over from her she would be able to combine her life at Snowberry with a life in London – and then she could once more become fully active in the WSPU's struggle for equality with men.

It wasn't an ambition Iris would understand. All Iris wanted was a country life of children, horses and dogs: something that was easily achievable and that marriage to Toby would bring. Whereas her own ambition – to be part of a force for change in the world – was well-nigh impossible when women weren't even able to vote and a political life of any kind was closed to them.

She dug her hands deep in the pockets of her gored skirt, well aware that all that was expected of her was that, like Iris, she married well; but, as marriage would mean surrendering all independence, it was something she most definitely did not want.

The minute Iris heard the sound of the Talbot approaching the house she hurried downstairs and outside to welcome her grandfather home. To her surprise Lord Jethney wasn't with him, which meant she could immediately tell him of how Snowberry had been graced all afternoon by the presence of Prince Edward.

'You will never, in a hundred years, guess who has been playing tennis at Snowberry this afternoon, Grandfather.' She slid her hand into the crook of his arm. 'Prince Edward! Oh, he was so nice! I thought him a little young for his age, but that may be because he's so angelic-looking. Buttercup-blond hair and the sweetest smile imaginable. He *loved* Snowberry. He told Rose he thought it was a cracking house!'

'By that I take it he meant he thought it was first-rate.'

Herbert Houghton was dressed for the glorious weather in a lightweight flannel suit and a jaunty panama hat. He patted her hand affectionately.

'But why was he here? Was he visiting Chanbury Hall or Sissbury Castle and did Lord Reighton or Toby's father bring him?'

'No. Let's have tea on the lawn and then I'll tell you everything. It's all very exciting, because it began with him almost *killing* Rose.'

Having so intrigued him she refused to say another word until she'd asked for tea to be brought out to them on the lawn. Soon the two of them were seated comfortably in cane chairs at either side of a small white-naperied table on which stood bone-china cups and saucers, a sugar bowl and milk jug, a Georgian silver teapot and silver tea-strainer.

The Earl, a man of equable temperament who was seldom ruffled, waited patiently for the granddaughter who was most like him to spill the beans.

Iris poured the tea and said, 'The Prince was driving from Dartmouth to Windsor and Rose was cycling down to the village to post letters when the Prince took a corner very badly.` As Rose veered out of his way he clipped her back wheel.'

'Dear Lord!' Her grandfather's geniality vanished at a stroke. 'Was she hurt?' He rose to his feet, full of anxiety. 'Where is she now? You should have told me this straight away, Iris.'

'Please sit down, Grandfather. Rose wasn't hurt – at least not seriously. She was winded and she's grazed her face. She's gone for one of her trudges and has taken the dogs with her.'

Vastly relieved her grandfather sat down again, but he was still slightly alarmed. 'Who was with the Prince?' he asked, thinking of possible repercussions. 'Did he have an aide-de-camp with him?'

'He had an equerry. Captain Cullen. David brought Rose back to Snowberry in his car and Captain Cullen walked back with the damaged bicycle.'

Her grandfather stared at her, confused. 'David? Did Prince Edward have two equerries with him?'

'No. The Prince asked us if we would call him David. It's a name he prefers.'

Her grandfather had just taken a sip of tea.

He choked on it.

When he could speak, he said, 'I think you're teasing me, Iris. I do hope the rest of your story isn't a tease as well, because if it is, it's very naughty of you.'

'Of course it isn't a tease!' Iris's nut-brown eyes were indignant. 'I think Captain Cullen was rather shocked by the Prince asking us to call him David, but he did, and it made things so much friendlier. I partnered David and Marigold partnered Captain Cullen in a game of doubles. Rose umpired and Lily was ball boy. It was tremendous fun.'

'It may have been tremendous fun, Iris, but as I wasn't here to act as his host, it was also highly irregular.' He frowned, deeply worried. 'If it should become known that the Prince, his equerry and four single young women had spent the afternoon playing tennis with no one else present, it would cause uproar at the palace. I can't imagine what his equerry was thinking of to have allowed it.'

Iris's elation ebbed a little. Her grandfather seldom worried about anything, and she didn't want him worrying now.

'It won't become known, Grandfather, because none of us – not even Marigold – is going to say a word about it to anyone. And Captain Cullen won't say anything either, because if he did he might lose his position as equerry.'

'Oh, he would. There's no doubt about that. One hint of

45

this afternoon's escapade to King George and heads – including Prince Edward's – would roll. The King is a martinet; even his most intimate friends are terrified of him. I suspect that's why Prince Edward so enjoyed his afternoon at Snowberry. His tennis match with the four of you would have been a delightful novelty after the rigidly correct behaviour demanded of him at Windsor and Buckingham Palace. I remember Jethney telling me what a great pity it is that the princes aren't allowed to form friendships with other boys their age. It must make for very lonely lives.'

Iris, remembering the expression in David's eyes as he said goodbye to them, and then the sudden hope that had flooded them when he asked if he could visit again, was quite certain that her grandfather was right and that, as heir to the throne, David carried a heavy burden of loneliness.

She was trying to imagine how it must be, holding a position so exalted that normal relationships were all but impossible, when Lily came running across the lawn towards them, a flaming smile of delight on her face.

'Grandpapa, you're home!' she gasped, as if he'd just returned from a round-the-world voyage. She kissed his cheek and knelt down on the grass beside his chair. 'Has Iris told you about Prince Edward's visit? It was so nice his being here. Just as nice as when Rory is here.'

Her grandfather chuckled. 'I'm sure Rory will be pleased to hear that. What have you been doing, sweetheart? You've got straw in your hair.'

'I've been feeding the rabbits and cleaning out the hutches. Where is Lord Jethney? Rose said he was coming for dinner and that you were bringing him home with you.'

'He is coming to dinner and I was going to bring him home with me, only he's been delayed. The coronation seems to have thrown the normal running of government into chaos – and there is still nearly a month before it takes place.'

Iris sucked in her breath. 'You're going to find this unbelievable, Grandfather, but I'd forgotten all about the coronation. It's going to be very weird seeing David in his ceremonial robes. Will he wear a coronet?'

'Will he carry a sword?' Lily asked, equally mesmerized at the thought of David playing such an important role in an event so historic it would have the attention of the entire world.

'He'll certainly be wearing a coronet. I don't know about the sword. Although the last coronation was only nine years ago, I can't remember how King George – who was the then Prince of Wales – was robed. I do know that the Prince of Wales takes precedence over all the other peers of the realm, but as Prince Edward isn't of age yet to be a peer, he can't wear a peer's robes. That being the case, I think it highly likely that the King will invest him with the Order of the Garter. There's no age barrier where that most ancient order of British chivalry is concerned.'

'And if he is invested with the Order of the Garter, what robes will he wear?' Lily asked, enraptured.

'He'll wear the Garter dress of white and silver with a blue velvet cloak and a big black velvet hat with white plumes.'

'Oh! He will look *wonderful*. I do wish I was going to be in the abbey to see him.'

'Even if you were, you would probably only get the merest glimpse of him. Very few people have a good view of what takes place.' The tea in the teapot was nearly cold and he rose to his feet. 'It's time for me to have a nap before dinner. Are the two of you coming indoors, or are you going to stay outside in this far too hot early-evening sunshine?'

'The present heatwave isn't too hot for me, Grandpapa.' Lily turned her face blissfully towards the brassy blue bowl of the sky. 'I just want it to continue like this throughout the rest of the summer.'

'The farmers wouldn't like that, sweetheart. We need a healthy amount of rain. We do need weather like this for the coronation, though. It's the reason blazing June is the traditional month for coronations and why, although King Edward died a year ago, King George is having to wait until next month to be crowned. June of last year simply wouldn't have given time for the arrangements to be made.'

Iris slipped her arm through the crook of his. 'Then let's hope the heatwave holds,' she said as, together, they began walking companionably back to the house.

# SIX

King George peered at the glass of Windsor Castle's barometer, tapped the case sharply to make sure that the needle
wasn't stuck, and set it again. The barometer read the same
as it had originally.

'The weather's going to break,' he said bad-temperedly to
David. 'I dare say it will still be the same on Coronation Day.
Rain is the one thing impossible to guard against.' He tugged
at his neatly trimmed spade-like beard. It was anointed every
morning with lavender water and David could smell its faint,
unmistakable tang. 'Come into the library.' His father's
command was as peremptory as always. 'There is an arrangement with regard to the coronation of which I have to apprise
you.'

David's heart sank. So far, his return home had gone
without a footman giving him the dreaded message that the
King wished to speak to him in the library. Dinner, too, had
passed off without incident. Since, after dinner, it was his
father's habit to shut himself away with his stamp albums,
David had been looking forward to a stress-free (if boring)
evening spent in the company of his mother, one of her ever-
present ladies-in-waiting and his sister.

Dutifully he followed his father down the portrait-laden corridor and into the library where all one-to-one talks with his father took place. As his father seated himself behind his large desk David stood in front of it, his legs astride, his hands clasped behind his back, midshipman fashion. It was what his father, who like him had had a naval training, expected.

'It's a damn nuisance you are not of age to be a peer and so I shall invest you with the Order of the Garter. After all, you can hardly take part in a thousand-year-old religious ceremony in naval cadet uniform, can you?'

'No, sir.'

'And your investiture as Prince of Wales will take place at Caernarvon Castle two weeks after the coronation.'

David blinked. To the best of his knowledge no Prince of Wales had had a formal investiture in Wales since the title was created, way back in 1301. A formal investiture in Wales – and at Caernarvon – would be a very big event; and he would be at the centre of it.

He felt violently queasy. He didn't like having all eyes on him. The coronation was going to be nightmare enough, without his having to endure another horrendous ceremony almost immediately after it.

'And afterwards you will begin carrying out public duties proper to your title,' his father continued relentlessly. 'When not at Dartmouth there will be levees to attend and civic and charitable banquets. Never forget how much is expected of you. You were born to a great destiny. Always remember the position that will one day be yours. You will not only be king of the greatest nation the world has ever known, and king of all her dominions beyond the seas, you will also be King-Emperor of India: the brightest jewel in the crown.'

The straitjacket of burdens and responsibilities that were his future was so daunting the very thought of it made David wince.

'I shall always do my utmost to make you proud of me, Papa,' he said stiffly, praying to God the interview would come to a close before more unpleasant shocks were lobbed his way.

His prayer went unanswered.

'Because of your new duties as Prince of Wales, your time at Dartmouth is to be cut short.'

David's heart tightened within his chest. 'But I've yet to go on my final training cruise, sir.'

'When your fellow cadets set off for North American waters you will not be with them. You will be being measured for your Garter robes. You will be being measured for your investiture robes. You will be being coached in the part you will play at the coronation. For your investiture the Chancellor of the Exchequer, Mr Lloyd George, will coach you in the Welsh language. You will be giving thought to the historic speech you will make. But now,' his father said, glowering at him, 'you will explain to me why Bertie was an atrocious sixty-first in his year group and why you, as his elder brother, have not been encouraging him to work harder.'

Even before he began, David knew it was useless explaining that he'd done his best to give Bertie every possible encouragement, but that it had been difficult when rigid rules forbade senior cadets from mixing with junior cadets.

Also, he was too loyal to say that, like him, Bertie found the curriculum massively difficult and that the reason for the difficulty wasn't their fault. Their fellow cadets had all had the advantage of a preparatory school education before going to naval college. He and Bertie had only had a private tutor who had abysmally failed to teach them subjects such as mathematics and science, which they should have had a grounding in.

'House rules mean Bertie and I can only meet up in a far corner of the playing fields and we can't do that very often, sir. And sixty-first isn't really so bad – not for Bertie. He really is trying to work harder.'

There was a deferential knock on the library door.

'*Come!*' his father barked deafeningly.

The door opened and a footman said nervously, 'Your Majesty, Lord Esher has arrived.'

The King's mood changed instantly. Esher was an old and trusted friend and an adviser he relied upon greatly.

'You may go, David,' he said, to David's vast relief. To the footman he added, 'I'll receive Lord Esher in here.'

Once on the other side of the library door, David hesitated. His mother and his sister would be expecting him to join them, but he was far too emotionally disorientated to want to do so.

The news that he was to leave Dartmouth before achieving his goal of the last four years – the final training cruise and graduation – had come completely out of the blue, as had his father's announcement that he would be embarking so soon on what would be a lifetime of public duties. What hadn't been mentioned were any plans for his further education – plans that must, surely, be in place.

That he was always the last person to know of the plans made for him rankled deeply. How long ago, for instance, had plans for his investiture at Caernarvon been made? The answer, he knew, would have been months and months ago.

Two footmen in brilliant livery, their hair powdered, were standing impassive-faced at either side of the library door. As he looked down the corridor he could see at least half a dozen more footmen at strategic points. At dinner that evening two of his father's equerries had dined with them, as had one of his mother's ladies-in-waiting. David assumed that there were times when his parents dined without the presence of courtiers, but he couldn't for the life of him remember them ever doing so.

At this moment, though, he for one wanted to be alone in order to mull over what his father had said and to indulge in the pleasure of reliving his afternoon at Snowberry. Although the presence of footmen would, in royal terms, still equate with his being alone, he wanted to be really alone, with no palace flunkies in his field of vision. At Windsor there was only one place for such absolute privacy.

The roof.

As boys, he and Bertie had often escaped to the castle's battlements, the excitement of the adventure intensified by the knowledge that they were doing something dangerous and utterly forbidden. It was years since he had made his way up the many staircases and along the warren of passages that led to an access door, but he remembered the way perfectly.

As he stepped out on to the vast expanse of lead he could see, ghostly in the moonlight, the dark expanse of the Great Park and, if he turned round a little, the twinkling lights of the little town of Windsor lying at the castle's foot. A little further away was the silken sheen of the river Thames winding its way languorously east, towards London. In the other direction, far too far away to see, lay Snowberry.

He leaned against an enormous chimneystack and lit a cigarette. The contrast between life at Windsor – or at any other of the royal palaces – and the kind of life he had glimpsed being lived at Snowberry, was colossal. When he thought of the careless informality he had enjoyed that afternoon, he knew he wanted to experience it again and again. The question was: how would he be able to?

He blew a plume of smoke into the air. As far as the immediate future was concerned he could detour to Snowberry when travelling back to Dartmouth in two days' time. Or he could if he were sure Piers Cullen would keep his mouth shut about it.

An owl swooped on to a turret a few yards away and

regarded him unblinkingly with yellow eyes. He stared back at it, deep in thought.

Though Piers Cullen had arrived at Snowberry obviously intent on swiftly removing him from it, he had behaved surprisingly well once the game of doubles had been suggested. Had that been because of Marigold? She was probably just the right sort of age for him. She was also as sexy as any Hollywood vamp. Whatever the reason for Piers acting so completely out of character, his doing so had made it impossible for him to tell the King of any future visits without hopelessly compromising himself.

David determined to leave for Dartmouth early enough to be able to spend a few hours en route with his new friends. That he now had people he could call friends filled him with a warm rosy glow. Whatever the difficulties of his future – a future that had been mapped out for him before he had even been born and which he couldn't alter in any way – he knew he would be able to come to terms with it if, unknown to his family and to courtiers, he had the solace of Snowberry and the friendships he had made there.

Especially his friendship with Lily.

At the thought of Lily his knees grew weak.

Not only did she look like an angel, she had the sweet, sunny nature of an angel. He wanted to see her again more than he'd ever wanted anything else in his life, ever.

And he would be seeing her again in two days' time.

The very thought made him feel like a new person. The isolation at naval college caused by his royal position no longer mattered. The fact that he couldn't choose for himself what his future would be no longer mattered in the same way. His dislike of anything that set him apart as a person requiring homage – as would most certainly happen at the coronation and at his investiture and afterwards on endless, innumerable occasions his whole life long – no longer mattered. At Snowberry he could forget all about his royal status and be treated like any other young man his age. At Snowberry, with Rose, Iris, Marigold and Lily, he could simply be himself.

Euphoria surged through his veins. He felt as if he could take on the world. The imminent abrupt ending of his naval training was a bad blow because, once he was no longer driving regularly between Dartmouth and Windsor, opportunities to visit Snowberry would be much harder to come by, but he was going to allow nothing to stand in the way of his finding them.

He dropped the glowing stub of his cigarette and ground it out beneath his foot. With a great flapping of wings the owl flew off to continue to hunt. As David watched it disappear into the star-studded darkness a quite different thought occurred to him. His father had been so irate at Bertie coming sixty-first in his year group that he had completely forgotten to take him to task over his own poor positioning in geometry and trigonometry.

A grin split his face and as he walked back to the access door he was whistling, as happy and as carefree as a lark.

Four days later, he had made up his mind that although his visits to Snowberry had to be kept secret, he couldn't possibly keep them secret from Bertie, so he arranged a meeting with his brother on the far edge of Dartmouth's playing fields.

Bertie was the brother nearest in age to him and since they had been brought up totally isolated from other boys until naval college, apart from seldom-seen royal cousins, there was a very close bond between them.

As Bertie came trotting across the field towards him, the expression on his face was anxious. It was an expression that was almost permanent, for if David had found much of his time at Dartmouth difficult, Bertie, far more introverted and even shyer, was finding it a nightmare.

'W-what is it, David?' he panted, floundering to a breathless stop. 'D-did the K-k-king ask about my class p-p-position?'

'Yes, he did, old chap. I told him you were sixty-first and that that was quite good where you were concerned and that you were working very hard.'

At the still agonized expression on Bertie's face he added a comforting fib: 'He said he was pleased about the way you were trying.'

Bertie's face lit up. 'D-did he?'

'Yes. That wasn't why I wanted to see you, though. I wanted to see you because the most extraordinary, *wonderful* thing has happened to me.'

Bertie couldn't imagine anything wonderful happening to either of them with the coronation hanging over their heads like the Sword of Damocles.

'W-what is it, David? Have you been m-made a cadet c-captain?'

David grinned. 'It's something far more wonderful than that, Bertie. If I tell you, you have to promise *on your life* that you won't tell anyone. Not even Mary.'

Bertie looked bewildered. Though Mary was three years younger than David and over a year younger than himself, they'd always treated her as an equal and had never had any secrets from her.

'Now, d'you promise me, Bertie?' David said, eyeballing him fiercely. 'Not a word to anyone. *Ever.*'

David was Bertie's hero and though it seemed a bit of a bad show that Mary wasn't to be in on David's secret he didn't have the slightest doubt about doing as David asked.

'N-n-not a word, old chap.'

David flashed him his uniquely charming grin and offered him a cigarette. As he was only fifteen and a half it was against the rules for Bertie to smoke, but he took the Capstan gratefully.

When both their cigarettes were alight, David said, 'I've met the most amazing family – and the most angelic girl.'

Girls were foreign territory to Bertie, but he knew that David, as Prince of Wales, would have to marry young because their father, when he had been Prince of Wales, had married young, as had their grandfather, when he had been Prince of Wales.

If their father and mother were already bringing suitable girls to David's attention it didn't surprise him in the slightest. All suitable girls had, of course, to be princesses of royal blood and as Germany had the largest clutch of royal princesses – nearly all of them cousins or second cousins or third cousins – he naturally assumed that David's most angelic girl was a distant German relation.

'I say, it isn't V-Victoria L-Louise, is it?'

Princess Victoria Louise was their Uncle Willy's daughter and both he and David liked her enormously because, although she wasn't very pretty, she was very easy to get on with. A match between the Emperor of Germany's daughter and the heir to the British throne would be a dynastic master-stroke.

'No. She isn't one of the Schleswig-Holstein mob either. Her name is Lily. Her father was Viscount Houghton. He died when she was a baby. She and her older sisters live with their grandfather, the Earl of May. Their home is called Snowberry and it's in Hampshire.'

Bertie blinked. If the Earl of May was a friend of their father he would have heard of him. But he hadn't. He knew their father certainly wouldn't want David becoming acquainted with the daughter of a mere viscount.

'B-but h-how did you m-meet her?' he asked, stumbling for clarification. 'W-where did you m-meet her?'

'I was en route to Windsor and I took a corner criminally

57

wide and knocked Lily's sister, Rose, off her bicycle. She wasn't seriously hurt but I couldn't just say sorry and drive on.'

'So you took her h-home?'

'Yes. Then I met her sisters Iris and Marigold – and Lily. Yesterday I went there again and met Lord May. He's just as nice as his granddaughters. They really are the most spiffing family, Bertie. I wish you could meet them, but I don't suppose you can. If two of us began going to Snowberry, the secret couldn't possibly stay a secret – and I have to be able to keep going there and being friends with the Houghtons, Bertie. I *have* to.'

'C-Cullen will find out.'

'Captain Cullen was with me. I think he's fallen for one of Lily's sisters. We all played tennis that first afternoon and he partnered Marigold in a game of mixed doubles. She's a redhead and a demon of a player. He won't say anything because he wants to keep going back there – I can tell – and if he did say anything, it would come out that he hadn't done so when the first visit took place. Then the King would dismiss him.'

Bertie didn't think it odd that David often referred to their father as 'the King'. It came more naturally to both of them than the word 'father' did.

'L-lady Houghton will t-talk. She's b-bound to. She'll want everyone to know that the P-Prince of W-Wales is a family f-friend.'

'No, she won't, Bertie. She's remarried and lives in Paris. Lily and her sisters won't talk either, because we're friends and they understand how very difficult it is for me to have a private life and how much I enjoy visiting Snowberry. They won't do anything to spoil the fun we all have.'

'F-fun?' Bertie looked even more bewildered. Since their grandfather King Edward VII had died, fun wasn't something either of them had had much experience of.

'Yes. Just being at Snowberry is fun. There's a lake, and when I visited on my way back here we all swam – or at least everyone but Marigold swam. She was in London, staying with her great-aunt, Lady Harland, who has a house in St James's Street.

'Marigold', he added, 'likes parties and dancing. Unlike Rose and Iris and Lily, she spends a lot of time in London.'

'She sounds pretty r-r-racy.'

David flashed him the smile that so totally transformed his face. 'I think she is. I also think Piers Cullen is pretty besotted with her. He was terribly moody yesterday. Just kept staring at Lily and barely speaking to anyone. He didn't make any objections to being there, though. I expect he was hoping Marigold would turn up.'

'After the s-swimming? W-what did you do then?'

'We had tea, picnic-style on the lawn. Lily's pet goat launched itself into the chocolate cake Millie had made, but it was so very funny it didn't matter.'

'M-Millie? Is she another s-sister?'

David dropped his cigarette stub to the grass. 'No. Millie is the cook. There is also a butler, William, who has been in service with Lord May since the two of them were young men, and though there are parlour maids and kitchen maids, there is no housekeeper. Rose acts as the housekeeper. She doesn't seem to mind. She's frighteningly capable and sensible and she doesn't let anyone get away with any nonsense – me included.'

'G-golly.' To Bertie it seemed a very strange set-up and he didn't know whether to be impressed by it, or alarmed.

'The Sinclair side of the family also have a home on the Isle of Islay. It's where Lily's cousin Rory lives. He often visits Snowberry for a week or so at a time – it was his swimming gear Cullen and I borrowed – and so he'll probably have to be let in on my visits there. But no one else is to know, Bertie.'

'N-no. Of course not.' Bertie tried to imagine what would happen if their father discovered David's secret. The thought of a rage that would be nothing less than apocalyptic made him feel giddy. He took a deep, steadying draw on his cigarette, waiting for David to tell him some more.

David didn't do so. He was staring dreamy-eyed into the middle distance, reliving the magical moment when he and Lily had left the picnic together.

'I'm going to take all the fruit and salad we haven't eaten down to the buns,' she'd said. 'Would you like to come with me?'

'The buns?' He'd wondered if she'd meant to say 'bins' and if clearing up in such a way after a picnic was a strange Snowberry custom.

'Buns is short for bunnies,' Rose had said, seeing his confusion. 'Lily's rabbits are totally spoiled, and be warned that one of them – the big black one – bites.'

'No, he doesn't.' Lily had put leftover salad and fruit into one of the otherwise now empty picnic baskets and risen to her feet. 'Nibbles just has bad eyesight and sometimes catches your fingers accidentally when you're feeding him.'

Rose and Iris had hooted with laughter.

Grateful that Piers Cullen was with Lord May, admiring Lord May's pride and joy, his Talbot motor car, David had risen to his feet and, hardly able to believe his good fortune, had fallen into step beside Lily as she began walking towards a part of the garden he hadn't yet been to.

'Are you getting very excited about the coronation?' she'd asked as they walked down a shallow flight of stone steps into what he saw was a lower lawn on the west side of the house. 'There was a piece in the newspaper this morning about all the magnificent street decorations that are being put up. It said that the twenty-second of June will be one of the most memorable days the country has ever seen.'

She'd smiled across at him, expecting him to respond with enthusiasm. Instead, so suddenly reminded of the ordeal that lay before him, he'd blanched.

Her expression had changed instantly. She'd come to a stop, saying in a stunned voice, 'What on earth is the matter, David? Aren't you looking forward to it?'

With anyone else – other than Bertie – he would have lied and said that of course he was. Instead he'd said unhappily, 'No. I'm dreading it. The ceremony is hours and hours long and there are so many things that could go wrong. At one part of the ceremony I have to pay homage to my father and I'm terrified of forgetting the words. Plus I shall be wearing heavy ornate robes and a coronet and I hate being dressed like someone out of medieval times and being stared at.'

At her look of horrified concern, he'd added miserably, 'I'm not very good at being royal, Lily. I just don't enjoy it.'

She didn't have to say how awful she thought that must be for him. He could see it in her eyes.

She'd said thickly, 'But you *have* to enjoy it, David. It's going to be your whole life.'

'I know.' He'd given a helpless shrug of his shoulders and they'd started walking again.

After a few moments she'd said, 'Perhaps if you thought of how much pleasure royal ceremony gives to hundreds of thousands of people, and how much pleasure you give to people when they see you dressed in magnificent medieval robes, you wouldn't mind wearing them quite so much?'

It was a point of view he'd never thought of before and he'd found it interesting. She hadn't, though, grasped the real crux of why his royal status filled him with such overwhelming despair.

By now they had reached the grassy pen where half a dozen rabbits were happily hopping about. He'd watched her as she filled feeding bowls with the fruit and salad they had brought with them and then, as she lifted one of the rabbits out of the pen and knelt on the grass with it on her lap, he'd said: 'It's not having any choice about things that's so difficult, Lily. I can't choose what I want to do, or be. Unless I die before my father, nothing in the world can prevent me from becoming king. My father didn't want to become king. He was in the navy and he wanted to stay in the navy, but once his father died he had no choice in the matter. Like it or not he's the King of England and he'll be the King of England – and of an Empire that straddles the world – until the day he dies.'

She'd had her head bent low over the rabbit. Then she'd raised it, her eyes meeting his, her hair tumbling in a riot of ringlets past her shoulders. 'I think that when you become king you'll be a very great king,' she'd said solemnly. 'I think you should be proud of such a privilege. Think of all the good you will be able to do. Think of being loved by so many hundreds of thousands – *millions* – of people. And all they will be wanting from you is that you do your best for them.'

As their eyes held his breath caught in his throat. He didn't know about doing his best for millions of people, but he did know that he wanted to do his best for Lily. He wanted to make her proud of him. He wanted her to love him, as he knew, beyond a shadow of a doubt, that he loved her.

The rabbit had hopped free of her lap and, sitting on the grass beside her, he'd taken hold of her hand.

Her fingers had curled around his.

And at that moment, Snowberry's lower lawn had become, for Edward, Prince of Wales, the Garden of Eden.

# SEVEN

The London home of Sibyl, Lady Harland, was *en fête*. It wasn't an unusual occurrence. Though she was seventy-two years old, Sibyl still loved a party. 'We'll be fourteen for dinner, with sixty more people invited to my little pre-coronation party afterwards,' she said in high satisfaction to Marigold as she inspected the flower arrangements for the evening with an eagle eye. 'You know I've scored quite a coup. The Prime Minister *and* the Marquess of Lansdowne.'

The Marquess of Lansdowne was the Leader of the Opposition in the House of Lords and, politically, he and Mr Asquith did not see eye to eye.

'It means', she said as Marigold looked a little mystified, 'that with luck there will be lively verbal fireworks at the dinner table. That means a memorable dinner party, and a memorable dinner party, dearest Marigold, is a successful dinner party.'

'Who else will be here?' Marigold asked, mentally filing Sibyl's advice away for future use, thrilled that the Prime Minister was to be the guest of honour at dinner. 'Will anyone close to King George be among the guests?'

'The only people close to King George are his courtiers

and sparkling dinner conversation is not their forte. They are all far too close-mouthed. Even if they weren't, what could they possibly have to gossip about that would be of interest? It isn't as if King George has a mistress tucked away. All the man is interested in is stamp-collecting and shooting. It's a wonder there is any wildlife left at Sandringham.'

Laughter bubbled in Marigold's throat. She adored her great-aunt Sibyl's salty conversation. She also adored the kind of people who frequented her great-aunt's town-house in St James's Street, close to St James's Palace. Everyone who came was a somebody, because, like herself, Sibyl had no time for nonentities.

'The Stainfords will be here,' Sibyl continued, tweaking a petunia into a more pleasing position. 'The Shaw-Stewarts; Strickland, the portrait painter; the Jethneys; young Mr Churchill, though not his very delightful wife, Clementine. She is *enceinte* and the baby is expected any day. Lord Conisborough and his new bride. She's an American and I'm told she is great fun.'

The news that Theo was to be one of the dinner guests sent adrenalin singing along Marigold's veins. The fact that he would be there with his wife didn't trouble her. She liked Jerusha. When, a few days ago, Rose had told her quite flatly that her flirtation with Theo was a cruelty to Jerusha she had been exasperated beyond words. 'I'm not trying to *steal* him from Jerusha, Rose. I don't want him to leave her and to marry me. I just want to enjoy feeling extra alive when I'm with him. I can't see what's wrong with that.'

An aghast Rose had told her that there was plenty wrong with it and that she was amoral. Afterwards, Marigold had looked the word up in a dictionary and thought Rose was probably right. For the life of her, though, she still couldn't see what all the fuss was about. Fascinating older men were always married and as it was fascinating older men she enjoyed being with – and as they so obviously enjoyed being with her – what was she supposed to do? Ignore them? Try as she might, she just couldn't see the sense of doing that.

What she did see the sense of was living life as *she* wanted to lead it, and not as other people thought she should lead it. What would Rose think if she suddenly started lecturing her about her WSPU activities? Or if she started taking Iris to task for having no other interests but horses and dogs? They wouldn't like it and – more to the point – they wouldn't take any notice of what she said, either.

Happy with the conclusion she had reached she wasted no more time thinking about Rose's disapproval. Instead she thought about the evening ahead and of how much fun being privy to the verbal sparring between the Prime Minister and her great-aunt's close friend, the Marquess of Lansdowne, was going to be. Politics didn't really interest her, but politicians – successful, powerful politicians – did. It was one of the reasons she found Theo Jethney so mesmerizingly attractive.

That evening she wore long emerald earrings, an emerald necklace given to her by her mother and an off-the-shoulder evening gown in shimmering black taffeta. Unless she was in mourning it was an unheard-of colour for a nineteen-year-old girl to wear – which was why Marigold was wearing it. Against the drama of the dress her Titian hair blazed like a candle-flame. To her chagrin she discovered that Viscount Conisborough's bride was also a redhead and looked no older than she was.

Though they were seated at opposite ends of the table, it was obvious that they were each stealing the other's thunder and Marigold half expected Delia Conisborough to shoot her a look of aggrieved fury. Delia didn't. She simply shot her a wide smile, her eyes showing nothing but friendly amusement.

There was no smile on Theo's face. As he looked towards her down the length of the table the expression in his eyes was one of grim urgency. Because she found teasing him great fun, she looked away, listening with rapt attention to what Mr Asquith was saying so that when the opportunity came for her to talk to him, she would be able to appear far more intelligent than she actually was – a ploy she had honed to perfection. All around her brilliant conversation ebbed and flowed and she wondered what kind of an impression Rose and Iris made when visiting Sibyl. Rose was quite intelligent enough to hold her own no matter what the subject of conversation, but as her political views were diametrically opposed to many of their great-aunt's regular guests Marigold couldn't quite imagine how Rose got on. If she had been here this evening, for instance, suffragette talk in front of the Prime Minister would not have gone down at all well. Apart from that, although she looked striking, Rose was incapable of flirting and, in Marigold's experience, their great-aunt's gentlemen guests – the Prime Minister included – adored it when she flirted with them.

As for Iris . . . The idea of Iris scintillating in a gathering such as the present one was impossible. Iris was not a sophisticate, and neither was she a beauty. The only person this evening who would have had time for Iris was Jerusha, for Jerusha's interests, like Iris's, centred almost entirely on domestic matters and country pursuits.

Lily, of course, didn't count, for she hadn't even been presented at court and wasn't yet 'out'.

As she heard Violet Rice, the Duchess of Stainford, say to Lawrence Strickland, 'I quite agree with you about Matisse. There is something of the decorative effect of a child's drawing about his work,' Marigold finally turned her head in Theo's direction, her eyes meeting his.

With a stab of shock she saw that he was looking over-wrought and the silent message he flashed towards her, as the rest of the table erupted in laughter at one of Margot Asquith's acidly sharp witticisms, was impossible to mis-understand. He wished to speak to her in private at the very earliest opportunity.

She hoped it wasn't going to be about something stuffily boring.

'The person I would most *love* to capture in pastels is Lily Houghton,' the Duchess of Staines was now saying. 'She has a most extraordinary quality.'

Marigold was distinctly miffed. The duchess was an acclaimed artist who had exhibited at the Royal Academy and had been likened to Holbein. Her delicate sketches of her friends were famous. Margot Asquith had sat for her, as had Princess Beatrice of Battenberg and Arthur Balfour who had been prime minister a few years ago. In fact it was hard to think of anyone celebrated or beautiful who *hadn't* sat for her.

When Marigold thought of how much she would like to see a portrait of herself hanging in the Royal Academy, as Margot Asquith's had, she began to feel more than miffed. She began to feel very cross. Then she saw the way Lawrence Strickland was looking at her.

Strickland was a portrait artist too, though in oils; and oils would, she knew, suit her flamboyant beauty far better than pastels or pencil.

Her eyes told him exactly what she was thinking.

He tilted his head a little to one side, looking back at her in a way that sent a very odd emotion snaking down her spine.

Like Winston, who was now discussing the tricky subject of Home Rule for Ireland with Ivor Conisborough, he was not a good-looking man, but had undeniable presence. It was a presence not given to him by his tailoring, which was abysmal. The sleeves of his dinner jacket were a good inch too short, as if, like a lanky schoolboy, he had outgrown it. There were traces of cigarette ash on his waistcoat; a speck of yellow paint on one of his thumbs. His hair was worn too long; his eyes were the colour of mud. His whole physique was awkward – too tall, too bony, too gangling.

She was riveted by him.

'We ladies will not be leaving you gentlemen to your port this evening,' her great-aunt said, rising to her feet. 'Not when I believe some of my party guests have already arrived. Winston, would you be so gracious as to give me your arm?'

'It would be my honour, dear lady.'

As they left the table and made their way towards the ballroom, Violet Rice again commandeered Lawrence Strickland. Marigold didn't mind. She knew she would be having a private word with him before the evening was over.

For the moment, though, it was Theo who was trying to have a private word with her. As they stepped into the ballroom and Jerusha began happily greeting a sea of people she knew, he began walking in her direction – and was waylaid by the Marquess of Lansdowne.

Marigold shrugged her shoulders philosophically and scanned the room to see whom she could most happily flirt with. There was no sign of Rory, which was a disappointment. Why her cousin preferred the isolation of the Isle of Islay to the excitement of London she couldn't imagine, especially when London meant the opportunity of meeting the most influential people of the day at his grandmother's.

She weaved her way among the guests, all of whom she knew from her debutante season, and caught sight of the Honourable Toby Mulholland, Iris's unofficial fiancé. Because his family home, Sissbury Castle, was so near to Snowberry, she had known him ever since she could remember. Even when they had been children she had found him dull company and as he wasn't startlingly handsome and certainly wasn't imbued with the glamour of power, she didn't particularly want to spend time with him.

He headed straight towards her and instead of asking if Iris was with her, as she had expected, he said, 'You look wonderful, Marigold. Make me the envy of every man in the room and waltz with me?'

Without being offensively rude, she didn't see how she could refuse.

As they took to the floor he said with a leer, 'I understand from a friend that you've acquired a rather racy nickname, Marigold. Nell Gwynne.'

She had been expecting his sole subject of conversation to be Iris. What she hadn't expected was for him to start flirting with her – and that, unless she was much mistaken, was what he was trying to do.

Instead of encouraging him, which she would have done with almost any other man, she said coolly, 'Is it racy?' She knew very well that it was and wondered who the friend had been. 'I thought I'd been given it because I have the same colour hair Nell had, and because I like oranges. When Nell first came to King Charles's attention she was selling oranges.'

Aware that his remark had annoyed her and that it wasn't going to lead to the sexually provocative conversation he'd been hoping for, he said, holding her a little tighter, 'Ah! I hadn't realized that was the reason. Is anyone taking you into supper, Marigold, or may I?'

No one had, as yet, asked if they could take her in to supper, but Marigold liked to keep her options open. 'I don't think that would be a very good idea, Toby,' she said as they rounded a corner of the ballroom and she saw that Jerusha was waltzing with Ivor Conisborough and Delia Conisborough was dancing with the Prime Minister. 'Aren't you curious as to where Iris is? You haven't asked.'

He chuckled. 'I'm assuming that as she isn't with you, she's at Snowberry.' And then, as she didn't give a little laugh back, he said, 'Confidentially, Marigold, Iris and I haven't been seeing much of each other since I joined the Coldstream Guards.'

Marigold stopped dancing so suddenly that he stumbled over her feet. 'Are you hinting that an engagement between you and Iris is no longer on the cards, Toby? Because if you are, the person you should be telling is Iris. It's stretching it a bit to say she has already bought a wedding dress, but she certainly thinks she'll be doing so soon.'

'Then she's being too quick off the mark. To tell you the truth, Marigold, over the last few months I've realized that though Iris is wonderful, she is no longer quite in my league. Now can we continue dancing? We're beginning to attract attention.'

'No, we can't continue dancing! Reason one is because you are a terrible dancer, and reason two is because I don't like the way you are talking about Iris!'

Leaving him flushed with embarrassment she walked from the dance floor, making a beeline for Theo as fast as her narrow-skirted, beaded evening gown would allow.

In white tie and tails, his night-black moustaches elegantly curled, his hair brilliantined to a glossy sheen, he looked splendid. He also looked to be under enormous strain.

She wondered if it was because of the brouhaha existing at present between the House of Commons and the House of Lords – he was, after all, a government minister – and hoped very much that it wasn't. She'd already suffered enough talk at the dinner table about the House of Lords' imbalance of hereditary Conservative peers to Liberal peers and the way that, because of it, many of Mr Asquith's Liberal policies were being blocked. She didn't want to hear about it again.

'Step out on to the terrace,' he said in a low voice as she came within earshot, looking all the while towards Jerusha who, now the music had changed, was being whirled around the floor in a Viennese waltz by the Shaw-Stewarts' son, Patrick. 'But don't draw attention to yourself.'

Marigold felt a flash of impatience. The evening was not turning out remotely as she had expected. Rory wasn't around to laugh and joke with. Her only dance of the evening so far had been with Toby chinless-wonder Mulholland and now Theo was seriously out of sorts and speaking to her as if she was one of the underlings at his ministry.

Severely miffed, she headed towards the French doors leading to the terrace.

Two minutes later he joined her in the darkness. She slid her arms up and around his neck, not wanting to waste a second of their illicit time together in boring conversation.

His mouth came down on hers firmly and sweetly, but he didn't prolong the kiss and caress her as he would normally have done. Instead, far too soon, he lifted his head from hers and held her a little away from him to look into her face.

'What I have to tell you is going to be very difficult for me, Marigold,' he said, praying to God that he would have the will-power to carry his decision through. 'More difficult than you'll ever know.'

Her pleasure at physical contact with him died. From his tortured expression it was obvious that what he had to say wasn't anything to do with the lack of Liberal peers in the House of Lords, or Home Rule for Ireland. It was something to do with the two of them – something she wasn't going to want to hear.

She stood very still, her hands pressed against his chest, waiting.

'We haven't been as careful as we thought, Marigold.' The rich resonant voice that spoke so commandingly on national and international matters was bleak. 'Your grandfather has given me a word of warning.'

She removed her hands from his chest. 'And?' she said, knowing very well that it would have been Rose who was behind her grandfather's cautionary words and not understanding what the fuss was about when with one smooth lie Theo could put all her grandfather's fears to rest.

'And, as your grandfather is aware that you have, in his words, "a crush" on me, it means a suspicion has been aroused. Our affair can't continue, Marigold. Continuing with it would be suicidal.'

She stared at him, unable to believe what she was hearing. 'I thought', she said, when she could trust herself to speak, 'that you were in love with me? That nothing like me had ever happened in your life before? That if necessary you would die for me?'

He groaned and, releasing his hold of her, passed a hand despairingly across his eyes. He'd never said anything to her that he didn't mean. In twenty-five years of marriage he had rarely been unfaithful to Jerusha – and on the occasions he had been, it had been with married women who knew the rules of the sport being played.

Marigold was different. In being young, single and virginal she had been off-limits and different right from the very beginning. But he'd been too intoxicated by her to care. So intoxicated he'd cast all reason and restraint to the wind.

Now the day of reckoning had come. Much as he wanted to, he couldn't divorce Jerusha and marry Marigold; divorce for a man of his class and social position was unthinkable. As for Marigold, if word got out that she was no longer a virgin, her reputation would be destroyed. No truly eligible young man would even consider marrying her. The life of the person he had come to care passionately about would be ruined – and he would be the one who had ruined it.

Overcome with remorse, he said unsteadily, 'I shouldn't have started this, Marigold. I took advantage of you in a way that was quite despicable.'

That he thought he, or anyone else, was capable of taking advantage of her, filled Marigold with indignation so hot it swamped all her other feelings.

'No one', she said fiercely, the tears she had been about to give way to now held in check, 'has ever taken advantage of me. Not you, Theo. Not anyone.'

He mistook her meaning, believing she was trying to ease the guilt he felt. 'You were a nineteen-year-old virgin, my darling,' he said thickly. 'My seducing you was unforgivable.'

She gave him a long, long look. She had been mad for him for over a year, and she was mad for him no longer. Instead, she was infuriated with him. That he would end their steamy romance merely because her grandfather had warned him off was incomprehensible to her. Theo's attraction had always been that he was such a powerful public figure. But a powerful public figure who couldn't allay an elderly friend's suspicions and fears wasn't, in her book, powerful at all.

Her disillusionment was deep – as was her desire to hit back at him.

'I'd never realized you thought you had seduced a virgin,' she said waspishly, 'but it is at least one burden I can lift from your shoulders.'

Her reaction was so unexpected – so unlike the pleas and tears he had braced himself for – that he was totally thrown. Bewilderedly, he said, 'I'm sorry, Marigold. I'm not following . . .'

'I wasn't a virgin when we started our affair,' she said, hoping the lie wouldn't show in her voice. 'I'm sorry, Theo. When we first went to bed together I thought you would be

73

able to tell.' She gave a careless, expressive shrug of her shoulders. 'When you said nothing, I thought it best for me to say nothing.'

Jethney couldn't breathe. Couldn't speak.

Seeing his reaction and satisfied with the body-blow she had delivered, Marigold turned swiftly away from him and headed towards the French doors.

As her hand touched the handle, he said, 'Take a word of advice from someone who cares very deeply for you, Marigold. Accept the first marriage proposal made to you before gossip means there will be no suitable offers. Once you are safely married you can discreetly indulge in as many love affairs as you please. As a single young woman you can't. A ruined reputation would be disastrous for you, my darling.'

Keeping her back towards him she turned the handle downwards and opened the door.

He said quietly, 'If you ever need help in any way, you know where you can come.'

The tears she'd held at bay for so long threatened to choke her. Not turning towards him – knowing that if she did she would lose all dignity and precious self-control – she nodded her head to show she had heard, then stepped into the brilliantly lit ballroom, leaving him alone in the darkness.

As the sea of Sibyl's guests surrounded her, the tears she hadn't shed burned the backs of her eyes. Her affair with Theo had mattered far more to her than she'd allowed him to believe. Its necessary secrecy had been intoxicatingly exciting and she didn't know how she was going to endure the boredom of life without it. The way that he had ended such a blissful affair so – to her – unnecessarily, was something she didn't think she would ever get over.

She caught the eye of Daphne Harbury, one of Rose's WSPU friends, and vowed such a thing would never happen to her again. In the future, where men were concerned, *she* would be the one who ended things.

'Marigold!' Daphne swooped down on her, angular and agonizingly plain. 'I don't suppose Rose is in London as well, is she?'

Marigold shook her head, hoping no one would think that, like Rose, she was a bosom friend of Daphne's and a fellow member of the WSPU.

Daphne's horsy face fell. 'What a shame. There's a terrific demonstration being planned for Sunday. I'm hoping to get myself arrested.'

As Marigold said, deadpan, 'I do hope you're successful, Daphne,' she saw Lawrence Strickland. He was leaning against the jamb of the ballroom's double entrance doors, his arms folded, one foot nonchalantly crossing the other at the ankle.

He wasn't watching the dancers.

He was watching her.

'Excuse me, Daphne,' she said, her stomach muscles contracting giddily. 'There's someone I simply must speak to.'

Leaving Daphne once again standing on her own, she headed straight for the double doors.

Strickland didn't look remotely surprised that she was doing so.

When she came to a halt in front of him, he didn't stand up straight or unfold his arms. He simply said, 'You want me to paint you.'

It was a statement, not a question.

'Yes.' Her mouth was dry, her heart hammering. 'I want to see my portrait exhibited publicly, at the Royal Academy, as Margot Asquith's was.'

He cocked his head to one side. 'I'll do so, but only on one condition.'

'What is that?'

'That I also paint you as a goddess of Greek legend, because that is how I see you.'

Marigold tried to remember the paintings she had seen in the National Gallery depicting ancient Greek nymphs and goddesses. As far as she could recall, the nymphs and goddesses in them had all been semi-naked – sometimes even completely naked. She wondered if that was the way Strickland wanted to paint her. Looking into his mud-dark eyes, she rather thought it was.

Common sense told her she should speedily walk away from him as, for entirely differing reasons, she had just walked away from Theo and, earlier, Toby.

She didn't.

Strickland was an acclaimed artist. If he wanted to depict her as a Greek goddess, it was an opportunity too good to miss. Besides, she looked wonderful naked. Theo, who had never seen a natural redhead before, had been mesmerized.

A slow smile split her face. Here was an adventure far more erotic and shocking than her adventure with Theo.

Knowing how deep the waters were that she was plunging into – and not caring – she said, 'I think that would be a splendid idea, Mr Strickland.'

# EIGHT

Rose and Iris were seated in cane chairs on the lawn, glasses of lemonade in their hands. Rory was on the grass beside them. 'I'm sure the two of you are telling me the truth about Prince Edward's visits to Snowberry,' he said, amusement in his voice, 'but you have to admit it takes a lot of swallowing.'

'He likes being here,' Rose said matter-of-factly. 'I think he's beginning to regard Snowberry as a refuge. It's somewhere he can forget about being Prince Edward and can simply be a young man called David.'

'And that's really what you call him?' Rory ran a hand through hair that was as turbulently curly and as flame-red as Marigold's. 'You don't call him Prince Edward, or sir or Your Highness?'

Iris giggled. 'No. He's David. And to him we are Rose, Iris, Marigold and Lily.'

'And what happens if anyone finds out about his visits? What if, when he's here, Tessa Reighton rides over from Chanbury Hall to spend time with Marigold? There would be no more keeping things secret then.'

Rose took a drink of her lemonade. 'If that happened,

and gossip got out and reached the palace, then his visits would come to a very swift end. King George would see to that. And if the visits mean as much to David as I think they do, it would be a great pity.'

Rory quirked an eyebrow. 'Especially if he'd fallen in love with one of you.'

Rose tossed her lemonade straw at him. 'Idiot,' she said affectionately. 'There's nothing like that about things at all – and besides, we're too old for him.'

'You, Iris and Marigold may be. Lily isn't.'

Rose's eyes widened and Rory knew that Prince Edward falling for Lily was something that had never occurred to her.

She said uncertainly, 'I don't think that's something that is happening, Rory. David is very shy.'

'Shy or not, I think it would be impossible for him – or anyone else – to spend time with Lily without falling in love with her. And they are the same age.'

There was an odd inflection in his voice and Iris wondered, not for the first time, if perhaps Rory was a little in love with Lily. She knew no one else would think it likely. Rory was twenty-six and his taste in girlfriends ran to the glamorous and sophisticated. They never remained long on his arm. Once they began thinking of engagement rings they were smoothly dropped and speedily replaced.

Rose said, 'Even if he is taken with her, nothing will ever come of it. Royalty only ever marries royalty. When did you ever hear of the heir to the throne marrying anyone other than a royal princess? It's never happened and it isn't going to start with the heir to the most prestigious throne in the world marrying a viscount's daughter.'

'Poor Marigold.' There was amusement back in Rory's voice. 'Can't you just imagine how much she'd love to have a sister who was Princess of Wales?'

'Dear Lord, yes!' Iris rose to her feet. 'Whatever you do, Rory, don't even put the idea of it in her head or she'll be planning her outfit for the wedding! And while you two continue to sit out here, baking in the sun, I'm going inside where it's cooler.'

She walked away from them towards the house, Homer loping after her, and when she was out of earshot Rory said, 'How is Marigold these days, Rose? Do you still have anxieties where she and Theo Jethney are concerned?'

'I did have until I spoke with Marigold earlier this morning.' With no father to turn to for advice, and with a grandfather who was very unworldly, Rory had always been Rose's sounding board if she had any family worries. 'She promised me she'll never flirt with Lord Jethney again and she told me that at your grandmother's party, she never even danced with him.'

Rory moved from the grass to Iris's vacated chair. 'Whom did she dance with?' he asked, knowing that where Marigold was concerned it was always best to try and stay one step ahead of the game.

'Toby, Patrick Shaw-Stewart, the Duke of Stainford.'

As the Duke of Stainford was so elderly as to be doddery, Patrick Shaw-Stewart pallid-faced and freckled and Toby uninteresting to anyone but Iris it didn't sound to Rory as if Marigold had had a very exciting time.

He didn't say so, though. It would only make Rose worry as to what Marigold might next do that would be exciting, for with Marigold there always had to be something. Her need to be the centre of attention was an annoyance to everyone in the family but him.

He understood. Marigold had been only three when her father had died and five when her mother had remarried and gone to live in Paris. They were abandonments that Rose, four years older than Marigold, had been tough enough to come to terms with and that Iris, always stoic and practical, had also accepted. Lily had been saved from damaging grief by being so young. For Marigold, though, things had been very different.

He could vividly remember her pathetic bewilderment when her father had died, followed by heartbroken crying; crying that hadn't ceased when everyone else's had. 'The little mite sobbed herself to sleep for months,' Millie had once told him. 'And when her mother upped and went off to Paris . . . well, that was terrible, truly terrible. She was so distraught, it made her ill.'

It was after that that the fibbing had started – something he thought Marigold still did – and that her urgent need for attention first appeared. She was forever putting on impromptu theatricals, singing and dancing for anyone she could persuade to sit down and watch her. Even now, if she could capture an audience, she would put on a *tableau vivant*, transforming herself into Hiawatha with the aid of a magnificent feather, or Joan of Arc, eyes raised up to heaven, one of her grandfather's antique swords clasped fervently in her hands. Another favourite subject was the beheading of Mary, Queen of Scots. Kneeling with a scarf around her eyes, her arms stretched out behind her, she always attempted extra realism by persuading Fizz or Florin to hide under her skirts as the Queen's little dog had done.

Rose's bafflement when she had first suspected Marigold of flirting with Lord Jethney, a man old enough to be her father, had not been shared by Rory. He found it perfectly plausible that when it came to falling in love, Marigold would seek a father figure.

He rose to his feet. 'It's time I was getting back to London. When Marigold is next staying at St James's Street, I'll keep an eye on her for you – and I'll let you know of any inside gossip I get about your friend Daphne.'

80

Rose stared at him. 'Daphne? Daphne Harbury? Why on earth should there be gossip about her? I don't know what you're talking about, Rory.'

'You didn't read yesterday's *Times*?' He frowned. 'No, I can see you didn't. Daphne Harbury was arrested after a suffragette demonstration. She's to appear at Bow Street Court tomorrow and according to the newspaper, it seems she'll very probably receive a prison sentence.'

Rose paled. 'Daphne is the daughter of an earl. Surely, considering who her father is, she'll be let off with a fine?'

'I'd like to think so, Rose, but I very much doubt it. The demonstrations have become far too violent and other aristocratic young women have been imprisoned. Not only that, they are on hunger strike being forcibly fed.'

Rose sucked in her breath. She'd been immured too long at Snowberry, far from suffragette activity. It was time she went back into the fray – and the first thing she had to do was to give Daphne moral support by being at Bow Street tomorrow morning.

She said decisively. 'I'm coming to London with you. Your grandmother won't mind me arriving at St James's Street unexpectedly. Iris will have to look after things whilst I'm away.'

That afternoon, with Rose en route to London with Rory, Iris took the dogs for a walk around the lake. She had something on her mind; something that was causing her intense distress. She was beginning to think that Toby was no longer as interested in her as she had believed him to be. Ever since he had joined the Coldstream Guards a little over a year ago it was almost as if the unspoken understanding that had existed between them for as long as she could remember had come to an abrupt end.

She came to a halt, staring out over the shimmering surface

81

of the lake. Toby had commandeered her as his best friend when, in the years before he had gone to prep school, there had been no one else near Sissbury for him to be friends with. She had always been the tomboy in the family and had loved racing her pony against his, swimming with him in Snowberry's lake, fishing with him in the river that ran through Sissbury's estate, climbing trees and making secret dens with him in Sissbury's woods. She had enjoyed all that far more than the boring dressing-up games Marigold always wanted to play.

Even after he had gone to Eton they had still been inseparable whenever he was at home and, as they had both grown a little older their friendship had made her feel special in a way that, being the plain Jane of the family, was very important to her. She might not be as academically clever as Rose, or as stunningly beautiful as Marigold, or as sweetly lovable as Lily, but Toby never spent time with Rose or Marigold or Lily. He spent time with her – and she had grown up hoping he would always do so.

Then he had joined the Coldstream Guards and had begun moving in a world far removed from that of Sissbury and Snowberry, which they had shared for so long. Instead of riding with the local hunt, he now played polo at matches in Surrey and Berkshire that she wasn't invited to; they were matches she knew would be attended by the kind of girls men regarded as being 'a catch'.

She bit her lip, well aware that she couldn't be described by anyone as 'a catch'. She hadn't even been 'a catch' the year she had been a debutante. That was the year when girls hoped to get engaged and it was certainly the year she had hoped for a proposal from Toby.

When she hadn't received one it had been a disappointment, but one she had understood, for his father, Viscount Mulholland, had been seriously ill that summer with typhoid fever. Though Toby had waltzed her around her great-aunt's ballroom at her coming-out ball in a manner that had caused happy speculation about the two of them, for most of her season he had been at Sissbury where his father had hovered between life and death for many weeks.

No one else had shown any interest in her at all.

At other debutantes' coming-out balls and parties she had been a wallflower, seated with the chaperones, an empty dance card in her hand. Or she had unless Rory had also been a guest; he had always come to her aid and ensured that, for a little while at least, she was the envy of a mass of other girls. Rory, though, was her cousin and so didn't really count.

She sighed, seeing spinsterhood ahead of her if Toby didn't propose. That spinsterhood very probably lay ahead for Rose – who was now twenty-three and still not within a mile of becoming engaged – was no comfort. Like the vast majority of militant suffragettes, Rose believed that remaining single was all part of the battle; that to gain full equality with men, women had to be independent of them. It was an attitude Iris, who longed for marriage and babies, found hard to understand.

As she continued to look out across the lake she found herself wondering again about the weekend Marigold had spent at their great-aunt's. Rose had been so relieved about Marigold getting over her infatuation for Lord Jethney that for the moment she'd ceased worrying about her. Iris hoped Rose wasn't doing so prematurely. There had been an air of suppressed excitement about Marigold when she had returned from London – and if Lord Jethney wasn't the cause, then, knowing Marigold, another man was.

Feeling the need of Lily's company, she headed back towards the house, Lily, like herself, rarely left Snowberry. She was generally out of sight, though, in a large attic room that had been converted into a studio with huge skylights. There she spent hour after hour modelling busts and heads in clay. Rose had expressed the opinion that once her debutante year was over, Lily was talented enough to apply for a place at the Royal College of Art. It was a prospect that Iris knew both elated and terrified Lily. It was also a prospect Iris doubted Lily would ever have to face, for nothing was more certain than that Lily would be inundated with marriage proposals during her debutante year, and that all of them would be highly suitable.

Lily would, just by being herself, ease the hurt that was in Iris's heart and, for a little while at least, take her mind off the anxiety as to when, if ever, Toby was going to pop the question.

Rory dropped Rose off at 4 Clement's Inn, just off the Aldwych. The headquarters of the WSPU was, as always, a hive of frenzied activity.

'It's good to see you again, Rose,' Christabel Pankhurst said to her as they squeezed into a comparatively quiet corner of the long inner office for a talk. 'You can see how busy we are.'

All around them a score of women were working like beavers, addressing envelopes, making banners, printing leaflets and manning phones.

'We intend stealing the show at the Coronation Procession of the Women of Britain on the seventeenth of June,' Christabel explained. 'We don't want the Women's Freedom League outdoing us, do we? You will be there, Rose, won't you?'

'I'll be there. As for tomorrow morning, I shall be at Bow Street.'

Hearing the steel in her voice, Christabel narrowed her eyes. 'Don't do anything that might get you arrested, Rose.

Not when there's so little time before the suffragette coronation procession – and when five days later it's the coronation itself. There'll be plenty of time for heroics afterwards.'

'If Daphne is given a prison sentence – and is sentenced to serve it as a common criminal and not as a political prisoner – then I shall protest, Christabel, even if it means missing the procession and the coronation.'

For a second she thought Christabel, who was the WSPU's chief strategist and whose word was law, was going to forbid her to. Then Christabel flashed the wide, vibrant grin for which she was famous. 'Quite right, Rose. If you can bring attention to the great indignity done to our members by being brought before ordinary courts when their offences are political, then do so.'

Her grin widened. 'Be sure to make it known that you are the great-niece of Lady Harland who is a friend to both the Prime Minister *and* his odious home secretary, Churchill,' she added wickedly. 'That will make the press really sit up and take notice!'

# NINE

'That odious man Churchill was here again this morning with the Prime Minister,' King George said, stamping fretfully from the dining room, David at his side. 'He takes far too much on himself. Do you know what the damned scoundrel wrote to me in his account of a Commons debate on the relief of unemployment? '"As for tramps and wastrels there ought to be proper Labour Colonies where they could be sent for considerable periods and made to realize their duty to the State." Well, that bit was all right, but then he had the damned impertinence to add, '"It must not, however, be forgotten that there are idlers and wastrels at both ends of the social scale."'

As he bore down on his study two footmen in blue and gold sprang into action, hastily flinging open the double doors. The King stormed through them, David in his wake. 'His views are those of a damned socialist, not a liberal!' he fumed, heading straight for the glass cabinets where his beloved Purdey shotguns were kept. 'What he advocates is nothing more than workshops, which have been tried in France and have turned out a complete failure.'

He lifted down one of the two shotguns that the people

of King's Lynn had presented to him and took it over to his desk. Then he slammed open the drawer that held his brass-cornered oak cleaning case. David was relieved. For an insane moment he'd thought the King was about to hunt down his perfidious home secretary and teach him a violent lesson.

'After I had written back, remonstrating with him, then d'you know what the bloody fellow did?' The King took an ebony cleaning rod from the case, a square bottle of oil and a Selvyt cleaning cloth. 'He wrote to me *again*, and in the most insolent manner.'

He pushed a piece of House of Commons headed notepaper across the desk to David.

Wishing he possessed just an eighth of Winston Churchill's nerve, David read:

Mr Churchill will feel a serious difficulty in writing letters in the future, after what has occurred, for fear that in a moment of inadvertence or fatigue some phrase or expression may escape him which will produce an unfavourable impression on Your Majesty. He therefore would earnestly desire that Your Majesty would give commands that the duty should be transferred to some other Minister who would be able to write with the feelings of confidence in Your Majesty's gracious and indulgent favour, which Mr Churchill regrets to have lost.

David thought the defiance of the reply, the way it succeeded in being both deferential and yet annoyingly mocking, very clever. It was the sort of letter he wished he was able to write. Aware, however, that this was not what his father would want to hear from him, he said, 'The man is a cad, sir. He's more belligerent now the Liberals are in government than he was when they were in opposition.'

87

The King made a satisfied harrumphing noise and David felt vast relief. For once in his life he had, it seemed, made the right response.

His father began disassembling the Purdey with practised ease, saying, 'Naturally Knollys advised a conciliatory reply.'

Lord Knollys was one of his father's two private secretaries, a man who had vast experience and who came from a long line of royal courtiers. An ancestor of the same name had been the Treasurer of the Household to Queen Elizabeth. Where pedigree was concerned, Knollys' was exceptional.

'How was that received, sir?'

'How d'you think it was received?' His father glared at him. 'It mollified him, damn him.'

Aware that if he didn't continue making right responses his father's wrath was going to be unleashed on him as well as on Mr Churchill, David said, choosing his words carefully, 'So will Mr Churchill be continuing with his Cabinet task of writing daily to you with a description of parliamentary proceedings?'

'Unfortunately, yes. Though Knollys didn't accept his doing so until he'd told him in no uncertain terms that he should have suppressed his remark about idlers and wastrels, bearing in mind that the cost of support in one case falls on the State and does not do so in the other.'

He rammed the cleaning rod down the barrel of the gun, saying, 'So now we come to you, David.'

David tensed, certain it was going to be about him coming forty-eighth in geometry and forty-fifth in trigonometry. To his great relief he was proved wrong.

'You're to stay in London from now on – and at Buckingham Palace, not Windsor. We can't have Lloyd George trekking to Windsor to give you lessons in the Welsh language. There's a formal rehearsal at the abbey tomorrow. Bertie needn't be there, of course. He'll be a spectator on the twenty-second, not a participant. I'll be there too, though I'm not leaving for the abbey until tomorrow morning.'

David's heart sank to his boots. The command to return to Windsor after only a week back at Dartmouth had come as a very welcome surprise, or it had until there had been a phone call from the palace just before he had left, confirming his time of departure and estimated time of arrival. The phone call had meant he hadn't been able to spend time at Snowberry en route. To compensate, he'd intended spending as much time there as possible on the way back.

Now that plan was also out of the window. Even worse, he had no way of telling when he would next be able to visit Snowberry.

Plucking up all his nerve, he said, 'Very good, sir. I'm looking forward to my Welsh lessons with the Chancellor of the Exchequer. I shall need to return to Dartmouth pretty speedily today, though, to tidy things up. An essay to put in. That kind of thing. I'll be back early tomorrow and go straight to Buckingham Pal—'

His father stopped what he was doing. 'ARE YOU DEAF, BOY?' he bellowed. 'YOU'LL LEAVE FOR THE PALACE *NOW*, DAVID. THIS MINUTE!'

For the King to have even mentioned the word deaf, considering his own deafness, was an indication how near he was to a full-scale explosion. Not only would arguing any further be as useless as arguing with a brick wall, it would also be highly dangerous.

'Yes, sir. I'm sorry if—'

'NOW!'

He left the room and, without even going to the White Drawing Room to say goodbye to his mother and to Mary, he left for Buckingham Palace, with Piers Cullen at the wheel of the Austro-Daimler.

'When will we be returning to Dartmouth, sir?' Piers asked as the car swooped smoothly down Castle Hill.

'God only knows. Perhaps never.' The bitterness in his voice was profound.

Piers hesitated and then said, 'And Snowberry?'

David looked out of the car window. It was a beautiful late evening. The sky was the smoky violet of deep dusk and in the town of Windsor gas lamps illuminated decorations already in place for Coronation Day.

'As soon as ever the hell I can.' His fine-boned jaw was set hard, his hands clasped so tightly between his knees that the knuckles gleamed white.

As the Daimler swept through the quiet streets he shot a quick glance towards his equerry and was touched to see that Piers, aware of the difficulties there would be when it came to visiting Snowberry in the future, was looking devastated on his behalf.

Such loyalty was touching and he warmed towards the man he often found a stiff and difficult companion.

'I have to have some corner of my life to call my own, Piers,' he said, his use of Piers's Christian name indicating how charged his feelings were. 'Snowberry gives me that. I'm not going to forgo it, no matter what the difficulties may be.'

'I'm pleased to hear that, sir.'

They lapsed into silence. An hour later, as the car eased into the dark courtyard of Buckingham Palace, David said, 'I shan't require your company any further tonight, Piers. Once inside the palace I'm going straight to bed. Finch will see to all I need.'

Finch had been his personal servant since David was a child, when he had served both him and Bertie as a nursery footman. Now, dependable and devoted, he acted as David's valet whenever David was at the palace.

The Austro-Daimler came to a halt and David stepped out into the warm night air. For a moment he looked un-lovingly at the forbiddingly austere palace façade. Despite the redecorations that had been taking place ever since his grandfather's death, the palace was not yet a home either to him or to his parents.

Previously their London home had been Marlborough House, which, though splendidly grand, had also managed to be what his mother described as *gemütlich*, German for comfortable and cosy. Buckingham Palace wasn't remotely *gemütlich*. Formed of four sides enclosing an inner court-yard, it was massive in size and there was no coherence to the interior. In a way that was both rambling and confusing acres of red-carpeted corridors and narrow passageways linked state apartments, picture galleries, throne room, grand drawing rooms, numerous small sitting rooms, bedrooms, landings and staircases.

His own suite was on the third floor overlooking the Mall. So far, he had spent only a handful of nights there. Glumly he set off on the long trek towards his rooms, enduring the acknowledging nods of knee-breeched footmen as they stood sentinel at every strategic corner of his route.

'It's a pleasure to have you back, sir,' Finch said wel-comingly after David had walked what had seemed to be at least half a mile. 'You've got a long heavy day ahead of you tomorrow, I understand.'

David was tempted to respond that now his father had deemed him old enough for public duties – public duties that would continue for the rest of his life – he had long heavy days ahead of him until eternity. It would, though, have been self-pitying and dear old Finch deserved something better from him.

'It's going to be a daunting day, Finch. His Majesty will be there and the Archbishop of Canterbury and no doubt the Prime Minister and a host of other people who will be involved in the ceremony on the twenty-second. I don't suppose it will be the real Crown of England that will be used in the rehearsal, though. I expect it will be a dummy.'

'Just as long as the dummy crown is the same weight, sir,' Finch said practically. 'When your grandfather was crowned he said the crown was so heavy he thought his knees were going to buckle. You look as if you could do with a nice cup of milky cocoa, sir. Shall I go about getting one?'

David nodded. Finch had been organizing comforts such as cups of hot cocoa ever since his nursery days. Until now he'd thought Snowberry perfect in every single detail, but it occurred to him that there was one detail it lacked, and that detail was Finch.

With his thoughts on Snowberry again, something else occurred to him. Something he had been wondering about more and more often. 'What happens if a royal prince wants to marry someone aristocratic but non-royal, Finch? D'you remember that ever happening?'

Finch paused in the act of brushing down the jacket he had helped David take off. 'Now, that's quite a question, sir. It mostly depends, of course, on whether the royal prince in question is heir to the throne or not.'

'Well, let's suppose that he is. What would happen? I expect there'd be an awful stink about it.'

'I believe there would, sir.' Finch hung the jacket up and then said, 'In that case I expect the marriage would have to be what I understand is called a morganatic marriage, sir.'

David was never surprised at the kind of information Finch had at his fingertips. 'What does that mean?' he asked, intensely interested.

'I think it means that the lady in question is never granted royal status, and that any children are excluded from the line of succession to the throne. Just which of your European cousins is in this predicament, may I ask?'

David tapped the side of his nose with his finger and grinned. 'Ah, now that would be telling, Finch, wouldn't it?'

Finch knew better than to pursue the subject. He was that rare thing, a royal servant who wasn't servile, but was always carefully respectful, even to the young man who, as a small child, he had dandled on his knee.

When David was finally on his own he took his mug of cocoa over to his desk and sat down. Then he took notepaper and a pen from the desk's middle drawer and began writing his first letter to Lily.

*My dear Angel*

He stopped. How could he address Lily in the way he felt about her when he hadn't yet told her how he felt?

He took another sheet of Buckingham Palace headed paper and started again.

*Dear Miss Houghton*

He stopped again. This was even worse. It was far too formal.

*Dear Lily*

Then, throwing caution to the winds, he took a fourth sheet of notepaper from the drawer and wrote:

My dearest Lily,

I was hoping to call in at Snowberry today, en route for Windsor, but due to circumstances beyond my control I wasn't able to. I can't even call in on my way back to Dartmouth as I had to leave Windsor for Buckingham Palace this evening in order to be near the abbey, ready for a day of coronation rehearsals tomorrow. It's all an awful bore, and I wish I didn't have to be there, but I do. How are the buns? Give

93

them some extra lettuce from me and do please forgive this fearful scrawl. I do miss Snowberry. And you.

David

He put the letter in an envelope, sealed it, rang for one of the twelve postmen constantly doing the rounds inside the palace and, when he arrived, gave orders that the letter be sent express. Then he crossed to the window and stared broodingly down into the lamp-lit darkness of the Mall for a long, long time.

The next day, when he arrived at the abbey, it was to find it a scene of chaos. People were milling about everywhere, some in uniform, some not. Choristers were trying to practise; vergers were swarming like flies and putting name cards on the hundreds and hundreds of seats; the dean was having an argument with the Duke of Norfolk who, as Earl Marshal, was responsible for the whole ceremony and who, in turn, was trying to have a conversation with the Lord Great Chamberlain, who was responsible for the conduct of royal affairs in the Palace of Westminster.

'You wouldn't think rehearsals had been going on for weeks now, would you, sir?' Piers Cullen said to him as a harassed-looking Archbishop of Canterbury approached the Duke with more problems.

'No,' David said, not knowing they had been.

A whole flotilla of choirboys from St James's Chapel nearly knocked him off his feet as they scurried past him in order to join the Westminster Abbey choirboys.

The Duke of Norfolk disentangled himself from the Lord Great Chamberlain and came striding across to him, the archbishop in his wake.

'Good morning, Your Royal Highness,' he said, sounding remarkably unharassed. 'A run-through of your homage speech is needed. I will deputize for the King. Now, what happens is this . . .'

Time after time, as other parts of the service were being rehearsed around them, David knelt before the Duke of Norfolk, nervously saying the vastly important words he had learned by heart.

'I, Edward, Prince of Wales, do become your liege man of life and limb, and of earthly worship; and faith and truth I will bear unto you, to live and die against all manner of folks. So help me God,' he said nervously.

'Now you rise to your feet,' the Duke said when he was eventually satisfied. 'At the actual ceremony you will touch the crown upon the King's head – it will be St Edward's crown, worn only at a coronation – and kiss him on the left cheek. That is all your homage is. After you, the peers will do homage. The next rehearsal at which you will be required will be the full dress rehearsal on the twenty-first.'

Grateful that his part was over for the day, David looked around for someone a little more knowledgeable than Finch when it came to the subject of morganatic marriages.

He could see the Prime Minister deep in conversation with Lord Lansdowne, who was carrying the royal standard, as he would be doing on Coronation Day. Asquith would, no doubt, know all about morganatic marriages, but David sensed that he wasn't the man to ask in case it set him wondering *why* he was asking.

A royal courtier would be a much better bet. Lord Knollys and Lord Stamfordham were both in the abbey, as was Lord Esher, but all three were intimate friends of his father. As he didn't want his father to know of his curiosity with regard to morganatic marriages, he made no move towards any one of them.

He suddenly heard an elderly voice saying plaintively, 'I really am going to have to sit down for a little while, Esher.

As the order of procession is to be just the same as it was when King Edward was crowned nine years ago, I really don't see why so many lengthy rehearsals are necessary.'

The weary peer was Lord Wainwright, a man of great age who, fifty years ago, had been a courtier to David's great-grandmother, Queen Victoria. If anyone knew about morganatic marriages, it would be Wainwright – and Wainwright was not a member of his father's inner circle.

As Esher moved away and Lord Wainwright sat down (most inappropriately on a seat inscribed with Mrs Asquith's name on the back of it), David sat down next to him.

'I have a query – purely academic – that I think you may be able to help me with,' he said with a friendly smile. 'I want to know what would happen if the heir to a throne wanted to marry a young lady who, though aristocratic, was non-royal.'

'Ah, you're talking, of course, of an heir to a *European* throne,' Lord Wainwright said, mistaking David for one of the many minions who were helping the Earl Marshal to organize the rehearsal. 'Well, there are plenty of examples to be found. Take Emperor Franz Josef's heir, the Archduke Franz Ferdinand, for instance. He wanted to marry Countess Sophie Chotek, who was not nearly royal enough. It caused a crisis lasting for more than a year, for when the Archduke was asked to choose between his lovely countess or succession to the Habsburg throne, he refused to.'

'Quite right,' David said stoutly.

Lord Wainwright, who loved an audience, smiled at him benignly. 'It took the prime ministers – two of them, because the Habsburg Empire straddles both Austria and Hungary – as well as a whole cluster of bishops, and an even bigger cluster of constitutional lawyers nearly a year to come to a workable conclusion.'

'Which was?'

'Which was that if Franz Ferdinand promised that his countess would never show herself either at court or in high social circles and would never make claims of any sort or seek to play a royal role, a morganatic marriage would be found acceptable.'

David breathed a sigh of relief. 'So Franz Ferdinand kept his Sophie and also keeps his right of succession to the throne?'

'Indeed he does. But any children he and Sophie have will not be allowed to succeed him, and when he and Sophie married not one member of his family was present.'

'How unspeakable.' David was outraged.

'Then of course there was the morganatic marriage of Queen Mary's grandfather,' Lord Wainwright said as a procession of heralds passed close by them.

'Queen Mary? D'you mean the Queen Mary who ruled in the fifteen hundreds and persecuted the Protestants?'

Lord Wainwright ducked to avoid his head coming into contact with the standard of England as the hereditary king's champion, who was carrying it, followed the heralds down the aisle. 'No, dear boy,' he said. 'Our present queen. When her grandfather, Duke Alexander of Württemberg, married a non-royal Hungarian countess he wasn't as lucky as Franz Ferdinand. Unlike him, he lost his right of succession to the throne, and so did his son, the Queen's father.'

Oblivious of the way David's jaw had dropped, he said, 'It made things very difficult for Queen Mary's father, who was given the title Prince of Teck, Teck being a subsidiary name of the House of Württemberg. He was quite fortunate in that Queen Victoria didn't view *ebenbürtig* in the same way the German courts have always done. When he fell in love with Princess Mary Adelaide, Queen Victoria's niece, Queen Victoria happily gave them her blessing.'

'*Ebenbürtig*?' David's head was reeling.

97

'It means of equal birth. The German royal families are sticklers for it.'

The standard of Wales was now being carried past them, followed by the standard of Scotland. David struggled to get his head around the amazing fact that his maternal great-grandmother had not been of sufficiently elevated birth for his great-grandfather to have been able to marry her and to keep his rights of succession. Why had no one ever told him of the skeleton rattling away in the family cupboard?

'Our present queen also owes a great debt to Queen Victoria's fair-mindedness,' Charlie Wainwright added as the standard of Ireland was carried past them. 'It was she who suggested that Mary of Teck would make a perfect future Queen of England. Because of not being *ebenbürtig*, her hopes of marrying into a European royal house had been rather thin until then.'

David goggled. Lord Wainwright was talking about his *mother*. That his mother might once have been considered not royal enough to marry into a royal house was a staggering revelation. He had always thought of her as the most regal, majestic person he had ever met. Which she now was, thanks to her marriage to his father – and that marriage, apparently, had been entirely due to his awesome great-grandmother, Queen Victoria.

Before he could gather his thoughts and ask something more, the Duke of Norfolk announced in ringing tones, 'After the standards will come the King's regalia and then the sword of temporal justice, which will be carried by Lord Kitchener, and the sword of spiritual justice, which will be carried by Lord Roberts.'

As the lords concerned took their places, David reflected on all he had just learned. His mother's family history meant that if he should wish to marry someone not of royal blood, she would surely be understanding. Archduke Franz Ferdinand's experience showed that it *was* possible for the heir to a throne to both marry a non-royal *and* to remain heir to the throne.

Even though the situation wasn't yet applicable to him, just knowing what the possibilities were made him feel quite giddy. If he were ever so fortunate as to have Lily fall in love with him, then the difficulties they would face would be difficulties that could be overcome.

As if on cue, there was a blare of trumpets and as shafts of sunlight fell upon the fawn and azure hangings and peers and prelates passed and repassed across the blue and gold carpet in front of the throne, David felt for the first time the grandeur and the sacredness of what was soon to take place there. He remembered what Lily had said about the splendour of royal ceremonial cheering the lives of millions of people and suddenly, instead of finding the role he had been born into a nerve-racking burden, he was filled with pride and honour.

'Ah, there you are, sir,' the Duke of Norfolk said, bearing down on him, and then adding to Lord Wainwright, 'If you'll excuse us, Wainwright. I would like His Royal Highness to go over his homage speech one more time.'

Leaving behind them a pole-axed Lord Wainwright, he bore David off for one final rehearsal.

# TEN

Lily was alone in her eyrie. Sunlight streamed in through the massive skylights her grandfather had had put in when she first asked if she could use the large attic room as a studio. Her turbulent hair was pinned carelessly on top of her head and she was wearing a flowered overall over one of her oldest dresses.

She was working in water clay on a bust. Though she usually liked people to sit for her, this time she was working from memory. The bone structure she was capturing was so delicately moulded it could have been that of a girl, but for the masculine stubborn set to the mouth.

She stepped back from her work table for a moment, assessing what she had done so far, wondering if she should, perhaps, have tried to capture David's likeness in paint, rather than sculpture. It was his expression she most wanted to convey, most particularly the melancholy she often saw in his eyes when he had to leave Snowberry for what he always termed his 'princeing' life at Windsor.

'*Weltschmerz* is the word for it,' her grandfather had said when she had tried to explain the expression to him. 'It means intense sadness caused by comparing the actual state of things with the ideal state of things. In Prince Edward's case, the actual state of things is the prison he was born into – and make no mistake about it, Lily, to be born heir to a great throne is to be born into a life so confining it can only be described as a prison – and the ideal state of things, which for him would be the freedom to live life howsoever he chose.'

She also wanted to be able to convey David's shy charm. It was a quality he seemed totally unaware of, and one that was quite spellbinding. Even Rose, who found charm in men intensely suspect, had fallen an instant victim to it.

Lily took more clay out of the clay-bin and set to work again. Several days ago he had written her a sweet, short letter telling her of how he was in London for a coronation rehearsal and of how he was missing Snowberry. And her.

She had never kept anyone's letters before, but she had hunted out a shallow japanned box that had once held biscuits and was prettily decorated with roses and butter-flies and placed the letter inside it. Since she had, two more letters had joined it. Letters she had told no one about as yet; not even Marigold.

She wasn't sure, but she thought that Marigold, too, had a secret. Even though she had so recently spent a long weekend in London, she had been back there twice in the last few days and each time she had returned home, Lily had sensed Marigold's inner excitement.

Rose was also spending nearly all her time in London.

Her friend, Daphne Harbury, had been given a three-month prison sentence and had been sent to Holloway.

'And Rose', Iris had told Lily, 'is lobbying everyone she can in order to get Daphne released – and via Great-aunt Sibyl that is an awful lot of powerful people.'

The door nudged open and Homer ambled into the studio and flopped down by her feet. Lily didn't mind. She liked it when Homer, or Fizz and Florin, kept her company.

As she continued to work, she thought about the forth-coming coronation. That David was the Prince of Wales still seemed strange to her and she wondered if it would seem a little less so after she had seen him on Coronation Day in full royal regalia.

She wouldn't be in the abbey, of course. Of their little family at Snowberry only her grandfather, a peer of the realm, would be in the abbey, dressed in what he termed his coronation 'full fig': his coronet and an ankle-length robe of crimson velvet topped by a shoulder cape of white ermine trimmed with the appropriate number of black sealskin spots.

Great-aunt Sibyl, who was a dowager marchioness, would also have a seat in the abbey. Rory, however, was joining Lily, Rose, Iris and Marigold at Sibyl's house, where, from one of its wrought-iron balconies, they would have a grandstand view of the coronation procession as it passed down St James's Street on its return to Buckingham Palace from Westminster Abbey.

She paused in what she was doing, rotating the turntable on which the bust stood in order to view it from another angle, grateful that as no one else would be with them, they would be able to talk freely about David as his carriage passed below their balcony. If their mother had been with them they wouldn't have been able to utter a word – or at least not a word that would indicate he was both a regular visitor to Snowberry and their friend. A secret of that kind was one their mother would be totally unable to keep.

There had been a rather fraught period of time when they'd thought their mother was coming over from France for the coronation, but as her second marriage rendered her ineligible for a seat in the abbey she had decided against it. She was a woman who liked being at the centre of things and, if she couldn't be, she preferred to give the appearance of negligent unconcern.

Lily continued looking at a section of the head from the left-hand side. She had been wrong to start on the cheek-bones so soon. Before working on the bust again, she picked up some callipers and began retaking measurements to ensure that all her basic proportions were exactly as they should be.

It was William who interrupted her. 'I'm very sorry to disturb you, Miss Lily,' he shouted through the speaking tube that linked Snowberry's ground floor to its upper floors, 'but Captain Cullen is here to see you.'

Lily stopped what she was doing and, with her heart slamming, crossed the studio to pick up the funnel-shaped end of the speaking tube. 'Is Prince Edward with him?' she shouted down it.

'No, Miss Lily. The Captain is unaccompanied.'

Lily's eyebrows pulled together in a puzzled frown. 'Did he initially request to see Marigold, William?' she asked, her heart returning to its normal rhythm.

'No,' William shouted, as if she were in the next county and not merely two floors above him. 'He simply asked if you were at home.'

'I'm sure you've made a mistake, William. Why would he ask to see me?'

'Perhaps he has a message for the family from His Royal Highness. With your grandfather being in London to collect his coronet from storage at Asprey's, and with Miss Rose and Miss Marigold also in London and Miss Iris out for a walk somewhere, I didn't like to say you were unavailable. Just in case.'

As she told William that she was on her way down, her heart began beating faster again. William's assumption had to be correct, though as Piers had specifically asked for her, she doubted if the message he was bringing from David was for the family as a whole. It was far more likely to be a message just for her.

Scrambling out of her flowered overall, she ran from the studio, Homer hard on her heels.

Piers Cullen was waiting for her in the middle of the drawing room, as ramrod straight and forbidding-looking as always.

'How nice to see you, Captain Cullen!' she said cheerily and a little breathlessly as she hurried into the room. It wasn't too much of an exaggeration. Not if he had a message for her from David.

Piers cleared his throat. From his first visit to Snowberry, when Prince Edward had invited the Houghton sisters to address him as David, he had been known by his Christian name as well.

'Piers,' he reminded her.

'Piers,' she said with an apologetic smile. Then she waited for him to give her whatever message it was he had come to deliver.

He didn't. Instead he said, 'It's a beautiful day, Miss Houghton – Lily. I wondered if you would like to go for a drive.'

She stared at him, wondering if she had heard correctly. 'A drive? Is David with you? Is he outside, waiting for us?'

'No.' He tried not to let his disappointment at her reaction show. It was, after all, quite understandable that she should think he was, as usual, accompanying the Prince. 'His Royal Highness is in London.' No way could he bring himself to refer to Prince Edward as David when Prince Edward had infuriatingly never invited him to. 'He will be there now until after the coronation.'

She nodded. David had told her that, in his letters.

As Piers Cullen said nothing further, she gave him a gentle prompt, 'So are you here to deliver a message from him?'

'A message?' He looked baffled. 'No. Prince Edward is in

rehearsals at the abbey again today and as I was not needed I thought . . . I thought perhaps you would like to go for a drive and that we could . . . could talk.'

The thought of being able to talk with him about David and about David's princeing life was irresistible.

She smiled sunnily. 'That would be lovely. Just give me ten minutes to change my dress and do my hair.'

As she left the room he could hardly believe his good fortune at having called at a time when there was no one at home from whom she'd had to ask permission. Of course, it would have been quite out of the question to behave as he'd just done – and as she had just done – if it had been any other girl of Lily's class and age. Well-brought-up girls of seventeen did not go out with a young man unchaperoned, especially when the man in question was several years her senior.

From his very first contact with the Houghton sisters and with Snowberry it had, however, been very obvious that the normal rules governing society simply didn't apply. It eased his conscience, as did the fact that his intentions were entirely honourable. Lily wasn't remotely the kind of young woman he had envisaged falling in love with, but her sweetness of spirit and *joie de vivre* were exactly the antidote his introverted, sombre personality craved. His intentions were to court her, to become engaged to her as soon as possible, and to marry her when she was eighteen.

She was the daughter of a viscount, not the daughter of a marquess or a duke; she wasn't too far above him in the class hierarchy for it to be an unreasonable ambition. Though his family weren't titled, they were ecclesiastically distinguished and, as an equerry to the Prince of Wales, he had status. Most importantly of all, she obviously liked him a great deal. No girl had ever been so pleased to see him as she had been when she so eagerly entered the room.

Now they were going to spend time together alone. He wondered where he should take her, where she would like to go.

He was still wondering when she came back into the room dressed in a raspberry-pink dress that had a nipped-in waist and a broderie anglaise collar and carrying a straw hat that had a raspberry-coloured silk ribbon around its brim. Her hair had been brushed and was once more worn down – which rather disconcerted him for it reminded him that she wasn't yet 'out'. He thrust the thought to one side, certain she would be presented before the summer was over.

'Goodness!' she said when she saw his car. 'It's even bigger than David's motor car!'

He was highly pleased by her reaction. 'Prince Edward's was a gift from his first cousin once removed, Kaiser Wilhelm. German cars are generally a little smaller than the ones being made in Britain.'

'Have you met Kaiser Wilhelm?' she asked as he opened the front passenger door for her. 'It seems so funny David having so many German relations. Nearly every aunt, uncle and cousin he mentions is German.'

'That's because his paternal great-grandmother, Queen Victoria, was entirely German by blood, if not by birth, and she double-looped her German heritage by marrying a German, Prince Albert.' He seated himself behind the wheel. 'Though Queen Mary was born at Kensington Palace, her bloodline is almost entirely German, too. Her father, the Prince of Teck, was German and her maternal grandmother was German.'

As he drove down the drive he hoped that his knowledge of royal genealogy was impressing her. 'It's the reason Prince Edward is so blond and Teutonic-looking,' he added for good measure, turning into the road.

Lily thought of David's pale gold, glassily smooth hair

and of the startling blueness of his eyes. He *did* look German, though not a raw-boned, beefily muscular German. Instead he reminded her of pictures she had seen of medieval Teutonic knights, full of valour and honour, their white mantles bearing the scarlet cross of St George.

She wondered if David spoke German; if the King and Queen sometimes spoke to each other in German.

'Good Lord, no!' Piers said, when she asked about the King and Queen. 'The King doesn't speak any foreign language.'

'Not even French?' Lily was shocked.

'Not even French.'

He began heading in the general direction of Winchester, happy that there was a subject that interested her and that he could talk about. More interested than he could even begin to imagine, she said, 'What about Queen Mary? Does she speak German?'

'Fluently. As does Prince Edward.'

Lily was entranced. Why had it never occurred to her that Piers Cullen could tell her such interesting things about David?

'Is that why there's sometimes the trace of an odd accent in his speech?'

'An odd accent in his speech?' He shot her a look of complete bewilderment.

'Yes. It was Rose who drew my attention to it. She thinks it sounds almost cockney.'

Comprehension dawned and he did something she hadn't thought him capable of. He gave a bark of laughter.

'It *is* cockney. Lala Bill, who was his nanny, is a cockney. She's still a royal nanny, only now she is nanny to Prince John.'

Prince John was the youngest of David's four brothers and not someone David had spoken about when at Snowberry.

Later, when they were having tea and cakes in a very

upmarket Winchester tearoom, she asked Piers about David's other brothers, and his sister, Princess Mary.

Though he had no intention of admitting it, Piers had had very little contact with David's siblings. The only royal personage he met with regularly was the King, who demanded constant reports as to his son's activities. Remembering the grave offence he was committing in not having told King George of Edward's visits to Snowberry, he blanched. If the truth came out his disgrace would be so enormous Lily's grandfather would never give permission for them to marry. Beneath the table he clenched his hands tightly. The truth wasn't going to come out. And he *was* going to marry Lily. His single-track mind ensured that any goal he set himself, he doggedly achieved.

Aware that she was still waiting for an answer to her question, he unclenched his fists. 'Prince Albert is a shy boy. Very nervous. A very bad stammerer. He hero-worships . . .' He paused. The words 'His Royal Highness' or 'Prince Edward' stuck in his throat when Lily spoke so easily of Prince Edward as David. 'He hero-worships HRH,' he said, feeling that HRH sounded informal enough to indicate close friendship.

'What about Princess Mary?' she asked, helping herself to an almond slice from the heavily loaded cake-stand.

He knew less about Princess Mary than he did about Prince Albert, but it was common knowledge at Windsor and Buckingham Palace that she was a far better rider than either of her two older brothers.

'She rides very well. She is only three years younger than HRH and so she and Prince Albert and HRH are good chums.'

'And Prince Henry and Prince George and Prince John?'

'Prince Henry and Prince George are tutored by Mr Hansell, who was HRH and Prince Albert's tutor until they went to naval college. As for Prince John . . .'

He came to a halt, wondering what the devil he could say about the youngest member of the royal family. There were so many wild rumours about John: that he was epileptic; that he was retarded. If he told her of them she might let slip to Prince Edward that he had and then there would be a row of unholy proportions.

'Prince John is the extrovert of the family,' he said.

This was true. Though he was not quite six years old, Prince John quite often upset the royal apple cart by escaping from Lala Bill and waylaying high-ranking courtiers and government ministers, greeting them in a way that was extremely disconcerting. 'Haven't you got a big, big nose?' he had shouted cheerily to the Prime Minister. To the Prime Minister's wife, Margot Asquith, he had said, 'You're a funny-looking lady, aren't you? Are you a witch?'

What made such remarks even worse, was that they were always so apt. The Prime Minister *did* have a big nose and Mrs Asquith, in the long, black, scarlet-lined cloaks she favoured, *did* look like a witch.

Piers told Lily of how John had once got hold of Princess Mary's paintbox and, after daubing himself like a Red Indian, had run whooping into the dining room when the King and Queen were holding a dinner party. He told her how John was now kept out of sight as much as possible, and that he wouldn't even be in Westminster Abbey with his brothers and his sister when the King was crowned.

Lily was appalled at the thought of John missing out on such an historic occasion and even more appalled when Piers told her of how Prince Albert had once been so terrified when told his father wished to speak with him in the library that he had fainted dead away, and of how the King had ordered that the pockets of Edward's suits be sewn up after Edward had put his hand in his pocket when speaking to him.

'I'd no idea King George was such a bully,' she said as they drove back to Snowberry. 'Poor Prince Albert. No wonder he stammers.'

Piers was rather taken aback. He had told the anecdotes because he had thought they were amusing. Compared to the Scottish Presbyterian strictness in which he had been brought up, Edward and Bertie's lives were, he thought, a piece of cake. He didn't say so, though. He said, 'Prince Albert is left-handed and is required to write right-handed. HRH says it causes him a lot of stress.'

'I'm not surprised it causes him a lot of stress!' Lily was furiously indignant. 'How would the person responsible for such a decision like it if someone forced them to write left-handed?'

The person responsible was King George, but Piers thought it best not to say so.

As they drew up outside Snowberry's rose-covered frontage Lily's grandfather stepped outside, his expression one of concern.

Piers sucked in his breath. Lord May had every reason to be displeased. Taking Lily out for a motor ride, when there had been no one to ask permission to do so, had been grossly out of order. Taking her out without anyone to chaperone her had been even more out of order. Fervently hoping he hadn't spoiled his future chances, he stepped out of the car.

'William told me whom you had gone out with, but not where you had gone to,' her grandfather said to Lily, and then to Piers, he said, 'Your action was extraordinary, Captain Cullen. I appreciate that over the last weeks you have become something of a family friend, but Lily is seventeen and not yet "out".'

As Piers flushed a deep red, her grandfather turned to Lily again. 'You should have known better, sweetheart,' he said with loving reproach. 'Another time – if there is another time – if I'm not here for you to ask permission, you must stay at home.'

'Oh, but I hope there will be another time, because I've had the most splendid afternoon, Grandpapa!' Lily's eyes had stars in them.

She turned to Piers. 'Thank you so much for such a *wonderful* afternoon, Piers. I enjoyed it hugely.'

Then, innocently leaving him under completely the wrong impression as to the reason for her enjoyment, she walked indoors, Fizz and Florin skittering around her in excited welcome.

# ELEVEN

For once when staying at Sibyl's at the same time as Marigold, Rose took very little notice of Marigold's comings and goings. All her thoughts were centred on how she could secure Daphne's release from prison. Her great-aunt had been as helpful as she could be.

'The first person to appeal to, of course, is Winston. As home secretary, he could order Daphne's release immediately. Unfortunately, it is highly unlikely he will do so. He's implacably opposed to the WSPU's violent methods of demonstration. However, nothing ventured, nothing gained, and I will ask him if he will meet with you.'

'How about the Prime Minister?' Rose had asked, remembering how taken with her Mr Asquith had seemed at one of her great-aunt's dinner parties a few short weeks ago.

'I'll do my best, but with the coronation only days away I doubt he will have time to be doing favours. If I were to tell him that you wanted to speak with him regarding Lady Daphne's imprisonment, he most certainly wouldn't find the time to meet with you.'

'But you will try, Aunt Sibyl?' she'd asked anxiously.

'I shall try.' Her aunt had pursed her lips. 'Not all my influential friends are anti Votes for Women, Rose. Let me make a list for you of those who will be only too happy to add their names to your campaign.'

The list had been impressive and heading it had been the name of Lord Jethney.

Quite how she felt at asking for Lord Jethney's support, she didn't know, and she decided that though she would meet with him, she would do so only after meeting everyone else who was willing to see her. The first person with whom Sibyl secured a meeting for her was the Home Secretary, Winston Churchill. The meeting took place in the House of Commons, and though he was courteously civil to her, asking after both her grandfather and Sibyl, he was as immovable as a rock when it came to the question of an early release for Daphne.

'Absolutely impossible, Miss Houghton,' he'd said implacably. 'Lady Daphne was sentenced in a court of law and must serve her time.'

A five-minute meeting she had with the Prime Minister at Downing Street was equally unsuccessful.

Mr Asquith had been most affable, taking both her hands warmly in his and saying how much he had enjoyed their last meeting at one of her great-aunt's dinner parties.

'What can I do for you, my dear?' he had asked when she was comfortably seated on a chintz-covered sofa in Number 10's drawing room.

Rose had wasted no time in preliminaries. 'A friend of mine, Lady Daphne Harbury, has been sentenced to three months' imprisonment in Holloway for taking part in a suffragette demonstration, Prime Minister,' she'd said. 'I'm here to plead that she be given an early release on the grounds that she should never have been sentenced as a common criminal. As a suffragette, she should be a political prisoner.'

113

He had been as immovable on the subject as his home secretary. At last, when she had risen to her feet, knowing she had failed utterly in her mission, he had asked her if she would like to look at the roses in Number 10's rear garden.

Knowing very well that the invitation had been made in order that he could take hold of her arm as he escorted her, she had declined.

In the end the only person who was helpful to her was Theo Jethney.

'My friend is not only on hunger strike and being forcibly fed, but she is in an underground cell so damp that if the forced feeding doesn't kill her, pneumonia will!' she said to him in passionate outrage. 'How can civilized men – men like King George and Mr Asquith and Mr Churchill – allow women to be kept in such appalling conditions?'

'The King and the Prime Minister and the Home Secretary don't make personal visits to Holloway,' Theo Jethney said drily. 'And the governors of Holloway aren't likely to enlighten them as to conditions there.'

They were in his office at the House of Lords. Rose was wearing suffragette colours. Green for hope. Purple for dignity. White for purity. In her purple narrow skirt, with a spray of vivid myrtle leaves pinned to her jacket and a wide white picture hat on top of her thickly waving auburn hair, she looked enchanting.

Partly because she did look so enchanting, partly because she was Marigold's sister and partly because he shared her outrage at the treatment being meted out to the suffragettes, Theo had set aside plenty of time for his meeting with her.

'Then someone else must tell them,' she said vehemently. 'That person must be someone they will listen to.'

'Do you think I am that person?'

'Yes. Neither Mr Asquith nor Mr Churchill will be as

dismissive, or as patronizing, to you as they were to me. The general public also needs to be made aware of the horrors taking place in Holloway. Force-feeding is a torture straight from the Middle Ages, yet newspapers treat it as a joke. Editors would soon change their tune if it was *their* daughters, or sisters, or mothers, who were being held down and violated in such an inhuman manner.'

Theo stood up and walked across to a window that looked out over the Thames. 'A year or so ago,' he said, looking not at her, but at the strongly moving river, 'when force-feeding first became an issue, Keir Hardie raised a question in Parliament, objecting to it strenuously on moral grounds. His fellow Members of Parliament roared with laughter. He said afterwards that if he hadn't heard that laughter for himself, he would never have believed that a body of gentlemen could have found reason for mirth and applause over such an issue.'

He turned away from the window and walked back to his desk in deep thought. At last he said, 'We cannot denounce torture in places like Russia and support it in England, but Members of Parliament, as well as the general public, have to come to an understanding that it *is* torture, and far from being a joke. The only way to achieve that, Rose, is via a sympathetic press. It needs a national newspaper to wholeheartedly and unequivocally denounce the horrors of force-feeding – and I think I know the newspaper most likely to.'

He seated himself once more behind his desk and drew out a small black notebook from its central drawer.

'The man you need to speak to is Hal Green,' he said, flicking pages. 'He's editor of the *Daily Despatch*, and the most bohemian editor in Fleet Street. He likes a controversial cause.'

'Would you arrange for me to see him?'

Theo flashed her one of his rare smiles and, for the first

time, Rose understood just why Marigold had been so dazzled by him.

'Nothing easier. I'll speak with him myself. Even hard-boiled Fleet Street editors like an invitation to the House of Lords every now and then.'

From a page in his notebook he copied Hal Green's telephone number on to a piece of paper and passed it across his desk towards her, saying, 'Is everyone well at Snowberry? I haven't visited recently and I'm rather missing Millie's meringues.' Then, before she had the chance to respond, he said, 'And Marigold? Is she in London in readiness for the coronation?'

'Yes, she's at Aunt Sibyl's.' With great difficulty Rose kept her voice as nonchalant as his. 'Her house is on the processional route. Lily and Iris are arriving tomorrow morning and I think Rory will be joining us there.'

'Good. The five of you will have a grand-stand view.'

He walked her to the door. 'I'll tell Hal Green to expect a call from you, and I'll speak to both Churchill and the Prime Minister.'

'Thank you.' The words came out stiff and stilted. In the seconds before he turned his head away she had seen the expression in his eyes when he had spoken Marigold's name and her shock was so profound she didn't know how she was still managing to behave normally.

He was in love with Marigold. A public figure with a flawless reputation, sophisticated and long married, he was as dazzled by Marigold as Marigold, for a time, had been dazzled by him.

She said goodbye to him. Never once had it occurred to her that Theo Jethney had already responded to Marigold's shameless flirting. Her fear had simply been that he might be tempted to. Now she had the horror of wondering just how intimate their relationship had been.

116

She walked down the Palace of Westminster's marble-floored corridors to the St Stephen's entrance, clinging to the word 'had'. Marigold was no longer infatuated with him. She had seen sense and the relationship was over. The bleak misery in his eyes was testimony to that. As Rose stepped out into brilliant sunshine she thanked her lucky stars that Marigold was not quite as foolhardy as she often seemed.

Marigold was a mile away in Chelsea, lying on her tummy upon a silk-covered couch in Lawrence Strickland's studio. With her weight on her elbows, her head at a coquettish tilt that ensured her mane of hair fell to one side in a riot of glorious golden-red waves and with her ankles crossed blithely in the air, she was as naked as the day she was born.

That she was didn't faze her in the slightest. On her first visit to his studio, when Strickland had said he wanted to do the classical Greek painting first and had asked her to take off her clothes, she had done so with the casual nonchalance of a professional artist's model. The only difference Strickland could see was that where professional models chatted to him about mundane things as he worked, most frequently their family and friends, Marigold was more interested in him.

'What is your background, Strickland?' she had asked him as she settled into the pose. 'Who are your family? Where are you from?'

'My family is my own affair,' he had said, sketching her outline in broad, confident strokes. 'As for where I'm from; I'm from Norfolk.'

Later, when it had become obvious to her that the fact of being born in Norfolk was the full extent of the personal information he was prepared to give – and that he wasn't at all interested in her, or any other woman, sexually – she had asked him about his work. Much to his surprise, he'd answered her questions. Later still, she had talked to him about herself.

'So you were how old when you lost your virginity?' he had asked, fascinated.

'Nineteen. But I didn't lose it, Strickland. I simply didn't see the importance of keeping it.'

He'd grinned. Her careless outspokenness about sexual matters was extraordinary coming from a girl of her age, class and upbringing. Though he mixed with the aristocracy, accepted by them because of his very great talent, he privately had a great deal of contempt for them. He didn't have contempt for Marigold, though. Marigold amused and intrigued him. Yet despite his private antipathy for peers, he couldn't help feeling sorry for her grandfather. From all he'd heard about Lord May, he was a decent old cove. Not the kind of man to deserve a granddaughter who was undoubtedly destined to go through life leaving a trail of scandal behind her.

'And who was the lucky man?' he asked as he captured the exact coquettish tilt of her head.

'Lord Jethney. He was passionately in love with me.' She didn't want to talk about Theo. She wanted to talk about the painting. 'What will happen to this painting when it's finished, Strickland? What will you do with it?'

'I've no idea,' he said truthfully.

'Couldn't you forget about a Royal Academy showing for the other portrait you are going to do, and enter this one instead?'

He cracked with laughter, thinking she was joking.

Not at all put out, she said, 'Why not? The Academy is always exhibiting paintings of classical nudes.'

'True,' he said, still chuckling. 'But the models for such pictures are professional models, they aren't members of the aristocracy. You would be instantly recognized and the furore would be enormous.'

'The furore would be fun. Who are you depicting me as? Penelope?'

'Persephone.'

Marigold, whose knowledge of Greek mythology was hazy, looked blank.

'She was raped by the god Pluto,' he said helpfully. 'He was the ruler of the Underworld. During one of his visits to the upper realms he saw a beautiful girl picking spring flowers, desired her, seized her and carried her off to his kingdom where she ruled as his queen.'

He removed a speck of tobacco from his tongue. 'Every spring he allowed her to return in order that, for a few short months, she could comfort her grieving mother.'

'So this pose – this lying on my tummy pose – in the finished painting will I be lying in a grassy meadow full of flowers?'

'Yes, unless I change my mind and depict you struggling in Pluto's arms as he carries you off.'

She shivered in shocked delight, not knowing whether he was joking or not, and not caring. All that mattered was that the painting was going to cause a sensation: a sensation she would be the centre of.

Iris was deeply unhappy. In two days' time she would be leaving for London with Lily and their grandfather. With Marigold and Rose they were to stay at their Great-aunt Sibyl's for a week so that they could conveniently attend all the coronation parties and balls that would be taking place: parties and balls at which she and Toby would be able to enjoy each other's company. Only she was no longer sure Toby wanted to enjoy her company.

She was in what was known as the estate room, a small room adjoining the library where all the paperwork dealing with the running of Snowberry's home farm and tenanted

119

cottages was kept. Since Rose had hared off to London to fight for Daphne Harbury's release, dealing with the estate correspondence had fallen to her. She had been surprised at how satisfying she had found doing it. But she wasn't finding it satisfying just now.

Just now all she could think of was that a proposal from Toby was growing unlikelier by the day.

She put her pen down, overcome by the suspicion that there were times when Toby came down from London to spend a few hours at Sissbury without telling her. A year ago, when he had first joined the Guards, if he visited Sissbury, he also popped over to Snowberry and they would have a game of tennis or mooch companionably around the lake with the dogs at their heels.

The sun streamed in through the estate room's windows and she was overcome with the longing to visit Sissbury and gain news of Toby from his mother. Lady Mulholland had never made any secret of the fact that she would welcome her as a daughter-in-law and a chat with her could well remove the doubt she was now feeling.

She didn't ask her grandfather if she could be driven to Sissbury in the Talbot. Instead she took the pony and trap. She enjoyed the sound of the pony's rhythmic trot and the feel of the reins in her hands and by the time she turned into Sissbury Castle's long drive she had recovered a great deal of her equanimity. It was understandable that Toby was unable to spend much time at Sissbury since joining the Guards and thinking he would do so without bothering to see her was idiocy on her part. As she left the pony in the care of one of Sissbury's stable boys, she convinced herself she was making a mountain out of a molehill.

It wasn't a conviction that lasted for long.

'Master Toby and his guests are on the terrace,' the butler said, as if her arrival was expected.

Iris sucked in her breath. That Toby was home and hadn't let her know was a hurt so deep it threw her completely off balance. If she went out to the terrace (as the butler was waiting for her to do) she would have to survive the excruciating embarrassment of having shown up uninvited. But if she left straight away (as she was desperate to do) Toby would know of her reaction, because the butler would, as a matter of course, tell him of her visit and abrupt departure.

When she had set off her intention had been to spend half an hour or so with Toby's mother. If she was to retain any dignity at all, it was what she had to do.

'I've come to see Lady Mulholland,' she said, struggling not to let her distress show.

'Her Ladyship is not at home.'

'Then please tell her that I called.' She was just about to make a quick, vastly relieved escape when Tessa Reighton burst out from the drawing room into the marble-floored hall, shrieking, 'Iris! How super to see you! We're having a swimming party in the ornamental pool. It's the most terrific fun. Some of the girls have changed into bathing costumes. It's all very risqué and a good job Toby's ma and pa are in London, otherwise the poor dears would have heart failure.'

She tucked Iris's arm in hers and began steering her into the drawing room. 'Such ages since I've see you. Most of the girls here are this year's debutantes – terribly young, all aged seventeen and eighteen. We twenty-one-year-olds are getting to be quite old maids, aren't we?'

She laughed merrily, as well she might considering that she was a natural blonde with stunning blue eyes and a head-turning figure. If Tessa was still an old maid, she was so only out of choice.

'I actually came to see Lady Mulholland.' Iris vainly tried

to extricate herself from Tessa's hold and stop the swift progress towards the open French doors. 'But as she isn't here . . .'

It was too late.

The large ornamental pool, with its three-tiered central fountain, was situated on the terrace and once they had reached the French doors they were in full sight of it – and everyone was in full sight of them.

A swift glance told Iris that even if Toby had invited her, she wouldn't have found it at all her sort of party.

Glasses and bottles of champagne stood on the terrace's wrought-iron tables. Three men, barefoot and with their trouser legs rolled to the knee, were in the pool, chasing and splashing half a dozen squealing girls. Three of the girls had their floaty summer dresses caught up to their knees, the others were in red and white striped bathing costumes that ended at mid-thigh to reveal a dizzying expanse of naked leg. They weren't much different to the flannel bathing suits she, Rose, Marigold and Lily wore when swimming at Snowberry, but in the vast tranquillity of Snowberry's tree-shaded lake their costumes had always seemed the essence of respectability.

This display, in the shallow water of the ornamental pool, was anything but respectable and Iris wanted nothing to do with it.

'Look who's here, everyone!' Tessa called out gaily. 'It's Iris! Isn't it a pity Marigold isn't here as well?'

Girls she didn't know called out for her to join in the fun.

Not only did Iris not know the girls, she didn't know the young men, either. They all looked typically ineffectual upper-class young men who brayed with laughter at the slightest thing. What Toby was doing surrounding himself with them she couldn't imagine.

She looked around for him, knowing she had no option

but to explain why she was there and why, as his mother was not at home, she was now about to leave.

'Has anyone a spare bathing cossie for Iris?' Tessa trilled in a manner that indicated she was more than slightly squiffy. 'A good-sized one. She's not a nymph, more a Venus.'

As someone snorted with laughter Iris's cheeks flamed scarlet.

'I'm not staying, Tessa,' she said, struggling to sound pleasant and reasonable. 'I'm just going to say hello to Toby and then I'm leaving.'

She didn't want to say hello to Toby, but good manners left her with no choice. The problem was that she couldn't see him anywhere.

'Toby!' Tessa waved furiously and a little unsteadily in the direction of the centre of the pool. 'Toby! Do stop horsing around. Come out from behind the fountain and say hello to Iris.'

Toby, saturated with spray from the fountain, reluctantly did as he was bid. He didn't do so alone. With him was a girl Iris recognized as being *Tatler*'s debutante of the year.

Until now she had believed he was keeping a low profile because he was as appalled by the wildness of the party as she was, and shocked that his fellow Guards officers had simply taken it over and that he'd lost all control of it.

Now she knew she'd been wrong.

'I'm glad you're here, Iris,' he said unconvincingly, letting go of the girl he had been holding. 'I did try to phone you to tell you I'd come down here, but the operator couldn't make a connection. It's Rupert's birthday tomorrow' – he gave a wave of his hand towards one of the young men in the pool – 'and we're all getting in trim for it by letting off a little steam.'

'Yes,' she said unhappily, not knowing what else to say. 'I can see that.'

He walked up to her. 'I'm sorry if your feelings are hurt, Iris. The whole thing was pretty spontaneous. If I'd known in advance I was going to be down here I would have let you know.'

'Yes,' she said again, knowing that he wouldn't have. 'Thank you for asking me to stay, Toby, but I won't, if you don't mind.'

Though she couldn't swear to it, she was sure his reaction was one of relief.

She turned away from him swiftly and he said, falling into step beside her, 'Did you come in the pony-trap or the Talbot?'

'The pony-trap. There's no need to walk me back to it, Toby. I'm fine, truly I am.'

He didn't protest and he didn't continue walking along beside her.

Less fine than she'd ever been before in her life she stumbled back to the pony-trap and then, with a hurting heart, made her way back to Snowberry, certain that whatever the future held for her, it no longer held the person she'd so long thought would be her future husband.

# TWELVE

David's stomach was a knot of nerves. It was Coronation Day and he was dreading every minute of what lay ahead. In a day of such long and ancient ceremony a host of things could go wrong and he knew his father would never forgive him if he made an error of any kind, and once the service was under way in Westminster Abbey, an error would be only too easy to make. All he would have to do was to move when he should be standing still, or stand still when he should be moving. As for the possibility of his forgetting any part of his homage speech: the very thought brought him out in a cold sweat.

'I'm afraid Garter robes are uncomfortably hot, sir,' one of the courtiers fussing around commiserated with him, mistaking the cause of the perspiration that had broken out on his forehead. 'It will be cooler in the abbey.'

David said nothing, but privately he didn't see how it could possibly be cooler in the abbey when the abbey would be packed to the rafters with thousands of guests invited from all over the world.

He stared at his reflection in a full-length mirror, not liking what he saw at all. He simply didn't have the physique to carry off robes so ornately grandiose as the Order of the Garter. Over a cloth-of-silver suit, worn with white stockings and white-satin slippers with red heels, he was wearing a flowing cloak of blue velvet lined with white taffeta and at his side was a sword in a red-velvet scabbard.

Even now his ensemble wasn't quite complete, for the finishing touch was a medieval Tudor 'bonnet', a floppy black velvet hat adorned with white ostrich feathers.

At the thought of it, his jaw tightened. Like all his family, he wasn't tall and was certain the flamboyantly plumed hat did him no favours.

He remembered again what Lily had said to him about the amount of pleasure given to the public by medieval pageantry and ceremonial robes and he took a deep, steadying breath. If he was to survive the role in life into which he'd been born, he had to begin cultivating positive mental attitudes towards the aspects of princeing he found so embarrassing – and Lily was showing him the way to do so.

'Prince Albert, Princess Mary, Prince Henry and Prince George are already in the state carriage, sir,' a senior courtier said respectfully. 'It's time for you to join them.'

David nodded, suddenly feeling much better about everything. The processional route on the return from Westminster Abbey was a circuitous one to give the maximum number of people the opportunity to be able to see it. Lily would be watching it pass by from an upper balcony at her great-aunt Sibyl's home in St James's Street. From there she would have a grandstand view. He was hoping that he would also have a view of her. Two nights earlier he had driven past the house so that he would be able to recognize it despite the crowds that, today, would be thronging the pavement in front of it.

'Sir?' the elderly courtier at his side prompted, an edge of anxiety now in his voice. 'The departure of carriages from the palace is timed to the second and—'

'I'm coming.' David took one last look at his reflection and picked up his Tudor bonnet. On this day his father was to be crowned King of Great Britain and Ireland and Ruler of the British Dominions beyond the Seas. It was going to be one of the most memorable days of David's life – perhaps the most memorable until the day when he would make the exact same journey to his own coronation.

Sharply, he pushed the thought aside. His father was only forty-six and with luck, if his father lived as long as had his grandmother, Queen Victoria, it would be another thirty-five years before his own coronation would take place.

He had seen his father earlier in the morning, but only briefly. Now, as he walked past his father's suite, his father came out into the broad, crimson-carpeted corridor to speak with him again.

Brusque as always, King George's remarks were not about anything of deep significance. They were about the weather.

'The barometer shows it's going to be overcast and cloudy with some showers and a strongish cool breeze, which will be better for the people lining the streets than hot sun,' he said, adding as an afterthought, 'Please make sure, David, that Harry and Georgie don't fidget in the carriage. There will be no one else riding in it but yourself – and Bertie and Mary, of course. The eyes of the world will be upon you and you must make sure that the young ones behave well.'

'Yes, sir. I will, sir.' He waited for his father to add something more fatherly and personal. His father didn't and, fighting disappointment, David continued on his way to where his all his siblings, apart from John, were waiting for him.

'G-g-goodness but I'm nervous,' Bertie said as he joined him in a gold carriage drawn by eight white stallions. Bertie was dressed in his cadet uniform and looked as ashen as if he were about to sit a naval exam. 'W-what time w-will Papa and Mama be s-setting off?'

'Ten-thirty. Harry and Georgie, you have to sit still.'

Harry and Georgie were in Highland costume and David, who always felt comfortably at home in Highland costume, envied them. 'We want to wave,' eight-year-old George said defiantly. 'Mama said we *had* to wave.'

'You can wave. But you have to wave while sitting still.'

The horses moved forward and the carriage lurched into movement.

'Oh g-g-goodness,' Bertie said again, a sheen of perspiration on his upper lip. 'This is it, David. W-we're off.'

As they crossed Buckingham Palace's courtyard the procession stretched ahead of them down the Mall as far as they could see.

'Look at the soldiers, Harry! Look at the soldiers!' Georgie squealed as a band of the Brigade of Guards swung into position behind them; following the band came marching members of the Highland Infantry.

Immediately in front of the carriage rode four troopers of the Household Cavalry, the pale sun glinting on the silver of their white-plumed helmets. Somewhere ahead of them in the 250-strong procession were the Prime Minister, the heads of foreign governments, church leaders and a whole cavalcade of foreign royalty – nearly all of whom were his relatives.

Troops in brilliant red ceremonial dress lined the route, standing shoulder to shoulder. Beyond them, the stands that had been set up in the Mall were so densely packed David didn't know how people were still able to breathe. With patriotic fervour, the crowds were waving thousands of flags.

He waved back, enjoying the sensation of making personal contact with such a vast throng. At the end of the Mall the procession streamed through Admiralty Arch and into Trafalgar Square where tier upon tier of seating had been erected. David could scarcely see Landseer's bronze lions for the flag-waving well-wishers clinging to them for a better view.

'I wish I was on a lion and waving a flag,' Georgie shouted across to him as amid a storm of cheers their carriage rattled on towards Westminster, Big Ben and the Houses of Parliament.

'You're not sitting still enough, Georgie.' Mary's coronet and ermine-lined robe of state made her look far older than fourteen, but not so old that she intimidated young Georgie.

'Phooey!' he yelled, launching himself on her and tickling her in the ribs.

David seized him by the scruff of the neck. 'One more *whisper* out of you, young Georgie, and I'll deck you!'

Like David, Georgie had charm that the rest of their family lacked and it came to his rescue. 'Sorry, David.' He shot David an apologetic grin and changed the subject. 'Just *look* at those decorations strung across the street! Aren't they whiz?'

Once in the abbey David was blessedly relieved of all responsibility for anyone but himself. The focus of all eyes and accompanied by a fanfare of silver trumpets, he walked up the ancient nave with a retinue of attendants, his plumed hat in his hand.

On either side heads bowed in acknowledgement and then, after a walk as long as eternity, he finally reached his chair in the south transept. Behind him, in crimson robes, the peers of the realm were seated, row upon dizzying row. Somewhere among them was Lord May, but he couldn't distinguish him among the sea of faces.

His brothers were now making their way to their places in the royal gallery, pausing to bow to him as they did so. Mary, looking very grave, curtsied deeply and in response he rose to his feet.

Immediately he knew that it was the wrong thing to have

done. The Earl Marshal had told him that once seated for the obeisances he was not to rise. His cheeks flushed and he wondered how many people had noticed his gaffe and whether his father would be told of it. After that, as those of the blood royal made their obeisance to him on their way to the royal boxes, his only acknowledgement was an inclination of his head.

Slowly, and with regal grandeur, the royal boxes began to fill. Opposite David thin shafts of sunlight fell upon the peeresses seated in the south transept. Above them, azure hangings served as backdrop to the galleried seating for Members of Parliament and their wives.

Finally, at eleven o'clock, there came the booming sound of guns and loud cheering from outside the abbey. David breathed in hard. His mother would enter the abbey first and he found it impossible to imagine what her feelings would be. Never, under any circumstances, did his mother show emotion. She would be rigidly in control of herself – and would expect no less of him. Determined not to let her down, he took another deep, steadying breath.

Through the abbey's great west door his mother's procession entered to the fanfare of the coronation anthem.

She was wearing a gown of white satin thickly embroidered with gold. Attached to her shoulders, her deep purple robe, lined with ermine and dotted with ermine tails, stretched out in a long train carried by the daughters of six earls.

David felt the blood drum in his ears. One day, the girl he married would also enter the abbey in such a way. The same magnificent anthem would be sung to greet her; the throne his mother was now standing in front of would be her throne. The girl in question, he fervently hoped, would be Miss Lily Houghton.

With a struggle he forced his thoughts away from the future and Lily, and back to the present. The atmosphere in the abbey had reached fever pitch, for the King's procession was now making its way down the blue-carpeted nave. There were ecclesiastics, heralds, attendants, high officers of his household and representatives of all the various orders of knighthoods.

They were followed by Lord Kitchener carrying the sword of temporal justice, Lord Roberts carrying the sword of spiritual justice, and the Duke of Beaufort carrying the sword of mercy.

Then came the Bishops of London, Ripon and Winchester, carrying the gold communion plate, the bible and the chalice.

After them came the King.

He was wearing a crimson surcoat and the crimson velvet robe of state, with an ermine cape over his shoulders. His massive train was borne by eight scarlet-costumed pages and he was flanked by twenty gentlemen-at-arms. Bringing up the rear of the procession were twenty Yeoman of the Guard.

The sheer majesty of his father's appearance took David's breath away. His father looked exactly what he was: a king-emperor, ruler of over a quarter of the earth's surface. How was he, David, ever to stand one day in his father's place? The very idea was beyond his imagination.

As his father knelt before the altar, the archbishop prepared to administer the coronation oath. David bit his lip, hoping fervently that his father's voice would be firm and strong.

It was.

After the oath, Holy Communion was celebrated and then came the most sacred part of the coronation ceremony: the anointing and crowning.

With the aid of the Lord Great Chamberlain and the Master of the Robes, King George's crimson robe was replaced by the austere plain white anointing gown. Then the choir began singing the anthem 'Zadok the Priest' and he was led to St Edward's Chair, used for coronations since medieval times.

The Dean of Westminster poured consecrated oil from an eagle-shaped ampulla into a spoon and then, as all those within the abbey held their breath in reverent awe, the Archbishop of Canterbury anointed King George on his hands, his breast and his head.

The King was then enrobed in a white garment of fine linen over which was placed an ankle-length coat of cloth of gold, lined with rose-coloured silk and fastened by a jewelled sword belt.

David glanced across to where his brothers were seated. Bertie was so white-faced and tense he looked as if he were about to faint. Harry and Georgie were round-eyed with wonder.

Now the crown jewels were being handed to his father. First the orb, a golden sphere set with precious stones and surmounted by a cross representing Christian sovereignty. Having received it, his father handed the orb back to the archbishop for it to be laid upon the altar. Then the archbishop put a ruby ring, representing the 'marriage' between him and the nation, on the fourth finger of the King's left hand. Next he handed him two sceptres, one surmounted by a gilded dove, symbolizing the sovereign's prerogative of mercy, the other by a cross, symbolizing kingly power and justice.

As the King held them vertically upright, the sceptre with the cross in his right hand, the sceptre with the dove in his left hand, the Dean of Westminster brought St Edward's crown, magnificent on a purple, gold-tasselled cushion, to the Archbishop of Canterbury.

Standing before the altar the archbishop dedicated the crown.

A shiver ran down David's spine. This was it. The moment of crowning. The moment that unless he died before his father, he, too, would one day experience.

Slowly the archbishop lifted the jewel-encrusted crown high and then, with great reverence, lowered it on George V's head.

Immediately the abbey erupted with threefold shouts of 'God Save the King!' Coronets and caps were put on heads. Trumpets sounded. Drums thundered. Cannon boomed from the Tower of London. Salvos of artillery erupted from the royal parks.

For David the worst part – the homage of the lords – began.

Symbolically taking possession of his kingdom, his father was led from St Edward's chair to the throne. The archbishop stepped before him, knelt and swore his fealty. Then it was David's turn.

With his Tudor bonnet exchanged for a coronet, David rose to his feet and moved forward, his heart beating like a piston. With his sword cumbersomely at his side he knelt at his father's feet and said in a voice that seemed to him to come from a million miles away, 'I, Edward, Prince of Wales, do become your liege man of life and limb and of earthly worship; and faith and truth I will bear unto you, to live and die against all manner of folks. So help me God.'

He'd done it. It was over. Unsteadily he rose to his feet. His father kissed him on both cheeks and for once David sensed great emotion in his father.

He, too, was overcome with emotion as, weak with relief at having his ordeal over, he watched the Duke of Connaught pay his homage, followed by a representative of each order of the peerage. Fervently he wished that Lily were in the abbey; that she, too, were experiencing the mesmerizing splendour of the sacred thousand-year-old ritual.

All through the far simpler ceremony of his mother's enthronement as queen consort, he thought of Lily and of the magical way she had so suddenly entered and transformed his life. Because of Lily his loneliness and desperate sense of isolation were things of the past. Because of Lily he was happy.

As the crown with the legendary Koh-i-Noor diamond blazing from its centre cross was placed on his mother's head, the peeresses put on their coronets.

His father then exchanged St Edward's crown for the imperial state crown and began making his way out of the abbey, the sceptre with the cross in one hand, and the orb in the other.

David felt as if his heart was going to burst with pride. It had been a wonderful service. A magnificent service. For the first time ever he began to wonder if becoming a king wasn't such a bad thing after all.

The horse-drawn gold carriage that was to carry him, his brothers and Mary by a circuitous route back to Buckingham Palace edged to a halt in front of the abbey's great west door. It was smack on a quarter past two and though the day was grey and windy the stands and tiers fronting the abbey were jammed to capacity with waving well-wishers.

David waved back with a shy smile and the crowds went wild. It was as if Bertie, Mary, Harry and Georgie didn't exist.

As his name was shouted out from every quarter, David was filled with euphoria. This part of princeing – making contact instantaneously with crowds of people he had never met, and never would meet – sent a surge of adrenalin through him. All he wished was that he wasn't dressed in such a preposterous rig. Then he would feel comfortable. A coronet was not agreeable headgear. Already it felt heavy. By the time they reached Buckingham Palace he knew it was going to feel like a ten-ton weight.

When the giant procession reached Trafalgar Square it didn't turn left through Admiralty Arch; it turned right, into the Strand, heading for Fleet Street. Every inch of pavement was packed with flag-waving spectators, many of whom had been waiting for the procession since the previous evening. Every window was open and jammed with people. To David, it seemed as if the whole world had zeroed down to a sea of furiously waving Union Jacks.

Up Ludgate Hill they went, and around St Paul's Cathedral. Then the mile-long procession began making its way back to the palace. The nearer they drew to Piccadilly the more taut became David's excitement and sense of expectation. By now the front of the procession would be passing Lady Harland's town house. Was Lily looking forward to waving to him as much as he was looking forward to waving to her?

Piccadilly Circus was mayhem. There were so many people wedged into it, David could only imagine that the rest of the country was empty. And then they were turning into St James's Street.

He pressed himself as close to the right-hand side of the carriage as possible and, ignoring the waving crowds on the pavement, he looked eagerly upwards.

There was the house.

There was the window.

There was Lily.

Not caring about being discreet he shouted her name, only to have it drowned by the shouts of the crowd and the triumphant sound of the band of the Brigade of Guards marching only yards ahead of him.

At the sight of him, Lily's face lit up. She leaned so dangerously far over the wrought-iron balcony that Rose had to grab hold of her and steady her. Though he couldn't hear her, he saw that she was shouting his name. But unlike everyone else that day, she was not shouting 'Edward!' but 'David!'

The carriage began taking him further and further away from the house and he twisted round in his seat, still waving towards her furiously.

'Is that her, David?' Bertie shouted across to him above the noise of the band and the crowds.

David nodded. 'Yes!' he shouted back. 'That's Lily! That's the girl I'm going to marry, Bertie! When I'm king, that's the girl who will be my queen!'

# THIRTEEN

'Dear Lord, so you weren't exaggerating.' Rory stared after the state carriage goggle-eyed. 'The Prince of Wales really *is* a personal friend of yours!'

'Of all of us,' Marigold said smugly as a carriage carrying Princess Louise, King George's sister, clattered down the street below their window.

'Maybe.' There was amusement in Rory's voice. 'But it was Lily's name he shouted. I was watching his mouth and I would swear to it. I'm also certain that it was Lily he was waving to.'

Rose laughed. 'I don't think so, Rory. David is far too well mannered. When he waved, it was to all of us.'

Rory quirked an eyebrow at Lily, who had the grace to blush.

Iris said anxiously, 'You must remember your promise, Rory. Not a word to anyone about David's visits to Snowberry. Absolutely no one, other than the five of us and Grandfather, must know about them.'

'We weren't even going to tell you,' Marigold said, eyeing one of David's German cousins with an appraising eye as he rode beneath their window, so close that despite his distinctive

Teutonic spiked helmet, she could even see the intriguing cleft in his chin. 'But we knew you'd be visiting Snowberry and that not telling you could cause problems. And then there's the fact that there is already a close and intimate bond between you and David.'

Iris and Lily stared at her blankly.

Rose said, mildly annoyed, 'Don't be silly, Marigold.'

Rory, well knowing Marigold's outrageous sense of humour, grinned. 'Which is?' he asked.

'Your bathing costume. David borrowed it the last time he was at Snowberry. I did suggest embroidering HRH on one of the legs, but Rose wouldn't let me.'

Rory roared with laughter, Iris and Lily burst into giggles and even Rose's mouth tugged into a smile.

'So, Rose, what d'you think the chances are of Prince Edward visiting Snowberry over the next few days, when I'll be there?' he asked.

'Not high. He won't be able to slip away unnoticed when every crowned head of Europe is a guest at Buckingham Palace.'

'Also it's his birthday tomorrow,' Lily said. 'There is to be the hugest party for him. He's never had a birthday party before at which so many relations will be guests. He says that if every one of them bring him a present it will be like all the Christmases he's ever had rolled into one.'

A frown puckered Rose's forehead. David hadn't mentioned his birthday when he'd been with them at Snowberry and it suddenly occurred to her to wonder if Lily and David were writing to each other.

It wasn't something she'd any intention of asking in front of Marigold, Iris and Rory, in case the answer was yes. She would ask Lily the next time they were on their own, though. If the answer *was* yes, quite what she would do, she didn't know. She couldn't very well tell the heir to the throne that she'd prefer it if he didn't write to her sister. All the same, his doing so would indicate that an especially close relationship was growing between him and Lily. A relationship that would cause ructions of seismic proportions when the palace became aware of it.

'So what now?' Marigold said, waving down to a carriage carrying eighteen-year-old Princess Maud and twenty-year-old Princess Alexandra, David's English cousins. 'The parties and balls don't start for hours yet and soon the only people left in the procession will be foreign royalty. Have we to go down and enjoy the atmosphere in the streets? The hoi polloi look to be having tremendous fun.'

To her great surprise, Iris was the first taker for such an adventure. 'Yes, let's,' she said eagerly. 'Let's make our way to Buckingham Palace, because that is where the greatest crowds will be. Once the King and Queen arrive back at the palace they will come out on to the balcony and there will be lots of singing of the National Anthem and lots of dancing by cockney pearly kings and queens. Rory will come with us to make sure we're safe, won't you, Rory?'

Rory ran a hand through his hair. 'I shall if you think my great-uncle won't mind.'

'Grandfather won't mind,' Marigold said airily, not caring overmuch whether he did or didn't. 'We'll need umbrellas with us, though, in case it starts to rain.'

'And in case we need help in getting through the crush,' Lily said impishly.

'I'm not sure you should go, Lily.' The worried frown was back on Rose's face again.

Lily looked at her aghast. 'Oh, *please*, Rose! I'll keep *very* tight hold of Rory's arm. I promise!'

It was Iris who came to her aid. 'It would be most unfair to make Lily stay here on her own, Rose,' she said reasonably. 'We'll all be together. She'll be quite safe.'

'On your head be it then, because I shan't be with you. I'm going to the Harburys to see Daphne.'

'She's been released from Holloway then?' As they all stepped from the tiny balcony and back into the room there was surprise in Rory's voice. 'I thought she had at least another month of her sentence to serve.'

'She had, but the Government used the coronation celebrations as an excuse to release her early without losing face. They had to find some excuse, Rory, for if they hadn't Daphne might well have died. She doesn't have the constitution for a prolonged hunger strike and the torture of force-feeding.'

Mindful of how grey and blustery the day was Marigold and Iris went to change into something a little warmer than the chiffon dresses they were presently wearing. Rose, already sensibly dressed in a high-necked blouse and navy-blue serge tunic – the tunic worn knee-length over a matching skirt, arrow-straight and tight at the ankle – secured a hat on her head with a mother-of-pearl hat-pin and picked up a pair of kid gloves.

'Bye,' she said to them, adding as an afterthought, 'and be careful on the streets. Whatever you do, don't lose each other.'

When she had left the room Rory said to Lily, 'So tell me about the Prince of Wales, Lily. Have you and he become special friends?'

Her cheeks flushed. 'We write to each other.'

'And he doesn't write to Rose or to Iris or to Marigold?'

She shook her head. 'No. Rose and Iris are much older than he is and even Marigold is a good two years older.'

Rory didn't know whether to be amused at the thought of his favourite cousin being the calf-love of the Prince of Wales, or alarmed. 'But you're not sweethearts, are you, Lily?'

This time Lily didn't merely flush. Her cheeks flew scarlet banners. 'No,' she said, avoiding his eyes. 'But we're *very*

140

good friends. David's never been able to have a really best friend before – not outside of his family. He loves being at Snowberry and when he can't visit he misses it terribly.'

She didn't say that he missed her most of all, but Rory was beginning to read between the lines.

'How the devil does he manage to visit Snowberry? I'd have thought every moment of his day is accounted for.'

'It is usually, but he manages to spend a couple of hours at Snowberry every time he travels between his naval college and Windsor, and because of all the arrangements that had to be made for the coronation, he's been able to do that several times.'

'But he doesn't travel alone, surely?'

'No. He has an equerry, Captain Cullen.' She gave him her seraphic smile. 'Rose thinks Captain Cullen rather likes Marigold. But then *all* men like Marigold.'

'You shouldn't be aware of things like that, young Lily – though if Cullen does have his own reason for surreptitiously visiting Snowberry, it explains why Prince Edward has been finding it so easy to do.'

Iris and Marigold re-entered the room. Iris was dressed in a mulberry-coloured coat-dress over a skirt not quite narrow enough to be fashionable, her matching hat sporting two small, but jaunty feathers. She made an attractive picture, but not a head-turning one.

The same could not be said of Marigold. Her skirt and bolero-top were a sizzling royal blue, the skirt so narrow at the ankle Rory couldn't fathom how she was managing to walk. Her pale-cream lace blouse had a dramatically large cameo at its high throat and on top of her glorious hair was a swooping, wide-brimmed hat laden with iridescent peacock feathers. She looked sensational and Rory knew that no matter how dense the crowd, every male head was going to turn as she passed.

He sighed. Escorting and chaperoning Iris and Lily would be a simple task. Accomplishing the same thing with Marigold was going to be a nightmare.

From where they were, in St James's Street, the only way to the front of Buckingham Palace was to walk down the length of St James's Street, make a very brief left into Pall Mall and then, not following the route the procession was taking, take an abrupt right into Marlborough Road, skirting St James's Palace. From there they would be able to enter the Mall about a third of the way down from Buckingham Palace; though if the tail end of the procession had still not returned to the palace by the time they reached the Mall they would then come to a complete halt, for it would be so jam-packed with spectators that walking up the Mall's grassy verges would be impossible.

'Come along,' he said, wondering how he could have been so rash as to have agreed to something so reckless – and how someone as sensible as Rose could possibly have sanctioned it.

As they stepped out into the street they were deafened by hoarse cheers for the Queen and King of Norway, the King's sister and her husband. In their wake came the carriage of King Ferdinand of Romania and his wife, Queen Marie, Queen Victoria's granddaughter. They didn't stand to watch it pass. Instead they began weaving their way through the crowds towards the bottom of the street.

For Iris and Lily, who seldom, if ever, journeyed any distance unless in a carriage or a hansom cab – and only then when suitably accompanied – the experience was exhilarating.

'No wonder Rose jaunts around London on her own by omnibus!' Iris shouted above the din to Marigold.

Marigold – who also jaunted around London unaccompanied, though nearly always by hansom cab – merely grinned. As far as she was concerned, the less Iris knew about her own adventurous activities when she stayed with Sibyl, the better.

Once in the Mall, even though the procession was still heading up it towards the palace, they managed to inch their way through the crush towards the spankingly new, glittering white-marble monument to Queen Victoria that stood on an island in front of the palace gates.

'If we can get to the palace side of the monument we'll be in the best possible position to see the royal family when they step out on to the balcony,' Rory shouted as, with Iris and Lily's arms firmly linked in his and Marigold hard on his heels, he continued to forge a way forwards.

'There's someone selling toffee apples!' Lily tugged Rory's arm urgently. 'I've never had a toffee apple, Rory. May I have one? Please?'

'Dear God!' Rory, as breezily unconventional as most of the rest of his family, was profoundly shocked. 'I can't have anyone seeing Lord May's granddaughters eating in the street. It simply isn't done, Lily. It's an absolute no-no.'

'We're not going to meet anyone we know in this crush.' Marigold held on to her hat as a couple of costermongers squeezed past them. 'I quite fancy a toffee apple. What about you, Iris?'

Iris had never been faced with such a dilemma. As conventional as Rose and Marigold were unconventional, in the normal way of things she would never in a million years have even considered eating in public. But today wasn't like any other day – and the toffee apples did look nice.

Seeing the expression on her face, knowing that it signified she was quite happy for them all to be seen behaving in just as plebeian a manner as the thousands of people thronging around them, Rory put his hand into his pocket.

Minutes later, toffee apples in hand, they were about twenty people deep from the front of the palace railings. Even though

143

carriages and bands from the tail-end of the procession were still rolling from the Mall into the palace courtyard, the crowd around them were lustily shouting for the King to make an appearance and the shouts of, 'We *want the King! We want the King! We want the King!*' were deafening.

'*And Queen Mary!*' a woman near to them shouted, and the chant, '*Queen Mary! Queen Mary! Queen Mary!*' was immediately taken up.

When the royal party finally stepped out on to the balcony from the grand gallery's centre room, the storm of cheers, whistles and applause was like nothing any of them had ever heard before.

'Oh gosh, Rory!' Iris shouted. 'I'm so glad we're here!' She squeezed his arm so tightly she nearly stopped the flow of blood. 'There's David! Just stepping out behind his mother! Oh, doesn't he look wonderful! Just like a prince from a fairy-tale!'

Rory looked towards Lily, to see how she was reacting to seeing her best friend the object of such slavish adoration and respect from so many hundreds of thousands of people.

As David stepped forward, into full view, the chants '*Three cheers for the Prince of Wales*' and '*Hip, hip, hurrah!*' were taken up.

Lily's eyes were fixed on David, but she wasn't joining in the chanting and she wasn't laughing with delight. Instead the expression on her delicately boned face was that of someone pole-axed, of someone stunned by a sudden, terrible realization.

Concerned, he bent his head to hers, his mouth close to her ear. 'What's the matter, Lily?' He cupped his mouth with his hand so that she would be able to hear him above the din all around them. 'Is it all too much for you? Are you feeling dizzy?'

She shook her head, not taking her eyes from David,

boyishly handsome in his Knight of the Garter robes and coronet, his blond hair gleaming as pale as barley beneath the sun that had, at last, made an appearance.

'No. It's just . . . it's just that for the first time I've realized just how far removed from our world David is. When I saw him in the procession it was as if he was in a pageant. Just something that was splendidly good fun. But now . . .' She turned her head away from his, looking around her at the vast throng that stretched in an unbroken sea all the way back down the Mall as far as Admiralty Arch. 'But now I see that we'll only ever be able to be friends at Snowberry. I'd never truly realized what being royal meant before.' She looked stricken and he thought he knew why.

If she, too, had been having stirrings of first love, seeing the Prince in full royal regalia, instead of his naval cadet uniform, would have been quite an eye-opener. As would seeing him the object of adulation of hundreds of thousands of people – millions, if British subjects overseas, listening in to accounts of the coronation on the wireless, were taken into account.

He said sympathetically, 'Snowberry is just a novelty to him, Lily. As is his behaving as if he can be friends with you and your sisters just as if he were an ordinary young man. He isn't an ordinary young man. He never can be. One day, like his father, he'll not only be King of Great Britain and Ireland and all her Dominions beyond the Seas, but Emperor of India as well. Queen Victoria has only been dead ten years and she was ruler of a quarter of the human race; I don't imagine the numbers have gone down much.'

He didn't add that looking at Edward now it was impossible to believe he was destined for such a momentous place in the world's history books. Young-looking for his age, without the Garter robes and coronet he could more easily be taken for a choirboy than heir to the greatest throne in the world.

145

Of all his cousins, Lily was Rory's favourite. The place she held in his heart was of such complexity he had never trusted himself to examine it too closely. He didn't now, but the look of devastation on her face turned his heart over and he said gently, 'If you had any romantic notions about yourself and Prince Edward, it's best you forget them, Lily love. Heirs to thrones marry where they are told to marry – and I rather think King George and Queen Mary will have already drawn up a shortlist of names for Edward to choose from.'

# FOURTEEN

'So what it really comes down to, May,' an exhausted George said late that evening when he and his wife were, at last, blessedly alone, 'is a Dane, a German or a Russian. The others are all just too problematical.'

Queen Mary, for whom the day had been just as exhausting and just as emotionally draining as it had been for her husband, had not the least desire to embark on a conversation as to which court of Europe would be the best hunting ground for a bride for their eldest son, but she didn't say so. George was her king as well as her husband. It was something she never allowed herself to forget and she always subjugated her wishes to his, no matter how mundane those wishes might be – as now, when she simply wanted to go to bed.

'The Danes.' She kept her voice free of any inflection of disapproval, well aware that it was very difficult to be disapproving of the Danish royal house. That she *was* disapproving was only because they were such a happy-go-lucky, informal lot. In Queen Mary's opinion, informality was a far from desirable quality when it came to being royal. The difficulty in saying so was that George's mother, Queen

Alexandra – still alive and well and living at Sandringham – had been, prior to her marriage, a princess of Denmark and the British royal family's ties with the Danish royal house were close.

'Another Danish princess, as Princess of Wales, would be a very popular choice,' she said diplomatically. 'The people took Motherdear to their hearts the instant she set foot on British soil.'

Despite all the problems Queen Mary had with her mother-in-law – her refusal, after King Edward's death, to move out of Buckingham Palace and into Marlborough House, for instance, and her perpetual lateness for absolutely everything – she was fair enough to give credit where it was due. Her mother-in-law had been an exceedingly popular queen consort and, despite her deafness and increasing lack of mobility, was just as popular with the general public now that she was Dowager Queen Consort.

'However,' May went on, 'there are things to take into consideration that didn't have to be taken into consideration in eighteen sixty-three when Motherdear's marriage to your father was arranged. The political situation was far less complicated then. Willy is so belligerent and his navy is growing at such speed that Mr Asquith thinks it will soon be comparable to ours.'

George made a noise in his throat that indicated just what he thought of his cousin's efforts to bring the German navy into anything approaching parity with the British navy. Ever since he had become Kaiser, Willy had been a thorn in everyone's flesh, plunging his stubby finger into every diplomatic pie he could find.

'A marriage between David and his daughter will unite Germany and Great Britain in a way no amount of treaties will ever do. Princess Victoria Louise is just the right age,' May continued, 'only a year or so older than David and I think

David likes her. They got on very well together when she came with Willy and Dona to the unveiling of Grandmama's memorial monument.'

They were in the small sitting room that linked their bedrooms. Irritably, George ran the tasselled end of his dressing-gown cord through his fingers. Princess Victoria Louise was a pleasant enough girl and there was a lot to be said for uniting Germany and Britain in such a way. Nicky wouldn't like it, though. Nicky, Tsar of Russia and his and Willy's first cousin, had just as fretful a relationship with Willy as George had.

Between the three of them they ruled over half the population of the world. It was something that had to be taken into account when deciding on a politically advantageous marriage for Great Britain. The question was: which would be more advantageous? A marriage uniting Britain more closely with Germany – who at the moment was in close cahoots with Austria–Hungary and Italy – or a marriage drawing Britain even closer to Russia?

May, reading his thoughts, said, 'You're thinking of the Romanovs, aren't you? You're thinking of Nicky's eldest daughter, Olga.'

He nodded. 'She's the right age, only a year younger than David, and if we want her as a bride for him we'll have to act fast. Nicky has told me he is already considering Prince Carol as a future husband for her.'

Prince Carol's mother was a granddaughter of Queen Victoria through the paternal side of her family, and on the maternal side she was a granddaughter of Tsar Alexander II. With such a strong Russian link May could well understand why the eighteen-year-old Romanian Prince had been singled out by Nicky as a suitable husband for Olga.

David, though, would be far more suitable, for there could be no comparison between the throne he would inherit and the throne Carol would one day inherit. As for family ties – always an important consideration in a royal marriage – Olga's paternal grandmother and Queen Alexandra were sisters. It was the reason George and Nicky looked so alike.

A disadvantage, though, was Olga's mother. German-born Alix would hate the thought of Olga ever leaving Russia. That any woman could be as possessive a mother as Alix was something May – who hadn't a maternal bone in her body – failed to understand. She said doubtfully, 'There's always unrest in Russia, George. We don't want to be linked to that unrest any more than we can help, and that might happen if the next Queen of England was Russian. That dear Olga has barely a drop of Russian blood in her veins is neither here nor there. She's a Romanov and the public will always remember it.'

George, who didn't like to be reminded, however obliquely, that his own blood was far more German than English, made another non-committal sound in his throat.

Aware that she had inadvertently touched a sensitive nerve, May moved swiftly on. 'What about the House of Mecklenburg-Strelitz?' She threw her personal preference into the ring as if it were an afterthought. 'The small courts of Germany have never failed Britain when it has come to the question of future queen consorts.'

'Nor have they.' George stopped running tassels through his fingers and looked at her fondly. Though May had been brought up at Kensington Palace, by birth she was a member of the German House of Teck and her connections to Germany were strong.

'Too minor,' he said regretfully. 'A minor royal house will no longer suffice, May. Not in this day and age. David will one day be a king-emperor, and his bride should be the daughter of one – and apart from myself there are only two king-emperors. Willy and Nicky.'

'So David's future wife is to be either the Kaiser's daughter or the Tsar's?'

George nodded. Whether, when a decision was made, the girl in question would be happy about the future arranged for her wasn't something that even crossed his mind. Royal marriages had always been arranged marriages. And what girl wouldn't want to be the future Queen Consort of Great Britain and Ireland and of all her Dominions beyond the Seas?

'I think', May said, abandoning all hope of a Mecklenburg-Strelitz marital match, 'that when the choice is put to David, he may well consider dear Nicky a more agreeable father-in-law than Willy.'

'David's preferences are immaterial, May. The question is: will a marital alliance with Germany be more beneficial, or less beneficial, than a marital alliance with Russia? And it is the Prime Minister's and the Foreign Secretary's opinions that will have to be taken into consideration, not David's.'

He walked away from her towards the door leading to his bedroom, saying, 'David will do as he's always done, May.'

'And that is?'

He paused, one hand on the doorknob. 'He'll do as he's told,' he said. 'Goodnight, dear May. God bless.'

In a separate wing of Buckingham Palace David, like his father, was in his dressing-gown. He wasn't about to go to bed, though. He was at his desk, writing to Lily, a glass of whisky and soda handily within reach.

Dearest Lily,

What a day today has been! I just wish you could have been sharing it with me, but as you couldn't I want to share it with you by writing down all my

151

thoughts and feelings before I turn in for bed. I saw my parents at 9 a.m. and the King showed me the Admiralty Order in *The Times* gazetting me a midshipman. I was frightfully bucked about it. Then I dressed in my Garter clothes and robe – and though I really do hate guying myself up as if I were living in the Middle Ages I remembered what you said about the pleasure it gives people and so I didn't mind too much at all – and then at 10.00 a.m. I left the palace in a state carriage with my sister Mary and the brothers.

We arrived in the abbey at 10.30 and then I walked up the nave and choir to my seat in front of the peers. (I tried to single out your grandfather and give him a nod, but there were so many old gentlemen all dressed in peers' robes that I couldn't distinguish one from another.) All the relatives and people were most civil and bowed to me as I passed. Then Mama and Papa came in and the ceremony commenced. There was the recognition, the anointing and then the crowning of Papa, and then I put on my coronet with the peers. Then I had to go and do homage to Papa at his throne, and I was very nervous . . . Then Mama was crowned.

After that we got into our carriage and had a long drive back. My coronet felt very heavy and we had to bow to the people as we went along, which made it even more uncomfortable. The highlight, dearest Lily, was seeing you waving to me from the balcony of your great-aunt's house. It was so sweet of you to do so and I shall always remember it.

Afterwards, I went out on to Buckingham Palace's balcony with the rest of my family to wave to the crowds and then later there was a most enormous banquet and it went on so long I thought it was never going to end.

Dearest Lily, I'm not very good at letter-writing. I do hope you don't think this the most awful drivel, but I'm dreadfully tired and I expect that doesn't help. I thought about you all day today, and I can't wait till I'm next back at Snowberry. It's only been a few days since I was there, but already it feels like weeks and weeks.

He paused, his pen hovering over the paper. He wanted to sign off by writing *Tons and tons of my very best love, David*, but knew he couldn't. Not yet. But soon he would be able to do so. Soon he would let everyone know how he felt about Lily, for he had decided the last thing he wanted was for there to be anything furtive about his love for her. With his heart in every word, he wrote: *Your very best friend, David*.

In the bedroom that was always assigned to her whenever she stayed at her great-aunt's, Rose, too, was wide awake. The day had seemed endless. First had been the long wait to see the coronation procession pass down St James's Street and the very odd experience of seeing David, looking so very regal in his Garter robes and coronet. Then there had been her visit to the Harburys. Neither of Daphne's parents had been home. As an earl and countess they had been among the eight thousand or so guests jam-packed into Westminster Abbey.

Daphne had looked shockingly gaunt, but her spirit had been as strong as ever. 'I wish I hadn't been given a special release because of the coronation,' she'd said fiercely. 'The Home Secretary only gave the order because he was frightened of the repercussions if I were to die – and I don't think he would have been worried about my dying if it wasn't for the fact that my father is an earl.'

153

Rose had taken hold of her hand, noticing how yellow Daphne's skin had become during the weeks of her imprisonment. 'When you were in Holloway,' she'd said, 'I spoke to Lord Jethney about the conditions in which you and other suffragettes were being kept. I told him that force-feeding – especially under the unhygienic and brutal conditions in which it is applied – was certain to end in a suffragette's death. He agreed with me that the general public have to become aware that force-feeding isn't some kind of a joke but a form of torture no country calling itself civilized should tolerate. He gave me an introduction to Hal Green, the editor of the *Daily Despatch*, who was pretty dubious at first, but I think he's going to help us.'

'What, come out publicly in support of the Cause?' The amazement in Daphne's voice had been total.

'Yes,' she'd said, 'and with banner headlines if I can keep him to his word.'

There, she thought, as she tried in vain to sleep, was the crunch. Would Hal Green keep his word?

He was the most unsettling person she had ever met. She had expected him to be a contemporary of Lord Jethney's, in his mid-forties or possibly older. She had also expected him to be – in manners at least – a gentleman.

He'd proved to be neither.

When she had arrived at the *Daily Despatch*'s offices in Fleet Street for her meeting with him, he hadn't been there.

'Mr Green won't be long, Miss Houghton,' said a forbidding-looking secretary who had been seated outside a large glass-fronted office. She had then risen to her feet and said, 'If you follow me, you can wait for Mr Green in his office. It will be more comfortable for you.'

When Rose had looked through the large glass windows and seen Hal Green striding into the outer room, she had assumed he was an employee. For one thing, he looked to

154

be in his early thirties, not his mid-forties. Tall and lean, he had the easy loose-limbed walk of an athlete. Dark hair fell low over his forehead. He was in shirtsleeves and waistcoat, his jacket slung casually over one shoulder as a working-man might carry it. When, to her amazement, he strolled into the office, she had said helpfully, 'Mr Green isn't here.'

'No problem.' He'd grinned at her, rounded the desk, flung his jacket over the chair behind it and sat down. 'Hal Green,' he'd said. 'I take it that you are Rose?'

Calling her by her Christian name, before they had even introduced themselves, had been a familiarity so astonishing it had taken her breath away.

'Miss Houghton,' she'd said crushingly and then, remembering why she was there and that he was the person with the power to carry the crusade for a change in the sentencing laws to untold millions of people, she'd added swiftly, 'It's very kind of you to meet with me, Mr Green. I believe Lord Jethney has told you why I'm here?'

'Yes,' he'd said, and she'd seen that his grey eyes weren't dark, as she had expected them to be, but extraordinarily light. 'You want me to cut my readership figures to zilch by coming out in whole-hearted support of a lot of foolish women.'

She had risen to her feet and said with ice in her voice, 'Lord Jethney has obviously misjudged your character and sympathies. You are not the kind of man I thought I would be dealing with, Mr Green.' She'd turned her back on him and walked towards the door.

He'd said with lazy amusement, 'You're not much of a fighter, are you, Miss Houghton?'

She'd whipped round, furious at having behaved in a way that justified his comment. 'I haven't come here to gain support in the battle for votes for women,' she'd said tightly. 'I realize that's a step too far for a national newspaper that panders to a predominantly male readership. My crusade is to end the injustice of suffragettes being imprisoned in the third division when, as political prisoners, they should be being held in the first division. I want Rule 243A brought to public attention and revoked.'

'Rule 243A?' He'd looked interested despite the fact that he'd now stretched his legs out in front of him and crossed them negligently at the ankle, revealing a glimpse of purple sock-suspenders.

Still standing, she'd glared down at him. 'A year ago,' she'd said, 'the Home Secretary, Mr Churchill, introduced a ruling that denies suffragettes the official first-division status available to political prisoners.'

He'd tapped a pencil against his teeth and said, 'Just why do you think suffragettes should be classified as political prisoners?'

'Because they are acting in the pursuit of a political cause – and that cause is to win for themselves the same lawful rights that men have.' She'd leaned forward aggressively, resting her hands flat on his untidy desk. 'Have you any idea, Mr Green, of the horrendous conditions that women and girls are being held in as third-division prisoners? Or of the treatment they are receiving?'

She'd proceeded to tell him of how Laura Ainsworth, because the feeding tube couldn't be forced up her nostrils, had been held down by five wardresses while a two-foot-long tube was forced down her throat; of how Lady Constance Lytton, after being force-fed eight times, had suffered a heart attack and now her health was irreparably damaged; of many more instances of treatment so brutal it could only come under the heading of torture.

'Over and above such horrors', she'd said, 'are the petty humiliations. It wasn't enough for the authorities that my friend Lady Daphne was held in solitary confinement and repeatedly force-fed, but she was provided with no water – apart from an enamel mug of drinking water – in which to wash.'

To her dismay she'd felt tears spring to her eyes.

Throwing his pencil on to the desk, he'd said, 'All right, Rose. I'm interested – and I think I can interest my chairman. It is controversial and controversy sells newspapers. Because it does, the *Daily Despatch* will launch a campaign rooting for first-division political-prisoner status for suffragettes.'

She'd been so thankful she hadn't even minded his use of her Christian name, though she had been furiously angry with herself for her last thought as she left his office.

That thought was that Hal Green's grey eyes were fringed by the blackest, thickest eyelashes she had ever seen on a man.

She pulled her bedroom curtains back. A couple of hansom cabs were heading in the direction of Piccadilly. Two men in white tie and tails were strolling past Rumpelmeyer's, the smart teashop and confectioner's on the far side of the street. Almost imperceptibly the night sky was lightening into dawn.

After such a long day, not being able to sleep was annoying, but not surprising after the evening she had endured. Their grandfather, exhausted after the long ceremonials in the abbey, had returned to Snowberry, taking Lily with him. Though Lily was not yet 'out', Rose had expected that under the very special circumstances of a coronation Lily would be staying in London and going with them to the many balls and parties arranged for the rest of the week, but she had been strangely out of sorts and had wanted to return to Snowberry.

So she hadn't had to worry about Lily. Iris and Marigold, however, had both, for very different reasons, caused her anxiety, Marigold excessively so.

The ball she, Iris and Marigold had been invited to that evening had been a fancy-dress ball, its theme: royalty. She had gone as Eleanor of Provence, Henry III's queen. Iris had gone as Queen Victoria. Marigold had refused to tell anyone what she was going as, which should have warned Rose that Marigold had every intention of being daring to the point of outrage. She'd had so much on her mind, though, with Daphne's poor physical condition and her worry as to whether or not Hal Green was going to keep his word, that Marigold had barely entered her thoughts.

The three of them hadn't left for the ball at the same time. She and Iris had left first, leaving Rory and Marigold to follow on after them. Needless to say, she hadn't had a glimmer of what royal personage Marigold was to be, but had assumed that as Marigold was such a spectacular redhead she would be going as one of the Tudors, most probably Elizabeth.

The first indication that the evening wasn't going to be a smoothly happy event was when Iris had emerged from her bedroom dressed as a young Queen Victoria. Queen Victoria had been short, dumpy and more than a little plain. Iris looked so like her that it was eerie. Her gown was of shot silk in brown and green, the brown the exact colour of her eyes and hair. With its low, scooped neck and crinoline skirt it should have been immensely flattering. Instead it merely made her look years older than she was and, like Queen Victoria, not remotely glamorous or head-turning. Nearly every other young woman of her debutante year had chosen to dress in a costume that was flattering. There were scores of Queen Elizabeths, a regiment of Anne Boleyns, a whole shoal of Mary Stuarts and a sprinkling of Lady Jane Greys. Delia Conisborough had come as Titania, Shakespeare's Queen of the Fairies. Margot Asquith had come as Catherine the Great.

In contrast to them Iris, wearing her hair as Victoria had worn hers, in a no-nonsense chignon in the nape of her neck, had looked a brown mouse and Rose, fearful that Iris's dance-card was going to remain empty yet again, had been vastly relieved when she'd seen Toby enter the room, dressed rather improbably as Henry VIII.

'Oh look, Iris! There's Toby!' she had said, grateful that Iris was now going to have a happy evening.

Iris had looked in the direction she was indicating and Rose had seen the exact moment when Toby registered their presence.

Instead of walking immediately across to them, his face lighting up, he had given them an embarrassed nod and had turned to speak to the girl standing next to him.

'What on earth . . .?' she had said, turning in amazement to Iris.

To her horror she had seen that Iris was fighting back tears. 'Toby and I are no longer as . . . as close as we used to be,' she had said stiltedly, her face a picture of misery. 'Please don't make a big thing out of it, Rose.'

'But what has happened, Iris?' she'd said, totally bewildered.

'I don't want to talk about it!' Iris had said fiercely.

Toby led the girl he had been speaking to out on to the dance floor and Iris had turned on her heel and blundered her way towards the boudoir being used as a powder room.

While Rose had been debating whether or not to go after her, she became aware of a surge of excitement coming from the direction of the grand staircase. The bemedalled and bejewelled throng around her had begun moving towards it to see what the fuss was about and, as they did, Rory, appropriately kitted out as Bonnie Prince Charlie, strode up to her, his face grim.

'Marigold has arrived,' he'd said abruptly. 'When it comes to being outrageous, she's outdone herself. I tried to talk her out of it, believe me I did, but it was like talking into the wind.'

From the top of the broad shallow stairs of the grand staircase had come a storm of laughter and applause. A second later the reason became obvious.

Lawrence Strickland led a white pony into the ballroom. Perched seductively side-saddle on its back was Marigold.

Her hair fell in a riot of fiery waves to her waist and was crowned by a majestic gold and pearl-encrusted headdress that looked as if it had been borrowed from a Covent Garden production of *Aida*. The upper part of her costume consisted of nothing but gold net, her nipples covered by strategically placed jewelled discs. Over a diaphanous ankle-length gold-coloured chiffon skirt, a band of broad gold satin girdled her hips. Her feet, with toenails painted gold, were naked.

There had been one brief second when Rose was so appalled, so dizzy with horror, she'd been rooted to the spot. Prince Maxim Yurenev – who, being a Russian prince, had dispensed with fancy dress and simply come as himself – had gallantly stepped forward to lift Marigold from the pony's back.

It was then that Rose had moved – and moved fast. As Marigold had gaily announced to everyone that she was the Queen of Sheba, she had seized hold of her, sending half a dozen golden arm bracelets tinkling down to Marigold's wrist.

'*Home!*' she had hissed between clenched teeth and Marigold, secure in the knowledge that she was the sensation of the evening, hadn't argued.

Though the two of them had been in a hansom cab and en route to St James's Street within minutes, Rose had known the damage was done.

Marigold, totally heedless of her reputation, had ruined it. When Rose had thought of what such shamelessness

160

might mean where Marigold's relationships with men were concerned, she'd been cold with fear. Marigold's flirtation with Lord Jethney had escaped catastrophic consequences only by a hair's breadth. But now she was quite obviously on close terms with the artist Strickland, who, if he wasn't unsavoury and dissolute, looked to be. How, and when, had she come to know him so well that he had agreed to be a part of her vulgarly sensational entrance? Or had it been Strickland who had suggested the idea to her? Then what of Prince Yurenev? Had it just been chance that he had been nearest to the pony when she had made her entrance? Or had he been expecting its arrival?

Over the rooftops the sky was the pale yellow of early dawn. Rose sighed heavily, not wanting to remember the hideous scene that had taken place between her and Marigold when they had reached home, quite certain that Marigold wasn't lying awake, thinking of it.

Marigold would, she knew, be sleeping deeply without a care in the world.

# FIFTEEN

David didn't have a moment to himself. The day after the coronation, Buckingham Palace was still jam-packed with foreign royalty, nearly all of them relations of one kind or another. There was a huge celebration party for his birthday and he had received shoals of incredibly expensive – and largely useless – presents. His favourite gift had been the card Lily had given him when they had last been together and which she had made him promise he wouldn't open until his birthday morning.

Home-made, it was a pencil drawing of the five of them picnicking on Snowberry's lawn the day her pet goat had demolished an entire chocolate cake. Though her figures were little more than stick figures, each one was instantly recognizable. Rose, highly indignant, her hands on her hips like a schoolmistress. Iris, vainly trying to shoo the goat away. Marigold, a huge wide-brimmed straw hat shading her face but quite obviously laughing fit to bust. Lily, her eyes wide, her hands to her mouth as if inexpressibly shocked at the naughtiness of her pet. She had drawn him, too; his peaked white and navy naval hat pushed to the back of his head;

his hands in fists on his waist as he surveyed the scene in delighted disbelief.

She had written on the inside of the card: *Dear David, We hope you will have a very happy birthday. From the four of us and Grandpapa and all the buns!*

He wanted to place it in a prominent position in his room, but knew it was too risky to do so. Instead he had placed it in the Book of Common Prayer his mother had given him on his twelfth birthday. It was a book no one else was ever likely to open – and when he was seen opening it, he would be credited with only the highest of motives.

It was a day when every second had been filled with being polite to aunts, uncles, great-aunts, great-uncles, first cousins, second cousins and third cousins, and often having to do so in German or, if not in German, then in French, the language that was the second language of everyone there – apart, from his father, of course.

The vast profusion of imperial, royal, grand-ducal and most serene highnesses, (not to mention imperial *and* royal highnesses) made for endless complications of precedence and by the time the grand banquet that evening had drawn to a close, his head was throbbing and he wanted only one thing in the world: to be away from chandeliers and champagne and at Snowberry with Lily.

With as much patience as he could muster, he listened to the luxuriantly mustachioed Tsar Ferdinand of Bulgaria telling him of how, when he and Franz Ferdinand had been travelling in private carriages aboard the Orient Express, the Archduke had impertinently had his carriage placed immediately after the engine in a position of precedence.

'But I got the better of him!' Ferdinand chortled. 'When he needed to pass through my carriage to reach the dining car, I refused him permission! The old fool had to wait until the

train reached a station, then alight and hurry along the platform to the dining saloon. When he'd eaten, he had to wait
until the train stopped at another station before he could
make his way back to his carriage!' He laughed so hard at the
memory he had to mop his rheumy eyes with his handkerchief.

David smiled dutifully, his thoughts still on Lily. He wanted
to be with her so much it hurt. He wondered if she was still
at her great-aunt's house in St James's Street, or if she had
returned to Snowberry. Wherever she was, he wanted to be
there.

The Tsar was now having a rant about the Kaiser, but
David wasn't listening to him. What he wanted was to slip
away from the banqueting table, get in his Austro-Daimler
and drive to wherever Lily was. He wouldn't be able to see
her, of course. It was nearly midnight and she would be in
bed. Just to be near her, though, breathing the same air she
was breathing, would be a comfort.

'You don't look well, my boy,' Tsar Ferdinand said suddenly,
forgetting whatever it was he'd been in the middle of saying
about Kaiser Wilhelm. 'Have you a headache? I get migraines.
They're beastly things. Is that what you have now?'

It wasn't, but Ferdinand had given him the idea he was
looking for. 'Yes,' he said. He motioned to the footman
standing behind his chair. 'The instant we rise from table
please offer my apologies to His Majesty and tell him I have
the most ghastly headache and that I've gone to bed.'

There were over a hundred people seated at the banqueting
table and when the meal came to an end he avoided all eye
contact with his parents and close relatives and left the room
as unobtrusively as he could.

Once in his own suite of rooms he said to a startled Finch,
'I need help, Finch. I need to leave the palace for a breath
of fresh air and I don't want company. D'you have any ideas?'

Finch, who had been seeing to his every want since he

was seven years old, said, 'Would you be walking when you go for a breath of fresh air, sir? Or motoring?'

'Motoring.'

'Then that's tricky, sir.' It was a massive understatement. No senior member of the royal family ever went anywhere alone – and certainly not in the middle of the night.

'It's important to me, Finch. I thought if I could borrow your motor car . . .'

Finch's car was his pride and joy. With great self-control he kept his face impassive.

'. . . and I wore your greatcoat and hat and left by a staff exit . . .'

'Is this "breath of fresh air" really so important, sir? There would be an unholy row if you were recognized and word got back to His Majesty.'

The imaginary headache that had been his excuse for leaving the banqueting hall was now a real one. David felt as if his head was in a vice. 'Yes, Finch,' he said, his face unnaturally pale. 'It is important.'

'Then so be it, sir. Do you know your way to the staff garages? My motor car is the little blue tourer. It'll be easy to spot. Only a handful of staff have vehicles.'

'And your greatcoat and hat, Finch?

'Are at your disposal, sir.'

Well aware that he was behaving exceedingly rashly, David made his way out of the royal apartments to the nearest back stairs. There, with no one about, he put on Finch's coat and hat, pulling the brim low down over his brow. Then, furtive as a thief, he left the palace by one of the many staff exits. Should he be stopped and recognized he had already decided on what his response would be. He would play squiffy with champagne and say it was all a stunt: a bet he'd had with Tsar Ferdinand as to whether his leaving the palace in such a manner could be done or not.

165

'Off for a little private celebration, Finchy?' one of the guards at the staff exit called out as he motored past him.

He didn't risk an imitation of Finch's voice. Instead he gave a thumbs-up sign and, seconds later, unchallenged, he was motoring down the gas-lit Mall.

It was still busy with revellers partying into the early hours. He grinned to himself, wondering what they would say if they knew who was at the wheel of the car driving past them.

Cutting down the side of St James's Palace into St James's Street he came to a halt outside the Harland town house. No lights were on. He wondered if Lily's bedroom was in the front part of the house, or the rear. He wondered if she was asleep or lying awake and, if she was, whether she was perhaps thinking of him.

A couple of dozen yards away a couple of elderly gentlemen were leaving White's slightly the worse for wear. White's members were invariably titled and also very often government ministers. Fearful of being recognized he pulled Finch's trilby even lower over his eyes. Without so much as glancing in his direction the men stepped into the rear of a chauffeured Rolls-Royce Silver Ghost.

He watched it drive off in the direction of Piccadilly and then once again turned his attention to the darkened upper windows of Lady Harland's London home.

He had hoped that just by being outside the house he would feel closer to Lily, but the sensation he yearned for eluded him. He couldn't easily imagine her within the house, because he had never been inside. Snowberry would have been different. Whether she was there or not, Snowberry would be imbued with Lily's presence.

The little car's engine was still ticking over and decisively he put it into gear. He would drive to Snowberry. He'd never driven such a distance at night before; even in daytime he'd

166

only ever driven such a distance when accompanied by Piers Cullen. A drive into Hampshire in the early hours would be a drive to remember – and he would be able to think of Lily all the way.

The route took him through Windsor and with very mixed emotions he looked up at the massive dark outline of the castle. Windsor, more than any of the other royal palaces, symbolized England's monarchical glamour and grandeur. Nine hundred years ago William the Conqueror had built a fortress on the huge chalk cliff above the Thames and throughout the centuries, from then to now, Kings and Queens of England had counted it one of their principal homes.

When he was king, no doubt he would do the same. As he continued to drive south-west, towards Hampshire, he thought of Windsor's sumptuously ornate drawing rooms – the white, the green, the crimson – and of how, though masterpieces by Rembrandt, Canaletto and Van Dyck hung on their walls, he far preferred the informality of Snowberry's drawing room, its French doors opening on to the long lawn leading down to the lake.

At last, in the orange glow of his headlamps, he saw that he was on the sharply curving road where his life had changed so monumentally when he had knocked Rose from her bicycle. His spirits soared.

He was nearly there; nearly on what he was beginning to think of as hallowed ground.

Snowberry's high wrought-iron gates were open and he drove between them, slowing his speed to a crawl so that he wouldn't waken Millie, or William, or the dogs.

No matter how carefully he drove the sound of his tyres on the gravel were horrendous. Panic-stricken, he came to a halt just short of the house. How the devil would he explain himself if he woke someone?

The house remained in darkness and he let his breath out

slowly. In the moonlit sky an owl flew low over Snowberry's ancient, red-tiled roof. The unmistakable shape of a fox darted from one side of the shrubbery-edged driveway to the other. He fumbled for his cigarette case and as he did so light flooded from one of the bedroom windows.

His heart slammed against his breastbone. Even at unconventional Snowberry no member of staff would have a bedroom at the front of the house. It could only mean he had disturbed one of the girls or their grandfather and, as he was certain the girls were still at their great-aunt's house in St James's Street, the chances were that it was Lord May who was about to come out of the house, probably with a shotgun in his hand.

For an insane moment he was tempted to swerve around and hightail it back to the main road. The car wasn't known at Snowberry. No one would realize he was its driver. But if he did hightail it, it would be assumed that the driver was a burglar, and Lily and her sisters would be unable to sleep at nights without anxiety.

At the thought of his darling Lily living in fear of a night-time prowler he gritted his teeth, knowing he had no option but to brazen things out.

As the massive front door opened he stepped from the car. Lord May was a reasonable and kindly man and, if David told him the truth about why he was parked outside Snowberry in the middle of the night, he might very well be understanding – and it would be a relief to tell her grandfather what his feelings for Lily were.

As fast as the thought came, it went. The figure standing in the darkness of the doorway wasn't that of a man – much less one with a shotgun. It was that of a woman. Fleetingly he wondered if it was Millie and then the voice he loved called out tremulously and with enormous pluck: 'Who is there, please? Who is it?'

168

'It's me, Lily! David!' Uncaring now of the sound of scrunching gravel he sprinted towards her.

She gave a gasp of both relief and pleasure and then she, too, was running; running until she reached him and ran straight into his open arms.

He had only ever kissed a girl once before, when he was nine and had shyly kissed his cousin Anastasia aboard the Russian imperial yacht at Cowes. Under any other set of circumstances, his kiss now would have been just as tentative and shy.

Only it wasn't another set of circumstances – and he didn't give a thought to being shy. As his arms tightened around her, his mouth closed on hers in instinctive unfumbling contact.

With a stab of shock she swayed against him and then, in total response, her arms slid up around his neck and her mouth opened beneath his.

Her lips were as soft as the petals of a flower. Her dark hair, plaited in a night-time braid, gave off the clean fresh scent of lemons. Her summer dressing-gown was of thin lace-edged cotton and the feel of her body, so unconstrained against his, nearly unhinged him. In his wildest dreams he had never imagined that physical desire could be so urgent and overwhelming.

There was no way he could hide his body's response to her. She pulled away from him slightly and even in the darkness he could see she was rosy with embarrassment.

'I'm sorry!' he gasped, utterly mortified. 'Oh God, Lily, I'm so sorry! I won't let it happen again! I promise!'

'It's all right, David darling. Really. It's just all so . . . strange . . . isn't it?' Her eyes looked into his with perfect trust.

'You mean our loving each other?'

She nodded. 'I thought perhaps it was just me that loved

you. I never dared to hope . . . because of who you are . . . that you would love me back.'

'I do, Lily.' His voice was raw with emotion. 'I love you more than you can ever imagine.'

She let out her breath in a long, deep sigh of happiness.

In the moonlight the delicate features of her face were absolute perfection. He said with awe, 'You're so beautiful, Lily. As beautiful as an angel.'

She pressed close to him again and as her body dovetailed with his in a way that was new and exciting to them both, he said devoutly, 'I'll love you always, Lily. I promise.'

'I shall always love you, David. I couldn't possibly love anybody else. Not ever.'

As he lowered his head once more to hers he knew that nothing, not his father, not the Prime Minister, not public opinion, would ever separate them. It may always have been traditional for the Prince of Wales to marry someone of royal blood, but it was a tradition that was going to be broken.

Later, he said huskily, 'I didn't expect to find you here, Lily. I thought you would still be in London, at your great-aunt's house.'

She slid her arms from around his neck, saying as he took her hands in his, 'Rose, Iris and Marigold are still there, but I came home with Grandpapa. What made you drive all this way when you didn't think I'd be here? Whose little motor car is that? Is it your brother's?'

'No. Bertie is still too young to drive. The car belongs to my valet, Finch, and I drove here because I wanted to be somewhere I could feel near to you – even if you didn't know I was there. I went to St James's Street first, but being there didn't make me feel the way I wanted to feel, and so I drove down here.'

'I'm so glad you felt like that, because I couldn't sleep for wanting to be near to you. Have we to walk down to the lake? Just in case our talking together so close to the house wakes Grandpapa.'

He nodded agreement and, hand in hand, they began walking towards the lawn.

'What on earth possessed you to come down to the front door and challenge me, when you didn't know I was the driver of the car?' he asked in concern as they reached the edge of the lawn and she slipped her feet out of her satin mules so that she could walk on the grass barefoot. 'Because it was me, I'm so glad you did, darling. But what if it had been someone else? What if it had been a burglar?'

'I didn't think about it being a burglar. I just thought it was Rory, or one of Rory's friends, and that they'd arrived here so late they didn't like to wake anyone in order to be let in.'

'Whatever you thought, it was a very brave thing to do – but promise me you'll never do it again, darling.'

She looked across at him in the darkness, shooting him a radiant smile. 'I promise. Isn't it wonderful being alone like this? I want to know so much about you, David. I want to know what life was like for you as a little boy. I can't imagine being small and being brought up in a palace.'

'I wasn't actually brought up in a palace. Until my grandfather died and my father became king, we lived mainly at York Cottage, on the Sandringham estate. It's a villa not much bigger than Snowberry – though not as ancient or as beautiful. Its rooms are tiny. That's one of the things my father liked about it. He says it reminds him of the cramped conditions he always lived in aboard ship when he was in the navy.'

'Did you like York Cottage?'

'Not very much. But that wasn't because of the size of the rooms. It was because I was never very happy there.'

'Why?' Her voice was fierce. 'I can't bear the thought of you being unhappy.'

171

He gave a wry smile. 'Not everyone is fortunate enough to have an upbringing like the one you, Rose, Iris and Marigold have enjoyed at Snowberry. You have always known that you were loved. Until now – with you – I've never been loved. At least not in any way that was shown.'

Remembering all that Captain Cullen had told her of King George's harsh temper, she squeezed his hand. 'That's beastly,' she said with feeling.

As if reading her thoughts, he said, 'It wasn't all my father's fault, though he terrified me when I was a child and often still does. The real misery was caused by my nanny. She was a real horror.'

They had reached the lakeside and she remained quiet, sensing he was about to tell her things he had never told anyone before.

Still in silence they walked out on to the small jetty. They sat down together at the end of it and he undid his shoelaces and pulled off his shoes and socks.

'Every teatime, when I was brought down from the nursery to visit my parents, she would twist my arm to make me cry just before we entered the drawing room.' He rolled up his trouser-bottoms. 'Naturally my mother would ask her to take me away again.'

His voice was so bleak and filled with such remembered pain, both physical and emotional, that she felt sick.

He plunged his feet into the cool water of the lake. 'It was always like that. Every day there would be arm-twisting and pinching. Poor Bertie came off even worse. She always kept him hungry and Bertie has suffered chronic tummy trouble ever since.'

'The woman was a sadist!' Lily's tender heart was outraged. 'Surely your parents must have realized there was something terribly wrong if you were crying whenever they saw you?'

'Oh, I suppose they just thought I was a difficult child.

172

People don't like crying, bawling babies, do they? Eventually, after three years of this torture, the nanny had a nervous breakdown and left and Lala Bill – who now looks after John – became my nanny.'

Lily, who couldn't imagine how, day after day, for three years, any mother could banish a crying child instead of taking it in her arms to comfort it, fumed silently. It wasn't up to her to tell David that his mother had ice in her veins, but she knew she would never feel the same about Queen Mary ever again.

He said with deep regret, 'I can't stay for much longer, Lily. It's going to be dawn in an hour or so and I have a busy day ahead of me. It's the traditional Coronation Fleet Review at Spithead tomorrow.'

They rose to their feet and he rolled down his trouser-legs, stuffed his socks into the pockets of his trousers and pushed his wet feet into his shoes.

Then he took her hands in his. 'There's something I have to ask you, Lily. It's the most important thing I've ever asked anyone – or ever will ask anyone.'

His eyes held hers pleadingly, his hair gleaming pale gold in the fast fading moonlight.

She waited trustingly, ready to do whatever it was he asked.

He said with a tremor in his voice, 'Will you marry me, Lily? Please, please say you will. I need you so very much, you see.'

Her bewilderment was total. 'How can I marry you, David? I'm not royal. I'm not even a little bit royal.'

His hands tightened hard on hers. 'That doesn't matter, Lily darling. All that matters is that I want to marry you – that I can't face the thought of life without you. Being royal is such a nightmare for me. I can't face the thought of it without you by my side. Once my father understands that

– and once he meets you and knows how sweet and wonderful and beautiful you are – he'll be only too happy to give his consent to our betrothal.'

'But . . . it would mean I would become Princess of Wales!' Her next thought pole-axed her. 'It would mean I would one day become *queen*!'

The horror in her voice was so naked he felt as if the ground was shifting beneath his feet; as if at any moment he was going to fall into a bottomless chasm.

'You wouldn't be queen for years and years, sweetheart,' he said, desperately trying to reassure her. 'My father is only forty-six. He'll probably reign for as long as Queen Victoria – and she reigned until she was eighty-one. Please don't think about any of that king and queen stuff. Just think of me and of how much I love you and how much I need you. Please say you'll marry me, sweet darling Lily. *Please!*'

The blood pounded in her ears and then, overcome by his all-encompassing need of her and by all the love she felt for him, she said with quiet certainty, 'Yes, of course I'll marry you, David. It's what people in love do, isn't it?'

With a sob of relief he caught her to him. 'Thank you, *thank you*, darling Lily.' He swung her round and round off her feet. 'We're going to be so happy, sweetheart!' Tears of joy filled his eyes. 'For the rest of our lives we're going to be the two happiest people in the world!'

# SIXTEEN

Though he'd had no opportunity to visit Lily again, Piers was still euphoric at how well things had gone on their afternoon out together. His heart beat faster whenever he remembered how pleased Lily had been to see him, and how she had been so interested in everything he'd said, hanging on to his every word.

His experience with her was so different from the stilted, unsatisfactory experience he'd previously had with young women that he knew he couldn't let her slip out of his life. Until now he'd barely given a thought to marrying. Now he could think of nothing else.

Because of the grand occasions taking place during coronation week he'd had no opportunity to contact his father and speak to him about his intentions with regard to Lily, but as soon as he and Prince Edward returned from the Coronation Fleet Review at Spithead, he was going to do so. Until then, he was deeply grateful that the review was an occasion absorbing all Edward's attention.

As Edward was being educated at the world's most prestigious naval college this wasn't, of course, too much of a surprise. Even he, an army, not a navy man, was impressed by the sight in front of them as they steamed out of Portsmouth's great dockyard and into the Solent aboard the royal yacht. There, in breathtaking magnificence, the entire British Fleet was arraigned in Review Lines, full flags flying, their upper decks manned.

'What a sight, May! What a sight!' Piers heard King George say to Queen Mary. For once he had to agree with his king. No country in the world had a navy to rival Britain's, not even Germany, where the shipyards at Kiel were building battleships as fast as was humanly possible.

'D'you know how many battleships and dreadnoughts are out there, Cullen?' David suddenly said to him. 'Thirty-two. And they are backed up by twenty-four armoured cruisers, sixty-seven destroyers, twelve torpedo boats and eight submarines. I wish I was serving as an officer aboard one of them.'

'Yes, sir,' Piers said, knowing that if such a day should come, he would be replaced as Edward's equerry by a naval officer.

The royal yacht was nearing the Lines and the world suddenly exploded in thunderous, deafening noise as twenty-one guns began firing a royal salute.

Only with great effort did Piers stop himself from wincing. As the smoke finally cleared away and the royal yacht began steaming slowly down the first of the Review Lines, he wondered how long his position as an equerry was likely to last. He certainly still wanted to be Edward's equerry when he married Lily. That way Edward would be in attendance at their wedding and, with luck, might be so as his best man.

They had reached the first of the battleships and three great cheers went up from the men lining her decks. At moments like this he liked to pretend that the cheers were for him. That his position and Edward's were reversed.

Only he wouldn't have Edward as an equerry, not even in his imagination.

He would have someone far more forceful.

He would have someone like himself.

Unlike Piers Cullen, Hal Green never indulged in daydreams. At thirty-two he was the youngest editor in Fleet Street. It was a position he'd gained via brilliant talent, tireless energy and family connections, for his uncle, Gerald Fielding, was the press baron, Lord Westcliff.

That nepotism was responsible for his position as editor of the *Daily Despatch* rode easily on Hal's shoulders for he knew that even without Gerald he would have become the editor of a newspaper of similar stature. His own hungry talent would have seen to that. The only difference would have been that the editorship would have taken a little longer to achieve.

He surveyed the morning's headlines, well pleased with them. The *Despatch*'s crusade for first-division status for imprisoned suffragettes was causing a furore, which was just what he had set out to achieve. Rose Houghton's visit had so piqued his interest about how suffragettes were being treated in the third division that he had applied to visit Holloway in order to see conditions for himself.

It had been a request that had been refused.

Hal hadn't been too concerned. Such a refusal, when publicized as he could publicize it, was all grist to his mill. Also, as he never took no for an answer, he knew he'd eventually get the visit he was after.

'I intend running a weekly page devoted entirely to suffragette issues,' he said in a telephone call to Rose. 'It will have the headline "A Woman's Voice" and feature articles by leaders of all suffrage societies and reports of any forthcoming suffrage activities. I'd like your friend, Lady Daphne, to write an article detailing her experiences in the third division – and I'd like to meet her. D'you think you could arrange that?'

'I can try,' she said crisply.

He severed the connection, his mouth quirking into a smile. Rose Houghton's masculine-style forthrightness and her obvious (though unexpressed) low opinion of men amused him vastly.

He tapped a pen against his teeth, wondering what her prose style was like. She wouldn't have had much education; girls of her class rarely did. She'd probably been educated by private tutors with a few 'polishing' months at a finishing school in France, where the only academic subject would have been French. Her eyes, however, were fiercely intelligent (as well as beautiful) and instinct told him that anything she wrote would be commercially compelling as well as incisive.

If he was right in his assumption, there was no reason why the *Daily Despatch* shouldn't be the first national newspaper to employ a female journalist. Doing so would tie in very nicely with the present campaign, and even when the campaign was over, there was room for a woman's slant on national topics. The controversy such an appointment would arouse would increase circulation figures, just as the controversy caused by the present campaign was increasing them.

He pushed his chair away from his desk and rose to his feet. He was due to meet with his uncle at the Savoy in half an hour and was going to add the possibility of Rose being employed by the *Daily Despatch* to their agenda. Gerald would be aghast, he knew, but he would talk him round to the idea.

Just as he would talk Rose Houghton round to the idea.

Stepping out of the building and into Fleet Street he ignored the chauffeured Daimler that was at his beck and call and began strolling in the direction of the Strand.

Lord Jethney was sunk in so deep a depression he could barely bring himself to be civil to people. With his decision to end his relationship with Marigold, all the joy had gone out of his life. Time after time he told himself he was being ridiculous. He was, after all, a very fortunate man. He came from a family that had been prominent since the time of the Tudors. He was well respected. He was wealthy. He was healthy. He had two handsome, intelligent sons and he had a wife who loved him. He had, in fact, all that a sane, reasonable man could wish for. But he wasn't happy, and in his blackest moments, he seriously wondered if he would ever be happy again. All because of a nineteen-year-old girl he had known since her birth; a girl who was young enough to be his daughter.

Sophisticated though he was, nothing in his experience had prepared him for Marigold. It had simply never occurred to him that a girl so young – and brought up as she had been brought up – could be so sexually provocative.

Never in a million years would he have thought that instead of disapproval, his reaction would be to fall head-long, crazily in love with her. He was forty-six. Men of forty-six didn't lose their heads in such a way. If and when they indulged in love affairs, they were always carefully in control of the affair. It didn't disrupt their lives, never disrupted their marriages, and they never, ever, became enslaved.

He, fool that he was, had become completely enslaved. It was only because Marigold's grandfather was one of his oldest, dearest friends that he had found the will-power to put an end to the insanity. Herbert Houghton was a man of integrity and honour and thought he, Jethney, was equally honourable. The prospect of Herbert realizing otherwise – him knowing that his hospitality had been taken advantage of and his granddaughter deflowered – was a horror so unspeakable he'd found a strength he would otherwise have been utterly unable to summon.

But it was when he had exercised that strength that the unimaginable had happened. Instead of being devastated that he was putting an end to their love affair Marigold had merely been petulant. Then, as if it wasn't of the slightest importance, she had told him that he hadn't been her first lover. Who, then, had been? The thought tormented him. Had it been someone he knew? Had it been one of his many close friends?

He strode towards the chief whip's office, his jaw clenched so hard his teeth hurt. Had it perhaps been the son of one of his friends? Someone young. Someone single. Someone who might still be in love with her and might ask her to marry him?

Clenching his jaw even harder he came to a halt outside the chief whip's office, wishing to God that he was still a bachelor. If he were, he wouldn't be suffering as he was now suffering. He would have put a ring on Marigold's finger and lashed her to him so tightly she would never have looked at another man again.

As he tried to order his thoughts before entering the office, a wave of shame washed over him. How, in the name of all that was holy, could he be thinking such thoughts? How could he be wishing he had never married Jerusha, who had never said, or done, an unkind thing to him in all the years of their married life?

Desperately trying to focus his thoughts on the subject of the meeting ahead of him – Lansdowne's proposition that the House of Lords should consist mainly of indirectly elected members – he put his hand on the brass door-handle and turned it, knowing that after his behaviour of the last few months he needed to be horse-whipped.

The Honourable Toby Mulholland was wrestling with the most difficult decision he had ever faced. Did he do what his family, and Iris and Iris's family, so clearly expected of him, and propose to Iris, or did he make it crystal clear that he was never going to do any such thing?

His platoon was in the middle of a training exercise in Windsor Great Park and as he automatically went through drills that were second nature to him, he passionately wished that he was at Sissbury. Sissbury and Iris were, for him, inextricably linked and, if he had to make a decision about her, it seemed only right that the decision should be made where, ever since they were children, they had spent so much time together.

He felt he should be at Sissbury for other reasons as well. Sissbury lay so close to Snowberry that at one point the two estates marched side by side for nearly half a mile, and this was the reason his father had always encouraged the idea of a romance between Toby and Iris.

'With May's son dead, and May not being a stickler for tradition, there's no absolute certainty who will eventually inherit Snowberry,' he had said bluntly to him when he was fifteen years old. 'The Sinclair boy is the nearest male relative, but he'd be out of the running if May had a male grandchild and I somehow don't see the eldest girl being early marriage material.'

As Rose at that time had only been fifteen, Toby had always been impressed by his father's very accurate foreknowledge.

Nothing had been said at that time about Marigold, but it hadn't been very long before it became obvious that Marigold was going to prove even less likely early marriage material – though for quite different reasons – than Rose. Lily, being the youngest daughter, didn't count at all in his father's scheme of things.

'Iris is the one,' his father had said. 'Marry Iris and there's no knowing what the future might bring.'

The idea of marrying with an eye to the Snowberry estate one day becoming one with the Sissbury estate had been repellent to him at the time, though now he could see the sense of it, especially when the girl in question was one he got on with so well.

Iris was, quite simply, his best friend. Ever since he was six and she was four, she had always been his best friend. They had learned to ride together; of all her sisters, she was by far the best horsewoman. Together they had solemnly trained their pet dogs to be gun dogs. They had learned how to fish together and had ridden out with the local hunt together. Their interests were the same. So he had never minded teasing references about being 'childhood sweethearts', or careless remarks about 'when Toby and Iris tie the knot'.

Or he hadn't until the last twelve months.

Though he hated to admit it, joining the Coldstream Guards had changed everything. For one thing, it had taken him away from Sissbury and plunged him into a life that was very different: far more sophisticated. Imbued with the glamour of being a Guards officer, he'd suddenly found himself knee deep in girls, and he had liked it. Suddenly, the thought of marriage to a girl he had known nearly from the cradle no longer seemed so attractive. Instead it seemed circumscribing. Put bluntly: he'd begun to have cold feet.

The crunch had come the evening of Lady Harland's pre-coronation ball. Marigold had looked absolutely stunning that evening and like every other red-blooded male in the room he'd wanted to be seen with her, to flirt with her, to find out if her very racy reputation was justified.

Whether it proved to be or not, he'd had no intention of becoming seriously involved with her. Unlike Iris, Marigold was not a girl any sane man would choose to become seriously involved with. She was, though, sexually exciting: merely dancing with her had sent the adrenalin racing through his bloodstream.

He'd realized almost immediately, of course, that she wasn't going to play ball. The way she had so pointedly brought Iris into the conversation had shown him that. Then he had made the remark that had brought his long-rumbling dilemma into full focus. By saying he and Iris no longer saw much of each other he had indicated quite clearly that a Sissbury–Snowberry wedding was no longer on the cards.

He couldn't know for sure that Marigold had passed on what he had said to Iris word for word, but he thought her arrival at Sissbury a few days later, in the middle of his party for friends he'd never bothered to introduce her to, was a pretty fair indication she had.

He continued drilling, wiping a bead of sweat from his forehead. God, that party! It had been harmless enough in itself. Everyone there moved in a pretty fast set and none of them would have thought it particularly wild. Wild was opium and cocaine. But he had seen the expression on Iris's face when she had been faced with the sea of champagne bottles and the squealing, giggling behaviour of the bathing-suited girls. Iris had thought it wild – and suddenly he had seen it through her eyes.

Taking advantage of his parents' absence to throw the kind of party he certainly wouldn't want them to know about had been a shabby thing to do, as had encouraging the drunk and near-drunk to cavort in Sissbury's beautifully ornate eighteenth-century fountain and pool. Sissbury deserved better of him than to be treated so cheaply. So although in front of his friends he had tried to laugh off Iris's unfortunate intrusion, he had known that she deserved better of him as well.

The worst part, though, had been Iris's bewilderment and hurt.

Then instead of easing that hurt he had compounded it at the Coronation Day ball.

He had known she would be there and even when he had stepped into the ballroom he still hadn't made up his mind as to how he was going to behave towards her. If he apologized, he would be setting their relationship back on the track it had always followed – and a proposal would still be expected of him.

Not apologizing to her and not behaving normally towards her would be to send the clearest possible signal that no engagement was to be forthcoming.

And that was what he had done.

The stricken look on her face when, instead of crossing the room towards her, he had turned his attention to the girl standing next to him, was one he knew he would never forget. When, absolutely mortified, he had turned to look again towards her, she hadn't been there. But before he could decide what to do about it, Marigold had made her outrageous, half-naked entrance. He had seen Rose bundle Marigold swiftly out of the house and, assuming that Iris had already left the ball ahead of them, he had sloped off for a lone supper at the Café Royal when the excitement had died down.

The question now was: was he going to continue on the course he had set himself, enjoying his bachelorhood and forgetting all about marriage to anyone for at least another ten years, or was he going to make things right between himself and Iris?

It was a hot day and as the drill relentlessly continued he perspired even more freely. He wiped his forehead with the back of his hand, remembering his family motto: 'Suivez raison'. Follow reason. And knew with a flash of blessed certainty what he was going to do.

Rory had never suffered any kind of inner turmoil. Like his favourite second cousin, Lily, he possessed a sunny nature that was rarely ruffled. Unlike Lily, he also possessed a great deal of Marigold's sexual chutzpah. Girls constantly flocked round him, but as soon as they assumed a claim on him they were dropped and disappeared without trace.

He spent a great deal of time in London, always staying, as did his cousins when in the capital, at his maternal grandmother's town house in St James's Street. It wasn't his favourite place to be, though. A Scot through and through, his favourite place in all the world was the place where he'd been born: the seventeenth-century Castle Dounreay, over-looking Loch Gruinart, on the Isle of Islay.

Islay's nickname was 'Queen of the Hebrides' and if Rory could have lived there year round, he would have. As it was, he was studying for his Foreign Office examinations and he knew that in the near future he could expect to find himself posted to any one of a score of European capital cities.

Until that day came, he was enjoying a vast number of London friendships and spending as much time as possible with his Houghton cousins. Usually such gatherings were nothing but fun and pleasure, but, though he hadn't let it show, their get-together on Coronation Day had seriously disquieted him and he was now lying wide awake in his bedroom at St James's Street, brooding over the Prince of Wales's visits to Snowberry.

What the devil was the heir to the throne doing paying visits to a private house which no one but his equerry knew about? Even worse, what was he doing playing Romeo to Lily's Juliet? It was lunacy of the highest order. Once the palace got to know of Edward's visits there would be an immediate end to them and his great-uncle would suffer the ignominy of being accused of luring the Prince to Snowberry in the hope of forging exactly the kind of romantic relationship now taking place.

Why his great-uncle hadn't seen the dangers and put an end to Prince Edward's visits, he couldn't imagine; unless, of course, the visits had been sanctioned by King George. Presumably it was because Lord May simply hadn't envisaged the Prince falling in love with one of his granddaughters.

Who could blame him for that, Rory thought grimly as he stared sleeplessly up at the ceiling.

What was needed was for a male member of Lily's family to have a few pertinent words with the Prince, pointing out to him that for his own sake – as well as the Houghtons' – his relationship with Lily had to end, as had his Snowberry visits.

The problem with this was that the only male members of Lily's family were her grandfather and himself. That it should be her grandfather who spoke to Prince Edward was obvious. That his great-uncle was too genial an old buffer for such a task was equally obvious.

Which left him.

On that grim thought, he punched his pillow, turned over, and tried, once again, to go to sleep.

# SEVENTEEN

Queen Mary was at Buckingham Palace, a royal residence she still didn't feel completely at home in. After the late King's death when, as his widow, Queen Alexandra should have moved out of the palace and into Marlborough House in order that the new King and Queen could move in, she had steadfastly refused to do so. Even Kaiser Wilhelm, a member of the royal family only Queen Mary had a partiality for, had urged her to behave as tradition demanded. It had been a complete waste of his breath. Though she was one of the most loved queens the country had ever had, in private life, and where selfishness, stubbornness and sheer awkwardness were concerned, 'Motherdear' had few equals.

After six months, when Queen Alexandra had still not moved out of Buckingham Palace and when the royal family, Queen Alexandra included, were at Sandringham for Christmas, May travelled back to London, taking advantage of her mother-in-law's absence to have her belongings moved into temporary quarters in the palace her husband always referred to as 'the Sepulchre'.

It had been an action so uncompromising that Motherdear's

removal to Marlborough House had taken place almost immediately.

Since then Queen Mary had not spent an idle moment. Sepulchre-like the palace might be – her late father-in-law had detested its musty smell so intensely that he had spent as little time as possible there – but she had been determined that it wouldn't remain so. What it needed was redecorating and renovating. She'd had very radical ideas as to how such work should be done.

'Each room devoted to a particular period of history and style of furniture?' her husband had said to her, his protuberant blue eyes full of doubt. 'Surely that will look very odd, May? Even museums aren't set out like that.'

'Maybe not,' she had said with stark simplicity, 'but I think that perhaps they should be.'

King George, who had other things on his mind – not least Mr Asquith's insistence that he create enough peers to ensure the passage of bills such as the Budget through the House of Lords – had said that he was sure she knew best, and returned his attention to the difficult question of how to deal with a querulous prime minister.

The problem troubling Queen Mary was a very different one and she was pondering it in the private sitting room leading off her bedroom. For once (it was something that happened rarely) she was alone, without a lady-in-waiting in attendance. Seated at her secretaire, she was in the middle of writing a letter to her late mother's sister, the Gränd Duchess Augusta of Mecklenburg-Strelitz.

Her elderly aunt had been a first cousin of Queen Victoria and, because of her age, was a vast reservoir of information on generations of royal marriages.

May looked down thoughtfully at the sentence she had just written: *And so it does seem so* *underline premature underline* *for us to be thinking of a bride for dear David when he has, as yet, barely left naval college.*

Remembering that Queen Victoria's daughter Vicky was barely fifteen when Crown Prince Friedrich of Prussia came to Balmoral to propose to her, she laid down her pen.

The marriage between Vicky and Prince Friedrich hadn't taken place until Vicky was eighteen. The diplomacy surrounding royal marriages could not be concluded in a matter of weeks, or even months, and three years was, she thought, possibly the average length of time negotiations would take – and in three years' time, David would be twenty.

Kaiser Wilhelm, the black sheep of the family, was just twenty when he had proposed to, and been accepted by, Princess Augusta Victoria of Schleswig-Holstein-Sonderburg-Augustenburg, who, to avoid confusion with the many other Augustas and Victorias in the family, was always known simply as Dona.

Closer to home, George's father, King Edward VII, was also only twenty when he had proposed to the seventeen-year-old Alexandra.

Taking into account such examples, it wasn't premature at all of George to have begun thinking about a suitable bride for David.

She picked up her pen again: *Though if we don't act now, the two prime candidates, Princess Victoria Louise and the Grand Duchess Olga, will very likely be snapped up elsewhere.*

She knew, without having to ask, which candidate her aunt would prefer. As a member of both the House of Mecklenburg and the House of Hanover, Aunt Augusta was most definitely going to favour a British–German wedding, rather than a British–Russian wedding.

There was another, far more pertinent reason why a German wedding would be preferable to a Russian wedding.

Olga's brother, the Tsarevich, was a haemophiliac. It was a bleeding disease passed down to sons through the female line and, in the case of the Tsarevich, was traceable back via his mother and grandmother to his great-grandmother, Queen Victoria. Though Olga and her sisters didn't suffer from the disease, just as their mother, grandmother and great-grandmother hadn't, it wasn't beyond the realms of possibility that they, too, were carriers of it.

Via a different daughter of Queen Victoria – Vicky, who had married Crown Prince Friedrich – the German royal house had a similar line of descent, but neither Vicky's son, the Kaiser, nor any of the Kaiser's sons, suffered from the hideous disease. For that reason alone, Queen Mary found the thought of a German daughter-in-law far preferable to the thought of a Russian one. She felt quite sure George would, too, when he was forced to face the hideous 'H' word he was so obviously blocking from his mind.

In his own suite of rooms, in an entirely different part of the palace, David was wrestling with problems that, if Queen Mary had known of them, would have stupefied her.

How was he to tell his parents that he had met the only girl he would ever want to marry? How was he to go about introducing her to them in order that they could see for themselves what an absolutely terrific, special kind of person Lily was? Before other kinds of obstacles could be overcome – Lily not being royal, for instance – he had to surmount the obstacle of how, and when, he had met her.

The truth was most definitely out. Once it was known what part Piers Cullen had played in enabling him to make secret visits to Snowberry, Piers would be disgraced and his army career over; although he felt no strong tie of friendship to Piers, it was something he couldn't let happen.

It would be far better if the King and Queen believed that

190

he had met Lily at a court function or that he had met her via a member of the royal family.

If Lily had been presented at court a case could have been made for his having first seen her then. But she hadn't been presented at court. The only member of the family he could think of who could believably have become acquainted with the Houghtons and introduced them to him was his second cousin, Prince George of Battenberg.

Though Georgie's father, Prince Louis of Battenberg, was married to one of Queen Victoria's grandchildren, Georgie was far enough removed from the throne to be free of royal protocol. He also, like all the Battenbergs, led a flamboyant lifestyle. It would be perfectly plausible that Georgie and Lord May's granddaughters were on friendly terms and, because there was only two years' difference between them and because Georgie had still been at Dartmouth when David had first gone there and the two of them had always got on very well together, it would also be easily believed that Georgie had introduced the Houghton girls to him.

The only question was whether or not Georgie, now a junior naval officer, would play ball.

David chewed the corner of his lip. Later that afternoon he was scheduled to accompany the King and Queen to the Crystal Palace, where Their Majesties were to give an immense tea party to a hundred thousand London children. As far as stunts went – stunts being the name of any official duty he was required to carry out – it promised to be more enjoyable than most, but he would have much preferred being at Snowberry.

He wondered if Lily had told Rose – and perhaps even Iris and Marigold – that he had asked her to marry him. He rather thought that she wouldn't have. Not yet. Not till he'd had the chance to speak to her grandfather.

When, he thought with frustration, was that going to be?

From now until his investiture as Prince of Wales at Caernarvon Castle he was either going to be accompanying the King and Queen on a string of post-coronation celebration visits to towns in Scotland, Ireland and Wales, or cooped up with the Chancellor of the Exchequer, Mr Lloyd George, grimly getting to grips with enough Welsh to see him through the investiture ceremony.

Remembering his desperate need for practice, he declaimed melodramatically as Finch came into the room: '*Mor o gan yw Cymru i gyd!*'

'Yes, sir,' Finch said, ever equable. 'What does that mean, sir?'

'All Wales is a sea of song.'

'I'm pleased to hear it, sir, but give me London any time.'

With his sombre mood dispelled by Finch's cheery banter, he flashed him a smile. 'Me, too, Finch. Me, too,' he said, determining to contact Georgie immediately and to cry off one of his meetings with Mr Lloyd George in order to shoot down to Snowberry and break the news to Lord May that he wished to make his youngest granddaughter Princess of Wales.

The opportunity didn't come for another five days and, when it did, he had little option but to be accompanied by Piers Cullen. Leaving the palace without his equerry – especially when he should have been in a meeting with Mr Lloyd George – would have attracted exactly the kind of attention he was anxious to avoid. He had expected Piers to be unhappy at having his career put on the line yet again, but instead he had seemed elated at the thought of a Snowberry visit.

David, knowing via Lily that Marigold was no longer in London but had been sent home to Snowberry in disgrace after an unfortunate costume choice at a fancy-dress ball, thought his equerry's elation was probably justified. Wryly, it occurred to him that if Piers were to marry Marigold, he would become Lily's brother-in-law. What his and Piers's relationship would be when he and Lily then married, he didn't know, but he did know it would be one completely beyond Piers's imagination.

The thought made him chuckle, as did the thought of Rose, Iris and Marigold acting as bridesmaids at the biggest royal wedding the country had seen since his parents' wedding eighteen years ago.

Piers was looking across at him as if he had lost his marbles. He didn't care. He was on his way to make the first public declaration of his intention to marry Lily and the knowledge gave him an all-pervading sense of optimism.

Once he had spoken to Lily's grandfather his cards would be very firmly on the table. Though there would still be a mountain to climb where gaining the King's permission – and the Prime Minister's approval – was concerned, it was a mountain that step by step, he would scale.

Because he was slightly built and blond and fey-looking, people thought he could easily be bent to their wills. Over the next few weeks and months they were going to find out that they were very, very mistaken, for he knew something about himself that other people still had to find out.

When he made up his mind about something, as he had now, no force on earth could make him change it.

Relegated to a passenger-seat while the Prince drove, Piers wondered if Edward was heading towards a nervous breakdown. For the past couple of weeks he had been unusually introspective, as if he had a lot on his mind, the burden being, presumably, the coronation – now safely over – and, still looming ahead, his investiture at Caernarvon. Chuckling to himself for no apparent reason was, Piers felt, yet another indication that the strain of the ceremonies the Prince now had to take part in was beginning to tell on him.

Sending a message to Mr Lloyd George, informing him

that because of a migraine he couldn't meet with him as arranged, was yet another example of odd behaviour. Not, of course, that Piers had minded. As far as he was concerned, any opportunity of seeing Lily was something he fervently welcomed and if, instead of getting to grips with the Welsh language, Prince Edward wanted to knock a tennis ball around with Rose or Iris or Marigold, that was fine by him.

The problem he was mulling over as they sped through the village adjacent to Snowberry was how he was to find enough free time from his duties to be able to begin to court Lily properly. He could, of course, ask to be released from duty as an equerry, but he didn't want to do that. It was being an equerry that made him special.

Lily had been absolutely entranced at the little bits of gossip he had been able to give her about King George, Queen Mary, Princess Mary, Prince Albert, Prince Henry, Prince George and Prince John. Now his ultimate goal was to have Prince Edward as best man at his and Lily's wedding. If, at the time of their wedding, he was still the Prince's equerry, then it was very likely that Edward would be so. If, on the other hand, he was no longer a member of the royal household, then the chances of such a social triumph were nearly zero.

Edward slowed down in order to turn in between Snowberry's massive permanently open entrance gates. Piers wondered whom they would find at home. The Earl, certainly. Herbert Houghton seldom left Snowberry. Neither, fortunately, did Lily. But if Prince Edward was to be engaged elsewhere while he snatched a few precious minutes alone with Lily, he had to hope that at least one of her sisters was also home.

His preferred choice was that the sister in question would be Iris. Unlike Rose and Marigold, he found Iris unthreatening. Rose he detested. She had a way of looking at him – as he suspected she looked at all men – as if he was of absolutely no consequence. All suffragettes were anathema to him and he believed that those, like Rose, who supported Pankhurst-style militant action should be locked away in Holloway.

As for Marigold . . .

His body went rigid at the thought of Marigold. Her bold-as-brass, flagrant sexuality was almost as abhorrent to him as Rose's suffragette militancy.

It was a horrific thought that when he married Lily, Rose and Marigold would become his relations-by-marriage and he dealt with it by determining that, as a married couple, he and Lily would have little to do with them.

'I want to have a few private words with Lord May,' Edward said, bringing the Austro-Daimler to a halt on the gravel in front of the house. 'I'll leave it to you to let the girls know we've arrived.'

They entered Snowberry to be informed by William that Lord May was in the drawing room and that Miss Houghton, Miss Iris, Miss Marigold and Miss Lily were down by the lake.

It was then that Piers became aware of just how extreme Edward's nervous tension was. It emanated from him in waves. Piers was mystified by it. Unable to take a short cut to the rear of the house via the drawing room and its French doors, he strode back outside, walking around the house towards the vast lawn leading down to the lake. Whatever the subject the Prince wished to discuss with Lord May, it was one that had put him in a great tizzy, but for the life of him Piers couldn't imagine what the tizzy could be about.

'Captain Cullen!' Iris was the first to notice him as he stepped down from the terrace steps on to the velvet-smooth grass. She rose from where she had been sitting, waving welcomingly.

He ground his teeth. The minute His Royal Highness Prince Edward had invited the Houghtons to address him as David, he'd had no choice but to be on similar Christian-name terms. Other than when Lily addressed him as Piers, he didn't like it. It offended his sense of dignity. Iris reverting back to a little formality wasn't, however, a good sign. Not when he wanted to make headway with his courtship of Lily.

In a rowing boat far out in the centre of the lake, Lily was with Rose. The boat was motionless, rocking gently beneath a sun so hot it was already making him perspire.

Marigold, he saw with a fierce tightening of his stomach muscles, was seated on the grass next to the remains of a picnic, her arms clasped around her knees.

Not troubling to rise to her feet she said as he approached, 'Are you here to see Lily, or is David with you?'

Taking satisfaction from the fact that Lily had obviously told her about their afternoon out together, he said, not looking at her, but looking out towards the rowing boat, 'I'm carrying out equerrying duties. Prince Edward is in the drawing room, having a few words with your grandfather.'

He showed no sign of joining Marigold on the grass, as David or Rory would most certainly have done, and Iris, who found him uncomfortable company, said with forced cheeriness, 'I'll go back to the house and ask for cane chairs and fresh sandwiches to be brought down.'

'There's no need.' The last thing in the world Piers wanted was to be left alone with Marigold.

With vast relief he saw that the rowing boat was no longer motionless, but that, having registered his arrival, Rose had begun rowing in the direction of the shore.

Ignoring Iris and Marigold, he walked away from them and out on to the lake's small jetty.

Seated in the stern of the rowing boat Lily looked as enchanting as ever. Her hair was held away from her face by two tortoiseshell combs and the lilac tea gown she was wearing was embroidered with flowers the exact violet shade of her eyes.

Her face shone with happiness as, brief minutes later, he

helped her from the boat. At the thought that whenever she saw him he would, for the rest of his life, see that kind of joy, Piers felt himself to be the luckiest man alive.

'HRH is having a few words with your grandfather,' he said, before he could be asked about the Prince's whereabouts. 'Probably something to do with the investiture. I imagine he is inviting him to be present at it.'

It was a possibility that had only just occurred to him, but expressing it enabled him to appear very much in the know.

Lily stumbled and his arm flew around her, steadying her. 'David is speaking with Grandpapa?' she asked, and he could feel her tension. It was almost as extreme as David's tension had been.

'It won't be anything you need worry about,' he said reassuringly, the blood surging through his body in a hot tide as he reluctantly removed his arm from her waist. 'All HRH has on his mind at the moment is his investiture at Caernarvon.'

Lily didn't look at all convinced, and her pale-cream skin was paler than he'd ever seen it. He wondered if she thought Edward was telling her grandfather that after his investiture he would no longer be able to visit Snowberry as often as he had been doing and if she thought it meant that he also would not be visiting as often.

'Shall we stay down here and wait for David to join us?' Iris asked. 'Or should we stroll back to the house and wait for him on the terrace?'

'The terrace, I think.' Rose began clearing the remains of their picnic into a large picnic hamper. 'There's something you should know, Piers,' she added as Marigold and Iris each took hold of one of the hamper's wicker handles and began walking towards the terrace with it. 'Our cousin, Rory Sinclair, is staying with us. At the moment he's over at Norbury, taking part in a steeplechase. I don't think he'll be back until early evening, but you never know.'

Piers's look of alarm was immediate. The possibility of visitors turning up at Snowberry while the Prince was also there had always been his deepest nightmare, for then there would be no way of keeping Edward's visits secret. Once the gossip reached the palace – which it would do in double-quick time – his days as an equerry would be over faster than light.

He steadied his rising panic by remembering that steeple-chases were day-long affairs and that Rose was probably right in thinking Rory Sinclair wouldn't be back at Snowberry until the evening. Just as he was beginning to breathe a little more easily, another thought hit him.

Instead of walking after Iris and Marigold, he said sharply, 'This Sinclair cousin of yours. He doesn't know about Prince Edward's visits, does he?'

Rose brushed her skirt free of grass. 'Yes,' she said, un-ruffled. 'I know we all promised to tell no one, but Rory is very close family, more like a brother than a cousin. We knew that he'd be visiting Snowberry and so, just in case David visited whilst he was here, we thought it best to put him in the picture. He won't gossip. Getting gossip from Rory would be like getting blood from a stone.'

Her certainty and her self-composure were so total he wanted to lay violent hands on her. *She,* God damn her, had nothing to lose if there was gossip. He had everything to lose. The mere thought brought him out in goose bumps.

As if what she'd said was of no consequence, she turned away from him and began walking after Lily, who was now hard on Iris and Marigold's heels.

He glared after her, fuming silently. His only comfort was the knowledge that Prince Edward's visits to Snowberry were soon going to be seriously curtailed – and might perhaps come to an end altogether.

# EIGHTEEN

'You want to marry Lily?' Herbert Houghton swayed on his feet, wondering if he was hallucinating. 'But, my dear boy...' He remembered to whom he was speaking. 'Your Royal Highness...' he said, desperately trying to gather his scattered wits. This, too, didn't sound right. Not when Prince Edward had specifically requested that he wasn't to be addressed formally when at Snowberry.

Aware, all too late, of the deep pit he had dug for himself by allowing the heir to the throne to visit Snowberry in the same free and easy manner that Toby Mulholland and other friends of his granddaughters visited, he tried again. 'Prince Edward... David... you cannot possibly want to marry anyone unknown to your family.'

His breathing, which had been terrifyingly erratic over the last few seconds, began to steady. It was a joke. A prank. Any minute now Rose, Iris, Marigold and Lily would come tumbling into the room, laughing fit to bust at the way Prince Edward had taken him in.

He was going to be very, very cross with them. Extremely cross. It was the kind of joke that could have resulted in him having a heart attack. He couldn't, of course, be cross with Prince Edward. That would be taking familiarity too far. With great effort he managed an indulgent smile, to show that he knew he was the victim of a prank and that he was taking it in good part.

The Prince didn't burst into chuckles, and the girls didn't burst into the room.

Instead Prince Edward said with terrifying seriousness, 'It's quite usual for someone of my position to have plans for their future bride put in place when they are only seventeen, or perhaps eighteen. The only difference in this instance is that I am choosing my future bride for myself. The girl I want to marry – the girl I *will* marry – is Lily.'

Herbert Houghton put his hand out to the nearest object to steady himself. It met with the corner of the ornate William and Mary mantelshelf. He gripped hold of it, hard.

'But Your Royal Highness . . . David . . . Lily isn't royal. She may come from a well-connected family, but she isn't even close to being royal. If the King were to know that you were even *considering* a commoner as a future bride . . .' The scenario he envisaged was so horrific words failed him.

'I know all these problems, sir. Truly I do.' David ran a hand over his glassily smooth hair. 'But they are problems I intend overcoming. Now that I have spoken to you and put you completely in the picture, I will be asking for the King's consent at the earliest, most suitable moment.'

'Oh, dear God!' The mantelshelf was no longer support enough for him and Herbert groped his way to a wing chair. What on earth was going to happen once the palace learned of the Prince's illicit visits to Snowberry and that he, Lord May, had known of them and had turned a blind eye? His own disgrace would be total, but what of Sibyl? Would his disgrace, and the social ostracism that would undoubtedly follow, extend to her? Would it extend to Rory?

It would certainly extend to his granddaughters. Rose, of

course, would take it in her stride, but then Rose didn't give a fig for high society and to be ostracized by it wouldn't trouble her at all.

Not to be invited to parties and balls would hit Marigold hard, though, and Iris's long-understood unofficial engagement to Toby Mulholland – of whom not much had been seen lately – might also be affected. Viscountess Mulholland was a snob. She wouldn't want as a daughter-in-law a girl whose family had offended the King. As for Lily . . . A thought that hadn't occurred to him before now did.

'Lily,' he said with what breath he could summon. 'Does Lily know you want to marry her? Does she know you are now asking me for my permission?'

'Lily and I are in love, sir.'

The pride in David's voice and his naivety as to whom he would and would not be allowed to marry smote Herbert's heart.

'She has probably guessed why I am speaking to you alone,' David added as Herbert struggled to think of words that would bring a return to sanity.

From outside there came the sound of Marigold's laughter and David broke eye contact with him as, beyond the French doors, Marigold and Iris came into view, walking up the steps to the terrace.

Hard on their heels was Lily and one look at her taut, tense face told Herbert she knew exactly what David had been telling – and asking – him.

At the sight of her David strode towards the French doors, all nervous tension gone.

Herbert summoned up the strength to totter after him, seeing with vast relief that Rose was also mounting the steps to the terrace and that Captain Cullen was only a yard or so behind her.

Rose's hard-headed common sense and Captain Cullen's

pragmatism would, surely, put an end to David's nonsensical daydream before he brought disaster down on all their heads by speaking of it to King George.

He envisaged talking to them without Marigold and Iris's – and possibly Lily's – knowledge. But as the scene unfolded he saw how euphorically Prince Edward was heading towards Lily, and with total helplessness he knew exactly what was going to happen next.

'Lily!' David strode past Marigold and Iris and made a beeline for Lily. Then, rooting everyone to the spot in thunder-struck incredulity, he seized both of her hands in his and, with his face ablaze with happiness, said, 'I've spoken to your grandfather, Lily darling. He's given us his blessing. All that remains is for me to speak to the King at the earliest opportunity.'

Herbert made a choking sound, for he most certainly had *not* given the proposed marriage his blessing. Marigold and Iris dropped the picnic hamper they were carrying so abruptly there came the sound of a wine glass shattering. Rose sucked in her breath.

None of them looked towards Piers Cullen.

If they had, they would have been given far more to think about than David's desire to make Lily Princess of Wales and, in due time, Queen Consort and Empress of India.

Piers Cullen was a man *in extremis*. Just as in one blinding, illuminating moment he had realized he had, for the first time in his life, fallen in love, so in an equal split second he now realized that his love was hopeless. Prince Edward, able to offer Lily vast wealth and a lifetime of royal privilege and glamour, had stolen her from him.

It was unthinkable. Unbelievable. But it had happened. And it had happened – had been happening – right under his very nose. His rage was absolute; his boiling hatred total.

None of it was directed against Lily. What innocent young girl would be able to withstand a proposal of marriage from a prince? That Lily *had* been unable to withstand it was obvious from the way she hadn't turned to him for help in getting out of the situation. That was all she'd had to do. Turn from Edward, to him. Slip her hand in his. Yet she hadn't. Instead she had clutched Edward's hands just as fervently as he was clutching hers.

All his life people had turned their backs on him. His mother had done so by dying when he was still a child. His father had done so by being such a rigid disciplinarian he'd grown up always expecting criticism and never praise. When, at thirteen, he'd been sent to Eton, he'd never fitted in; he'd never made friends. The army had been his life-saver, but even then he had remained a loner. Girls had never been attracted to him and he'd had such low self-esteem that he hadn't blamed them. Then the miracle had happened and, via his father's friendship with Lord Esher, he had been appointed as equerry to the Prince of Wales.

His hopes of becoming invaluable to the Prince, of being treated by him as a friend, had swiftly been dashed to pieces. Edward, he had quickly come to realize, resented his constant presence. He, in turn, had come to resent Edward's scrupulously polite but off-hand treatment of him.

Then Edward had knocked Rose Houghton off her bicycle and afterwards, at Snowberry, when Edward had invited the Houghtons to dispense with all formality and to call him David – something he had never invited *him* to do – his resentment had rocketed sky-high.

He had coped with it because, for the first time in his life, he had found someone who made him feel good about himself; someone who didn't make him feel unattractive; someone he could at last open his heart to and love.

Now his rare and precious happiness was at an end.

Vaguely he heard Iris say in a stunned voice, 'Have I completely misunderstood, or has David just asked Grandfather for Lily's hand in marriage?'

Marigold was clapping her hands and behaving like a child at Christmas, saying, 'Oh, but of course he has! Isn't it marvellous? Isn't it just too spiffingly *wonderful*?'

Only Rose was firmly keeping her thoughts to herself and there were white lines of tension at either side of her mouth as she crossed the terrace and stepped into the house.

Piers fought down wave after wave of nausea as everyone else, Lily's grandfather and Edward included, followed her.

No one turned to look towards him. He might just as well have not been there.

Struggling for self-control he bit his lower lip so hard he tasted blood.

# NINETEEN

Iris had never previously been glad to see the Austro-Daimler disappearing down Snowberry's drive, but she was glad now, for the drama of the past hour had been all too much for her to take. David, explaining that he had to get back to Buckingham Palace before his absence was noticed, had just left for London as happy as a lark.

Whatever happened in the future, Iris knew that she and Rose would no longer be able to regard David as a kind of adopted nephew whose visits to Snowberry were innocently pleasurable to him and harmless to them. The shock of knowing that he and Lily had fallen in love had brought home a truth all of them had been avoiding.

David wasn't an adopted nephew, or a younger version of Rory. He was a royal prince. Not any old royal prince, either, but the Prince of Wales; a prince who was the heir to the throne.

'As heir to the throne, sweetheart,' her grandfather was now saying gently to Lily, 'much as he may want to marry you, he can't marry you. I'm sorry, tootsums, but there it is.'

Lily regarded him lovingly, and without the least distress.

'Both David and I know that gaining King George's permission isn't going to be easy, Grandpapa.'

She was kneeling by the side of his chair, sitting back on her heels. 'David knows he is expected to marry a foreign princess, just as his father and grandfather did,' she said matter-of-factly, 'But he doesn't want that kind of an arranged marriage, and he wants his father to be aware that he doesn't want it, before he begins arranging one.'

She turned her head to include the rest of them in what she was saying. 'Things are always being arranged for him without his being told about them. He didn't know about his investiture until he was told Mr Lloyd George would be giving him lessons in the Welsh language.'

Their grandfather, realizing he was being totally ineffective, looked towards Rose for help. She didn't let him down.

'Neither you nor David is facing up to reality, Lily,' she said briskly. 'It isn't that it's not going to be *easy* for David to gain King George's permission for you to marry, it's that it's going to be impossible. It isn't just a tradition for the heir to the throne to marry foreign royalty; it is something that is set in stone. You are a commoner. A commoner has *never* married the heir to the British throne.'

'That's not strictly true,' their grandfather said unhelpfully. 'Elizabeth Woodville, Edward IV's queen, was a commoner. As was Jane Seymour, when she married Henry VIII.'

None of them ever lost their patience with their vague, mild-mannered grandfather, but Iris was aware that Rose was close to doing so.

'That was a long time ago, Grandfather,' she said through gritted teeth. 'A long, *long* time ago!'

'Oh! For goodness' sake!' Marigold erupted out of the chair she'd been sitting in and threw her hands up in the air. 'What is the matter with you all?' Her green cat-eyes flashed fire. 'You should be overjoyed that David is in love with Lily and wants to marry her. It means she will become a *princess*! Think of what that will mean. Think of the jewels she will be given! Think of all the eligible foreign royal bachelors Rose, Iris and I will be introduced to!'

They were all quite used to Marigold being appalling, but from the agonized expression on their grandfather's face, even he knew she had just surpassed herself. Before he, or Rose, could give her a piece of their minds, Lily took them all by surprise.

Rising to her feet, she said quietly, but with underlying steel in her voice none of them had ever heard before, 'You are quite wrong, Marigold, if you think I've told David I will marry him because I want to become a princess. It's the very last thing on earth I want to be. David has told me about being royal and it's not at all what it seems.'

Showing maturity Iris hadn't witnessed before – and that she knew Rose hadn't been aware of either – she'd said, 'It's a life of unremitting duty and David is dreading it. He hates being dressed up in ceremonial finery and having people deferring to him. That is why Snowberry is so important to him. He can be himself here. That is why he needs me to marry him. He simply can't face the thought of his future without me there to help him.'

Iris realized then that they must all begin thinking of Lily in quite a different way.

'And I'm not going to let him down,' she continued as they all, even Marigold, listened to her in respectful silence. 'Too many people have let him down. He had a nanny who was so sadistic she eventually ended up in a mental home. He has a mother who didn't even *notice* how he was being physically abused. King George has always been absolutely beastly towards him. His tutor didn't teach him any of the things he needed for his entry to naval college and so he's always had to struggle like mad not to be bottom of the class.

No one but me has ever loved him. I *do* love him. I am *not* going to let him down. I don't want to be Princess of Wales, but if I have to be in order for David to face a future he can never escape, then I shall be.'

'If King George gives his consent,' their grandfather said gruffly.

'Yes.' She reached down to where he was seated, squeezed his hand and left the room, saying she was going to feed her rabbits.

When the door closed behind her, Rose said, 'We are just going to have to wait on events now, aren't we? We have to hope that Marigold's shameless Queen of Sheba exhibitionism the other evening doesn't make gaining royal consent even more of a problem – which it will if word of it reaches the palace.'

'"Shameless exhibitionism"?' Their grandfather looked bewildered. 'But I thought Marigold went as an eastern queen? Surely she looked delightful?'

'I did, Grandfather,' Marigold said provocatively.

Rose eyeballed her and, ignoring their grandfather's remarks, said, 'If there is to be the faintest of faint hopes for David and Lily there have to be no more scandalous escapades, *of any kind*, Marigold. Is that understood?'

'Natch.' Her agreement had been given easily, but as she turned away from Rose a look of panic darted through her eyes, confirming Iris's suspicions that on her recent visits to London, Marigold had, once again, been behaving in a way that would ruin David and Lily's hopes utterly, if it became public knowledge.

'I'm going back to St James's Street,' Rose said, bringing their family conclave to an end. 'Hal Green wants to meet with me to discuss doing some journalism pieces. It's an enormous opportunity. No one else is ever likely to ask me.'

Marigold said that she was going to change into riding clothes and ride over to see Tessa Reighton.

Their grandfather said he was going to put a newspaper over his head and have a snooze in order to soothe his shattered nerves.

Iris didn't mind being left on her own. Not when she had so much to think about. She went into the kitchen to make sure Millie knew that David and Piers were no longer at Snowberry and that she needn't take them into account when she made afternoon tea, and then she'd rounded up Homer, Fizz and Florin and set off for a long, thoughtful walk.

Soon, with Homer plodding on beside her and Fizz and Florin skittering about in the undergrowth, chasing rabbits, she was in the woods at the far side of the lake. Out of sight of the house, she neither heard the little two-seater roar up Snowberry's elm-lined drive, nor saw, as he stepped from the motor car minutes later, that the driver was Toby.

'Miss Houghton, Miss Iris and Miss Marigold are not at home,' William said to him helpfully. 'Miss Lily is in the west garden.'

'No problem, William. I've come to visit Lord May.'

'Lord May is, I believe, in the drawing room.'

Informality at Snowberry was such that Toby merely said it was good to see William looking so well, then he set off for the drawing room unannounced.

Herbert was so deeply asleep he nearly jumped out of his skin when Toby woke him.

'What the deuce!' he spluttered, sending *The Times* flying in all directions. 'Oh, it's you, young Mulholland. What the devil do you mean giving me a start like that? I've had enough shocks for one day without having to suffer any more.'

'I'm sorry to hear that, sir.' Toby was uninterested in what kind of day Lord May had had. 'But I think I'm probably about to give you one more.'

'Then sit down. If you want a drink, please help yourself.'

'I don't, thank you – not this minute. As for what I've come to say I rather think we should be standing. It's a little formal, you see, sir.'

Herbert didn't see, but if rising to his feet was the only way of sending Toby on his way and once again having peace and quiet, then it was a price he was prepared to pay.

He hauled himself out of his comfy wing chair. 'Right,' he said with unusual grumpiness. 'Spit it out, young man.'

It wasn't quite the intro Toby had been hoping for, but as it was obviously the best he was going to get, he straightened his shoulders, took a deep breath, and plunged straight in.

'I wish to marry Iris and before I pop the question to her, I would like to make sure you have no objections.'

'Objections?' It was the second time in less than three hours that Herbert had been asked the same question – though the first time round it had concerned a different granddaughter and been phrased a little differently. This time, however, there were no insuperable difficulties to take into account. This time he could give his answer without fear of the consequences.

'No, young man. I have no objections whatsoever – though I must say I think it has taken you a long time to come up to scratch. However, better late than never. Iris is a grand girl. I just hope for your sake that she's still interested in you.'

'Yes, sir.' As he thought of all that was at stake, there was deep feeling in Toby's voice. 'So do I.'

Iris walked free of the woods and on to the rising meadow-land lying beyond them. The heat, which hadn't relented over the last few days, was intense. There were articles in the newspapers saying that temperatures were at record heights and that weathermen were forecasting they would continue to rise. How much further they could rise Iris couldn't even begin to imagine.

While she had been in the woodland the heat hadn't disturbed Fizz and Florin, but now, out on the hillside, even they were flagging. Knowing it would be unfair to them to go any further she came to a halt and, sitting on buttercup-thick grass, she hugged her knees and looked towards Snowberry.

There were so many things making her heavy-hearted. Worst of all, of course, was Toby no longer loving her – and not only no longer loving her, but no longer even wanting to spend time with her as a friend.

The moment at the Coronation Day ball when he had entered the ballroom and then, on seeing her, had turned away, had been as agonizing as a knife wound. She knew she would have to get over her searing sense of loss, but had no idea of how to set about it. Toby had been too central to her life for her to draw a line under things as Rose and Marigold would do if they were in the same situation.

As for the future . . . She couldn't imagine anyone else falling in love with her. She simply wasn't the kind of girl men lost their hearts to. Her year as a debutante had shown her that.

Since a future without a husband and babies was too bleak to contemplate she forced herself to think of the other things causing her anxiety. Lily having fallen in love with David, and David wanting to marry her, were top of the list. As it was obvious to everyone but David and Lily that, short of a miracle, such a marriage would never be allowed, both of them were plummeting headlong towards heartbreak. Lily had a heart that, like her own, wouldn't easily mend. Once given, it would, she was sure, be given for life.

As to what the repercussions were going to be once David had spoken to King George, they were anyone's guess. They wouldn't be good, though. Especially not for her grandfather.

It was another prospect so awful she didn't want to dwell on it.

Her final anxiety was Marigold, for she was quite sure that Marigold was involved in something that, if it became public knowledge, would prove so scandalous it would end Lily and David's relationship even before King George ended it.

Was it another married man? According to Rose, Marigold had come to her senses just in time where Lord Jethney was concerned. But what if she hadn't?

Whereas Lord Jethney used to visit their grandfather on an almost weekly basis, now they never saw him at all. Was that because he and Marigold had begun meeting in London, whenever Marigold was staying with Sibyl? When Rose had stressed how important it now was for Marigold to remain scandal-free, if her look of panic *hadn't* been because she was still seeing Lord Jethney, what had it been over?

From where she was sitting she could see Snowberry's gabled roofs and upper mullioned windows, but the lower part of the rear of the house, and the terrace and terrace steps, were obscured by the trees. A small portion of the lawn, just before it reached the lake, was visible, and as she pondered whether or not she should share her concerns over Marigold with Rose, she saw someone striding purposefully across it.

Apart from the fact that it was male, the figure was too indistinct for her to recognize. It wasn't her grandfather, though, because he couldn't walk that fast. David and Piers Cullen had left a good hour earlier for Buckingham Palace, so it wasn't likely to be either of them. Which meant it must be Rory.

She wondered if he was walking so fast towards the lake because he was desperate for a swim in order to cool off. In retrospect, it was what she should have done, instead of walking in heat that was close to being unbearable.

Homer, who had been lying at her feet, now flopped down by her side. Grateful for his company, she gave him a loving pat. There was no sound, apart from a couple of finches squabbling in a nearby clump of gorse.

She was once more worrying about what it was Marigold so clearly had on her mind when Fizz pricked up her ears and looked expectantly down to where the woods gave way to the hillside. Seconds later Florin was all attention, her stubby tail wagging in delighted anticipation.

Certain the person they had heard approaching was Rory, Iris remained where she was, her arms around her knees. Rory would have to know about David's proposal of marriage to Lily sometime, but she thought it best that she didn't tell him. Rory and Lily were very close. It was something Lily would want to tell him herself.

A figure emerged from the woodland. Barking welcomes, Fizz and Florin raced towards him. Preparing to give an equally warm welcome, Homer ambled off in their wake. Iris, almost frozen with shock, rose slowly to her feet.

Toby waved. Not waving back, a pulse beating fast in her throat, Iris waited for him to cover the distance between them.

'Your grandfather told me you were walking the dogs,' he said, coming to a halt a foot or so away from her. 'I guessed you might have come up here.'

Toby was behaving as if nothing had gone wrong between them simply because he didn't know any other way to begin saying what he had come to say. But that was lost on Iris. Her memory of him emerging from behind Snowberry's fountain with his arm around the debutante of the year, and the

213

even ghastlier memory of the Coronation Day ball, were too vivid and too recent.

Aware of how deep her hurt was, he abandoned the here-we-are-back-to-normal approach he'd hoped would act as an ice-breaker.

Plunging straight in, as he had with her grandfather, he took both her hands in his. 'Please forgive me for my stupidity of the last couple of weeks, Iris. I don't know what got into me. Whatever it was, I'm now free of it – and it won't come back. I promise.'

There was an expression in his eyes she had never seen before; an expression that sent the blood surging through her body in a hot, dizzying tide.

'I want us to be friends again.' His hands tightened on hers. 'I want us to be more than friends, Iris. I've done quite a bit of thinking and I now know what it is I want in life. It's not what I previously thought. It isn't a career in the Guards, and running with a fast set and having lots of different girlfriends. The doctor has given my father only another few months to live, and when he dies I don't want Sissbury to be run by anyone else but me. It's what I've been brought up to do. It's what my father has trained me to do.'

He put his arms around her, drawing her close. 'And I want to do it with someone who loves the things I love.'

His eyes, usually so light, were dark with passionate intensity.

'The things I love are Sissbury – and Snowberry. Horses. Dogs. A country life. What I'm trying to say, dearest Iris – what I'm trying to ask – is will you marry me?'

'Oh! Yes, Toby!' Her plain face was so radiant it was beautiful. 'I've always wanted to marry you! I've never wanted anything else!'

Vastly relieved, he lowered his head to hers, kissing her in a way she had only previously dreamed of.

Half an hour later, as they walked back down the hill, the dogs at their heels and their arms around each other's waists, he complimented himself on a good afternoon's work.

He had healed his friend's heartbreak. He had resolved his future. Buying himself out of the Guards would be no problem. And when he began managing Sissbury, he would begin managing Snowberry for Lord May, running the two vast estates in tandem. He could foresee no difficulty about doing so. May, increasingly infirm and mentally vague, would be deeply grateful to him for his help.

He stepped from the woods with Iris, full of *joie de vivre,* certain that with such a set-up in place, the chances of his and Iris's first-born son inheriting Snowberry were high; so high as to be almost a certainty.

# TWENTY

Marigold didn't enjoy her afternoon tea with Tessa Reighton. All she could think about was how, if it was shown publicly, Strickland's depiction of her as Persephone would end any hopes, however faint, of Lily one day becoming the Princess of Wales. Not in a million years would the stuffed shirt who was King George permit even a platonic relationship between his son and the sister of a girl who had so scandalously posed naked. Where David and Lily were concerned, the notoriety she had been so looking forward to would be a death-knell.

Which meant there would never even the faintest hope of her one day becoming the sister-in-law of the Prince of Wales. Even worse, it meant she wouldn't be his sister-in-law when, after his father's death, he became king. Placed on the scales against a season's notoriety, it was an awful lot to lose – and she most definitely didn't want to lose it.

It meant she had to speak to Strickland – a near impossibility when Strickland never answered his telephone and when she was confined at Snowberry after her Queen of Sheba escapade.

'I've had a spiffing time, but I must go,' she said to Tessa, while Tessa was still in the middle of telling her about her latest romantic conquest. 'Hope everything turns out brilliantly for the two of you.'

Forty-five minutes later she was back at Snowberry, where, instead of immediately having a private chat with her grandfather, wheedling out of him permission to return to her aunt's, she found herself standing next to him with a champagne flute in her hand as he toasted Iris and Toby on the announcement of their engagement.

Remembering how iffy Toby had been about his feelings for Iris only a few short days ago it was a surprise, to say the least. It wasn't, though, a surprise she intended brooding over. Not when she had so much else on her mind.

'I need to have a word with you, Grandfather,' she said when the toasts were over and Toby and Iris were looking deep into each other's eyes and drinking from each other's champagne flute. 'I want your permission to go back to Great-aunt Sibyl's for a little while. It's very important that I do so. For my classes.'

'Classes?' Her grandfather stared at her, mystified.

'Classes,' she said firmly. 'I'm taking art classes with Mr Strickland, whom I know you will have heard of, because he is one of the most famous artists in the country. Also I'm taking . . . I'm taking . . .' She thought furiously, desperately searching her mind for something that sounded remotely possible. 'I'm taking Italian classes at the Berlitz.'

'Are you, my dear? *Are* you?' Herbert was fascinated. His brow wrinkled in a frown. 'But didn't Sibyl send you back here, to Snowberry because you'd misbehaved? Something about not being appropriately dressed at a fancy-dress ball? If that is the case, she may think it a little soon for you to be returning to St James's Street.'

Marigold slid her arm through his and gave it a hug. 'Dearest Grandpa, I went to the ball as the Queen of Sheba and so I was *very* appropriately dressed. The Queen of Sheba would hardly have gone to a ball dressed like Rose, would she? Anyway, it wasn't Aunt Sibyl who insisted I came back to Snowberry. It was Rose. *Please* telephone Aunt Sibyl and tell her that I've served my penance.'

He patted her hand. 'If it means that much to you, my dear, *sono molto contento*.' He smiled.

Not having a clue as to what he had just said, she smiled back.

Inwardly, though, she wasn't smiling at all. When had her grandfather learned Italian? If he was going to start speaking it to her, she was going to have to learn it in earnest – or tell him she was dropping Italian in order to study German. But as she was living in the hope of soon having a whole raft of royal German relations-by-marriage, perhaps German wasn't such a bad idea.


'So you are once more in town for an indefinite period?' Strickland said, blowing a plume of Turkish cigarette smoke into the air.

Although they were in his studio and he was wearing a paint-spattered smock, he wasn't working. He was perched on the corner of a table that was crowded with brushes, palettes and tubs of paint, one long-limbed leg swinging free.

'I'm here for as long as it takes me to convince you not to go ahead with the painting. Or at least not with the Persephone/Pluto painting. I'm simply not going to sit for it any more. A portrait of me in my presentation gown would be all right. But I've decided that being painted without even a wisp of chiffon is just too vulgar for words.'

She was wearing a tawny-coloured narrow skirt topped by a diaphanous yellow-bronze tunic pulled in at the waist and tightly belted by a broad snakeskin belt; her only jewellery was a heavy amber necklace. He couldn't decide whether she was trying to look Russian, or to look Romany.

She certainly looked distinctive and, as always, provocatively voluptuous.

He grinned. He could believe a lot of things about Marigold, but not that she had been overcome by a sudden attack of quiet good taste.

'What if I told you I no longer needed you to sit for the painting in order to finish it?'

Though she was doing her best to try to appear unperturbed, he could see that she was seriously concerned.

'I don't want that painting to be shown, Strickland.' She remembered how paganly beautiful she looked in it and added, 'Or at least not until a family matter has been resolved.'

More intrigued than ever, he stubbed his cigarette out. 'Unless you tell me why you've got cold feet, that painting is going to be publicly exhibited within weeks.'

'You're a bastard, Strickland. Has anyone ever told you that?'

'Plenty of people, but none of them of your age, sex, or upbringing. Now why don't you tell me what is behind all this? You love feeling wicked, so why this sudden loss of nerve?'

Accepting defeat, aware that he knew her far too well to be fobbed off without being told at least a smidgeon of the truth, she sank down on to the studio chaise longue and said, 'It's because one of my sisters has the chance of marrying someone really, really distinguished and as a family we can't risk the slightest whiff of scandal. Otherwise it will all be off and her life will be ruined.'

She didn't add that if scandal robbed her of the chance of living within the palace circle, her life would be ruined also.

He regarded her thoughtfully. Marigold was the granddaughter of an earl. Her great-aunt, Lady Harland, was a dowager marchioness and a hostess in the grand manner. The Prime Minister often dined at her home in St James's Street, as did the Leader of the Opposition, the Marquess of Lansdowne. Prince Louis of Battenberg was another regular guest. King Edward VII had been, in Sibyl's words 'a very dear and close friend'. Rumour had it that in their younger days, her friendship with the late King had been so close as to be best described as intimate. Under the present reign, even Queen Mary was known to have visited her for afternoon tea.

With such a family background he couldn't imagine Marigold referring to anyone as 'really, really distinguished' unless they were a duke, or the heir to a dukedom. Or unless they were royalty.

His sludge-coloured eyes gleamed as he considered which member of the royal family could possibly fill the bill. There weren't many to choose from. The Prince of Wales was surely too young to be contemplating marriage. Prince Albert, being even younger, could also be discounted and the three other princes were mere children. And besides the person would have to be a more minor royal.

One name immediately came to mind. His Serene Highness Prince George of Battenberg. George's mother, a granddaughter of Queen Victoria, had married into the German House of Hesse, but she and her husband, Prince Louis, lived in England.

Georgie was the right age, in his early twenties and with his royal background he could certainly be classed as being 'really, really distinguished'.

Strickland grinned to himself. If the suitor in question was Georgie Battenberg, Marigold had nothing to worry about. The Battenbergs were a very flamboyant family. Marrying a bride whose sister had posed as Persephone wouldn't worry Georgie a bit.

Still deep in thought he reached into his smock pocket for his packet of cigarettes wondering whether, if the mysterious suitor wasn't Georgie, it was a foreign royal. There were plenty to choose from, especially at the moment when so many royal visitors, in London for the coronation, hadn't yet returned home.

Of the plentiful Russian contingent, Prince Maxim Yurenev, who had lifted Marigold from the pony's back when she had arrived at the fancy-dress ball as the Queen of Sheba, was by far the handsomest and most glamorous.

'Your sister's distinguished lover wouldn't be Prince Maxim Yurenev, would he?' he asked, making a stab in the dark.

'No.' Though it would have been sensible to have led him up the garden path, Marigold didn't. 'Prince Yurenev is in love with *me*,' she said.

Strickland nodded, well able to believe that having once had his arms around a near naked Marigold, Maxim Yurenev was eager to repeat the experience. Also, as Marigold had so obviously entered a Russian phase, it explained why she was dressed as she was.

'A Russian husband would suit you,' he said, deciding the subject of the 'really, really distinguished person' had run its course. 'And Yurenev is a Romanov. He must have palaces galore in Russia.'

While in banishment at Snowberry Marigold had received lots of long telephone calls from Maxim, all urging her to return to London at the soonest possible moment. She said carelessly, 'He's heir to one of the greatest fortunes in Russia. His family have a huge palace in St Petersburg and other palaces on their vast estates in Central Asia.'

'So trying to persuade me not to exhibit Persephone isn't the only reason you are back in London. You're here to indulge in a Cossack-style love affair as well?'

Laughter bubbled up in her throat and she forgot all about being cross with him for not promising to keep Persephone under wraps.

'I'm going to do what I damn well please, Strickland. May I have a cigarette?' As they settled back into their habitual easy camaraderie she said, as if talking to a best girlfriend, 'Now tell me all the gossip. What happened at the fancy-dress ball after Rose hustled me home? Was I the talk of the evening?'

The next day, in the company of her great-aunt, Marigold left for a Saturday-to-Monday at Belden Castle, the principal seat of the Duke and Duchess of Stainford. The weekend was one she was intensely looking forward to.

Strickland, who had been at Belden several times, had told her that the footmen were as splendidly liveried as those at Windsor and that the vast rooms and endlessly long corridors were studded with paintings by Gainsborough, Reynolds and Holbein. 'Don't be a philistine about the tapestries,' he had said warningly. 'They are Gobelin and priceless.'

Despite Strickland's attempts to educate her in art history, it wasn't Belden's glut of artistic treasures she was looking forward to seeing. Maxim was a close friend of the family and had told her that he, too, would be one of the guests.

What she hadn't expected when she went downstairs with Sibyl for pre-dinner cocktails, looking sensationally eye-catching in a searing pink beaded gown that clashed spectacularly – and deliberately – with her hair, was that Lord and Lady Jethney would be at Belden as well.

Theo, looking splendid in full evening dress, visibly tensed with shock at the sight of her. Jerusha's eyes widened in happy surprise.

'Marigold! How wonderful!' Leaving her husband's side she crossed the room and taking Marigold's hands in hers she kissed her affectionately on both cheeks. 'Are Rose and Iris guests as well?'

'No. Rose is in town, doing some suffragette-type journalist

222

thing, and Iris is at Snowberry. She's just become officially engaged to Toby Mulholland.'

All the time she was speaking, she was looking over Jerusha's shoulder at Theo. A shutter had come down over his eyes, leaving them expressionless, but his mouth gave away his inner feelings. It had narrowed into a tight line of pain. Seeing it gave her intense satisfaction. She wanted him to hurt. She wanted him to hurt just as much as he had hurt her.

'How lovely,' Jerusha said, speaking of Toby and Iris. 'They've always been sweethearts, haven't they? Will it be an autumn wedding, or are they going to wait until the spring?'

Marigold neither knew, nor cared. Maxim Yurenev was walking towards them, a cocktail glass in either hand. 'I've got something rather fun for you to try,' he said, handing her one of the glasses. 'It's called a Gimlet. Tell me what you think of it.' To Jerusha he said courteously, 'Would you like to try one, Lady Jethney?'

Jerusha, who seldom even drank champagne, smiled gently and shook her head. 'No, I don't think so, Prince Yurenev.'

Sensing that the extraordinarily handsome young Russian wanted Marigold to himself and that there was possibly a burgeoning romance in the air, she excused herself. In a gown of midnight-blue taffeta, tall, thin and elegant, she returned to where her husband was still looking across at Marigold, his broad-shouldered, deep-chested body as taut as stretched wire.

'I've bribed a footman to change the place-setting names at table, and so we will be seated next to each other.'

Maxim had been educated at Oxford and his accent was very faint and more French – the language all the Russian aristocracy spoke fluently – than Russian. 'It wasn't an easy task,' he continued, acutely aware of the way her shimmering evening gown was clinging to her hourglass curves. 'The dinner table seats eighty and is set for at least forty.'

Like every other man present he was impeccable in white tie and tails, though where several other stiff shirt-fronts were fastened with mother-of-pearl or gold studs, Maxim's shirt was fastened with exquisite diamonds, as was his white piqué waistcoat.

Marigold, sensing that Theo's eyes were still on her, took a sip of her Gimlet – which she liked very much indeed – and turned the full force of her attention on Maxim. 'How wonderfully clever of you,' she said in her bewitchingly husky voice. 'I'd much rather be seated next to you than next to one of the Duke's elderly friends. As it is my first time at Belden, d'you think there is time, before dinner, for you to show me the gardens?'

Maxim, well aware of Marigold's reputation for being fast, felt a rising in his crotch. 'I think there is time for me to show you the Italian terrace garden.' His eyes, as they held hers, were very narrow, very bright, very dark.

He took the glass from her hand and deposited it, with his own glass, on the tray of a nearby footman. When they stepped into the garden he wanted his hands free . . . and hers.

Fifteen minutes later, as the guests began making their way into a state dining room so majestic it rivalled the state dining room at Buckingham Palace, Maxim and Marigold were still in the garden, deep in a passionate embrace.

Neither of them was aware of being watched.

Theo, with the excuse of wanting a last puff on his cigar before escorting Jerusha into dinner, was standing on the terrace, jealousy and self-hatred raging through his massive frame like a roaring fire.

He had to get over her. He had to stop caring.

He ground his cigar stub beneath his heel and with his hands bunched into fists headed back into the castle, knowing that if he didn't get over her, he would never have peace of mind again.

# TWENTY-ONE

Queen Mary was enjoying a few moments of blessed solitude. She had had a restless night, her mind teeming with the challenges she was facing in her new position as a crowned queen consort. The coronation was over, thank goodness, and had gone very well. George, in particular, had looked magnificent. Despite not being very tall – none of the men of the House of Saxe-Coburg-Gotha were known for their height – he had looked every inch a king-emperor.

It was early dawn and she had opened the drapes so that pale yellow light spilled into the room. Seated at an Empire writing table that had once been Queen Victoria's, she pondered the next two hurdles to be overcome.

First was the investiture of David as Prince of Wales at Caernarvon; it was an occasion she had very mixed feelings about, for it hadn't been George's, or even the Prime Minister's idea, but that of Mr Lloyd George, the Welsh Chancellor of the Exchequer, who also happened to be constable of Caernarvon Castle.

There had been no formal investiture of a Prince of Wales for centuries and her great regard for historical accuracy baulked at the staging of a royal and religious ceremony that gave the false impression of a long unbroken tradition. As there was little historical regalia in existence, new regalia – a coronet, a rod, a ring, a sword, a mantle with doublet and sash – had had to be made.

The rod, ring and sword had been made of Welsh gold and featured the traditional symbol of Wales: the red dragon. This pleased her sense of what was appropriate, but didn't ease her reservations about presenting as time-honoured tradition something that was, for the most part, newly invented.

George, however, had had no reservations about holding the investiture at Caernarvon and she had kept her feelings of disquiet to herself. She never, ever, disputed with George. Not about anything.

The sunrise was now the colour of ripe apricots. Enjoying its beauty, she thought about the second, far greater hurdle that lay ahead.

In four months' time she and George were to leave for India to receive the homage of their Indian subjects.

Unlike the investiture at Caernarvon, the coronation durbar to be held in Delhi was George's idea. The grandeur and splendour would, she knew, be colossal. No other king-emperor and queen-empress had ever stepped foot on India's great sub-continent. She and George would be the first to do so. Even thinking about the magnitude of the occasion took her breath away.

A satisfied smile touched her mouth as she reflected how extraordinary it was that, having been born a very minor, semi-royal princess, she had reached such dizzying heights. It was certainly something that couldn't have been predicted. The morganatic-tainted blood she had inherited from her father, whose own father had forfeited the throne of Württemberg by marrying a non-royal countess, had debarred any reigning

German prince from asking for her hand. As for the other royal houses of Europe, there had been very little hope of her marrying into one of them. As a serene highness, not a royal highness, she hadn't been royal enough to marry a royal prince – and yet was considered to be too royal to marry someone who wasn't.

It had been her mother's cousin, Queen Victoria, who, in order to resolve a sticky problem of her own, had been her salvation. Aunt-Queen's sticky problem had been her grandson, 28-year-old Prince Albert-Victor. Prince Eddy, as he was known within the family, had been George's elder brother. Second in line to the throne, he'd been sadly lacking in the qualities desirable in a future king. He could no more concentrate than fly to the moon. Nothing caught his interest. He was indifferent about everything except indulging in hopeless love affairs.

'How *can* darling Eddy believe himself in love with Princess Hélène of Orléans?' Queen Mary clearly remembered her mother saying way back in 1890. 'He is heir-presumptive to the throne and she is a Roman Catholic. Does he know *nothing* about the British Constitution?'

Eddy, as everyone was well aware, knew nothing about anything, and it was his grandmother's opinion that what he needed, in order to make up for his many deficiencies, was an exceedingly strong-minded and sensible wife. Someone who would, in his grandmother's words, 'give dear kind Eddy backbone'. Which was where she, May, had come in, although, as she learned much later, others before her had been given the opportunity also, for with Princess Hélène ruled out as a bride because of her Roman Catholicism, Queen Victoria had taken matters into her own hands.

Her first choice of bride for her heir-presumptive had been his cousin, Princess Alexandra of Hesse. The prospect of a future as Queen of England hadn't tempted Alix who, instead, had married yet another royal cousin, Nicholas, thereby becoming Tsarina of All the Russias.

Queen Victoria's second choice had been eighteen-year-old 'Mossy', Princess Margaret of Prussia. She, too, had been uninterested in Eddy. That Queen Victoria had then trained her sights on a young woman whose morganatic blood had precluded any European royal from asking for her hand was typical of her enlightened way of thinking. It was a way of thinking for which Queen Mary had cause to be very, very grateful.

She hadn't been in love with Eddy, but she had been familiar enough with the royal way of doing things to know that being in love wasn't a necessary requirement for a successful royal match.

What mattered was that they knew each other well; they had known each other since childhood. Even more importantly, marriage to Eddy would bring her all the things she had so long been starved of. Instead of being on the periphery of the royal circle, as wife of the heir-presumptive she would be at its heart. Dignity and respect would be hers in abundance, as would wealth and jewels.

The latter was important to her for wealth and jewels had been sadly lacking so far in her life, her parents being so short of either commodity they had once been obliged to leave England in order to live more frugally in Italy.

When, at Queen Victoria's bidding, Eddy had proposed to her at a house party at Luton Hoo, she had accepted him unhesitatingly. How could she have done otherwise when by marrying him she would one day be queen?

She rose to her feet and crossed to a small satinwood table crowded with silver-framed photographs. The most recent was one of herself in coronation robes. Yet the king at her side was not Eddy, as she had believed it would be, but George. For Eddy had died from pneumonia a mere six weeks after their engagement, and the brilliant future that had lain before her as his fiancée had vanished with such speed her head had reeled.

With George now the heir-presumptive, Queen Victoria saw no reason why May should not still become her grand-daughter-in-law and a future Queen of England, and sixteen months later, at Queen Victoria's bidding, George had proposed to May. Once again she was a royal highness destined to be a queen. And this time her husband-to-be had been far more to her taste.

Between herself and George there had always been fond family affection and on their marriage the affection had turned into devotion. Being alike in many ways, they suited each other. Both of them were intensely reserved and undemon-strative and they were of one mind when it came to carrying out their duties as king and queen.

She turned her attention to a photograph of George taken shortly after the announcement of their engagement. A bluff, uncomplicated, straightforward man, he was also a disciplin-arian and a martinet, his main fault being his inability to curb his temper. It was so explosive she often thought that when they were at Buckingham Palace his angry bellow was loud enough to be heard at Windsor and, conversely, that when they were at Windsor, it was loud enough to be heard at Buckingham Palace.

It was a character defect she had schooled herself to take in her stride, knowing that if Eddy had lived, she would have found his apathy, which bordered on mental retardation, far harder to endure.

There came the sound of the palace coming to life. Any moment now her breakfast tray would be brought in and her woman of the bedchamber would arrive with a batch of correspondence needing attention. Her day, which with her strong sense of duty she thought of as her working day, would begin.

David's investiture robes were scheduled to arrive mid-morning and she wanted to be present when he saw them and tried them on. She found her eldest son an odd boy, restless in a way she couldn't understand and, until now, very unenthusiastic about being centre-stage at Caernarvon. Being centre-stage was, though, something he would simply have to get used to. Not doing so, when he would one day be king, was unthinkable.

'I wondered, Mama, if I might have a word with you alone about something very, very important before I try on my robes.'

Queen Mary's unmaternal nature prevented her from having anything but a remote relationship with her children. Try as she might, she simply never knew how to communicate with them. David, for instance, was now fiddling with his tie. The fact that he was doing so out of acute nervous tension was completely lost on her. She simply found it an irritating habit. His statement that he had 'something very, very important' to say to her annoyed her also. The task in hand was the trying-on of his investiture robes. Any problem he had was something he should be talking to his tutor at Dartmouth about.

'I'm sure it is something that can keep, David,' she said stiffly. 'Or that it is probably something you should be speaking to your cadet captain about. As for speaking to me alone, apart from Lady Airlie and Lady Coomber we are alone.'

Lady Airlie and Lady Coomber were the ladies-in-waiting in attendance on her.

David's disappointment was intense. There was always

someone in attendance. He could count on the fingers of one hand the times he'd been truly alone with his mother. If it wasn't her dressers, it was one of her four women of the bedchamber, peers' daughters who performed the same function as the equerries of the King's household.

Lady Airlie and Lady Coomber were not women of the bedchamber. They were ladies of the bedchamber and ranked more highly. Their function was to attend his mother on her grander and more impressive engagements – which indicated his mother would be en route to such an engagement the minute the little matter of his investiture robes had been taken care of.

Taking him by surprise, she said suddenly, 'As the man from Ede and Ravenscroft hasn't yet arrived with your robes, please tell me what it is you wished to say.'

David looked towards Lady Airlie and Lady Coomber, and then, as he couldn't possibly tell his mother about Lily in their presence, he thought up an alternative subject fast. 'I was wondering, Mama, why you chose to be crowned as Queen Mary, instead of being crowned as Queen May.'

Queen Mary wasn't accustomed to being questioned by her children – or by anyone else – but on this occasion she summoned up patience.

'I couldn't possibly have taken the name May. It isn't one of my Christian names, merely a name used in affection by the family because I was born in the month of May.'

'But why Queen Mary when Victoria is your first name?' He was genuinely puzzled.

'Both the King and I were in agreement that being called Queen Victoria would cause too much confusion.'

'You could have been known as Queen Victoria Mary. There wouldn't have been any confusion then.'

This was something Queen Mary was well aware of. Until the question had arisen of what name she would be known by as queen, she had always signed letters and official papers with the first two of her eight Christian names, liking both the look and the sound of them. George, however, hadn't.

'I detest double-barrelled names,' he'd said bluntly. 'I never liked Eddy's given name of Albert-Victor. I doubt anyone else did either, apart from Queen Victoria, who wanted both her name and her beloved Albert's to be perpetuated together. It was why Eddy was always known as Eddy. It's a diminutive of Edward, his last name,' he'd added, just in case she had forgotten.

That she would have liked to have been crowned as Queen Victoria Mary was not something Queen Mary was about to share with her eldest son. It would have been a criticism of George's decision.

'I much prefer Queen Mary,' she said crisply to him. 'It's beautifully short and simple.' Then, as the man from Ede & Ravenscroft was announced, she turned away, signalling that the conversation was over.

David dutifully allowed himself to be dressed in the robes that someone – he didn't know who – had deemed suitable for the grand ceremonial of his investiture. The result was almost more than he could bear. His breeches were of white satin trimmed with gold brocade and knee rosettes. His doublet, barely reaching his thighs, was of crimson velvet worn with a gold sash and edged in ermine. The mantle was of purple velvet. Worn with an ermine cape fastened with gold clasps, it fell into a cumbersome train behind him.

He looked ridiculous. This time he knew that even Lily would agree with him.

With his face pale and set, he said tautly, 'None of this fantastic costume has any historical significance, Mama. It's ridiculous. What will the cadets at naval college say when they see me in it? I look like a player in a pantomime and I absolutely and utterly refuse to wear it.'

'You can't refuse to wear it, David, and you must stop taking things so seriously. I quite agree that the costume has no historical precedent, but as a prince you are obliged to do certain things that may often seem a little silly.'

The prospect of having to do things that 'often seemed a little silly' for the rest of his life filled him with despair. 'I don't mind the ceremony, Mama,' he said, trying to meet her halfway. 'I wouldn't even mind wearing my Knight of the Garter robes at it. But not these.' He indicated his white satin rosette-trimmed knee breeches in distaste.

'I think what you are forgetting, David, are the political aspects of your investiture. Mr Lloyd George is a radical. He shocked your father inexpressibly a few years ago with a speech attacking inherited privilege. His suggestion that a royal ceremony be revived after many centuries wasn't done out of respect for the monarchy.'

She smoothed her white-kid gloves over the backs of her hands. 'As a Welshman, Lloyd George suggested it because he knew it would appeal to the national pride of the Welsh – and that it would please his constituents and win him polit-ical support.'

China-blue eyes, with more than a hint of steel, held David's steadily. 'As a new and inexperienced king, Papa needs to be on good terms with Mr Lloyd George. He is, after all, chan-cellor of the exchequer, and may very well be the next prime minister. In carrying out the role assigned to you at the investi-ture, and doing so without causing unnecessary waves, you will greatly help Papa in dealing with a very difficult man.'

It was emotional blackmail of a very tall order and he caved in beneath it.

'All right, Mama,' he said in defeat. 'For Papa's sake, I won't cause waves. But I do need to talk to you as soon as possible about something truly important.'

With one problem satisfactorily dealt with, Queen Mary

was feeling magnanimous. 'What is this oh-so-important subject, David?'

'It's about my future, Mama.' He blushed furiously. 'It's about getting married.'

To his stunned amazement, instead of looking horrified, she looked pleased. 'I'm glad you realize an early marriage will be beneficial to you. It's a subject Papa is eager to talk to you about.'

With that, happy that the tricky conversation King George wanted to have with David wasn't going to be quite so tricky after all, she exited the room, Lady Airlie and Lady Coomber attentively in her wake.

# TWENTY-TWO

Rose was in a tea shop in a small street just off the Strand. Seated opposite her, as if a tea shop was his usual watering hole, was Hal Green. The tea shop had become their usual rendezvous. It suited Rose, who felt uncomfortable at the attention she aroused at the *Daily Despatch* when closeted with Hal in his office.

'That last article was surprisingly good,' he said, helping himself to a toasted, lavishly buttered crumpet.

'Why "surprisingly"?' Much as she was beginning to like him, her eyes flashed fire.

He grinned. He loved goading her. It had become his major pleasure in life. 'Because young women whose education has consisted of a finishing school in France – or did you perhaps go to one in Germany? – aren't usually capable of writing to a brief. Or, I should think, of writing so well.'

'Have you had vast experience of women writing journalistic pieces to a brief, Mr Green?' she asked, annoyed that he assumed her education had consisted of nothing further than learning to arrange flowers and speak a foreign language, and pleased that he thought she wrote well.

He demolished the crumpet and pushed his chair a little

away from the table so that he could stretch out his legs and cross them at the ankles.

She wondered if he was again wearing purple sock suspenders, but couldn't see because the gingham-clothed table hid his feet.

His grin deepened. He had attractive laugh-lines at the outer corners of his black-lashed eyes and a cleft in his chin that, though she tried hard not to let it, always riveted her attention.

'Perhaps not. But then I've never had one turn up in my office the way that you did.'

Rose brushed a crumb from her skirt. She was dressed in suffragette colours, something she always did when meeting with him in London.

He was beginning to find the constant green, purple and white theme a little tedious. 'Don't you ever wear any other colours?' he asked, changing the subject.

'No. I regard wearing the colours of the WSPU equivalent to the wearing of a military uniform.'

He cracked with laughter.

That he was running a national campaign demanding that imprisoned suffragettes be given the status of political prisoners and yet privately still thought the suffragette movement a joke enraged her. The urge to kick him was so strong she could hardly contain it.

Her bag was on the table and she reached out for it, about to snatch it up and storm off in high dudgeon. He covered her hand with his.

The effect was like a bolt of electricity shooting through her.

'I'm sorry for laughing.' His grey eyes darkened with sincerity – and with something much deeper. 'I think suffragettes like Daphne Harbury are just as brave as soldiers who wear the uniform of their country.'

In turmoil with emotions she had never experienced before, she released her hold of her handbag. He removed his hand from hers.

'What did you think of the *Daily Despatch*'s royal correspondent's coronation coverage?' he asked, as if he hadn't touched her, as if nothing extraordinary had happened between them. 'It was a bit flat, wasn't it? Competent, but didn't convey to the reader the exhilarating sense of being there. I think if I'd let you run loose with it, you would have done much better.'

It was such a compliment she didn't know how to respond.

He cocked his head to one side, looking at her measuringly, a lock of straight black hair falling low over his brow. 'I could ask you to cover the Prince of Wales's investiture,' he said musingly. 'As you are not the *Despatch*'s official royal correspondent I wouldn't be able to get you into Caernarvon Castle, of course. Still, if you did your homework, had all the details of the ceremony to hand and were at Caernarvon itself to soak up the atmosphere on the streets, I think you would turn in something that would be a welcome addition to the royal correspondent's piece. What do you think? Do you think you could do justice to Prince Edward's big day?'

'Yes.' She was so overwhelmed by the thought of being able to report on the investiture, she forgot all about being angry with him.

He took a pocket-watch out of his waistcoat pocket and clicked it open. 'Time to be going, I'm afraid.'

She thought what his reaction would be if she told him of her close friendship with Prince Edward and, as he paid the bill, giggles fizzed in her throat.

'I'm still curious about your finishing school, Rose,' he said as they stepped out on to the pavement. 'Was it in France, or was it in Germany?'

'Neither.' She smiled sunnily. 'It was in Oxford – and it wasn't a finishing school. It was St Hilda's.'

The elation she felt as his eyebrows shot high sustained her as she journeyed by train back to Hampshire.

She was doing so alone. Since Marigold had returned from her Saturday-to-Monday at Belden Castle she had been seeing Prince Maxim Yurenev every day. As Great-aunt Sibyl approved highly of Prince Yurenev and was sure their mother would likewise, Rose hadn't interfered. Marigold was so sexy that someone was always going to be in love with her and, unlike Lord Jethney, Maxim Yurenev was a bachelor who was not only handsome, but a Russian royal as rich as Croesus.

As the train rattled through Berkshire it occurred to Rose that her title-loving mother could very well end up with two daughters bearing royal titles. Lily as the Princess of Wales, and Marigold as Princess Yurenev. As Iris would one day be Viscountess Mulholland, the only person letting the side down was herself, and she had no intention of marrying anyone.

Unbidden, Hal Green's image blazed into her mind's eye. She banished it. She was a militant suffragette and militant suffragettes did not embroil themselves in romantic relationships. Her reaction when his hand had covered hers had been a freakish aberration. Even if it hadn't been, not in a million years could she imagine her mother accepting as a son-in-law a very common-sounding plain Mr Green.

Nor in a million years could she imagine Hal Green putting himself in the position of being anyone's son-in-law, for if any man was blatantly not the marrying kind, that man was Hal.

When she arrived back at Snowberry it was to find that Lord Jethney was to dine with them.

'It's been weeks and weeks since he was here,' her grandfather said in high satisfaction. 'He asked if all you girls were now at home and I told him that you and Marigold were in London, staying with Sibyl. He'll be very pleased to find that I was wrong about one of you.'

Another guest expected at dinner that evening was Toby. Rose suppressed slight irritation. Now that he and Iris were engaged, she was going to have to get used to Toby being always at Snowberry. The snag was that she and Lily wouldn't be able to talk about David in front of him.

'Where is Lily, Grandpa?'

The investiture was on Saturday and it was now Wednesday. If she was to gather unique background information before leaving for Caernarvon, she was going to have to do so fast.

'In the studio, working on her bust of Prince Edward.'

Without even pausing to remove her hat, she set off for the top of the house.

'Sorry to interrupt you, Lily,' she said breathlessly five minutes later. 'But Mr Green has asked me to go to Caernarvon to report on David's investiture. The *Despatch*'s royal correspondent, who has a press pass, will be doing the main piece. As I don't have a press pass and won't be inside the castle, I'm to report on the atmosphere on the streets. I want to do much more, though, and wondered if you would be speaking to David before Saturday? He does telephone you, doesn't he?'

Lily flushed rosily. 'Every evening at six. How wonderful that you will be writing about David for the *Daily Despatch*. It will amuse him no end. He's dreadfully nervous about it all. He hates wearing ceremonial robes and apparently the robes he will be wearing on Saturday are just the product of someone's imagination – not historically traditional at all. David says they are quite ghastly.'

She put the loop tool she had been working with down

240

on her work table and wiped the clay from her hands with a cloth.

'Do you want to speak to him? What sort of thing is it you want to know?'

'I'd love to speak to him and I want to know anything he can tell me. The info about the robes is interesting. I bet the *Despatch*'s royal correspondent doesn't know David's robes aren't historically traditional. When I hand my piece in, Hal Green's eyes are going to pop.'

Now that her hands were free of clay, Lily gave her a welcome-home hug. 'Do you always use Mr Green's Christian name as well as his last name when speaking about him? It seems an odd thing to do. It makes it sound as if he's a friend as well as an employer.'

'He isn't a friend, though we do have a quite friendly relationship. He just always calls me – and probably everyone else – by their first name. Very properly I always call him Mr Green, but because he calls me Rose, I don't actually *think* of him as Mr Green.'

Lily gave a gurgling laugh. 'How do you think of him, Rose? You're not a little in love with him, are you?'

'Most certainly not!'

Her denial was so vehement it only confirmed Lily's suspicions.

As they left the studio and walked downstairs Lily hugged her sister's arm. Rose had always been the academic in the family and had never shown any interest in the opposite sex. It had been Iris's dour prediction that, like a lot of her fellow members in the WSPU, she never would. That the interesting-sounding Mr Hal Green was changing Rose's attitude towards men was, as far as Lily was concerned, a very good thing.

For Rose, Iris and Lily there was underlying tension at dinner as they all strove to keep the conversation away from the subject of the Prince of Wales. Because of the investiture, it was an impossibility.

'Hal tells me you are going to be in Caernarvon in three days' time,' Theo Jethney said, smiling across the table at Rose. 'I never thought, when I suggested you met with him, that this kind of thing would be the result. I'll be present at the ceremony,' he continued. 'As will Jerusha.' His smile died. 'That is, she will be if she is well enough.'

Rose's eyes widened.

Iris laid down her knife and fork.

Lily gave a small sound of concern.

They were all so accustomed to Theo dining informally at Snowberry unaccompanied by Jerusha it hadn't occurred to any of them that her present absence was caused by illness.

Aware of their alarm, Theo said quickly, 'It's nothing serious. Just headaches. She's been getting them for a while now and when she has them they lay her low for a day or so at a time. The doctor says they are nothing to worry about.'

Rose frowned, not liking the sound of headaches that lasted a whole day. She was about to suggest that perhaps a second opinion should be sought, but Theo was asking Iris and Toby if they intended marrying locally or if they were going to have a London society wedding.

'To please my mother – and Toby's – it's to be a society wedding at St Margaret's.' Iris's nut-brown eyes glowed with happiness. 'Grandfather is to give me away and Rose, Marigold and Lily are to be my bridesmaids.'

'Splendid.' Theo cleared his throat and for a second Rose thought he was going to ask after Marigold.

He didn't do so, but looking across the table at him, Rose knew that he wanted to. And she knew that if Marigold had been home, Theo would not have been dining with them.

As the conversation continued to revolve around Iris and Toby's wedding plans, she wondered what Theo Jethney's reaction would be when he learned of Prince Maxim Yurenev's interest in Marigold.

She wondered what the chances were of Marigold marrying in St Petersburg's great Kazan Cathedral with the Tsar and Tsarina of Russia heading a roll-call of royal guests.

# TWENTY-THREE

The day was stiflingly hot. As David stepped from the royal train into the horse-drawn open carriage that was to take him through the thronged, spectator-filled streets of Caernarvon to the castle, the heat rose from the ground in suffocating waves. He wasn't as yet wearing his velvet, ermine-caped cloak, but he would be wearing it on his return journey and he wondered how he was going to survive beneath it without melting away.

Minutes earlier, before Bertie had stepped into the carriage that was to follow his and which Bertie would be travelling in with their mother and their sister, Bertie had said with deep feeling, 'R-r-rather you than m-m-me, David.'

It had been sympathy he'd appreciated.

His mother, ramrod straight and magnificently regal in a floor-sweeping gown of silver brocade, her matching hat piled high with fluttering ostrich feathers, had given him a brief encouraging nod.

His sister, Mary, had whispered, 'Jolly good luck when you speak in Welsh, David.'

As he seated himself in the landau, next to his father, David wished she hadn't mentioned it. He was feeling nervous

244

enough as it was without being reminded of all the luck he was going to need when the time came for him to launch into his 'All Wales is a sea of song' piece.

His father, wearing the tricorne hat and gold-epauletted and gold-adorned uniform of an admiral of the fleet made a noise in his throat that could have meant anything.

Then the noise began.

It erupted the second their carriage emerged into full view. Every inch of pavement on the streets leading to Castle Square was jam-packed with flag-waving spectators and every last one of them was shouting and cheering at the top of their lungs.

When they reached the square the procession halted and the cheering intensified as the King knighted Caernarvon's mayor. Then it was back into the landaus for a climb up Castle Hill amid a sea of waving Welsh flags and Union Jacks. In many respects it was like a rerun of the procession on Coronation Day, but with one huge, momentous difference. On Coronation Day, it had been King George who had been centre-stage, with Queen Mary coming a very close second.

Today, David was centre-stage. It was *his* investiture. He was in Wales as the Prince of Wales, and though there were cheers in plenty for the King and Queen, the cheering he was receiving was far greater.

At first he felt so overcome at being the focal point of attention for so many thousands of people, he simply wanted to die of shyness. But then all his natural friendliness came to the fore. He liked people – and these people liked him. He remembered Lily telling him how, as Prince of Wales, he was in a position to effortlessly bring great happiness to people who would often have waited hours and hours to see him pass by.

Uncertain at first, and then with greater confidence, he

began to smile and wave – and, for the first time ever, the people he was destined to rule became aware of his scintillating charisma.

Once within the picturesque ruins of the ancient castle he waited with the Garter King of Arms as the King and Queen were seated, together with Bertie and Mary and all the civic and military dignitaries who had been in the procession. Then, as the sun beat down from a cloudless sky, preceded by the Garter King of Arms and accompanied by a fanfare of trumpets, he began walking up the great outdoor transept to where, beneath a magnificent canopy, his father waited for him.

During his approach, as he paused to make three successive bows, he forgot about the fanciful doublet and hose he was wearing.

He forgot about everything but the solemnity of what was about to happen.

Winston Churchill, the Home Secretary, sonorously proclaimed his titles. As well as Prince of Wales he was Earl of Chester, Duke of Cornwall, Duke of Rothesay, Earl of Carrick, Baron of Renfrew, Lord of the Isles and Prince and Great Steward of Scotland.

When the impressive roll-call came to an end, the regalia of the Prince of Wales was carried forward on tasselled cushions and the ceremony of investiture began. He was robed in the purple-velvet mantle. His father put the coronet studded with pearl and amethyst on his head and kissed him on both cheeks. He handed him the sword of Welsh gold as a symbol of justice. As a token of duty he put on to the middle finger of his left hand the ring featuring the Welsh dragon. Finally, he handed him the rod as a symbol of government.

Welsh voices rose in song as his father then led him by the hand through an ancient archway to the battlement tower known as Queen Eleanor's Gate. There, where hundreds of years ago Edward I had presented his baby son to the people of Wales as their prince, he, too, was presented.

This was the moment when he had to speak to thousands of people in Welsh. The heat was so overpowering that he felt close to fainting. Nerves gripped him with such ferocity he thought he was going to be sick. He thought of Lily. He thought of how much he loved her and of how much she loved him. He thought of how much he wanted her to be proud of him.

Loudly and clearly he declaimed, '*Diolch fy nghalon i Hen wlad fy nhadau.*' Thanks from the bottom of my heart to the old land of my fathers.

He sensed the appreciation of the vast throng packed like sardines into Castle Square below him and how they were all willing him to do well. By the time he came to *Mor o gan yw Cymru i gyd* – All Wales is a sea of song – he was happily confident that even Mr Lloyd George himself couldn't have done better.

The cheering was thunderous. Hats were thrown into the air. Flags were waved.

As David waved back he wondered if Rose was among the crowd in the square or if she was in one of the streets he would shortly be passing through on his way back to the royal train. The knowledge that he had a personal friend among the vast sea of ordinary people cheering him filled him with happiness so deep he had no words for it.

Accidentally knocking Rose from her bicycle had changed his life. It had shown him what a loving informal home life could be like. At Snowberry he'd experienced being treated as an ordinary young man – something he'd previously only dreamed about. Most importantly of all, it had given him Lily, and he knew that with Lily by his side he would be able to carry out whatever royal duties were asked of him.

His father touched him on the arm. It was time to turn

and lead the ceremonial procession out of the castle for another carriage-ride through Caernarvon's flag-decked streets.

Just as on Coronation Day, after he'd paid homage to his father, now that the difficult part of the day's ceremony was over he felt vast, euphoric relief. Or at least he did until he remembered the interview he still had to have with his father.

It had been his own decision to leave asking for the interview until after his investiture was over. 'The King will be in a much better mood then, darling,' he'd said over the telephone to Lily. 'He's always tetchy, but he's tetchier than ever just before a big ceremonial event. Once the investiture is over – especially if it's gone well – he'll be far more receptive to the kind of news I shall be giving him.'

In the couple of days since their telephone conversation he'd realized he had a problem they'd never previously thought of. Though Lily was old enough to have been presented at court, she hadn't been. She wasn't yet a debutante. She wasn't officially out. Until she was, in society's eyes she was off-limits as far as romance was concerned. His father was a stickler for proprieties. It would not go down well that David had taken no notice of them.

Because his father was the King, David couldn't simply speak to him any time that he wished. Occasionally, of course, if they were out together on a shoot for instance, conversation would take place between them, but it was always to do with the task in hand – or about the weather. (His father, like many of his subjects, was obsessed with the subject of the British weather.) If their exchange wasn't about the task in hand, or the weather, the King would usually proffer a criticism of some sort, complaining about his poor marks in maths at naval college. Good marks, which he quite often got in French and German, were never mentioned.

The morning after the investiture he wrote a letter to his

father saying he would like an interview with him, sealed it and gave it to a footman to deliver via miles of Buckingham Palace's red-carpeted corridors. Then he clenched his hands together until the knuckles shone white and fought the excruciating nerves paralysing his stomach.

The interview took place in the library, as did all interviews with his father, whether at Windsor or Buckingham Palace or Sandringham. David paused outside the door before entering, reminding himself of all the things that were in his favour. Though he was only seventeen, his mother had indicated that his father was in favour of his marrying young. And he wasn't about to ask for permission to *marry* at seventeen. He was about to ask for permission to become betrothed at seventeen. The problem would not be his age, but Lily's non-royal status. Praying that his father was going to be reasonable, he dug his nails into his palms and allowed a footman to open the door and announce his arrival.

The instant he entered the room he sensed with vast relief that his father, happy that the investiture had gone well, was in a good mood.

'You did remarkably well yesterday, David,' he said genially as David stood before his desk, legs apart and hands clasped behind his back. 'I've received compliments on your behalf from both Mr Lloyd George and Winston Churchill. Mr Lloyd George has assured me that you have forged a lasting bond of affection with the Welsh people and that you won the admiration of all those who witnessed the ceremony yesterday.'

Compliments from his father, even though they were compliments he was passing on from someone else, were rare. David flushed with pleasure.

'It was Mr Churchill's opinion that you possess a voice which carries well and is capable of being raised without losing expressiveness.'

David was an admirer of his father's bullish home secretary and his pleasure deepened.

'So now, with your investiture behind us, we come to your immediate future.'

'Yes, sir. I believe Mama may have mentioned to you that I wished to speak about it. Something very extraordinary and wonderful has happened to me and—'

'It was indeed a most extraordinary and wonderful occasion. The first investiture of a Prince of Wales on Welsh soil for over six hundred years – and now I have a pleasant surprise for you.'

King George stroked his immaculately clipped Van Dyck beard.

David yearned to interrupt him and to begin telling him about Lily, but knew better than to do so.

'Because of your disappointment at not being able to finish your time at Dartmouth with the traditional training cruise, I have arranged a three-month tour for you aboard the battleship *Hindustan*.'

He waited for a sign of gratitude and pleasure. David was completely unable to oblige. 'Three months, sir?' All he could think was that it would be a three-month separation from Lily. Clutching at straws he said hopefully, 'Will this be sometime next year?'

Having not met with the reaction he had expected, his father frowned. 'Not at all. You will be going to sea as a junior midshipman in three weeks' time. The *Hindustan* is commanded by an old navy friend of mine, Captain Henry Hervey Campbell. He's a splendid chap. You will have a grand time and learn a great deal.'

'Yes, sir. I'm sure I shall.' David knew that it was absolutely pointless to object to the plans that had been made for him. He licked dry lips, his heart hammering. 'I have some news of my own, sir. It's going to come as rather a surprise to you.'

King George seldom listened to what the person he was talking to was saying, and his son was no exception. 'When you return from your three months aboard the *Hindustan*, you are going to have to put in some work reading up the subjects you will be studying next year at Oxford.'

'Oxford?' The ground shifted beneath David's feet. '*Oxford?* But I've never been led to believe I would be going to Oxford! I'm not an academic. I'm not interested in academia. Oxford would be a complete waste of my time and—'

'In the early part of next year, before you go up to Oxford, you will be going to France to learn something of French politics and to polish up your language skills.'

The ground wasn't merely shifting beneath his feet now; it was opening into a yawning chasm. How, with such a programme before him, would he ever be able to spend time with Lily? Oxford would mean three years away from her. It would also be three years spent in an environment totally at odds with the kind of environment he flourished best in. He needed physical exercise. The kind of physical exercise he'd been accustomed to as a naval cadet. If he'd been given a choice he would have chosen to remain in the navy. But he never was given a choice. And he knew that as far into the future as he could see, he never would be given one.

Which was why Lily was so important to him.

Lily represented the normal world. The world where people made their own decisions with regard to their future. The world where friendships were made because people liked each other, not because it was to the advantage of one of them to fawn over and pay homage to the other.

Irritably, his father, his good humour fast evaporating, shifted a couple of Fabergé paperweights into different positions on his desk. 'In France you will be staying with the marquis de Valmy and his family and will be there in-cognito, travelling as the Earl of Chester. Mr Hansell and Finch will accompany you. The marquis, who has the advan-tage of having been a close friend of your grandfather, has two sons close to you in age, one of whom will act as your equerry.'

It was all getting worse and worse. With desperation in his voice David said, 'I do appreciate all the time and trouble that has gone into making all these arrangements for me, but I have news of my own that might mean rethinking some of them.'

'Rethinking some of them?' King George blinked. Not even his ministers ever suggested he should rethink any-thing. '*Rethinking* some of them? What the devil do you mean?'

Well aware that he had lost the advantage of his father's earlier good mood, David screwed his courage to the sticking point. 'I'd like to talk to you about my future marriage, sir.'

Amazingly, his father calmed down an edge. 'Harrumph,' he said into his beard, believing that after the conversation they'd had on the subject, Queen Mary had then spoken with David. 'You're not going to want any *rethinking* done on the subject of your marriage, are you?'

Not knowing what thinking anyone had done on the subject of his future marriage, David couldn't answer him, but the way his father had phrased the question didn't bode well. It indicated that, without his knowledge, plans for a future Princess of Wales were already under way.

The thought froze him in fear. The plan for him to spend three months aboard the *Hindustan* was reasonable, con-sidering the coronation had meant he couldn't go on the much longer training cruise that traditionally rounded off an educa-tion at Dartmouth. Even the plan for him to go to Oxford was understandable, if unwelcome, as was the plan for him to spend time in France, brushing up his French. But if plans were already in hand as to whom he should marry . . .

He felt so dizzy the walls of the library seemed to be moving around him. It was 1911, not 1811. Surely not even his father would have begun negotiating an arranged marriage for him without having spoken to him about it first?

He remembered that his mother's marriage to his father had been at Queen Victoria's suggestion and that neither of them had had any say in it. Heirs to thrones never did have much say as to whom they married. But he was going to be different, because he was going to have *every* say in whom he married.

Determination flooded through him, giving him courage he'd never felt before when confronting his father.

Without waiting for a reply, King George said, 'I'm glad you are being sensible about this issue, David. You may think seventeen is a little young to be thinking of marriage, but royal marriage negotiations take time and an official engagement at eighteen, followed by a wedding at twenty-one, would be very acceptable timing.'

'Yes, sir. I quite agree. I—'

'Olga is a dear girl . . .'

So it was the Russian connection his parents had in mind for him, not a German connection – and it was not even to be Olga's younger sister Tatiana who, of all the Tsar's daughters, he had always felt closest to.

'Papa! Please stop. Please stop until you have heard what it is I've come to tell you.'

His urgent use of 'Papa', instead of 'sir', finally stopped King George in his tracks.

'Papa, I've met someone.' There was a bead of sweat on his upper lip. The blood was pounding in his ears and his heart was racing like a steam train. 'She's a wonderful girl. Absolutely tip-top. I so want you to meet her and I so want to marry her.'

There. It was out. He had said it. He felt so weak with relief he had to put a hand on the desk to steady himself.

'What did you say?' King George cupped his ear. 'Olga's a wonderful girl? Of course she is – and it wouldn't matter if she weren't. She's your uncle Nicky's eldest daughter and there can be no better political alliance for Great Britain at the moment than with Russia – not the way Germany is building up its navy.'

Once more David summoned up all his courage. 'You've misunderstood me, Papa. I wasn't referring to Olga. The girl I've met and whom I love with all my heart isn't royal, though she does come from a very good family.'

This time it was King George who looked as if he needed to steady himself.

'What did you say?' His eyes bulged until they looked as if they were going to leave their sockets. '*What* did you say? You've met a girl? How in all that is holy can you possibly have met a girl? You're talking like a fool, David! Are you ill? Have you a temperature?'

'No, sir.' Thanking his lucky stars that Georgie Battenberg had agreed to play ball and that he wasn't going to have to go into explanations about how he'd knocked Rose from her bicycle, he said, 'Georgie Battenberg introduced us. She comes from a spiffing family and—'

'And nothing! Are you telling me you have become acquainted with a young woman without my knowledge? Are you? *Are you?*' The King slammed a fist so hard on the desk the paperweights jumped and skidded.

'It happened accidentally, sir.' That much at least was true. 'Lily is a unique and special person, Papa, and I love her with all my heart.'

Behind his beard, King George's face went white. 'Don't tell me you've been such a fool as to have *told* this girl you love her?'

Fear of his father was something David had grown up with. It was fear he felt now, but he had no intention of showing it, or giving in to it.

'Yes,' he said unhesitatingly, looking his father straight in the eyes. 'I've asked her to marry me.'

King George made a choking sound, his face no longer white, but puce. He clawed at his stiff high collar, struggling to free himself from it. Horrified, certain his father was about to have a heart attack, David sprang forward to help him.

Still struggling for breath, the King fended him off violently, hurling him backwards with such force he slammed into a glass-fronted bookcase.

Glass splintered.

Dazedly David struggled to remain upright, uncertain whether shards had pierced his jacket and, if he moved, would pierce his skin.

King George lunged towards him and, as David braced himself, shot past him. Yanking open the double doors he spluttered at the footmen on duty, 'Fetch Lord Esher to me! Fetch him to me *now*!'

The doors crashed shut again and he turned to face David.

'Never', he bellowed, 'would I have believed a son of mine could be capable of such imbecilic behaviour! Have you completely forgotten who you are? This isn't Romania! You can't go shilly-shallying off, falling in love where you please! When you marry, you marry a royal princess. A royal princess who will bring political advantages to the table. And that means Grand Duchess Olga. As heir to the greatest throne in the world – and on the outside chance of your proposal being turned down – you do *not* propose marriage to *anyone* in person. Not even Olga. Someone will do that for you. Now get out of my sight! Get out! *GET OUT!*'

Pale and shaking, David had no alternative but to do as he was commanded. The minute he was out of view of the footmen, or of anyone else, he leaned against a wall, a fist pressed hard against his mouth. To say that the interview had not gone as well as he had hoped it would was an understatement. His father, true to form, had been utterly unreasonable. When he thought of how his father hadn't even allowed him to explain who Lily was, he didn't know which emotion was uppermost. Anger or despair.

He sucked in a deep steadying breath. Lord Esher was his father's most trusted adviser and he knew why his father had sent for him. It was so that Esher could advise him on how best he could be extricated from the mess that, in his father's eyes, he had got himself into.

He bit hard on his knuckle. An approach from the palace to Lily's grandfather would put an end to everything. Then a drilling by Lord Esher, or by the King's private secretary, might well convince Lily that it was in David's best interest for her to sever all contact with him.

His head hurt and his eyes smarted. He blinked hard, struggling to think clearly. That disastrous interview with his father wasn't the end of everything. It was just the beginning. His father now knew what the situation was. He wasn't going to permit himself to be harried into an arranged marriage. He was going to marry the girl of his choice; the girl who had won his heart and whom he would love for as long as he lived.

Future interviews with his father would now start from that basis and no matter how long it took before his father accepted Lily as a future Princess of Wales, David was utterly determined that eventually he would do so.

Feeling much calmer and no longer shaking, he eased himself away from the wall and began walking in the direction of his own apartment. The first and most important thing he had to do was to ensure that neither Lord Esher, nor anyone else, spoke on the King's behalf to Lily's grandfather.

He came to a sudden halt, his eyes widening.

*No one* from the palace would speak with Lord May, for the very simple reason that the King hadn't given him the chance to tell him anything at all about Lily, or about her family.

Quite simply, apart from the fact that she came from a good family, his father had not the slightest idea who she was. And that was the way he was going to keep things until his father agreed that he could marry a non-royal for love.

He entered his own apartment and, as Finch fussed around him, his thoughts continued to race. He urgently needed to speak with Georgie Battenberg, so that Georgie was pre-warned about not disclosing Lily's identity. He also needed to speak with Piers Cullen about the same thing. Piers, of course, would need very little persuasion to keep mum, for if his part in visiting Snowberry became known his career as an equerry – and possibly even his army career – would be over as fast as light.

He sipped at the mug of cocoa Finch had handed him.

Most of all he needed to speak with Lily in order to let her know that he had spoken to his father – and that he would probably have to do so several times before his father accepted the idea of a Princess of Wales who would only become royal upon her marriage. He needed to tell her, too, that in three weeks' time he would be leaving for a three-month tour of duty aboard the *Hindustan* and that plans were also in place for him to spend time in France and then, the following autumn, to go to Oxford for three years.

He couldn't tell her any of those things over the telephone. He needed to speak to her face to face.

He pondered the chances of doing so after the scene he'd just had with his father and knew that they were zero. From now on every move he made would be watched and monitored. At the moment, however, his father was closeted with Lord Esher. No one was spying on him – or no more than was usual. Piers Cullen was on three days' leave visiting his widowed father, and the equerry standing in for him was inexperienced and could easily be given the slip.

Decisively he put down his half-drunk mug of cocoa. 'I'm going AWOL for three or four hours, Finch.'

'Absent without leave, sir? Will that be with a migraine, sir?'

He shot Finch a quick light smile. 'If you think that serves the purpose, Finch.'

Thirty minutes later, at the wheel of his Austro-Daimler and unaccompanied, he was speeding out of London in the direction of Hampshire.

Another hour later, as the light smoked to dusk, he was roaring up Snowberry's elm-lined drive and Lily was running from the house to meet him.

'I heard you the minute you turned in from the lane!' she shouted, racing over the gravel towards him.

He sprang from the car, all cares and concerns temporarily forgotten. She was wearing a faded blue dress she often wore when working in her studio. It had a creamy lace collar and its skirt bore traces of paint marks that had refused to launder out.

He opened his arms wide and, not caring who might be watching from the house, she ran into them as if he had just returned from a war.

In the little privacy the two of them had ever had together he had become very practised at kissing and as he kissed

258

her now, fiercely and deeply, she clung to him as though she would never, ever, let him go.

He never wanted her to let him go. He never wanted to be anywhere but with her.

At last he reluctantly raised his head from hers and said, looking down into her eyes, 'I've a lot to tell you, Lily darling. Let's go down to the lake. There's no one down there, is there?'

She shook her head. Her glossy hair was held away from her face by a ribbon tied at the nape of her neck. The temptation to undo it for the pleasure of watching her hair cascade free was almost too much for him.

'You were *wonderful* at Caernarvon, David,' she said as, her hand in his, they began walking in the direction of the lake. 'I've begun a newspaper-cuttings book.'

He squeezed her hand tightly, loving the way she made him feel six feet tall. He didn't pursue the subject of Caernarvon, though. Instead he said tautly, 'I've told the King that I love you, Lily darling. I've told him I want to marry you.'

Anxiety flooded her face. 'What did he say? Was he very disappointed you wanted to marry someone who isn't a princess?'

He hesitated and then, choosing his words carefully, said, 'He was a little disappointed, but then we'd known he would be. It's going to take him a little time to come round to the idea, but I'm sure he will do eventually.'

'Does he want to meet me? Does he want to speak with my grandfather?'

There was no eagerness in her voice at the prospect of meeting the King. Only acute apprehension.

The dusk was deepening, the air still warm. He said gently, 'He will want to meet you, darling. But not just yet. At the moment he still needs time to accept that my marriage is going to be different from the usual run of royal marriages.'

They had reached the jetty and, as had become their habit, they sat down on it, taking off their shoes and plunging their feet into water that, in the twilight, was the colour of indigo.

He wrapped his arm around her waist. 'You know how I've told you plans are always being made for me and without my knowledge until it's too late for me to object to them? Well, it's been happening again. On a grand scale.'

Both his voice and his face were sombre and she knew that whatever his news, it was news he didn't like.

He hugged her tightly. 'I'm to leave in three weeks' time for a three-month tour of duty aboard the battleship *Hindustan*. Next spring I'm to go to France. I'll be mainly in Paris, staying with the de Valmy family. The marquis de Valmy was a good friend of my grandfather's. Then, in the autumn, I'm to go to Oxford – and I'm dead-set against doing so. Mainly because while I'm there we'll hardly ever be able to see each other, but also because I'm just not cut out to spend three years studying under the tutelage of a lot of stuffy dons.'

She bit her lip, wondering what she could say that would make him feel better about things. At last she said tentatively, 'When you come down from Oxford we'll both be twenty-one. When we're twenty-one we won't need anyone's permission to marry.'

Her head was resting on his shoulder and he hugged her even closer, kissing her hair. 'I will,' he said glumly. 'It doesn't matter how old I may be, I will still have to have the King's permission – as will Bertie, Harry and Georgie when it's their turn to want to marry.'

He didn't mention John, and she had far too much on her mind to wonder why it was he never did mention his youngest brother.

She said, trying to be optimistic, 'Perhaps when your father has got used to the idea of you marrying me, he'll think differently about you spending three years at Oxford?'

'Perhaps.' But there was no confidence in his voice. To block out the thought of how violently opposed his father was to his marriage to anyone other than the Grand Duchess Olga, he hooked his finger under her chin and, tilting her head to his, kissed her long and lingeringly.

Her lips were as soft as velvet, her body supple and pliant against his. As he thought of how long it could be before she became his wife he groaned, hardly able to bear the thought of such an agony of waiting. He wanted to marry her now. This minute. He wanted to make her irrevocably his before negotiations for a wedding between himself and Olga got under way.

'I love you, Lily darling,' he said thickly. 'I love you with all my heart. You are my peace and my future and I simply have to get the King's permission for us to marry. I *have* to!' He ran a hand through hair so blond that in the twilight it looked silver. 'How am I going to manage all these months away from you? First at sea? Then in France?'

'We may not have to be separated all the time you are in France. My mother is the marquise de Villoutrey. She and my stepfather have a home in Paris and a chateau about twenty miles south-west of Paris, near Versailles. I could stay with them for the whole of the time you are a guest of the de Valmy family.'

It was so unexpected it took a second for him to register the significance of what she'd said. When he did, his mood changed instantly. He sprang to his feet, dragging her upright with him.

'But that's *brilliant*, Lily! I'm not going to be in France as the Prince of Wales. I'm to go there incognito, as the Earl of Chester. It's one of my lesser titles. It means I won't be under constant scrutiny as I am here. Do you know what that means, dearest darling Lily?' Jubilantly he swung her round and round off her feet. 'It means that the King has unwittingly given us the most fabulous present. It means we're going to have time alone together in the most romantic city in the world!'

# TWENTY-FOUR

It was the dog days of August. At 95 degrees in the shade, the heat was almost unbearable. All Marigold's friends had left London for long vacations elsewhere. Everything was stagnant. Nothing was happening. Marigold's boredom threshold – always low – had not only been reached, but was no longer in sight.

'Iris is no company because all she can talk about are her wedding plans,' she said in high dudgeon to Strickland as he worked on the portrait she hoped would one day hang in the Royal Academy.

The other painting, the Persephone/Pluto painting, was propped against a wall and her nudity looked so scandalously glorious Marigold found it hard to take her eyes away from it.

She continued with her list of complaints. 'The brides-maids' dresses are to be swooning lilac. Lilac! Rose's hair is a rich mahogany colour and so it will probably suit her, and the colour will be perfect on Lily, but it won't be perfect on me. It will make me look a fright. As if all that isn't bad enough, Rose is hardly ever around. She's too busy with her journalism work. The editor of the *Daily Despatch* was so pleased with her report of Prince Edward's investiture that he's asked her to do a piece on the strike at the Victoria and Albert Docks.'

Strickland laid his brush down and reached into his smock pocket for his Turkish cigarettes. 'A strike is a bit different to a royal event. She won't be going down to the docks in person, as she went to Caernarvon, will she?'

As Strickland was taking a break, Marigold relaxed her pose. Unlike the pose she had adopted for Persephone, it was very modest. Strickland had positioned her seated daintily on the studio's chaise longue, a bouquet of tea roses in her lap, her hair swept up in a fashionable chignon. The evening gown he had considered appropriate was one her aunt had bought for her. It was of yellow satin overlaid with silk net heavily embroidered with silver thread and silver bugle beads. She looked soignée, very beautiful and, at a pinch, respectable.

She said, 'Going down to the East End was the first thing she did. But not to speak to the dockers – though she will be doing that. The people she's gone to speak to first are the wives. There is no strike fund, you see, and they are the ones who are going to have to earn enough for food and rent. Rose', she added a little unnecessarily, 'is on the side of the strikers. She's a socialist.'

'Most militant suffragettes are.' He blew a plume of blue smoke upwards. 'I take it she didn't go into the East End alone?'

'I don't think so. I think she took her friend Daphne Harbury with her.'

'She should have taken a man. She'll certainly need a man with her when she visits the docks. Your cousin Rory would be a good choice. I take it her editor doesn't know what she intends doing? If he does, and if he hasn't warned her against it, he's a damned fool.'

Something close to a glazed expression entered Marigold's eyes. She had met Mr Hal Green and had known instantly that though he was many fascinating things, he was certainly not a fool.

The meeting had been accidental.

Two days earlier she and Rose had been leaving St James's Street at the same time. Marigold had been on her way to the Savoy, to meet Prince Yurenev for lunch. Rose had been on her way to Clement's Inn for a meeting with Christabel.

'We may as well travel as far as the Savoy together, Rose,' she'd said. 'Though if we do, it will have to be in a cab. I'm not travelling on a bus. Not even for you.'

In London they seldom spent any time at all with each other and travelling the short distance down St James's Street and through Trafalgar Square and into the Strand together had been something of a novelty.

As the hansom drew to a halt outside the front entrance of the Savoy, Rose had said, 'I'm getting out here with you. Clement's Inn is only a short walk away.'

It was then, as they had been about to step from the carriage, that one of the most handsome men Marigold had ever seen strode up to offer them his hand.

She had instantly assumed she was the attraction. She had begun dressing in as Russian a way as was possible and instead of a hat in a colour complementing her turquoise silk walking-dress, she was wearing a matching exotic-looking turban with a white cockade. To say that she was eye-catching was an understatement.

As she had flirtatiously accepted his proffered hand she'd heard Rose, who was behind her, catch her breath, and had assumed it was in shocked criticism at her having allowed a stranger such an intimacy.

Then, to her stunned disbelief, Rose had allowed him to help her from the hansom, too, and, though obviously cross about it, had even allowed him to pay their cab fare.

With the transaction over, she'd made introductions.

'Mr Green, my sister, Marigold,' she'd said, sounding unusually flustered. 'Marigold, Mr Green. Mr Green is the editor of the *Daily Despatch*.'

Until then Marigold hadn't given a moment's thought to Rose's editor and, even if she had, her mental image of him would have been totally at odds with the reality. Tall and loose-limbed, with straight hair so black it had a blue sheen, he looked the kind of man it would be both exciting and a little dangerous to know. What he didn't look to be was the kind of man Rose was likely to know.

'I'm very pleased to meet you, Miss Houghton,' he'd said with an easy smile and an even easier manner. 'I've heard a lot about you.'

'From Rose?'

He'd shaken his head and at the amusement in his eyes she'd known immediately that gossip had reached him of her Queen of Sheba appearance at the fancy-dress ball.

Unfazed, she'd flashed him her most bewitching smile. 'Are you about to enter the Savoy, Mr Green?' she'd asked with her usual careless disregard for proper behaviour. 'Because if you are, perhaps you would like to escort me inside? Rose', she had added, 'is on her way to the WSPU offices in Clement's Inn.'

It was then that the real surprise had come.

He hadn't taken her up on her offer.

Instead he had said pleasantly, 'I, too, am on my way towards the Aldwych. I shall look forward to meeting you again sometime, Miss Houghton.'

With that he had turned his attention from her to Rose, who, to Marigold's amazement, seemed quite happy to be the object of it.

As she watched the two of them walk away together it occurred to Marigold that they were walking extremely close together and that though it couldn't have been intentional,

Rose's dove-grey walking costume fitted her like a second skin, drawing attention not only to her wasp waist and the pleasing curve of her hips, but also to a pair of extremely neat ankles.

'I said that if her editor hasn't warned your sister against going down to the docks, he's a damned fool,' Strickland repeated, aware that Marigold had gone off into a world of her own. 'It's time we got back to work.' He stubbed his cigarette out. 'You haven't griped about your youngest sister yet. What is she up to? Is the aristocratic boyfriend who cannot be named still on the scene?'

'Yes. In spirit if not in actual fact.'

He began painting again, saying drily, 'He's dead, then?'

Laughter fizzed in her throat. 'No. He's at sea.'

'Ah!' Strickland's hooded eyes lit with fierce satisfaction. 'Then I know who he is!'

'You can't do!' Marigold tried to sound calm, but doing so wasn't easy.

Strickland was on gossiping terms with everyone who was anyone in London. If he let the cat out of the bag none of her sisters would ever forgive her.

'But I do. It was obvious right from the first that you wouldn't be fighting shy of scandal in order not to lose a mere marquess or an earl as a prospective brother-in-law. Knowing you as I do, I don't think you'd even be fussed at losing a duke. So your insistence on remaining scandal-free until your sister has been walked down the aisle can only be because she has snared a prince, and when it comes to a prince of the right age – especially one who is at present at sea – only one fits the bill.'

Marigold wasn't given to panicking, but she was on the verge of doing so now. What was going to happen at the next dinner party Strickland was invited to and at which the Prime Minister or the Foreign Secretary was present?

Would he be able to resist becoming the centre of attention by revealing the riveting information that the Prince of Wales was in love with – and wanted to marry – Miss Lily Houghton? It was a secret so explosive she doubted if anyone would be able to keep it, unless they had a vested interest in doing so.

Queasily she said, 'Well, as you know his identity, you can well understand why it needs to be kept secret until there is a public announcement.'

Strickland stopped painting, his interest intense. 'So how near is that to happening? Has royal permission been given?'

'Not exactly.' There were times when Marigold was astonished at how truthful she could be. 'But King George does know they want to marry.'

'I wouldn't have thought it was too much of a problem. I think royals having to have the King's consent to marry is carried a bit far at times. If Prince George of Battenberg wants to marry Lily, the only consent needed should be that of her legal guardian. Which is probably your mother, though it may well be your grandfather. I'm not *au fait* with guardianship legalities.'

'Prince George of Battenberg?' Marigold was so stunned – and relieved – by the realization that Strickland hadn't been talking of David she nearly betrayed the fact by the tone of her voice.

His eyes sharpened and she said swiftly, 'How bright of you to have guessed so correctly.'

He lit another cigarette, plastering it to his lower lip. 'You gave it away when you said he was at sea. Prince George is in the navy – not surprising when you consider that his father is a vice-admiral and Commander-in-Chief of the Atlantic Fleet. Which is an odd thing for a German to be,' he added, 'even though he is related to the King.'

Marigold wasn't interested in royal genealogy. Her relief

that Strickland had got things so wonderfully wrong was too vast.

'Where are you spending the weekend?' he asked, suddenly changing the subject. 'Are you going down to Snowberry?'

'To be bored to death by talk of Iris's wedding? No, thank you. Maxim has been invited to Marchemont. A Romanov aunt of his has taken it for the summer and he's wangled me an invite.'

Strickland began painting once again. 'You Houghton girls do have a lot of leeway, don't you? I don't know of any other single girl of your age and class who could go haring off to a house party in Dorset given by someone unknown to her family. I'm painting a portrait of Lady Diana Manners at the moment and she complains bitterly that she can't even have a meal out with an admirer without having a married couple accompanying them as chaperones.'

'We have leeway because our father is dead, our mother lives in France and our grandfather is blissfully unaware that the freedom he gives us is anything out of the ordinary.'

Strickland chuckled. 'It's out of the ordinary enough for your baby sister to be unofficially betrothed to a prince; for your eldest sister to be in paid employment by a national newspaper, wandering around such places as the East End and docklands; and for you to be spending a house-party weekend with a Russian lover. It seems to me the only one of you four girls doing things by the book is Iris.'

'Iris always has done things by the book. She's very pleasant and very dull. And Prince Maxim Yurenev is not my lover. Though he may well be so after this weekend.'

Marigold had never understood the fuss that was made about losing virginity before marriage. To her, virginity had always seemed an unnecessary encumbrance and she had been ecstatically happy when Theo had relieved her of it.

The problem, now she knew how delicious lovemaking

269

was, was that not making love was extremely tedious, especially when she had an admirer as ardent as Maxim. And she wouldn't be risking scandal by going to bed with Maxim. He was a Russian royal prince. He wouldn't tell. In which case, all that would happen was that her reputation would remain exactly as it had been ever since her debutante year. She would be regarded as being 'fast' and 'not quite the thing', but nothing worse. It was a conclusion that could lead to only one decision.

Two days later, as she packed her weekend case, her excitement was at fever pitch.

Marchemont was more a faux French chateau than an English country house. Against a wooded hillside fairy-tale turrets and steeples pierced the skyline. The vast parkland ran down to the sea and nearer to the house, on terraces and amid flower-filled parterres, peacocks strolled and white doves fluttered.

Her hostess, Princess Zasulich, wizened and weighed down by twelve ropes of perfectly matched pearls reaching down to her knees, greeted her warmly without having the slightest idea as to whom she was, apart from the fact that her favourite nephew had wished her to be invited. As she continued greeting some of her other thirty guests it was her private opinion that Maxim's bohemian-looking *chère amie* was probably an actress. She didn't mind. The girl would add a little spice to the weekend. And in Princess Zasulich's opinion, a little spice was always welcome.

Though it was customary for the bedroom of a married lady, if unaccompanied by her husband, to be sited conveniently close to the bedroom of her lover, such considerations were never shown to single young women of class. Actresses, however, were a different matter, and as Princess Zasulich was convinced Marigold was a member of the *demi-monde*, Marigold was delighted to discover that Maxim would have very little distance to cover when he left his room for hers.

Until he did so, there was an afternoon and an evening to be got through and she knew none of the other guests, all of whom were either Russian or French. Maxim, a regular guest at Marchemont, offered to walk her around the grounds.

'If we were in Russia, we wouldn't consider Marchemont's parkland very large,' he said as they unobtrusively slid away from a game of croquet that was engaging everyone else's attention. 'But everything is vaster in Russia. The parkland at Verechenko, my family's country home on the edge of the Black Sea, is as large as an English county.'

'Is Verechenko as superbly landscaped as Marchemont?' she asked, her hand tucked intimately in the crook of his arm as they walked so close together their hips almost touched.

'There are lakes, grottoes, fountains, panoramas. Perhaps one day you will see it for yourself.'

Marigold made no response. Maxim in London – or in Paris, Berlin or even St Petersburg – was one thing. Maxim on the shores of the Black Sea – somewhere so distant she wasn't even sure where it was – was entirely another.

A little later, as they wandered through Marchemont's magnificent orangery with small, brilliantly coloured tropical birds flying above their heads, he again began rhapsodizing about Verechenko. She wondered if he was doing so because he had an ulterior motive; if he wanted to gauge her reactions to his descriptions of Verechenko because he was considering proposing to her and because, if she accepted him, he intended Verechenko to be their principal home.

Mentally, she tried out what it would be like to be addressed as Princess Marigold. It sent a thrill through her so urgent she didn't see how she would be able to refuse him. To be known as Princess Marigold in London society would be wonderful. She wondered if people would curtsey to her.

Then she thought of having to leave England for Russia. From all she'd heard about Russia, that wasn't an enticing prospect. Also, though Maxim could give her a title and a magnificently wealthy lifestyle, he didn't have the added frisson of being politically powerful – and that frisson was one that meant an awful lot to her.

She thought of Theo and dug her nails into her palms.

At her Great-aunt Sibyl's dinner table, influential people such as Lord Lansdowne had spoken quite openly of Theo one day becoming prime minister. No Russian prince was likely to become the Russian prime minister. Even if such a thing were to happen, the real power would always be in the hands of the Tsar who ruled as an autocrat. In Britain it was different. Britain was a constitutional monarchy and the prime minister held far more real power than did the king.

The thought of never again sitting in on the kind of political conversations she so frequently witnessed at her great-aunt's, together with the thought of living thousands of miles away on the shores of the Black Sea, made the prospect of becoming Princess Marigold a tad less appealing.

Maxim as a prospective lover was, though, very appealing.

She came to a halt beneath an orange tree. 'I'm not in a hurry to return to the croquet match,' she said huskily, turning to face him.

Her mouth was ripe, her lips parted, her invitation blatant.

An expression flashed through his eyes that she couldn't read, to be followed by one she read very clearly.

'Neither', he said in a low taut voice as he pressed her back against the tree, 'am I.'

His mouth came down swift and hard on hers. His knee pressed against the silk of her skirt, forcing its way between her legs and his hand cupped her breast, his thumb moving over the thin material covering her hard, erect nipple.

It was as if a mask, there because polite society required

272

it to be there, had slipped and something very primitive – something very Russian – had been unleashed.

It wasn't the kind of lovemaking she had experienced with Theo, who had always been tender and considerate, but as every nerve-ending she possessed screamed out for him to finish what he had begun, Marigold knew it was the kind of lovemaking she was more than ready for.

# TWENTY-FIVE

It was the second week of September and Lily was in her habitual place of retreat: her studio. Her bust of David stood on a black-slate plinth beneath the huge skylight and her eyes turned to it frequently as she began work on a new sculpture: a tern in flight.

David hadn't yet seen her finished bust of him and she wasn't sure how he would feel about it when he did, for the mood she had struggled hard to convey was one of boyish wistfulness: the *Weltschmerz* in his eyes that both Rose and her grandfather had been so aware of when first meeting him.

It was an expression that was now only seen when he was leaving Snowberry – and not always then, for when he took his leave he did so in the certainty of returning. She knew, though, that his underlying wistfulness at never being treated the same as other young men – at always having homage paid to him – would never leave him; that it had become an intrinsic part of his personality.

She was still at an early stage with her tern-in-flight sculpture and because she was finding it impossible to block David from her thoughts, it wasn't going well. Fretfully she laid down the tool she was working with.

For David, once it was publicly acknowledged that they were a couple, life would be easier. The things he found intolerable in royal life would no longer be intolerable to him when he had her by his side. For her, though, life wouldn't be easier at all. Instead it would become difficult on a scale impossible to even imagine.

For a start, all privacy would be gone. Like David, she, too, would be on constant, life-long public display. The prospect filled her with a horror so deep she felt physically sick. David had told her that his mother was seldom without a lady-in-waiting in attendance on her. Would she be expected to have a lady-in-waiting? If she did, how would she suffer someone's constant company, unless the someone in question was one of her sisters?

She picked up a damp towel from her work-top and wiped clay-sticky hands on it. Even for love of her sister, Rose would never give up her suffragette activities and her exciting burgeoning journalistic career in order to be a lady-in-waiting. Court life would hold no charms for Rose at all.

Marigold would adore the glamour of being a lady-in-waiting, but when the initial novelty wore off she would resent the fact that she wasn't the centre of attention. Playing second fiddle to anyone, and especially to her baby sister, simply wasn't in her nature. There was also the troubling question of Marigold's naughtiness with men. How could she hope to have a moment's peace of mind if she was constantly worrying about whether Marigold was behaving herself or not?

The sister most suitable for court life was Iris, who was always dignified and who never, under any circumstances, behaved badly. Iris, however, was marrying Toby at Christmas and she didn't think he would be pleased at the prospect of Iris regularly disappearing for three-month stints as a lady-in-waiting.

Homer, who had been lying at her feet as she worked, sensed her inner turmoil and hauled himself to a stand in order to offer what comfort he could. She stroked his silky head. Not in any way at all was she looking forward to the kind of future that would come with marriage to David, but loving him as she did, neither could she bear the thought of his lonely misery if she wasn't with him.

She spoke her thoughts out loud to Homer. 'To be able to survive his royal burden, he needs to be able to share it,' she said to him. 'And so if King George consents to our becoming betrothed, my future will be just as mapped out as David's future is.'

Homer licked her hand encouragingly. As no one else seemed to understand, it was encouragement she was grateful for. Rose hadn't actually *said* she disapproved, but Lily sensed she was appalled at the thought of becoming so closely connected to royalty and was fervently hoping that the King would withhold his consent and that no official announcement of an engagement would ever take place. If it did take place she was certain Rose would think her entirely unprepared for the catastrophic changes that would follow.

Marigold, of course, was feverishly hoping that King George *would* give his blessing and that an announcement would be made as soon as possible, but she knew it hadn't even crossed Marigold's mind to sympathize with her over the loss of freedom that would then follow. All Marigold would ever see was the glitter that came with the title Princess of Wales. The burdens that also came with that title would completely pass her by.

Iris only saw that if King George gave his assent she and David would be able to marry and be together for the rest of their lives. The idea that she was going to find it crucifyingly difficult to live in the public eye was not something that had yet occurred to her favourite sister.

276

There came the sound of the speaking tube being cleared and then Millie shouted into it: 'I've just baked a Victoria sponge cake, Lily. Would you like me to bring a slice up to you, along with a cup of tea?'

'That would be smashing, Millie,' she shouted back down in response. 'Homer is with me, so will you cut a slice for him, too?'

Millie gave an ungracious reply and, despite all her anxieties, Lily's generous mouth curved in a smile. Millie didn't as yet know of David's marriage proposal and when the time came to tell her of it, Lily was fiercely hoping Millie's free and easy attitude would remain unchanged. The prospect of Millie bobbing a curtsey to her was simply too bizarre.

The skylights reached down to the floor and she walked over to the window-seat fronting one of them, sitting down on it with her arms circling her knees. Homer, who always sat wherever he wanted, eased himself up on the padded seat and lay facing her, his big brown eyes intently holding hers.

'If David were a younger brother my life would still change but not so catastrophically,' she said to him, her lovely face grave. 'It is the fact that one day he will become king that brings all the problems. Yet David doesn't want to be king any more than I want to be a queen. He says his sister Mary is the one who should be inheriting the throne. He says that Mary is far cleverer than him – and far cleverer than any of his brothers.'

Homer made a noise she took as indicating sympathy and then Millie entered the studio carrying a tea tray.

'There's some post as well,' she said, nudging the tray on to Lily's cluttered work bench. She handed over a distinctive cream envelope embossed with the Prince of Wales's cipher. 'It's from Prince Edward,' she said unnecessarily. 'That's the second letter this week.'

'That's because the *Hindustan* is in port at the moment.'

'How long will it be until he's visiting Snowberry again?'

'Not until the end of October, when his tour of duty is over.'

'Well, it will be nice to see him again.' Millie spoke as if she was speaking of Rory and Lily felt a stab of amusement at how unnecessary her worry had been that Millie's attitude might change if she became a royal.

When Millie had left the studio and while Homer was demolishing a very generous slice of cake, Lily opened David's letter.

My own beloved Angel,

We are now in Portsmouth and will soon be en route for Torbay. After that we'll be heading for Scotland and then to Queenstown, Ireland. After about a month, it will be back to Portland for the final few weeks. I can't tell you how much I'm counting the days away, knowing that every day I cross off my calendar is a day nearer to being with my darling girl again. I so miss our talks together; being able to tell you anything and everything and the way you always make me feel as if nothing – not even being Prince of Wales – is too difficult. You make me happier than I've been in my whole life until now. I love you with all my heart, darling Lily. All I want to do is to be the kind of prince – and when I'm king, the kind of king – that you want me to be. I want you to be proud of me, dearest sweetheart, and I will do anything and everything to make sure that you are.

You'll be happy to know that the Captain is working me really hard! I now keep watch both at sea and when we are in harbour. I've learned how to run a picket boat. I serve in a turret during battle practice and the Chief Yeoman is teaching me how to read flag signals. So you'll see that I have very little free time! I must finish quickly as the bell is signalling a change of watch. Millions and millions of thanks for everything, my angel.

Tons and tons of love, your D

She sat for a long time on the window-seat, her work forgotten, the letter in her hand. There was something ineffably boyish about his letters to her, a boyishness she was certain he would retain no matter how old he became. And his vulnerability – his need of her – shone through every line. Love for him flooded through her. Other people might let him down, but she would never do so. Never, ever. She would ensure he became the most popular Prince of Wales the country had ever known – and that one day he would become England's greatest king.

'And so I think I *would* like to be Princess Marigold Yurenev – but only as long as Maxim promises to spend at least six months of the year in England. I think that's a quite reasonable demand, don't you?'

Lily and Marigold were alone in the drawing room. Lily was stretched out on a sofa, a cushion behind her head, a book in her hands. Marigold was leaning against the mantelpiece, one foot balanced on the fender, the line of her thigh effortlessly provocative. As there wasn't a male within miles Lily felt the pose just went to show that Marigold was never *deliberately* sexually alluring. She just was, and that was all there was to it.

'I don't know, Marigold.' She put the book face down on her lap. 'It all depends on how much he loves Russia. What did he say about where you would live when he asked you to marry him?'

'He hasn't asked me yet – but he will. He's crazy for me. So crazy I can wind him round my little finger.'

She was smoking in a defensive, *noli me tangere* way, one arm held loosely against her waist and the other, the one with the hand holding the cigarette, slanted across her breast.

Lily regarded her thoughtfully. It wasn't like Marigold to be tense and she wondered what was troubling her.

'What's the matter, Marigold? If he loves you, and you love him, what is the problem?'

'There isn't any problem.' Marigold thought of the Persephone painting and her arm pressed a little harder against her waist. Maxim was a passionate Slav, not a buttoned-up Englishman. Even if the painting were to become public knowledge, it was something he would take in his stride.

Aware that Marigold was protesting just a little too much, Lily frowned, wondering if Marigold was as much in love as she wanted everyone to believe.

'I know that Prince Yurenev's family is fabulously wealthy,' she said, troubled, 'but that isn't why you are considering marrying him, is it?'

'Well, naturally it's one of the reasons! I would hardly be considering marrying him if he was an out-of-work docker, would I?' There were times when Marigold could hardly believe Lily's naivety. 'Don't come over all goody-goody on me, Lily. Not when you're living in the hope of marrying David who, as Prince of Wales, will be showering you with a king's ransom of jewels.'

Lily rarely lost her temper, but her eyes flashed fire. 'I'm not marrying David because of who he is, Marigold. Who he is, is a detriment, not an inducement! I'm certainly not marrying him in the hope of being drowned in jewels. I don't even *like* costly jewellery. I'm marrying him because he needs me and because I love him. I would still be in love with him if he was a . . . a . . .' She was about to say docker, but David didn't have the build of a docker. 'I would still love him if he was a gardener!'

Crossly aware that Lily was speaking the literal truth, Marigold moved away from the fireplace and ground out her cigarette in an onyx ashtray, saying, 'Whether you like expensive jewellery or not, you're going to have to get used to being draped in it.'

Next to the ashtray on the occasional table was a copy of *Tatler* and she slewed it around so that Lily could see the picture of Queen Mary on its front cover.

'*That* is how you will be expected to wear jewels, Lily. No matter what the occasion, day or evening, Queen Mary is always simply *drowned* in them!'

After Marigold had left the room, Lily walked across to the small table and looked down at the picture of Queen Mary. She was as festooned with jewels as a Christmas tree. A pearl and diamond tiara graced her wheat-coloured hair. Long diamond and ruby earrings fell from her ears. Around her neck were several ropes of waist-length pearls. A magnificent ruby and diamond brooch was pinned to her breast, as was the Garter and several other Stars and Orders. A cluster of diamond bracelets circled her wrists. She should have looked ridiculous; instead she looked breathtakingly majestic.

It was how a queen was expected to look. It was how, if she and David were given permission to marry, she would one day be expected to look.

The thought was daunting, so daunting she felt something close to despair.

Even though it was mid-September the heat that had blistered the country throughout the summer continued with temperatures far higher than normal. Reading *The Times* Court Circular page beneath the shade of Snowberry's cedar tree, Lily learned that King George, who had been grouse-shooting in Yorkshire on the estate of his friend, Lord Ripon, had now moved his shooting party across the

281

moors to the Duke of Devonshire's estate at Bolton Abbey; Queen Mary was in residence at Windsor; and the *Hindustan,* on which the Prince of Wales was currently serving, had left southern coastal waters for Scotland and the Firth of Forth.

Dearest, darling Angel,

We are just about to sail north to join the Home Fleet. Captain Campbell is continuing to work me very hard. I even help coal the ship, which is a filthy, back-breaking job. You wouldn't think I look forward to doing it, but I do, because it's the only duty on which I'm allowed to smoke! The general rule is that tobacco and alcohol are prohibited for midshipmen until they are eighteen – which is a pretty dud show, don't you think?

Though I'm enjoying being at sea, I'm missing you terribly, darling Lily, and can't wait for the end of October when my tour of duty will be over. Nearly every night I dream of Snowberry and all the good times I've had there and sometimes the temptation to jump ship and head straight for Hampshire is almost more than I can bear. It's only six weeks since we parted, but it seems years and years and there is still another six weeks to go before my tour of duty is over. When it is, there will only be a week, perhaps even less, before my parents leave for India and their great Coronation durbar in Delhi. (My father isn't actually going to be crowned again in Delhi, but he will receive the homage of Indian princes and rulers while seated upon a throne and wearing a new crown made especially for the occasion. His coronation crown, the Crown of State, isn't allowed to be taken out of the kingdom – not even by him!)

What all this means is that I'm going to have very little time in which to speak to him again about wanting to become officially betrothed to you. I'm not sure, but I don't think he believed I was serious when I asked him for his consent the first time. I'm hoping the twelve-weeks gap will have allowed him to get used to the idea and that when I speak to him again he will be more prepared to listen to me and that he will understand what a splendid thing our getting married will be.

I promise you, darling Lily, that it won't be long before our betrothal will be made public and when it is I will be the happiest man in the whole wide world. I'm counting off the days until I see you again.

Tons and tons of love,

your very own, very loving, D

'Will David be accompanying the King and Queen when they go to India for their durbar?' Rose asked Lily a few days later when on one of her fleeting visits to Snowberry from London.

'No. I'm not sure where he will be, but wherever it is, Windsor, or Buckingham Palace or perhaps even Sandringham, he'll be working hard preparing for his entrance exam to Oxford.'

They were in the studio and Rose regarded the clay sculpture of David's head thoughtfully. 'Even though he doesn't want to go there?'

'Even though he doesn't want to go there.'

Turning away from the sculpture, Rose looked towards her. 'And when is it he goes to France?'

Lily, who was still dissatisfied with her tern-in-flight sculpture, took fresh clay from her clay bin. 'I'm not sure of the exact date,' she said, spraying the clay with water, 'but the King and Queen return from India on the fifth of February, and he's to go almost immediately afterwards.'

'And while he is there, you are going to be there also – staying with Mama?'

Lily nodded, trying – and failing – to concentrate on what she was doing.

Rose pursed her lips and, sensing how strong Rose's disapproval was of what she and David intended, Lily put the clay back in the bin.

'This is perhaps the only time we'll *ever* be able to spend time together as an ordinary couple in love,' she said defensively. 'It is King George's wish that David travels to France incognito as the Earl of Chester and he'll be staying in a private home. It is a circumstance that is never likely to happen again. It's a heaven-sent chance for us to be together and one we can't possibly not take advantage of. Surely you can see that, Rose?'

Her eyes pleaded for Rose to be understanding – and Rose *did* understand. She was also extremely worried. David had already spoken to the King about his wish to marry Lily, and though neither she, nor, she suspected, Lily, knew exactly what the King's response had been, they did know he hadn't given his royal consent to the marriage. The outcome hadn't come as a surprise to anyone apart from Lily and David who, it seemed, were still behaving as if it was only a matter of time before King George changed his mind and a public announcement was made. Their distress when they were forced to face reality was, Rose knew, going to be colossal.

Concern for Lily's future happiness wasn't Rose's only concern. She was now spending far more time in London than she was at Snowberry. At first this had been because of her renewed commitment to her suffragette activities. David's proposal to Lily had meant these had been curtailed to behind-the-scenes activities to avoid the risk of arrest and notoriety, but they still took up a good deal of her time and now, as well as doing everything she could to further the work of the WSPU at 4 Clement's Inn, she was also writing regularly for the *Daily Despatch*.

It was a way of life she was revelling in, but she was only able to enjoy it because Iris had taken over all her responsibilities at Snowberry, which was something she had long wanted Iris to do. What was concerning her was that since Iris's engagement to Toby, it was Toby who seemed to be taking over the running of Snowberry. It was a situation her grandfather was very happy with, but Rose knew it had only come about because she had begun spending so much time in London – and for that, she couldn't help feeling a certain amount of guilt.

She was also concerned about Marigold, who, having decided she could overlook the inconvenience of spending part of every year in Russia, was behaving as if Prince Maxim Yurenev had already proposed.

'Let's hope he does so soon,' Rory had said to Rose the last time he had visited St James's Street, 'because gossip is that Marigold's relationship with Maxim has become red-hot.'

She'd blanched, knowing the term 'red-hot' meant Marigold's virginity was in question.

'But how', she'd asked unsteadily, 'would anyone know how intimate their relationship has become? Has Maxim been talking?'

'Not to me,' Rory had said grimly. 'But you need to tell her to cool things down, Rose. Remind her that virginity matters and that as yet she isn't even wearing an engagement ring.'

It was a conversation Rose still had to have with Marigold and, as Marigold was failing in her promise to remain scandal-free, it was a conversation she wasn't looking forward to.

She said now to Lily, 'Even though the King refused to give his consent to a marriage between yourself and David, I would

285

have thought that now he knows how David feels about you, our entire family would have come under close palace scrutiny. And we haven't. According to Iris, Grandfather has received no telephone calls from the King's private secretary, and neither have there been any letters.'

Lily fiddled with the tern's wire armature. 'That's because King George doesn't yet know my identity. He questioned Piers, of course, as to who it was David was in love with, but Piers said he didn't know and was unaware of David having formed a romantic relationship. If he'd admitted he knew of it he'd have lost his position as David's equerry. David says it is best his father doesn't know who I am until he's agreed in principle to a well-born non-royal marrying the heir to the throne.'

Rose, who had believed David's conversation with his father had been far more explicit, stared at her, deeply shocked. 'But that doesn't sound as if King George is anywhere near to giving his consent! How can he be, if he doesn't even know who you are?'

She sat down suddenly on the window-seat as if the strength had gone from her legs. 'If David has indicated to you that his father is likely to agree to his marrying you, I think he's being very naive, Lily. I hate to say this to you, darling, but I don't think the King is ever going to come round to such an idea. Never, ever.'

# TWENTY-SIX

'Never!' King George stormed to his private secretary, Lord Craybourne. 'Never have I been faced with such impertinence! And from my own son! He's met a girl and wishes to make her Princess of Wales. I've never heard such poppycock!' Seizing hold of a book that was on his desk he threw it against the nearest wall with all his strength.

Lord Craybourne was long familiar with the King's violent outbursts and his vitriolic temper. This time, though, he had to admit that the King's rage was justified. His own rage, though he couldn't give vent to it, was nearly as intense.

Fifteen minutes earlier, at the King's request, he had come into the library to discuss with him the arrangements for his durbar. Instead of broaching the subject of the durbar the King had suddenly revealed that in the middle of July the Prince of Wales had proposed marriage to an unknown girl.

It was information so bizarre, so preposterous, that he was still having difficulty assimilating it. One thing he hadn't had any difficulty assimilating was that as it was now the last week in October, the incident had taken place three months ago. That he, the King's private secretary, was only now being put in the picture, he found almost too extraordinary to be believable.

'May I ask who else is privy to this information, sir?' he had asked, white-lipped.

'Esher,' the King had snapped in response.

Craybourne's bloodless lips had tightened. Though King George hadn't volunteered *when* he had confided in Lord Esher, he intuited it had been several weeks ago; that on hearing the news from Prince Edward, the King's immediate response had been to send for the man he regarded as his closest friend.

The fact that Esher, the Deputy Constable and Lieutenant-Governor of Windsor Castle, had been told when he, Craybourne, had not, was, in his eyes, disgraceful. As the King's private secretary, his role was that of the King's chief adviser. He was the channel of communication between the King and his Government. He briefed and advised the King on all constitutional, governmental and political matters. He, not Lord Esher, should have been the first person the King had confided in. But not only had the King *not* confided in him first; he hadn't even informed him until three months after the event in question!

'It seems incredible to me, sir, that Prince Edward could have met any young woman often enough to have formed a relationship of any kind,' he said, keeping his feelings in check only with the greatest difficulty. 'Surely his equerry—'

'Cullen knows nothing.' King George spat the words, his face a choleric purple. 'Absolutely nothing. He was aghast when I confronted him with what David had told me. According to David he was introduced to this ... this *strumpet* ... by Prince George of Battenberg.'

He strode up and down the room, slamming a fist repeatedly into his palm. 'Prince George admits introducing a female friend of his to David when on a visit to Dartmouth early this year. He says she was with a party of *her* friends – and that the girl David has become so obviously infatuated with must be one of them. *His* friend married a Canadian in August and has gone to live somewhere in Saskatchewan. He doesn't know where.'

'She must be traced. I'll speak with Canada's governor-general immediately.'

King George came to an abrupt halt in the centre of the room. 'Grey mustn't know why you're doing so. There mustn't be a whisper of this affair to anyone, Craybourne.'

'Of course not, sir. But the sooner we know the identity of the young woman in question, the sooner we can put an end to this situation.'

Though his face was impassive, his voice without an inflection of any kind, Craybourne was inwardly seething. Prince Edward had gone to the King to ask his permission to become betrothed and King George, instead of controlling himself until Edward had told him the young woman's name, had so violently lost his temper that David had prudently decided it was safer not to divulge it. And the farcical quagmire they were now in was the result.

Lord Grey, Canada's governor-general, would see to it that the information required was speedily with them, but because the King had chosen not to confide in him for so long, an unconscionable amount of time had been lost.

King George returned to his desk and abruptly sat down behind it. 'I want official negotiations immediately put in place for a marriage between David and the Grand Duchess Olga. I've already had the Tsar's unofficial written approval for such a union, but my cousin changes his mind according to whoever it was he last spoke to. Under the present circumstances, the sooner an official announcement can be made, the better.'

The possibility of a marriage that would link Britain more

closely with Russia had been discussed at length some months ago and had Craybourne's wholehearted approval. It would be taken as a personal affront by the Kaiser, who had a very marriageable nineteen-year-old daughter, but that was no bad thing. If anyone needed taking down a peg or two, it was Kaiser Wilhelm II.

'Now,' King George said, 'about my durbar and my state entry into Delhi. Why the devil am I to enter the city on a horse? Surely an elephant would be more appropriate? On ceremonial occasions Indian princes always ride on elephants. It's a centuries-old tradition and, as India's king-emperor, it is what will be expected of me.'

'I believe the decision was taken on the advice of the Viceroy, sir. It is Lord Hardinge's opinion that for reasons of safety and security horses are preferable to elephants.'

Aware that the King was about to robustly protest, he added, 'Elephants are notoriously unstable beasts, sir. Hardinge says one ran amok and rampaged through the crowd earlier this year in Rajputana. The death toll was eighty-nine.'

Whatever protest King George had been about to make remained unsaid.

'Who will be riding on either side of me as I make my state entry into the city? The Viceroy and India's Secretary of State?'

'Yes, sir.

The King gave one of his habitual 'harrumphs'. Where his durbar was concerned, he had little to worry about. Though arrangements had had to be made on a mind-bogglingly vast scale, they were all in place. It wasn't the durbar that was ruining his peace of mind. It was his eldest son.

When his business with Lord Craybourne was finished and he was again on his own, he remained at his desk, his hands clasped tightly together, his brow furrowed, his lips pursed. All his children had always been somewhat of a mystery to him, but David had now become incomprehensible.

Even if, on an afternoon of free time at naval college, he'd met up with Georgie Battenberg and then been introduced by Georgie to several young women, how had he managed to form a relationship with one of them? The aspect of the situation that so puzzled Craybourne also mystified him.

Though David had obviously managed to give Captain Cullen the slip when he'd gone to meet Georgie, he couldn't possibly have given him the slip on a regular basis. He had no doubts at all that Cullen had been entirely ignorant of the meeting. The man's bewilderment when he'd been told of it had been so profound it couldn't possibly have been simulated.

The devil of it was that he'd never expected David to act in such a monstrous way, not when he'd been made aware of his unique position in life ever since nursery days and when the concepts of duty and responsibility had, ever since, been ceaselessly drummed into him. George's grandmother, Queen Victoria, had terrified his father, Edward VII, and his father had, in his turn, terrified him. It was a legacy King George felt was only right and proper when the parent in question was the sovereign, and he had always rigorously ensured it had been maintained. Or he thought he had. Now, having been confronted in such a way by David, he wasn't at all sure that he'd terrified David enough.

He pushed his chair away from his massive desk and rose to his feet. Even as a child there had been a perversity about David that his younger brothers and his sister hadn't possessed.

Brooding on David's disturbing difference he crossed to the cabinet where his Purdey shotguns were kept. Removing one of them he took it back to the desk with him and withdrew his gun-cleaning kit from one of the desk's deep lower drawers. Cleaning his guns always soothed him, though he doubted it would have the power to do so this time.

Kings of England were notorious for having bad relations with their eldest sons; it was for very good reason that George III couldn't bear to have his son, the future George IV, within his sight. It wasn't a situation he had ever imagined happening to himself, but David was already becoming an irritation in a way that he doubted the far more tractable Bertie ever would be.

He began disassembling the gun. Bertie, for instance, would never describe any ceremonial clothes he was required to wear as 'a ridiculous outfit', which was how David had referred to his investiture costume. Also if Bertie were heir to the throne he would never immediately change the subject whenever the words 'when you become king' were mentioned to him, as David so infuriatingly did.

He rammed a cleaning rod down the gun's barrel. Just as English history was full of kings who had deplorable relationships with their eldest sons, so too it was full of instances where the second son, not the first, had eventually inherited the throne.

Henry VIII, one of the most well known of English kings (though not the best loved) only succeeded to the throne after his elder brother, Arthur, had died suddenly of an undefined illness at the age of fifteen. A hundred years or so later, Charles Stuart inherited the throne, becoming Charles I, when his elder brother, another Henry, died of typhoid. Far closer to home, he himself was a second son, only becoming heir to the throne when his beloved elder brother, Eddy, had died of influenza aged twenty-eight.

He picked up a cleaning cloth, reflecting on how different English history would have been if Arthur Tudor and Henry Stuart had lived, and how different his own life would have been if Eddy had not died. He wasn't remotely imaginative, but May had been betrothed to Eddy at the time of Eddy's death and the thought of May being a sister-in-law to him, not a wife, made the hair at the back of his neck stand on end.

He began polishing the inside of the Purdey's choke. Such reflections on what-ifs where second sons were concerned were nonsensical. It wasn't a situation that was going to afflict David and Bertie. However more tractable Bertie might be, he didn't have the makings of a king. His stammer saw to that.

A spasm of temper flooded through him. Why Bertie persisted in stammering when he knew how intensely annoying everyone found it, he couldn't understand. It wasn't as if Bertie hadn't been taken to task about it. '*Spit it out, boy!*' he roared at him every time Bertie spent five minutes trying to say something that should have taken only seconds. No matter how much he bellowed, it never made any difference. Bertie only stammered worse than ever.

And David, as well as having an admirable speaking voice – even Winston Churchill, famous for his oratory, had commented on how well he had spoken at his investiture – also had great appeal.

Appeal some unknown girl had immediately latched on to.

He flung down the cleaning cloth in exasperation. If David's escapade with the friend of one of Georgie Battenberg's friends was anything to go by, the sooner he was safely betrothed and married, the better. He only hoped Nicky wasn't going to shilly-shally over a public announcement of David and Olga's betrothal. Nicky was a terrible vacillator and when push came to shove, he wouldn't want one of his dearly loved daughters leaving Russia, no matter that she'd be leaving it to become Princess of Wales and the future Queen of England.

As for David . . . David was going to have a very big surprise if he thought he was going to return from his tour of duty aboard the *Hindustan* and immediately speak to him yet again about this damned girl he wished to marry. The less that was said between them, the better it would be. In five days he and May were to leave for India aboard the *Medina*, the latest addition to the P & O fleet and a vessel blessed with a suitably Eastern-sounding name. In those intervening five days he would refuse to see and to speak with David. And by the time he and May returned from India the girl in question would have been located and bought off and David would, if he knew what was good for him, have forgotten all about her.

# TWENTY-SEVEN

Theo Jethney was a man with a great deal of care on his shoulders, for Jerusha was not well. Always very slender, she had now become rake-thin. The headaches that had plagued her for well over a year were increasing in both number and severity and none of the doctors he had taken her to had been able to put an end to them. All of them, from their family doctor to the consultant he had taken her to in Harley Street, had said the same thing. Jerusha's problem was her age. Though she was a little young to be so, at forty-five she was already menopausal. Headaches often afflicted women during the menopause. When her hot flushes began – as they were bound to do at any time – the headaches would cease.

Although he was able to express his anxieties about Jerusha's health to friends in a general way, he had no one he could discuss the specifics of it with. He could hardly discuss Jerusha's early menopause with the Prime Minister, the Home Secretary, or any other of his male friends. Herbert, for instance, would be completely at a loss, and embarrassed. What he needed was a close female relative and he didn't have one.

What he could do, he did. No matter how heavy his governmental workload, he ceased the habit of staying the night in town. However late the House sat, he always returned to his Hampshire estate, giving Jerusha the comfort of his presence every single moment he possibly could.

His guilt at having been so obsessed with Marigold was total. It wasn't that his feelings towards her had changed. His feelings for her were something completely beyond his control and he was certain that they would never diminish. What had altered, though, was that she was now no longer uppermost in his thoughts. His thoughts were all of Jerusha. He couldn't bear seeing her lying in their darkened bedroom, a cold compress against her eyes as she bravely rode out yet another bout of crippling pain.

The only time he now ventured out into society – and he only did so when Jerusha was deep in an exhausted sleep – was when he visited Herbert at Snowberry. With Marigold as permanently at Sibyl's as Rose was, it was something he could do with his old ease.

There wasn't quite the same old ease about Snowberry, though. There was something in the atmosphere that he couldn't quite put his finger on: a kind of suppressed tension. As it was tension Marigold wasn't there to cause, he could only imagine that Iris's forthcoming wedding to Toby Mulholland was responsible for it.

Iris was certainly a young woman transformed by love. Always the plain Jane of the family, radiant happiness ensured she was a plain Jane no more.

'I've never been so happy in all my life,' she had confided to him on one of his visits, 'and a Christmas wedding is going to be perfect. Wouldn't it be wonderful if it snowed?'

Herbert, too, was deeply happy at the prospect of Iris marrying Toby. 'I was at the boy's christening,' he'd said to Theo as they sat companionably together in the drawing room, brandies to hand. 'He's been in and out of Snowberry ever since he could walk.'

'Do you intend that he should run the estate?' he'd asked, knowing how much his aged friend had previously relied first on Rose, and then on Iris, to do so.

Herbert had chuckled. 'That's the best part of having him as a grandson-in-law. He's been raised to run Sissbury and so managing Snowberry will be no problem for him. At one point the Snowberry estate runs side by side with Sissbury's.'

That was convenient, Theo had to admit. And not just for Herbert.

Not liking the way his thoughts were going, he had changed the subject, asking after Rose and then, because it would have seemed extremely odd not to have done so, asking after Marigold as well.

'Rose is now a very independent modern young woman,' Herbert had said with pride. 'Your friend Mr Green thinks very highly of her. She writes regularly on suffragette issues, has also reported on the investiture and other important events and, this week, her subject was the effect the new National Insurance Bill will have on domestic servants.'

'So it was Rose who was responsible for that piece, was it? There was no byline.' It had intrigued him that there hadn't been. 'Why was that?' he'd asked, surprised that Hal wasn't making capital out of publishing straight news items written by a woman.

Herbert's response had begun happily enough, but then tailed off into confusion. 'Oh,' he'd said, 'it was thought best Rose didn't bring attention to herself. Not at the moment. Not when Lily and—'

He'd broken off so suddenly that for a second Theo thought he'd been taken ill.

'Not when Lily has not yet been presented and when having a sister doing something so scandalous as writing for

297

a national newspaper might rebound on her,' he had finished, flustered.

As Lily couldn't now be presented at court until next summer, and as she probably wasn't fussed about being presented at all – it was reasoning that had bewildered Theo. He had, however, put Herbert's odd reply down to the fact that he was growing increasingly vague and confused – which was the main reason Toby would be managing the estate for him – and that it wasn't the first time he'd lost track mid-sentence.

Making a quick recovery, Herbert had changed the subject. 'As for Marigold,' he'd said, swirling the brandy around in his glass, 'it would seem she is on the verge of becoming a princess. Prince Maxim Yurenev has been her constant escort for some time now and I believe a spring wedding is in the offing. It's a match that will please her mother – he's one of the richest young men in Russia – and that sort of thing matters to her. It will mean Marigold living for much of the year in St Petersburg and the Crimea, though, and I don't like the prospect of that. The dear girl never fails to keep me entertained. Did you know she was learning Italian?'

Theo hadn't known and he thought it rather unlikely. If Marigold was in the process of learning a foreign language, surely the language she would be learning was Russian?

He didn't have to wonder how he felt about the prospect of her marrying Prince Yurenev. He knew how he felt. He felt a sense of inappropriate, colossal loss. To get married at the earliest opportunity was, though, what he had advised her to do. And she would be deliriously happy at becoming a princess. All in all, it was the very best thing that could happen, for without a shadow of a doubt he knew he would never again play a romantic part in her life, or anyone else's.

Jerusha's ill health had shown him very clearly how much

she meant to him, and where his loyalties lay. He would never be unfaithful to her again. The thought of causing her more pain than the agony she was already suffering was unthinkable.

Lily liked the fact that after a long period of absence from Snowberry, Lord Jethney was again a frequent visitor. In the first week of December he arrived when there was no one at home but herself. She had been working on her tern-in-flight sculpture when William had called up through the speaking tube that Lord Jethney was in the drawing room.

'No one else is here, I'm afraid,' she'd said minutes later, hurrying into the drawing room still wearing her working smock. 'Grandpapa is in Winchester for the day and Iris is in London for the final fitting of her wedding gown.'

'Ah, yes.' He was dressed at ease in a tweed suit and a soft-collared shirt. 'Only another five days until the big day.' He smiled at her fondly. 'Jerusha and I are looking forward to it immensely.' Eyeing her clay-spattered smock he said apologetically, 'You're working and I've interrupted you. I'm sorry.'

'I was ready to be interrupted.' Her coal-black hair was swept into a loose knot on the top of her head and she brushed a straying corkscrew curl behind her ear. 'I'm working on a new sculpture, a tern in flight, and try as I may I can't get any sense of movement into it.'

'You're probably being too hard on yourself.'

She grinned ruefully, her cheeks dimpling. 'I don't think so. You should see it. It's the most leaden object you could possibly imagine.'

'I'd like to see it. May I?'

She hadn't meant to be taken quite so literally, but it would be embarrassing to retract the invitation and he was, after all, almost a member of the family.

It was only as they walked into her studio that she realized he would see far more than the tern: he would also see her finished bust of David. The thought came too late for her to change her mind. He was already walking over to the work so obviously in hand.

He stood silently in front of it for a few minutes. Lily may have thought her work leaden, but that wasn't the description he would have given it. Though far from finished the tern already soared, with only a slender curving rod holding it fast to a base of simulated rock that would eventually, like the tern, be cast in bronze. He remembered that she was hoping to become a pupil at the Royal College of Art and hadn't the slightest doubt that when she applied she would be immediately accepted.

'What is going to be of the most importance to you next year, Lily?' he asked. 'Becoming a pupil at the Royal College of Art or being presented at court and enjoying the season?'

To his astonishment her eyes took on an expression that was almost sombre. 'I won't be applying to the Royal College,' she said, her eyes on the tern and not on him. 'Though I shall, I think, be being presented.'

There was something in her voice that told him the subject was one she didn't want to discuss and, being a sensitive man, he didn't pursue it. He was imbued once again with the sense of secrets being kept at Snowberry, secrets even Herbert wasn't disclosing.

'If you should ever want a buyer for this sculpture,' he said, deeply sincere, 'you needn't look any further, Lily.'

She blushed rosily, immensely pleased at how much he liked it.

Theo stepped back from the tern and looked around him. At what he saw, he went rigid. 'Dear God!' he said when he had recovered his breath. 'When did you do this, Lily? It's stunning! It's absolutely magnificent!'

The bust had been cast in bronze by a local blacksmith

and Theo's immediate opinion was that it should be on exhibition at the Royal Academy.

'It's the Prince of Wales, isn't it?' The question was entirely unnecessary for Lily had caught Prince Edward's very essence. But how, without him having sat for her, had she done so? Until his investiture at Caernarvon the Prince had been deemed too young to play a public role and so there had been barely any photographs of him in the press. That had all changed at his investiture, of course. Every newspaper in the land had then carried reams and reams of photographs of him and, in all of them, in his spectacular robes and with a coronet on his pale gold hair, he had looked the very incarnation of a fairy-tale prince.

But the bust Lily had sculpted wasn't of a fairy-tale prince. Nothing about it signified his rank. It was, though, Edward to the life – and not what was fast becoming his public image, but the young man behind that image. The young man of whom Theo had been privileged to catch only a glimpse on a few fleeting occasions. That Lily had achieved such a likeness without having seen the Prince in the flesh astounded him.

He was still trying to get over it when there came the sound of the speaking tube being cleared and William shouted into it, 'Master Rory has arrived, Miss Lily. He's in the drawing room.'

Relieved at the interruption, and hoping that now she wouldn't have to answer any questions about her bust of David, Lily took off her smock and threw it over the back of a paint-marked chair.

'Now he's sitting his Foreign Office exams Rory is always visiting,' she said, making for the door. 'He'll be glad you are here. He always asks after you.'

What Theo Jethney's reply was she didn't know, for as they went down the stairs her thoughts were full of David.

The last few months of separation had been hard, and even though David had now finished his tour of duty aboard the *Hindustan*, they were still painfully apart because, before leaving for India, King George had decreed that the moment David stepped ashore he was to be accompanied to Sandringham where, for the duration of the winter, he was to study the subjects he would be taking at Oxford. David had written to her of his frustrations.

So as well as Captain Cullen, Mr Hansell, my old tutor, is here, keeping a steely eye on me. Just in case Cullen is questioned again, and just to be on the safe side, I no longer want him knowing when and how we see each other. That means the only way I can get to Snowberry to see you is if I do so without him. The only way I can do that is if I sneak out after everyone has gone to bed and if I get back in the morning before breakfast. But to be honest, my dearest darling, I don't think I can manage the distance from Norfolk to Hampshire and back in the time, although I am going to give it the best try I possibly can.

I love you to distraction, Lily darling, and miss you every single minute of every single day. Tons and tons of love and 'des milliers de baisers les plus tendres'!!!

Your ever-loving D

PS See, I am already brushing up my French ready for that wonderful day when we will be together in Paris!

Paris. Whenever she thought of the two of them being there together her heart sang for joy.

As they entered the drawing room, Rory, splendid in Highland dress, strode to meet them, his eyes lighting up with pleasure at the unexpected sight of Theo. They shook hands warmly and then Rory's eyes turned to Lily.

It was then that Theo received yet another shock in what was turning out to be a very surprising afternoon, for there was no mistaking the expression in Rory's eyes. He not only loved his cousin Lily but, whether he knew it or not, he was *in love* with her.

Theo wondered if the emotion was reciprocated. If it was, it was a future wedding that would please Herbert just as much as Iris and Toby's wedding was pleasing him. Although Rory and Lily's family relationship was close, it wasn't too close. English law permitted cousins to marry and Rory and Lily weren't first cousins, which might have caused a little comment, but second cousins.

He found himself hoping very much that there would be a happy outcome for the two of them and then he excused himself and headed out of the house to where his chauffeured Lanchester was waiting.

Seconds later he was heading back where he belonged. At Jerusha's side.

303

# TWENTY-EIGHT

A small village wedding would have made Iris just as happy as a smart London do, but she wasn't destined to have one. Thanks to her mother's and Toby's family's insistence, she had a glorious, over-the-top high-society wedding.

It took place, as did all grand weddings, at St Margaret's, Westminster. St Margaret's stood between Westminster Abbey and the Houses of Parliament, and all direct descendants of peers had the right to marry there. Both Iris's parents and Toby's parents had done so, as had a great number of their guests.

Though it was a Christmas wedding, the sky was a piercing clear blue, a perfect backdrop to the ancient white stone of the church's elegant Perpendicular Gothic façade.

Crowds of sightseers and well-wishers thronged the grassy square in front of the church, as guests continued to arrive. There was a murmur of recognition as Lord Jethney and his wife stepped down from their carriage, Lady Jethney heavily swathed in furs.

Next to arrive was the Prime Minister and his wife. Neither Iris nor Toby had ever met Mr Asquith, but his long-standing friendship with Iris's great-aunt had ensured his presence, which was adding immeasurably to the grandness of the occasion.

Great-aunt Sibyl had also insisted that several other notable Members of Parliament were invited to her great-niece's wedding and, with the exception of a minister who had already left for a long Christmas break in Switzerland, all had graciously accepted.

Winston Churchill and his wife Clementine were already seated inside the church, deep in happy memories of their own wedding which had taken place at St Margaret's three years earlier.

Despite it being mid-winter, the church was a bower of greenery. Red-berried sprays of holly twined around glistening white Portland stone pillars; hot-house Christmas roses scented the air; silver-ribboned poinsettias clustered at the foot of each and every ancient pew.

By the time Toby and his best man arrived the pews were full and stately organ music was playing. Toby looked remarkably relaxed. As he walked down the aisle he acknowledged several people with a slight inclination of his head and a swift confident smile.

Rory shot him a smile back. They'd never been close friends, but because of his close associations with Snowberry he, like Iris, had known Toby for ever and he couldn't have been happier that Toby and Iris were now marrying.

The atmosphere within the church became expectant as Iris's mother, the marquise de Villoutrey, arrived and, accompanied by her French husband, was led by the head usher to the front pew on the left side of the church. Moments later the groom's immediate family arrived and were conducted to the front pew on the right-hand side of the church, Viscount Mulholland cutting far less of a dash than his suave and handsome counterpart and Lady Mulholland, despite being clothed from head to foot by Lucile, looking positively dowdy

305

in comparison to the bride's mother, who, dark-haired and dark-eyed, was dazzling in sable and black pearls.

From outside the church came the sound of shouted good wishes and cheers. At the realization that his bride had arrived at the door of the church, Toby flexed his shoulders. The organist began to play the opening bars of the wedding march from *Lohengrin* and all heads turned in readiness to catch a first glimpse of the bride.

In the vestibule there was a flurry of last-minute activity. Iris's coronet of fresh orange blossom and her voluminous tulle veil – the veil her mother had worn when she had first married – was carefully adjusted. Her wedding gown of shimmering white satin fell into a long train behind her and Rose and Lily carefully spread it to its fullest so that it would follow Iris in a ripple of perfection as she walked down the aisle.

Marigold was attending to her own needs. The bridesmaids' wide-brimmed straw hats were violet, to complement the colour of their lilac satin dresses. Shallow-crowned, they were wreathed with white tuberoses and ivory camellias and Marigold tilted hers so that it dipped flatteringly low over her eyes.

'You look beautiful, tootsums,' Herbert said to Iris, so emotional at the prospect of giving her away there were tears in his eyes.

'You can't cry, Grandpapa,' Lily chided. 'Not in front of the Prime Minister.'

Rose, who was chief bridesmaid, handed Iris the small white-parchment prayer book she had chosen to carry instead of a bouquet. It was a gift that had been delivered to Snowberry a week earlier. Inside it was written: *To my dear friend, Iris, with deep affection, David.*

'Are you ready, sweetheart?' Rose asked.

Eyes glowing, face radiant, Iris slipped a hand through the crook of her grandfather's arm, and nodded.

With her sisters walking behind her and a gloriously robed St Margaret's clergy and choir processing in front of her, Iris stepped from the vestibule into the nave of the church and began walking down the aisle to where Toby was waiting for her.

Beautiful and historically ancient as St Margaret's was, Marigold couldn't help reflecting how much more magnificent and awe-inspiring a Russian Orthodox wedding in Kazan Cathedral in St Petersburg would be, especially as she would be able to count on having the Tsar and Tsarina in attendance.

As she walked down the aisle, hating the colour of her dress and looking forward to the moment when she would be able to change into something more flattering to a redhead, her eyes flicked along the packed pews, seeking for a glimpse of Maxim.

He was seated two rows further back than Great-aunt Sibyl, near enough to close members of the family for the deduction to be drawn that he would, very soon, be a part of it.

As her eyes lingered on the back of his head and his distinctively broad shoulders, she experienced a spiralling sense of sexual excitement.

A week ago, and after rapturous lovemaking when they were both guests at Marchemont, Maxim had stroked a finger down the naked length of her spine and said with post-coital reverence that he would give a fortune to have a painting of her looking as she did.

She had chuckled throatily and told him that if he really wanted that, she could make all his wishes come true.

The next day, when the two of them were back in London, she had taken him to Strickland's Chelsea studio and Strickland had unveiled his painting of her as Persephone.

Maxim's jaw had dropped.

Strickland hadn't blamed him.

For one thing it was a magnificent example of a romantic mythological subject: the kind of thing that had made the reputations of Sir Frederick Leighton and Dante Gabriel Rossetti. Unlike Sir Frederick he hadn't, however, depicted Persephone in Hades, or, like Rossetti, broodingly caressing the pomegranate that symbolized her captivity.

Apart from a storm cloud looming in an upper corner of the painting – a dark cloud in which Pluto could just be discerned in a chariot drawn by four jet-black horses – there was nothing dark or sinister about his depiction of the goddess.

Lying naked in a grassy meadow, as if blown lightly there by the wind, his Persephone was still joyously unaware of the fate about to befall her. Her chin rested on the back of her hand, her head at a pert angle; her warm wide mouth was curved in a beguiling smile; a careless torrent of Titian-red waves and curls was decorated with flowers; her legs were kicked up behind her in joyous abandon, the ankles crossed. As a painting in the Classical style it was imbued with gaiety and was lyrically lovely.

As a painting that could be recognized as a portrait of one of Lord May's granddaughters, it was also breathtakingly scandalous.

For a long moment Maxim had been too dumbstruck to speak and then, beneath his immaculately clipped moustache, a slow smile had split his face.

'It is magnificent,' he had said. 'Wonderful. On the walls of my palace in the Crimea are paintings by some of the most famous artists in history. A Rubens, a Botticelli, two Rembrandts – even a Caravaggio. Now they will be joined by something much more modern: a Strickland. And the Strickland will always mean much more to me – far more than I can ever express.'

Etiquette had demanded that in Marigold's presence money

was not discussed. Marigold hadn't minded. She had known Strickland wouldn't sell the painting for anything less than a breathtaking sum and all that mattered to her was that Maxim was as uncaring of her having posed in the nude as she herself was and that though the painting would not be on public display it would be on private display – and would become a Yurenev family heirloom.

As she drew level with the row of pews in which he was seated she looked towards him so that their eyes could meet. He didn't respond, but kept looking straight ahead to where the clergy and choir were now taking up their positions.

She knew why, of course. If their eyes had met in such a way everyone in the rows behind him would have seen and would have considered it not at all the thing. That he could be so conventional irritated her; but something else was annoying her far more.

He was seated next to 22-year-old Lady Anne Greveney, eldest daughter of the Duke of Culmnor. Anne was an un-expected friend for Iris to have, being a beauty who had appeared on the front cover of *Tatler*. The friendship had begun when Iris had been unwillingly launched on her debu-tante season and, in an ante-room full of hundreds of other debutantes, had found herself seated next to Anne prior to their presentation to Their Majesties.

Marigold didn't care for Anne – and she particularly didn't care for the way Anne was sitting so intimately shoulder to shoulder with Maxim.

Another couple of steps and they were out of her field of vision. Ahead, she could see Toby turn and, as Iris approached, Marigold saw him flash her sister a confidence-boosting smile. But that wasn't what was making her heart beat erratically high in her throat; Theo was seated at the end of the pew she was about to walk past. Next to him was Jerusha.

Marigold could only see a glimpse of Jerusha's face, but against the rich luxuriance of her furs, it was shockingly pale.

She felt a surge of concern. Lily had told her that Jerusha hadn't been very well of late – something to do with having become prone to headaches – but it hadn't occurred to her that Jerusha was actually *ill*.

Theo's elbow was resting on the edge of the pew. If she widened the distance between herself and Rose and walked a little further to the left of the aisle, the skirt of her bridesmaid's dress would brush the sleeve of his astrakhan-collared coat.

The urge to do so was overpowering.

Though he didn't turn his head by even a millimetre, she could sense his tension as she drew alongside his pew.

Why, when she was on the point of accepting a proposal of marriage from Maxim – who was younger, handsomer, far more glamorous, far richer and royal into the bargain – did Theo still have such a profound effect on her? It was exceedingly annoying.

Her skirt brushed his arm and crossly she hoped it would fill him with a million regrets for the way he had ended their relationship.

A couple of steps later and their bridal procession came to a halt. With her grandfather standing to her left, Iris took her place next to Toby. Toby's best man stood to Toby's right and Rose, Marigold and Lily stood a little behind the bridal couple.

Iris turned, handing her prayer book and net gloves to Rose, and the ceremony, conducted by the rector of St Margaret's, began.

Rose tried to give it all her concentration, but it was hard. Just when life was, in many ways, better than she'd ever dared to hope it could be, a whole raft of new concerns had replaced old ones. True, she was now living the kind of independent lifestyle she had only been able to dream about a year ago, when she had still been tied to Snowberry; but because of the unresolved issue of David and Lily's romance, though she was still wholeheartedly committed to her suffragette activities they were curtailed to back-room work and planning. Planning that did not always come to fruition.

The rector said, 'Who giveth this Woman to be married to this Man?' and as her grandfather stepped forward Rose reflected that there were some occasions when plans not coming to fruition were a relief.

Christabel's pet project, the storming of Buckingham Palace, for instance, had still not taken place. 'But it will,' Christabel had said determinedly, 'and in the not too distant future.'

When it did, Rose knew that Hal would expect her to take part in it and to write a first-hand account for the *Daily Despatch*.

Hal.

No one and nothing – not even Lily's romance with the Prince of Wales – was disturbing her peace of mind quite so much as Hal Green. Try as she might, she just couldn't banish his image from her mind. He intrigued and aroused her. And because she was so unfamiliar with it, it was the last effect that disturbed her the most.

Her most passionately held belief had always been that to effect political change, women needed the independence of being single – and this meant she had always avoided the temptation of a romantic relationship.

In a loud clear voice Toby said, 'I take thee, Iris Elizabeth Amy, to my wedded wife, to have and to hold from this day forward, for better for worse, for richer for poorer, in sickness and in health, to love and to cherish till death do us part, according to God's holy ordinance; and thereto I plight thee my troth.'

The words were heart-stoppingly beautiful and for the first time Rose realized she had only resisted temptation because the temptation had never been very great.

Which was not the case now.

# TWENTY-NINE

For David, the one mitigating factor about spending time at Sandringham, two hundred miles away from Lily, was that Sandringham was his grandmother's home, and had been ever since she had come to England forty-eight years ago to marry his grandfather. The eldest daughter of the King of Denmark, Alexandra had been heralded on her arrival as the 'Sea-King's daughter from over the sea', and the British people had not only fallen instantly in love with her but, even though she was now deaf and lame and the Dowager Queen, remained in love with her.

David understood why, for unlike his mother and father, who found it impossible to show affection, his grandmother did so with effortless ease – and was rewarded by always receiving it. As a child, living with his parents at York Cottage, in Sandringham's grounds, the highlight of David's year had been when his grandparents had descended on the Big House for Christmas.

As lights blazed and carriages arrived carrying the scores of guests King Edward loved to be surrounded by, he and Bertie would scamper up to the Big House to be, for a short time at least, part of all the fun that always surrounded his genial, pleasure-loving grandfather. It was fun that lasted for far too short a time and, when his grandfather died, the fun had died also.

His grandmother, though loving and sweet-natured, was hampered socially by her deafness and instead of throwing parties she lived quietly, attended by a large household staff, her unmarried daughter, Princess Victoria, and two devoted courtiers, her lady-in-waiting, Miss Charlotte Knollys, and her comptroller, Sir Dighton Probyn.

Though Bertie, Mary, Harry, Georgie and Johnnie had come to Sandringham over Christmas and the New Year this year, because they were staying at York Cottage, not the Big House, it had still been a staid Christmas.

His father had written to him from northern India where he was busy shooting tigers: *That means that you will be able to give all your time to your studies. There is only another month until you leave for Paris and once there your concentration must be on everything French, not only the language, but French history and French politics.*

He had gone on to tell him of how, while he was in Nepal, Queen Mary was enjoying a fortnight as the guest of the Maharajah of Rajputana, visiting the Taj Mahal and floating down the tiver Chumbal in a launch.

Then he had added:

We expect to return to Portsmouth aboard the *Medina* on the 5 February. By then Bertie will be back at Dartmouth and Harry and Georgie will have returned to school at Broadstairs. You, being still at Sandringham, will be able to meet us – as will your grandmother and Aunt Toria – and I would like you to do so in your uniform as a midshipman.

314

It was typical of his father that there was no mention of John. If a subject was anathema to him, he behaved as if it didn't exist. Which was why there was also no mention of the violent scene that had taken place between them before David had left for his tour of duty aboard the *Hindustan*.

What steps his father had since taken to find out Lily's identity he had no way of knowing. He only knew that whatever they were, they hadn't been successful for, according to Lily, life at Snowberry had continued undisturbed.

For the moment, with the visit to Paris looming so very near, that was just the way he and Lily wanted it. There would be time enough to reveal Lily's identity when Paris was safely behind them.

'Come along, Johnnie,' he said to the youngest brother he never saw unless he was at Sandringham. 'If you want to toboggan, you have to help pull the sledge.'

Six-year-old Johnnie, so warmly dressed for the weather that all that could be seen between his tweed flat cap and his knitted muffler were his eyes and the pink tip of his nose, gave a whoop of laughter.

'Are we pretending we're husky dogs, David?' His eyes were bright with merriment. 'I've seen photos of husky dogs pulling sleds.'

David paused in the task of seeking out the steepest of Sandringham's gentle slopes. 'I draw the line at pretending to be a husky, Johnnie, but we could pretend we are Antarctic explorers trying to reach the South Pole.'

Johnnie loved dressing up and playing make-believe. If Johnnie had had to dress in David's fanciful investiture costume, he would have been as happy as a lark. Johnnie, however, was never seen publicly and so there was never any call for him to wear anything ceremonial. Unless he had dressed himself up as a soldier – and Johnnie loved pretending to be a solder – he either wore a sailor suit or a tweed jacket and kilt.

'We'll need a flag if we're going to reach the South Pole.' Johnnie made a great show of hoisting the toboggan's rope over his shoulder and hauling hard on it. 'Have you got a flag with you?'

'No, but we can bring a flag tomorrow.' It occurred to David that Johnnie would expect to find a literal pole stuck in the snow and that he had, perhaps, created a difficulty for himself. In the summer, when Johnnie gardened and planted seeds, the gardeners speedily planted bedding plants so that he never had to wait for his seeds to flower. For Johnnie, seeds flowered overnight. If they were pretending to reach the South Pole, Johnnie would expect there to be a tangible pole for them to reach.

David grinned to himself. Sandringham was a royal house. There would be spare flagpoles lying around all over the place. He'd ask the gardeners to site one in a suitable place.

'I think this slope might do to toboggan down, Johnnie,' he said, mindful that he'd promised Lala Bill he wouldn't take Johnnie out of sight of the house. 'We can pretend it's a crevasse.'

He often wondered what he would do if, when out with Johnnie on his own, Johnnie were to have one of his falling fits.

'Don't try to move him,' Lala Bill had told him. 'If there are cushions nearby, put some under and around his head so that he doesn't hurt himself. When the fit is over, put him somewhere he can lie down and sleep.'

If Johnnie had a fit while they were out in the snow, the snow would act as a cushion and afterwards, when Johnnie came round, he would be able to lay him on the sledge and take him back to Sandringham that way.

It occurred to him that he'd never talked about Johnnie to Lily. Not doing so had been simply habit. He'd been brought

316

up – as had Bertie, Mary, Harry and Georgie – *never* to talk about Johnnie and what was wrong with him, to anyone. Lily, though, would understand. The word epileptic wouldn't frighten her. She and Johnnie would get on like a house on fire, and when the day came that he could wangle permission for it – or simply didn't need permission for it – Johnnie would love visiting Snowberry; he would especially love playing with the buns.

He positioned the sledge at the top of the long glistening slope.

'Now put your arms around my waist, Johnnie, and hold tightly,' he said, taking up front position on the sledge as Johnnie clambered on behind him. 'Are you ready?'

'I'm a great explorer!' Johnnie shouted. 'I'm Captain Scott! I'm Captain Scott!'

'OK then, Captain Scott. One! Two! Three! GO!'

He pushed off.

Johnnie squealed with glee.

And they went swooping down over the hard-packed snow. Two brothers, having fun.


As the *Medina* entered the English Channel King George stamped his feet and slammed his gloved hands together in an effort to keep warm. Snow was falling heavily, the wind was bitingly cold and as the Home Fleet steamed to meet the *Medina* in order to escort her up the Channel and into Portsmouth the King thought longingly of the heat and colour and vibrancy of the continent he had just left and which he doubted he would ever see again.

India.

It had been a life-changing experience. On the vast plains outside Delhi, the durbar had taken place in two adjoining amphitheatres, the larger one holding a hundred thousand spectators and the smaller and grander one for the princes, rulers and notables of the Indian Empire. The amphitheatres were joined by a wide dais in the centre of which was a series of marble steps leading up to two thrones of solid silver encased in gold. There, with May beside him, he had received homage from the princes of his Indian Empire.

As the long glittering line of rajahs and maharajahs passed before him it was borne in on him that the oriental obeisances being made were very different to the obeisances he had received at his coronation in Westminster Abbey. In India, to be the emperor was on par with being a god. According to the governor-general, when the durbar had ended and he and Queen Mary had descended the steps and departed, a vast crowd had rushed across to the steps they had walked down and had prostrated themselves on them, pressing their foreheads against the marble.

To be regarded as semi-divine was something that couldn't possibly be forgotten.

Now that the coast of England was in sight there were other things that couldn't be forgotten, though he fervently wished they could be. He was returning not only to miserable weather, but to grave constitutional problems. Home Rule for Ireland was a nightmare that wouldn't go away. The country was widely beset by industrial unrest. The suffragettes were as militant as they ever had been. His cousin Willy was bellowing that the German navy would soon be mightier than the British navy, and fear of German aggression was, according to Mr Asquith, being felt not only in the corridors of power but on the streets as well. Last, but by no means least, there was David's nonsensical desire to marry a non-royal girl he barely knew.

Absolutely nothing had come of the enquiries that Craybourne had put in hand in Canada. Georgie Battenberg had been spoken to again and had been unable to throw any further light on the subject. It was as if the girl didn't exist.

As if that little mountain of problems wasn't enough to contend with, he and May were sailing home to a family in mourning.

Snow had coated his moustache and beard and bad-temperedly he brushed it away with the back of a leather-gloved hand.

On the day after his great durbar ceremony, his eldest sister, Princess Louise, her husband the Duke of Fife and their two daughters, Princess Alix, aged twenty, and Princess Maud, aged eighteen, had been sailing aboard the P & O liner *Delhi* en route to Egypt. Off the coast of Morocco it had foundered with the loss of many lives and though Louise and her family had not been among the fatalities, they had spent long hours in the sea in life-jackets before being rescued.

A couple of weeks later, while on the Nile cruising towards Khartoum, Fife had died of pneumonia.

'Which of course he wouldn't have had if he hadn't spent so long in the water!' George had fumed to May when the wireless telegram had arrived telling them the news. 'Apart from the thanksgiving service at St Paul's all our homecoming festivities will have to be given up – and the thanksgiving service isn't going to be too jolly, not when everyone will be wearing black!'

'Nearly there, sir,' Admiral Sir Colin Keppel, who was standing next to him on the bridge, said respectfully.

King George, who had no real desire to be nearly there, made his habitual harrumphing noise.

The only good thing about this particular return home was that it was now over six months since David had dropped his bombshell about wanting to marry, and since then, because of David's tour of duty aboard the *Hindustan* and George's refusal to meet with David in the interim before he and May left for India, nothing further had been said between them on the subject. Six months was a long time and young men, as he knew (not from personal experience but from his late brother's experience), were capable of falling in and out of love with alarming rapidity.

As a flotilla of small boats came out of Portsmouth harbour to greet the *Medina,* he remembered May 1890, when Eddy had been head over heels in love with one of their many cousins, Princess Alix of Hesse, who, refusing his proposal of marriage, had gone on to marry yet another cousin, Nicky, and become Tsarina of All the Russias.

It had been the opinion of their grandmother, Queen Victoria, that it would take Eddy years to get over his heartbreak.

Within a month he had fallen violently in love elsewhere. Whereas Alix was extremely suitable as a future Queen of England, his next love, Princess Hélène of Orléans, was not. Not only was she a Roman Catholic – and no member of the Royal Family could marry a Catholic without losing all rights to the throne – she was also the daughter of the comte de Paris, the pretender to the French throne. Which meant that even if it were not for the religious difficulties, there would have been political difficulties.

Great efforts had been made in order to try to overcome both obstacles. Queen Victoria, together with her prime minister and several senior ministers, had conferred long and hard as to what Eddy's constitutional position would be if Princess Hélène renounced her religion and turned Protestant. It was Hélène's father who had brought the matter to a close by announcing that under no circumstances would his daughter forsake the church of her birth. Eddy had declared that in order to marry Hélène he would abdicate his rights to the succession. Hélène had tearfully said that under no circumstances could she allow him to do so.

By the spring of 1891 the affair was at an end.

By the summer Eddy was passionately in love with Lady

Sibyl St Clair-Erskine, the second daughter of the fourth Earl of Rosslyn. By December he was betrothed to May.

With such a track record in the family it was highly likely that David was long over the girl he had, six months ago, been insistent on marrying. By now, he probably didn't even remember her name.

As the *Medina* edged into her berth Piers Cullen waited with the royal party for the moment when they would be able to step aboard her for the family reunion. Princess Victoria, King George's sharp-tongued unmarried sister, was huddled deep in sombre mourning furs. Queen Alexandra, petite and aged and, behind her long crêpe veil, still delicately beautiful, was almost child-like in her impatience to be reunited with the son she still referred to in private as 'her darling Georgie boy'.

Her grandson wasn't showing any such signs of impatience.

From where he was standing, a couple of feet behind Prince Edward, Piers could see tension in every line of his body. He knew why Edward was so on edge. He was steeling himself for the inevitable interview with the King. Piers had not the slightest sympathy for him. All he felt was a well-hidden, deep and jealous hatred.

It galled him to the depths of his being that someone he regarded as being so insignificant should be treated with such deference; should have such vast wealth. Edward's revenue from the duchy of Cornwall alone was in the region of £90,000 a year, and he didn't even have the expense of an establishment of his own. As for his future: how much more glittering and fantastic could it be? When his father died he would be Edward VIII, King of Great Britain and Ireland and of the British Dominions beyond the Seas, Defender of the Faith and Emperor of India. And what had he done to earn any of it?

The answer was absolutely nothing. Everything he was, everything he had and would have, was his simply by right of birth. Even just thinking about it made Piers want to choke, and when he thought of the adulation Edward had begun to receive since his very public exposure at the coronation and at his investiture, he had to run a finger around the inside of his collar in order to give himself a little more air.

How could such a narrow-shouldered, slight figure arouse such universal admiration? It wasn't as if Edward were even tall. He was barely five feet seven. What kind of masculinity was that? More to the point, why the devil did he want to marry the one girl he, Piers, wanted to marry? It was almost, he thought, his hands clenching into fists as the *Medina* slid into her berth, as if Edward was doing it to deliberately spite him.

That wasn't possible, though. Edward needed him. He was, after all, the only person outside the Houghton family who knew his secret.

Grimly he wondered how Edward would manage in France without him.

'The whole point of Prince Edward's visit to France is that he will return home fluent in the language,' King George had said to Piers shortly before he had left the country for his durbar. 'That being so, the elder son of the marquis de Valmy is to act as Prince Edward's equerry while the Prince is a guest of the de Valmy family. It will ensure he doesn't fall back on speaking English – and that he doesn't run the risk of speaking French with the kind of John Bull accent the French find so offensive.'

Had the King meant that Edward would be at risk of picking up a John Bull accent from him? Piers had fumed, as only he could fume, over what he felt sure was a slur on his linguistic ability. He had, however, welcomed the thought of a break from his equerrying duties. Edward's stay in France would turn Edward's long separation from Lily into a separation of even longer duration. During that separation Piers was going to lay siege to Lily.

The gangway was being lowered and as the royal party gathered closer together, preparatory to boarding, he felt a surge of steely confidence. He would explain to her, as no one else could, that King George would never give his consent to a marriage between her and Edward. He would open her eyes to the fact that Edward was still a mere boy and that whatever he had said to her, the words carried no weight. He would point out to her that he himself was far from being a mere boy. When he said he loved her – which he did – she could rely implicitly on that love leading to a very speedy, secure marriage, something he knew all young girls yearned for.

He would tell her that he absolutely forgave her for having her head turned when Edward had asked her to marry him. After all, what young girl wouldn't want to be a princess and a future queen? Then he would tell her again that any such hope was a lost cause.

He remembered her studio at Snowberry – a studio he had never been invited to enter. He would point out to her that even if the traditions as to whom a Prince of Wales could marry were different, it would be unthinkable for a Princess of Wales to dabble with paint and clay. As his wife, however, she would always be able to and he would stress to her how important he thought it was for a woman to have a hobby.

It was now time for them to board and as they did, shielded from the snow by giant umbrellas, he was obsessed with the thought of how he was going to make Edward pay for all the slights he had suffered at his hands. For the way Edward had never treated him as a friend, although he had instantly treated the Houghton family as friends. For the way he had never invited him to call him David. For the way he had snatched Lily from under his nose.

He ground his teeth together so loudly that Sir Dighton looked across at him in alarm. Piers was too deep in thoughts of revenge to notice.

# THIRTY

Pale February sun streamed into the white, gold and yellow drawing room of the marquis de Villoutrey's elegant home in Neuilly, in the sixteenth arrondissement.

It was a drawing room very different to Snowberry's. Instead of comfortable chintz-covered sofas, it was filled with Louis Quinze furniture upholstered in heavy brocades. No jigsaw puzzles lay unfinished within easy access. No chessmen stood waiting for play to be resumed. It was a stiffly elegant room of mirrors and candelabra where gold leaf gleamed and glowed. It was the kind of formal setting Louise de Villoutrey much preferred to Snowberry's haphazard cosiness.

'How is Iris?' she asked Lily. They were seated on opposite sides of a low glass-topped table that was set on a centrepiece of ebony cherubim, enjoying coffee from black and gold Sèvres china.

Lily, perched uncomfortably on a gilt-framed spindly-legged chair that wouldn't have looked out of place at Versailles, shot her mother a wide smile. 'Ecstatically happy. Though she's spending quite a lot of time at Sissbury, she isn't living there yet and won't be until Toby has said a final goodbye to the Guards.'

'Who will act as housekeeper at Snowberry when Iris isn't there to do so?'

'Oh, we already have a new housekeeper. Millie's sister. Tilly. She used to work for Lady Conisborough, but the Conisboroughs live a quite grand lifestyle. Lord Conisborough is a financial adviser to King George and as Tilly has a weak heart, it all became a bit too much for her. The gentle pace of Snowberry suits her far better and if she isn't feeling up to snuff, Millie just takes over from her.'

Her mother pursed her lips. It sounded very lackadaisical, but then things at Snowberry always were. She ran things very differently. At both Neuilly and at the de Villoutrey chateau in the Loire valley, the male staff wore a livery of black suits with waistcoats striped with red and, on formal occasions, navy tailcoats collared and cuffed in crimson. The embarrassing lack of formality at Snowberry was why, when she and Henri had been in England for Iris's wedding, they had stayed with Sibyl.

'And Rose?'

'Rose is fine, Mama,' she said. 'She loves living in London at Great-aunt Sibyl's and she loves the feeling of financial independence she gets from her journalism.'

At the mention of Rose's freelance work for the *Daily Despatch*, her mother shuddered. With such a history, Rose was never going to make a suitable marriage. Even worse, she didn't even think Rose *wanted* to make a suitable marriage. Iris, however, had already done so, albeit not very excitingly, and Marigold appeared to be on the verge of making a marriage *par excellence*. 'It was a shame', she said, ignoring her coffee and fitting a Sobranie into a long amber holder, 'that Prince Yurenev had to leave the wedding reception for Marchemont so suddenly. We had only just begun to talk together when the message came that Princess Zasulich had been taken ill. He's very charming. Sibyl, who knows him very well, absolutely adores him.'

As Maxim Yurenev was a Russian royal, exceedingly handsome and sinfully rich, Lily wasn't surprised that he had made such a favourable impression. She tried to give the subject her attention but it kept straying to David, for now that both of them were in Paris, all she could think of was when – and how – they would be reunited. Before they left England they had envisioned their reunion as being relatively simple to arrange. In reality it was proving to be the very opposite, for her mother was allowing her to go nowhere unaccompanied.

Louise, having lit her cigarette, was studying the Russian imperial eagle distinctively stamped on it. It conjured up lots of delightful images. Marigold and Maxim's initials entwined beneath the Yurenev crest and decorating table linen, bed linen, stationery; perhaps even the buttons on the livery of their household staff. There would be visits to St Petersburg and audiences with the Tsar and Tsarina. Perhaps next time the Russian royal family visited Britain aboard the imperial yacht *Standart*, Prince and Princess Yurenev would be invited aboard.

The prospect of a Russian royal son-in-law was so intoxicatingly heady it almost – but not quite – overshadowed the news she had been saving until family matters were out of the way.

'I have the most *amazing* news, darling. News you are going to find *incredible*.'

Lily did her best to look interested, but her thoughts were still on David. Their plans had been that under the guise of visiting the Louvre, or Notre-Dame Cathedral or the Eiffel Tower, Lily, accompanied by Marguerite and Camille, her two stepsisters, and David, accompanied by Luc de Valmy, who was acting as his equerry, would meet up 'accidentally'; they would then persuade those accompanying them to give them some time together on their own – and to be silent afterwards at having done so.

The blow to this plan had been that Marguerite and Camille weren't in Paris. 'Such a nuisance, *ma petite chérie*,' her mother had said on greeting her. 'They now go to finishing school in Lucerne and won't be home until Easter – and finishing school is something I would like to talk to you about, Lily. But perhaps a little later, *que penses-tu?*'

It was something Lily had no need to think about, but she didn't say so. She'd been too devastated at knowing it was going to be her mother, not her stepsisters, who would be accompanying her when she went sightseeing.

'So far only a very few people know what it is I am about to tell you,' her mother said with a wave of her cigarette-holder. 'Though I am sure word will spread very quickly; *c'est certain.*'

Lily was only listening to her with half an ear. Accustomed to the freedom of movement her grandfather had always given her and which she, Rose, Iris and Marigold had always taken for granted, it hadn't occurred to her that her mother, who had always been too absent a parent to be a diligent one, would take the responsibilities of chaperoning so seriously. It was unexpected, to say the least – and it wasn't the only thing that was unexpected.

'Though I am here incognito, I've still had to pay my respects to President Faillières,' David had said with something like despair in his voice when, announcing himself to the butler as her cousin, he had telephoned her hours after her arrival. 'It was a very formal occasion, just the kind of thing I thought I wouldn't have to endure. The British Ambassador Sir Francis Bertie was there, and President Fallières presented me with the grand cordon of the Légion d'Honneur. It was all very nice, but, oh darling Lily, I didn't want to be in the Élysée Palace! I wanted to be with you, walking hand in hand on the banks of the Seine!'

328

It had been a cry from the heart and Lily's hand had been trembling when she replaced the receiver.

'. . . so, because of Henri's friendship with Guy, you are going to have the *extraordinary* privilege of meeting him in circumstances of the utmost informality.'

Lily struggled to bring her thoughts back from the urgent question of how she and David were to achieve the reunion they had dreamed of for so long.

'But surely even in France people don't take themselves so seriously,' she said, assuming the person being spoken of was a friend of her stepfather's and not caring about the circumstances in which they were to meet – or even if they met at all.

Her mother blew a thin plume of blue smoke into the air and said with exasperation, 'I don't believe you are listening to me *at all,* Lily! Henri's friend, the marquis de Valmy, has been asked to act as host to the Prince of Wales. Prince Edward is going to be staying with the de Valmy family in order to perfect his French and study French history and French politics, and . . . *your coffee, Lily!*'

The cry of warning came too late.

Lily's reaction was so extreme that she spilled coffee down her dress and on to the Aubusson carpet.

Instantly a footman was on hand to blot the carpet. Lily, uncaring of her ruined dress, said urgently, 'Did you say we would be visiting the de Valmys? Will we be doing so soon? Will we be doing so this week?'

Satisfied that the carpet was receiving proper attention, Louise said, 'We shall be dining *en famille* with the de Valmys in three days' time. It is the most *amazing* opportunity for us to become informally acquainted with the Prince. Guy says he is shy, but has a most attractive manner. He is staying with the de Valmys incognito, as the Earl of Chester, but royal protocol will still have to be followed and so please don't initiate a conversation with him, Lily. Allow him to speak to you first.'

She stubbed her Sobranie out in an onyx ashtray. 'Also, because he is shy, it doesn't mean he will be approachable. His mother is the most unapproachable woman in the world. I've never been part of the royal circle, but I have friends who are and they say that every time they meet Queen Mary the ice has to be rebroken afresh. Familiarity, even with her ladies of the bedchamber, is simply not in her nature. She is stiffness and formality incarnate. As King George is similarly rigid in manner I don't expect Prince Edward to be much different.'

The thought of David being even the teeniest little bit unapproachable was so funny it took all of Lily's self-control not to giggle. Even harder was not telling her mother how different to his parents David was; how he was the most approachable, wonderful person in the whole wide world.

As the footman finished blotting the carpet and her mother surveyed his handiwork she fought hard not to tell her all about David knocking Rose from her bicycle. About his visits to Snowberry. About how much they loved each other.

It was a battle she won, for she knew it was a secret her mother would be unable to keep. But until David received King George's permission for them to marry, it was a secret that simply *had* to be kept.

'*Il doit être pulverisé maintenant avec un mélange d'une part glycérine et de deux parts d'eau chaude,*' the footman said to her mother.

'*Oui. Immédiatement,*' her mother responded, and then she said to Lily. 'When Jacques has sprayed the carpet with his magic mix of glycerine and warm water no one will be any the wiser about this little mishap. But not a word to Henri, Lily. *Tu comprends?*'

Lily understood very well.

She also understood that David could have no idea his host and her stepfather were on such close terms. If he had, it would have been the first thing he would have told her when they had spoken on the phone. She now had to telephone him with the news that though their reunion wouldn't be a private one, they would at least be seeing each other in three days' time.

She took her opportunity two hours later when her mother, aware that she would soon be reciprocating the de Valmys' hospitality and playing hostess to her future king, was in deep discussion with her chef.

To the de Valmys' butler who answered the telephone Lily said she was a cousin of the Earl of Chester and wished to speak with him.

Seconds later David was on the line, saying tautly, 'Lily? Is everything all right, sweetheart? Are you able to escape on your own for a little while?'

'Not at the moment, but I do have news. In three days' time I am to be a dinner guest of the de Valmys! My stepfather and the marquis de Valmy are close friends. Isn't it wonderful? It means that it's going to be far easier to see each other than we ever dreamed!'

She spoke fast, not wanting to be caught on the telephone by her mother who would assume she was speaking with Rory and might very well ask to have a few words with him.

David, aware of the danger, was equally fast and abrupt in his response. 'But that's smashing news, darling! Absolutely brilliant! Except it means we won't be able to rush into each other's arms and we will have to be fearfully formal with each other! We *have* to meet alone beforehand. Try to think of a way, Lily. It will kill me if after all this time apart I have to treat you as a stranger when we meet, and instead of kissing you as I long to do more than you can ever imagine, I can only shake hands with you!'

At the thought of how hard it would be for her, Lily's heart tightened.

'David . . .' She heard the sound of her mother's footsteps approaching and what she was about to say remained unsaid. Instead she said swiftly, 'I have to go, David. But I'll do my best to think of a way we can meet. I promise!'

Hurriedly she replaced the receiver, turning to her mother with a quick bright smile. 'Just another call from Rory. He wanted to know if I'd been cycling or horse-riding yet in the Bois de Boulogne.'

She hated telling lies, but hopefully she would be able to make amends for it in the not too distant future.

'As you know, Mama, I haven't, but I'd love to be able to. Perhaps in the morning I could borrow Marguerite's bicycle, or Camille's, and go for a ride in the park?'

It wasn't an unreasonable request. The Bois de Boulogne, a park bigger than London's Hyde Park, was so near to the de Villoutrey mansion it could be seen from all the west-facing windows.

Louise's thoughts were still on the menu she had arranged with her chef. Would lemon ice-cream be more suitable than lemon sorbet? Still pondering the problem, she said, giving Lily only half her attention, 'But who would go with you?'

'I don't need anyone with me. At home, I cycle all over the place on my own.'

Deciding that the Prince would probably prefer ice-cream to sorbet, Louise said, still distracted, 'Perhaps if Jacques were to accompany you . . .'

Lily hugged her mother's arm and, careful not to agree to the Jacques suggestion, said, 'Thank you, Mama,' as if her mother had given permission with no strings attached.

Before her mother took it into her head to speak to Jacques then and there, Lily changed the subject to one she knew would divert her mother's attention from him. 'Will you be reciprocating the de Valmys' invitation, Mama? Will Prince Edward soon be dining here, at Neuilly?'

Later that day, when her mother was taking an afternoon rest, she telephoned David with the news that she would be in the Bois the following morning.

'Meet me at the north end, by the entrance to the Jardin d'Acclimatation.' His voice was unsteady with emotion. 'Oh, darling Lily! I can't believe that after all this time we are actually going to be together again!'

She didn't spoil things for him by telling him about Jacques. Jacques was a problem she still had to deal with.

To her great relief it was a subject not raised at dinner that evening. Instead, Louise's conversation revolved solely around their good fortune at being able to meet Prince Edward in such an informal manner. Even her stepfather was impressed by it.

'Though if I had given it any thought, I would have realized it was always on the cards that Guy would some day be asked to act as his host,' he said. He was wearing a swallow-tailed coat and white waistcoat even though they were dining *en famille*. 'King Edward VII was a great lover of everything French, Lilli. We Parisians loved him, for he was as Parisian in tastes and manners as if he had been born here. Your present king is very different. If a country is not part of the British Empire, King George has no interest in it. In France we have great hopes that when Prince Edward is king, things will be very different.'

It was strange hearing David being discussed in such a way. She had never before thought of him as being cast in the same mould as his grandfather, but that was because all her memories of King Edward VII were of an overweight, elderly man. He had been genial, though, and had made friends with people who had been born far from the royal circle: people like the German-born financier Sir Ernest

Cassel, who came from a Jewish middle-class family; and his yachting friend, Sir Thomas Lipton, a self-made man who had been born in one of the poorest parts of Glasgow and whose father had been a greengrocer.

His charm, too, had always been blazingly apparent. David had inherited it in full, just as he had inherited King Edward's lack of class-consciousness. In the nine and a half years he had been on the throne, King Edward had established himself as a great international statesman. The Entente Cordiale, the formal alliance that bound England firmly to France, was due almost entirely to his personal efforts at fostering goodwill between England and France. It was the kind of statesmanship she was sure David would, one day, emulate.

The problem of Jacques was solved the next morning when Louise announced she had a raging toothache and was going immediately to her dentist. She did so chauffeur-driven and, in case she should feel faint and need a strong arm, accompanied by Jacques. No mention was made of the permission she had given for Lily to cycle to the Bois. No mention was made of the original plan that Jacques should accompany her. Toothache had put all such considerations clean out of Louise's mind.

Sympathetic as Lily was where her mother's pain was concerned, she couldn't help feeling vast relief. She had permission for what she was about to do – and hours and hours ahead of her in which to spend time alone with David.

With a grey coat buttoned up to her throat, her coal-black curls crammed into a red beret and a matching wool scarf around her neck, she wheeled Camille's bicycle out of the *hangar de bicyclette* and adjusted her coat so that she had enough leg-room in which to pedal.

The sky was steel-coloured, promising snow. With her heart beating fast, her anticipation white-hot, she cycled down the drive and into the wide boulevard beyond, the crisp air whipping roses into her cheeks.

David's anticipation was just as feverish. He, too, had had more than a little difficulty in leaving for their rendezvous unaccompanied, but Luc, who until now had gone with him everywhere, had been understanding. Like David, he, too, hated being nannied and he didn't see why Edward shouldn't have a little freedom if he wanted it. Though Edward hadn't said so, he suspected Edward wanted to see a girl. Luc was eighteen, French – and entirely sympathetic.

David's sense of freedom as he cycled at top speed towards Neuilly was euphoric. The only other times he had experienced anything like a similar freedom had been on his clandestine drives to Snowberry from Windsor, but those drives hadn't had the edge of danger he was now experiencing as he skimmed past horse-drawn carriages, narrowly missing motor cars and crowded motor buses.

He had chosen the Jardin d'Acclimatation as a meeting point because it was the easiest place in the park for Lily to reach from the de Villoutrey mansion. Originally it had been only a zoo, but now there were some children's amusements and, in good weather, pony rides.

As he waited, David stamped his feet to keep warm. Lily would use a side entrance to the Bois leading from the boulevard Maillot and he could easily meet her there without any risk of missing each other. He mounted Luc's bicycle again and, as the first snowflakes began to fall, he pedalled like a maniac to meet the only person in the world who made his royal life bearable.

Cycling along the busy boulevards of Neuilly was very different to cycling down the country lanes around Snowberry and Lily was relieved her mother lived so close to the park. She whizzed between the open gates of the side entrance, grateful to see that unlike the boulevards, the pathway leading to the Jardin d'Acclimatation was near-deserted. There was a boy bowling a hoop, two girls roller-skating and, in the distance, a cyclist racing towards her as if his life depended on it.

Even though he was dressed for the weather as she was in an overcoat, and had a cap pulled low over his forehead and a scarf wrapped so high around his neck that half his face was hidden, she knew who it was.

'David!' she shouted. '*David!*'

Taking a hand off the handlebars, he waved furiously.

A smile of blazing joy split her face. After all the months of painful separation they were about to be together again. Her happiness was so deep she thought she was going to die of it.

They raced towards each other and then, just when it seemed they were going to collide headlong, David swerved to a halt and Lily slammed on her brakes. Ecstatically they let their bicycles fall to the ground and hurtled towards each other, catapulting into each other's arms.

'Lily! Oh, God! Lily, darling Lily!' He yanked his scarf away from his face. 'Darling girl, there were times when I thought this moment was never going to come!'

She clung to him as though she were drowning, unable to even begin expressing how deep her own fears had been. Then there was no time to even think of speech.

His mouth crushed hers and he was kissing her as though he would never stop.

The girls on roller-skates had headed back to the park gates when snow had begun falling, but the little boy with the hoop watched them wide-eyed.

David and Lily were as oblivious of him as they were of the snow. All that mattered to them was each other. When David finally lifted his head from hers, he said thickly,

336

'I love you, Lily. I love you more than anything in the world.'

'I know.' Her voice was husky with emotion. 'I love you the same way, darling David. I love you with all my heart – and I always will. Always and for ever.'

The snow was falling fast now, flakes settling on their eyelashes and cheeks.

'There's a small café in the Jardin d'Acclimatation.' He was still hugging her tightly. 'We'll be able to get hot chocolate there. Maybe hot chocolate with a shot of almond liqueur.'

'It sounds wonderful.' She smiled sunnily at him, all the love she felt for him shining in her eyes.

He didn't want to take his arms from around her, but if they were to go to the café he had no choice. 'To the bicycles then,' he said, releasing his hold of her with the deepest reluctance. Flashing her the grin that had won the hearts of the public in hundreds of thousands on Coronation Day and at Caernarvon, he added, 'I'll race you, sweetheart.'

Later, as they sat at a small zinc-topped table in the otherwise deserted café, he said, 'As your stepfather and my host are bosom pals we're going to have no problems seeing each other. It's all the greatest possible good luck.'

'It's beyond good luck. It's surreal.' She giggled. 'My mother has already taken it for granted that you will be dining with us in the very near future and she and her chef have the menu planned down to the smallest detail.'

Her hands were clasped on the table-top and he covered them lovingly with his. 'If I tell Luc that my sightseeing of places like Notre-Dame and the Eiffel Tower and the Louvre would be more enjoyable if you came with us, I don't think his father would object. In fact, I rather suspect Guy de Valmy would quite like to foster a close relationship between the future King of England and the stepdaughter of his closest friend.'

It was a thought that hadn't occurred to Lily. Her eyes rounded. 'You mean we may even find ourselves *encouraged* to spend time together and to flirt with each other?'

He grinned roguishly. 'If you think about it, it would be a pretty reasonable reaction on Guy's part – and on your mother's. No mother would object to her daughter spending time in the company of the Prince of Wales – and having high hopes as to where that might lead. Although Guy has to let my father know where I go, and who I see, dining and spending time with the family of his friend, the marquis de Villoutrey, will ring no alarm bells.'

She, too, appreciated the naughtily amusing side of the situation, but David's mention of King George reminded her that it was seven months since he had first told the King he was in love with someone non-royal and since then, when the King had refused to give permission for such a marriage, no headway at all had been made.

She said pensively, 'Do you think your father has forgotten all about you falling in love with someone and wanting to marry her? It seems such a long time since you were last able to talk to him.'

'I doubt *he's* forgotten about it, though he may hope *I* have. I think that's what his strategy in avoiding meeting with me is all about, because it *is* a strategy. By his reckoning, I won't have seen you since I went on my tour of duty aboard the *Hindustan*. He's banking on the fact that by the time we do have another private conversation together, I won't even bring up the subject of wanting to marry – or at least, wanting to marry someone of my own choice.'

'So when he finds out differently, when he finds out you still feel the same about me after all this time, do you think that will make him realize that you are truly in love and not just infatuated, and that he will then give us his blessing?'

He looked down at their clasped hands, avoiding her eyes.

338

He'd never been frank with her about how adamant his father's objections to his marriage to a non-royal were – objections that had the whole weight of English history behind them – in case, once she realized, she felt things were hopeless. Instead, he had always been at pains to assure her that once his father got used to the idea, everything would be all right.

He said now, passionately hoping it would prove to be true, 'I'm sure he will give us his blessing, angel. Especially so once he knows your identity and has met you. The only reason that hasn't happened already is that I wanted us to enjoy Paris together. We wouldn't have been able to, not in the way we are now doing, if it was public knowledge that you were soon to become the Princess of Wales.'

At the thought of how her life would change when that day came, a little shiver ran down her spine. How on earth would she cope with all the formality and stiff etiquette and being watched all the time? How would she cope with not being able to paint or sculpt whenever she wanted to?

She looked across at David and, seeing the happiness that flooded his face simply because they were together, she knew that she would cope because he needed her to do so. Overcome with love for him she unclasped her hands and squeezed his tightly. 'I've never visited the zoo here, David. Have we time to take a look around?'

'I think most of the animals will be in their sleeping quarters keeping out of the snow. We could cycle down to the lake, though. It will look pretty smashing with the snow falling on it.'

It did look pretty smashing. With the trees around the edge of the lake laced with white and ice on the water glimmering and shimmering, it looked ethereal.

Leaving their bicycles at the edge of the pathway so that they could walk along the lakeside with their arms around each other, David said with a catch in his voice, 'I never knew people could be this happy, Lily. It's like living in a fairy-tale. A fairy-tale that is going to have a very happy ending.'

She leaned her head against his shoulder, not caring about the snow that had settled on his coat. There was something on her mind; something she needed to ask him.

She hugged his arm. 'When we were in the café, you said you thought your father was banking on the fact that when you next spoke together, you wouldn't even bring up the subject of wanting to marry – or at least, of wanting to marry someone of your own choice . . .'

'And?' He shot her a loving smile.

'And I wondered what you meant by saying you want to marry someone of your own choice.'

He gave a rueful shrug. 'He wants me to marry my uncle Nicky's daughter, Olga. Nicky isn't my actual uncle, of course. He's my father's cousin, which I suppose makes him my first cousin once-removed, or my second cousin. I don't know which. I've been brought up to refer to him simply as uncle, just as I always refer to the Kaiser, another cousin of my father's, as Uncle Willy.'

Lily stopped walking, bewildered. 'If your uncle Willy is Kaiser Wilhelm, who is your uncle Nicky?'

'Uncle Nicky is the Tsar.' He burst out laughing at the incredulity on her face. 'When we're betrothed you're going to have to get used to hearing kings and queens, and even emperors and empresses, being referred to as uncle, aunt or cousin, because in one way or another I'm related to nearly every crowned head there is.'

'So Olga, who your father wants you to marry, is a princess?'

'Yes, though in Russia, princesses are referred to as grand duchesses.'

He could see that she was still struggling to take in what he was saying.

On the left-hand side of the path was a large cedar, the

branches so thick and heavy the ground beneath was still clear of snow. He led her over to it and as she leaned against the tree's great trunk he took off his gloves and shoved them into his coat pockets, and then took off her gloves and did the same thing with them.

'This bee my father has got in his bonnet about my marrying Grand Duchess Olga is nothing for you to worry about, sweetheart. If it wasn't her he had in mind for me, it would be someone else. Probably Uncle Willy's daughter, Victoria Louise. If it wasn't for the fact that I'm headlong, hopelessly, *passionately* in love with you, darling Lily, then I'd probably let such arrangements go ahead, if only because that's the way things have always been done in royal circles. But I *am* headlong, hopelessly and passionately in love with you, and that is *not* how it is going to be. Not for this prince. So don't look so concerned. I love you, darling Lily, and I'm going to love you until the day I die.'

His words were so reassuring all her fears fled. She slid her arm up and around his neck and he gave a moan of desire, unbuttoning his coat and then hers and pulling her close against him.

His kisses were passionate and urgent and the blood surged through her body like a hot tide. When his hands slid up from her waist to her breasts she didn't pull away from him. She was his without reservation and, sensing it, he fumbled in desperate need with the long line of pearl buttons running down the bodice of her dress.

With one hand around his neck, she used the other to help him free her breasts from her corset top and her chemise.

His fingers touched her soft warm flesh, his thumbs brushed her pale pink nipples, and as delicious sensations she'd never dreamed of pulsed through her body, she knew that if they had been in another place – somewhere warm and private – she would have been unable to refuse him anything he asked of her.

'You are so beautiful, Lily,' he whispered, looking down at her body in awe. 'You are the most beautiful thing I have ever seen.'

A flurry of snow blew in over the lake, sending swirls of it beneath the cedar tree. She shivered, and though it was the hardest thing in the world he'd ever done, he pulled her coat around her once again.

'We have to go, darling,' he said, knowing that if they didn't, they would die of pneumonia. 'Next time when we meet alone, it has to be indoors. The Louvre or Notre-Dame.'

She giggled, knowing the lovemaking they were now enjoying would be impossible in the Louvre, and more than impossible – sacrilegious – in Notre-Dame.

Something else occurred to her as well. Everyone who met David described him as being shy, but she knew differently. When it came to loving her, David wasn't shy at all.

She returned to Neuilly filled with a happiness so deep it almost hurt.

It lasted only a few precious minutes.

Hearing her enter the house, Louise, pale from her morning of torture at the dentists, hurried downstairs to meet her.

Ignoring the snow coating Lily's beret and the shoulders of her coat, she said, 'I've just had dreadful news from your grandfather, Lily. Jerusha Jethney died early this morning.'

342

# THIRTY-ONE

The minute Edward left for France, Piers raced down to Snowberry to see Lily.

'She isn't here,' Iris said to him politely as they stood facing each other in the drawing room.

'Where is she?' His manner was as abrupt and taciturn as always. 'When will she be back?'

'She won't be back for several weeks.' Iris ran the tip of her tongue nervously over her bottom lip, grateful for Homer's presence as he sat beside her and eyed Piers watchfully, sensing the strained atmosphere.

Piers blanched. He'd been counting on the fact that with Edward away in Paris he would have a clear field in persuading Lily to see how senseless Edward's proposal to her had been.

He slammed a clenched hand into his fist. Homer gave a low, warning growl.

Iris put a hand down to the top of his head to reassure him that things were still all right.

'Where has she gone? It's urgent that I see her. Absolutely imperative.'

She looked into his thin, tense face, wondering how it was someone could let their manner make them so unlikeable.

'The last few months have put quite a strain on Lily and she's gone to stay with relatives,' she said pleasantly, knowing very well what Piers Cullen's feelings for Lily were, and why he wanted to see her, and having no intention of telling him that Lily was in Paris.

'An address, Iris,' he snapped, as if he were a policeman speaking to a suspect.

Iris, who heartily wished Toby was with her instead of being at his barracks in London, stood her ground.

'I'm not going to give you her address, Piers, because I know she wouldn't want me to.'

He breathed in hard, his nostrils whitening. 'You don't like me, do you? Just like everyone else, you're polite on the surface, but you don't like me one little bit.'

For a second Iris felt absolute compassion for him. 'That's because you make yourself so unlikeable,' she said gently. 'If you just spoke more pleasantly to people and—'

'I don't need a woman to teach me how to speak to people!' His fury was incandescent. Lily would never have spoken to him in such a way. Lily respected him for what he was. A strong man, with a strong manner. Totally unlike the ineffective boy she had so foolishly agreed to marry.

He was just about to demand Lily's address again when Homer growled for a second time, his hackles rising.

This time Iris did nothing to restrain him.

Knowing he was beaten, knowing he would get no more information from her, he swung on his heel, slamming doors behind him as he stormed from the house. The only relatives of Lily that he knew of were her great-aunt Sibyl and Sibyl's grandson, Rory Sinclair. As her great-aunt apparently lived year-round in St James's Street, it had to mean that Lily was with the Sinclair branch of the family – and he knew exactly where the Sinclair family home was

344

sited. It was on the banks of Loch Gruinart, on the Isle of Islay.

He went by rail to Inverness, changed there for a train on the local line to Tarbert and from there he caught a Western Isles ferry to Islay.

In the cold and damp of February he could never remember a more miserable journey. The sea was rough; the ferry basic in the extreme. Even though he was a Scot himself, he couldn't for the life of him work out why Rory Sinclair was happy to make the journey as regularly as he did.

As he stood freezing on Port Askaig's jetty, asking where he could find a taxi, the only thing keeping his temper in check was the certainty that within a very little while he would be with her again. This time she was going to listen to him. This time she was going to see sense.

There was, it turned out, only one motorized taxi on the island and as well as smelling of stale cigarette-smoke, it gave him a preposterously uncomfortable ride.

With his thoughts centred entirely on Lily he took little interest in the magnificent scenery. As they crossed the island from east to west, the driver said in a thick Scottish burr, 'There be Loch Indall on your left, sir.'

Piers noted that it looked more like a bay than a loch, but was otherwise uninterested. He was trying to imagine Lily's surprise when she saw him. Her look of delighted pleasure.

The driver turned inland on a narrow single-track road. There was moorland on either side of them criss-crossed by rivulets of shining water. After a much shorter time than it had taken to drive from Port Askaig to Loch Indall another sea loch opened in front of them.

'Gruinart,' his driver said helpfully. 'Castle Dounreay be nearly at the mouth of the loch.'

He'd known, of course, that his destination was a castle. What else would an annoying prick like Rory Sinclair have as a home?

It proved to be an extremely pretty castle, which made Piers even angrier than ever. As they drew up to it a flock of geese flew low across the sky. He wondered if there were many sightings of Golden Eagles on Islay. In the Highlands, where he had been brought up, the giant birds could quite often be sighted, circling high in the mountains and then swooping down at ferocious speed to kill their prey.

'Wait for me,' he said curtly to the driver. It wasn't because he anticipated being with Lily only for a short time; he didn't. But he was hardly going to be invited to stay the night and he couldn't rely on anyone being willing to give him a lift back to Port Askaig and the nearest hotel.

To his stunned surprise it wasn't an old family retainer who opened the door to him, but Rory. If he was surprised at being faced with Rory – who he had assumed was in London, beavering away in the Foreign Office – Rory was pole-axed at being faced so unexpectedly with Piers.

'What the devil—' he began, hardly able to believe his eyes.

Piers didn't waste time in being polite. 'I believe Lily is staying with you,' he said bluntly. 'I need to speak with her.'

'You need to *what*?'

'I need to speak with Lily.'

Rory, resplendent in tweed jacket, kilt and sporran, led the way into a drawing room that didn't look very different to the drawing room at Snowberry. There were comfy sofas and chairs covered in chintz, a half-finished jigsaw puzzle on a table, a log fire roaring away in a fireplace big enough to roast an ox.

Rory crossed the room to where a silver drinks tray stood on a Georgian sideboard. Removing the stopper from a cut-glass decanter, he poured a generous three thimblefuls of whisky into two glasses.

'Lily', he said, handing one of the glasses to Piers, 'isn't here. What made you think she would be?'

Piers blinked, his disappointment so shattering he could hardly assimilate it. 'I went to Snowberry to see her and Iris told me she was staying with relatives. The only relatives I know of are yourself and your grandmother.'

Rory didn't correct him. If Piers didn't know that Lily's mother was alive and well and living in Paris, he wasn't going to enlighten him. Like Iris, he, too, knew exactly what Piers's agenda was with regard to Lily – and though he hated the thought of Lily becoming engaged to the Prince of Wales, he felt downright revulsion at the thought of her becoming engaged to Piers Cullen.

'I've no idea where Lily is.' It was a lie, but he'd no problem at all in telling it. He took a deep swallow of his whisky. 'I think it's time someone told you that you're wasting your time where Lily is concerned. She isn't interested in you.'

'That's where you're wrong!' Piers knocked back his whisky in one great gulp. 'She was on the point of accepting a proposal from me when Edward stuck his oar in!' His eyes were black and bitter. 'And all to what purpose?' he continued, letting fly with his feelings. 'He'll never be allowed to marry her. Not in a million years. I want her to see what an absolute impossibility such a marriage is and I want her to understand that I know why she accepted his proposal. Any girl her age would have her head turned if a prince proposed to her. But it doesn't mean she's in love with him, because I don't believe she is.'

'You don't know a damn thing about Lily!' Rory's own

feelings where Lily and David's love affair was concerned were too emotionally charged for him to suffer listening to Piers spout on about it. 'You've built something up in your mind that has absolutely no foundation in reality. Stop pestering her. Stop visiting Snowberry. You may be damned right that permission will never be given for Edward and Lily to marry, but if he isn't able to marry her, she isn't going to turn to you!'

'She'll turn to me because I'm going to forgive her.'

'Forgive her? *Forgive her?*'

It was such a pompous, sanctimonious, self-righteous remark that Rory couldn't contain himself. He slammed his glass down on the nearest surface, bunched his fist and sent it straight-armed into Piers's jaw.

Totally unprepared for it, Piers went flying, sending tables and the lamps on them crashing to the floor.

Amid broken glass he struggled to his feet and launched himself at Rory, who was ready and waiting for him. It was a fight that could have gone on for hours, for both were tall and tough and superbly fit, but the uproar could be heard all over the castle and half a dozen people ran from different directions into the room.

When a six-foot-three, seventeen-stone ghillie, who had been in the kitchen paying his respects to the cook, joined in with the task of trying to separate them, the fight was over.

'You'll regret this, Sinclair!' Piers shouted as he was forcibly escorted out to the waiting taxi, blood still pumping from his nose. 'I'm going to marry Lily! You just wait and see!'

'Like hell you will!'

Piers clambered into the taxi and as the driver fired the engine, Rory tore himself free of the ghillie's restraining hold.

He raced towards the car, but the driver was too quick for him and was already picking up speed.

Coming to a floundering defeated halt in its wake Rory shouted after it at the top of his lungs, 'If Edward doesn't marry her, Cullen, it won't be you she'll then marry! It will be me!'

Two weeks later, when he was back in London, Rory gave Rose an edited account of what had happened.

'I know I shouldn't have behaved like that, Rose,' he said as they sat over cups of tea in a small café near the Foreign Office, 'but I was so damned mad with him, I could have killed him.'

'If you had, Lily's hopes of marrying David would have gone straight out of the window. Can you imagine the head-line? "Friend of Prince Edward kills Equerry".'

Rory gave a wry smile. 'Your editor chappie would be pleased by it. You'd be able to write nearly a first-hand account.'

Not wanting to think about Hal, she changed the subject, 'Iris had a run-in with Piers at Snowberry before he hared off to Islay. It was over the same thing. He wanted to know where Lily was. I can't help wondering if we should tell Lily – warn her. *We* all know Piers has become obsessed by her, but Lily, bless her heart, hasn't a clue.'

'Oh, let's talk about something else, shall we? I was sorry to miss Lady Jethney's funeral. She was a lovely lady and I shall miss her. Were there lots of prominent members of the Government there?'

Rose nodded. 'The Prime Minister was there, as was Winston Churchill and the new Home Secretary. The really touching thing was how many ordinary, local people were there. The church where the service was held dates from the fifteenth century and it was so packed that people were standing in crowds outside it in order to pay their respects.'

She didn't describe Jerusha's coffin, laden with a wreath

of yellow roses from her two sons and with a wreath of white roses from Theo. Nor did she even attempt to describe Theo's grief. Beneath his beaver-collared coat his massive shoulders had been bowed, his face ashen as the words of the Twenty-third Psalm filled the church. Afterwards the congregation had sung Jerusha's favourite hymn, 'Abide With Me'.

Marigold, who had been standing next to her, had sung the hymn with tears streaming down her face. Their grandfather had taken hold of her hand, squeezing it comfortingly. Iris hadn't trusted herself to sing at all.

When the service was over Rose had returned to St James's Street with Marigold. Marigold had wanted to be back in London because she was dining with Maxim that evening, and she had wanted to be back in London because she had an early morning meeting the following day with Hal. This time their meeting was to be in his office at the *Daily Despatch*.

As she and Rory left the café together she thought about that meeting and how difficult she now found it to control her feelings when she was with Hal. He had wanted to see her to brief her about the next newspaper piece he wanted from her.

'I want you to write a woman's impressions of the luxury liners now ploughing to and fro across the Atlantic,' he'd said, pushing his chair away from his desk and stretching his legs out in front of him, crossing them casually at the ankles.

Though she'd tried not to look, she hadn't been able to avoid seeing that his socks that day were not purple, but a deep wine-red.

'But they are not a new thing,' she'd said, disappointed the brief wasn't more challenging. 'They've become quite commonplace.'

'The liner due to sail on her maiden voyage next month

isn't commonplace.' He'd flashed her a smile that had turned her knees to jelly. 'The *Titanic* is the biggest liner ever built. She's gigantic, Rose. She has a swimming pool, a ballroom, a gymnasium, Turkish baths. They say she's unsinkable. Harland and Wolff are allowing the press aboard her a week before she sails and I have a press pass here for you.' He'd leaned forward and handed her a small white card.

She'd said, becoming interested, 'Where is she berthed?'

'Southampton.' There'd been amusement in his voice. 'Nice and handy for your home at Snowberry.'

She hadn't responded. She now found it so difficult being in his company that she was always stilted with him, terrified that if she wasn't there would be a repetition of the time his hand had touched hers and then all her emotions would again be plunged into jangling chaos.

He had watched her intently as if trying to read her mind, his grey eyes concerned. 'You don't seem to be yourself, Rose.' Rising to his feet he'd rounded the desk to where she was sitting and put a hand gently on her shoulder.

A tremor she hadn't been able to control had run through her.

When he spoke it was in a manner quite different to his usual casual familiarity. 'I'd like it if you would have dinner with me tonight, Rose. Nothing to do with work. Just the two of us and champagne and perhaps a little dancing . . .?'

It was an invitation she had known would come – and because she had known it would come, she had given a lot of thought as to how she would handle it. None of her practice runs had been as hard as this, though, when he was so near to her she could hardly breathe for wanting to step into his arms.

'No, thank you,' she had said in a voice that didn't seem like hers at all and that couldn't have been more stiffly polite if she had been refusing an offer of a cup of tea.

'Then perhaps tomorrow night?'

'No.' Her throat had been tight and dry and for a dizzying second she'd thought she was going to be unable to continue; but then, standing by her belief that romance had no part to play in the life of someone as militant as she had determined to be, she'd risen to her feet and said, 'Please don't ask me again because the answer will always be the same.'

As if she had slapped him a shutter had come down over his face. Then, his eyes unreadable, he'd stepped away from her, saying, as if the scene between them had never taken place, 'The luxury liners piece. You'll do it?'

'Of course.' And with the press pass clutched in her hand she'd left the office, trying not to think of how wonderful an evening it would have been, dining and dancing with Hal.

'She turned me down flat.'

Hal was having his usual weekly lunch at the Savoy with his uncle, Lord Westcliff. Quite often the lunches were 90 per cent business. Lord Westcliff was a press baron who, even with someone he was as fond of as he was of Hal, didn't indulge much in small talk. Hal, however, had never before discussed his love life with him. That he was doing so now showed how deep his feelings for the girl in question were and how much her rejection of him had hurt.

'If she's a suffragette, as you say she is, maybe she would have turned any man down flat.'

Hal knew very well what his uncle was insinuating. He shook his head. 'No, she isn't a lesbian. If she was, I'd have sensed it long ago.'

Lord Westcliff took a drink of excellent Margaux and speared a mushroom. 'Then maybe there's a man in her life already.'

Hal, uninterested in eating, pushed his barely touched plate of beef bourguignon to one side. 'No, I don't think that's it either.'

'Then what the devil do you think?'

Hal said ruefully, 'I think she doesn't find me at all appealing – and that wild horses wouldn't tempt her to spend time with me over a candle-lit dinner table.'

The chill of February had turned into a very mild March and Marigold had persuaded Maxim to take her out in a rowboat on the Serpentine. Hyde Park was her favourite London park and though it was as full as usual with nannies pushing prams, apart from their own boat the lake was deserted.

Marigold, in a caramel-coloured coat with a fox collar and wearing a fox-fur hat, was reclining on a seat at one end of the boat as Maxim, just as elegantly and inappropriately dressed for boating, was manning the oars at the other end of it.

It was very peaceful, with no sound but the rhythmic splash of the oars. It was, Marigold felt, the perfect setting for a proposal of marriage and as Maxim rested the oars in the rowlocks and said, 'Marigold, my sweet, there's something very important I have to say to you,' she was almost certain that the moment she had been waiting for had, at last, come.

'Yes?' She smiled across at him expectantly, the fox fur emphasizing the colour of her hair and her flawless cream and apricot complexion.

He tilted his head a little to one side as if wondering how to begin and then he leaned towards her a little, his hands clasped between his knees. A ruby ring glittered on the little finger of his left hand. He said: 'In two days' time my engagement to Lady Anne Greveney will be announced in *The Times*. Obviously I want you to be the first to know.'

She blinked, wondering if she had heard aright and then, satisfied that she had, she said crossly, 'I don't like being teased, Maxim – and a tease that isn't even funny.'

'It wasn't meant to be funny, and it wasn't a tease.'

For a second she was too pole-axed to move and then she sat bolt upright, the colour vanishing from her face 'But you can't marry Anne Greveney!' The idea was so preposterous she felt as if she were going to faint. 'You're in love with me! It's me you're going to marry!'

He shook his head, the spring sun highlighting the Slavic lines of his face, the faint hollow under the high cheekbones, the sensual mouth. 'No,' he said. 'I'm not, Marigold. I'm going to marry Anne. But that doesn't mean anything need change between us. There'll be a month or two when we won't be able to see each other – I'm taking Anne to St Petersburg and the Crimea for our honeymoon – but once we return to England the two of us can continue nearly exactly as we have been doing.'

It was how a man would speak to a paid mistress – to a prostitute – and with a searing flash of insight she realized that was exactly how he regarded her, only she hadn't been paid with money, but with gifts. She also knew, without even being told, that Anne Greveney hadn't slept with him and wouldn't until their wedding night, and that the day she, Marigold, had tumbled with such abandon into his bed was the day she'd ensured she would never become Princess Yurenev.

She sprang to her feet, oblivious to the violent rocking of the boat, oblivious to anything but her rage at his unfairness in regarding her as being unmarriageable simply because she'd allowed him to become her lover.

'Sit back down,' he said sharply. 'You're going to have the boat over.'

'You're a bastard, Maxim Yurenev!' The boat rocked more wildly than ever.

Recklessly she launched herself at him with her fists and he went flying backwards. The boat tilted down to the waterline. Marigold fell to her knees and grabbed hold of one of the rowlocks. Maxim had no such luck, and with nothing to seize hold of, he slithered into the lake.

Water slopped into the boat, which then righted itself. Marigold hauled herself on to the seat she had knocked Maxim from and freed one of the oars from its rowlock.

Maxim floundered to his feet and, waist-deep in the water, lunged for the boat.

Marigold didn't hesitate. She plunged the oar into the water and used it like the pole of a punt to push the boat away from him.

Russian expletives poured from his mouth.

Marigold didn't care.

She slammed the oar back in the rowlock and, now there was enough room between them for her to do so, began rowing towards the boathouse.

Beside himself with rage, still swearing like a Russian peasant, Maxim waded after her.

The boat nudged the jetty and came to a halt. Marigold stepped from it, adjusted her hat and, without even looking over her shoulder at Maxim who still had a good distance to cover, she marched away from the lake and out of the park.

Once back at St James's Street she told Sibyl that she had chucked Prince Yurenev and that if she heard stories that it had been the other way around, she wasn't to believe them. Then, not wanting to be in town when his engagement to Anne Greveney appeared in *The Times* and she became the object of pity or, worse, derision, she left for Snowberry.

A week later, while she was glumly sitting in the kitchen talking to Millie, Toby walked in on them, Fizz and Florin at his heels.

'Iris is in the estate room,' she said to him, 'getting this month's accounts in order.'

'I wasn't looking for Iris.' He was dressed for a morning's

shooting in a Norfolk jacket, breeches and a pair of sturdy shoes with leather gaiters.

'Are you on leave?' she asked unnecessarily.

He nodded. 'A long weekend. I wondered if I could have a word with you.'

Marigold, who had always been sure that Toby wouldn't prove to be a faithful husband, and remembering how he had once flirted with her, frowned.

Millie, who was creaming butter and sugar for a cake and who could read her like a book, shot her a quick glance.

'It's important, Marigold.'

Hoping he wasn't going to be embarrassingly predictable, she rose reluctantly to her feet and led the way out of the kitchen.

Once in the passageway beyond, and out of hearing of Millie, he said, 'I don't know how to go about telling you this, Marigold, but some friends of mine were at a party at Marchemont at the weekend, guests of Maxim Yurenev.'

Relieved that he hadn't wanted to speak with her in order to make a pass, but furious that he thought she'd want to hear about Maxim, she said swiftly, 'I'm not interested.'

'I think you will be.' He ran a hand over his straight hair. 'He was showing a painting off to them – and to his other male guests. It was of the goddess Persephone and like most paintings of classical goddesses she was completely starkers. My friends said they'd have known you had posed for the painting even if Yurenev hadn't told them you had. Apparently there was a lot of laughter and some very lewd comments.'

Marigold put a hand to the wall to steady herself. No matter how ignominiously Maxim had jilted her, no matter how humiliating his soaking in the Serpentine, it had never occurred to her that he would seek revenge in such a despicable way.

She thought of how fast news of the painting would spread. She thought of what Rose and Iris's feelings would be when they heard about it; of how it would destroy any hopes of Lily ever becoming the Princess of Wales. She thought of how bewildered her grandfather would be. Last, but by no means least, she grieved for the lovely, lovely painting. It hadn't been painted for men to laugh at and make lewd remarks about. It had been painted to be admired. That Maxim was now making such a travesty of it hurt her to the very depths of her being.

She said unsteadily, 'Please don't worry about anyone else seeing it, Toby. I'll get it back. Iris and Rose and Grandfather need never know about it.'

His relief was colossal. The idea of such a scandal coming within even a mile of Iris was what had prompted him to ask for emergency weekend leave. He didn't ask how she was going to get it back. All he wanted was to be able to call those who had seen the painting liars, and for no one to be able to refute his allegation.

'Thank you for telling me, Toby,' she said, her thoughts already on Strickland. If anyone could get the painting back from Maxim, Strickland could. All Strickland had to do was return the money Maxim had paid for it.

Not even bothering to say goodbye to Toby, she ran along the passage and up the stairs to her bedroom. There was a London train leaving from Winchester in forty minutes. If she didn't bother packing a bag and if her grandfather's chauffeur took her to the station, she would be able to catch it.

Strickland wouldn't let her down. He'd become too good a friend for that. If he acted as fast as she was acting, the painting could be in his hands before nightfall.

Strickland put down his brush, took the cigarette out of his mouth and said with utter certainty, 'Yurenev won't sell it back to me, Marigold. From the sound of it, he's getting too much pleasure out of ruining your reputation with it.'

So agitated she was on the verge of hysterics, Marigold flung herself down on to the chaise longue. 'But you've got to try!' Her green-gold eyes were desperate. 'What's going to happen to Lily and David if you don't? There won't be the slightest hope left for them!'

'David?' It was the first time she'd put a name to her younger sister's secret romantic attachment. 'I thought your sister's romance was with Georgie Battenberg?'

'It isn't. It's with Prince Edward. Don't change the subject, Strickland. You've *got* to get the painting back from Maxim. You've *got* to.'

Strickland, who hardly ever showed emotion of any kind, was still reeling from the idea that for nearly a year Marigold's younger sister had been involved in a secret liaison with the Prince of Wales.

'I'll try,' he said reluctantly, knowing it was the least he could do in the circumstances, but not believing for one moment that he would be successful. 'Where shall I contact you? St James's Street or Snowberry?'

'St James's Street – and don't let the bastard run rings round you, Strickland. You didn't paint Persephone to be sniggered at. You painted her to be adored.'

Not knowing whether Prince Yurenev was in London or at Marchemont, Strickland phoned the Prince's London home first.

'His Highness is not in residence,' a butler said primly.

'Is His Highness at Marchemont?'

'I'm not at liberty to say, sir. Goodbye, sir,' was the stuffy response.

He rang Marigold and got Marchemont's telephone number from her. Five minutes later Princess Zasulich's butler was informing Maxim that there was a telephone call for him.

'Strickland? If you're touting for work and want to paint a portrait of my fiancée you're out of luck. She's already sitting for Sir John Singer Sargent.'

Strickland gritted his teeth. Singer Sargent was always stealing possible clients from him and he couldn't stand the man. Not congratulating Maxim on having obtained Singer Sargent's services, he said bluntly, 'I'd like to buy Persephone back from you. I imagine it's an embarrassment to you now that you've become engaged to someone other than Marigold and I'd like to include it in an exhibition of my paintings to be held in Paris in the autumn.'

'You're a liar, Strickland.' Maxim's voice was as hard as nails. 'You're acting as an errand-boy for Marigold. Well, you're wasting your time. She's as mad as a hatter, a bitch and a trollop and I'm going to make sure everyone who is anyone knows it. She damned near drowned me and she's lucky not to be facing an attempted murder charge!'

He slammed the receiver down so hard Strickland winced.

For several minutes he pondered on whether or not to make the journey to Marchemont and attempt to speak to Maxim face to face. Common sense told him he would be wasting his time.

He lit a cigarette and pondered some more. It was quite obvious Maxim wasn't going to return the painting to him, no matter how much he might offer for it. Even though he was the artist, in Prince Maxim Yurenev's eyes he simply didn't have enough clout.

Who, then, caring for Marigold enough to involve themselves in such a task, did have the clout?

The answer came instantly. Lord Jethney.

Jethney had once been passionately in love with Marigold. He was a government minister. He had the ear of the Prime Minister and, more importantly, would have the ear of the Russian Ambassador to Great Britain and the English

Ambassador in St Petersburg. If anyone would be able to twist Maxim Yurenev's arm, that man was Theo.

With hope beating high in his breast he lifted the telephone receiver again from its rest, wondering just how he was going to open such a tricky conversation.

# THIRTY-TWO

'Could you ever imagine we would be as lucky as this?'

Holding hands, David and Lily walked along the banks of the Seine, as carefree and as unnoticed by anyone as the other young lovers doing exactly the same thing.

'No.' She gave a loving laugh. 'But you are supposed to be in the Louvre with Mr Hansell, listening to a lecture on seventeenth-century French painting.'

'Not on a spring day as warm as this, sweetheart.' He stopped walking and turned her towards him. 'The best thing about our playing hookey is that even if it's discovered there won't be a row about it. Both Guy de Valmy and your mother are intent on fostering a love affair between the two of us. Everything is so perfect I sometimes think I've died and gone to heaven.'

She put a hand up to his face, touching it gently. 'Everything is always going to be perfect between us, David. Even being royal won't spoil things for us – not when we have each other.'

He drew her close, kissing her deeply, so grateful for her love he didn't know how he could even go about expressing it. What he had said about thinking he had died and gone to heaven had been no exaggeration. The last few weeks had been sheer bliss. The de Valmy family were absolutely ace.

Luc de Valmy was a good sport and though as his equerry he was supposed to accompany him at all times, he happily took himself off whenever David gave him the nod that he'd like him to do so. Combined with Guy de Valmy's desire for a permanent relationship between the future King of England and the stepdaughter of his closest friend, it had made spending time alone with Lily as easy as falling off a log.

He said now, as they strolled past a flower stall massed with sharply yellow daffodils and vivid-eyed polyanthus, 'Guy wants to take me to the races at Longchamp. He's planning on turning it into quite an occasion. You and your mother and stepfather are to be invited as well as many of his other friends.'

He shot her a wry smile. 'It's an opportunity for him to let people know that I'm his house guest. It will be rather fun, though. I love horse-racing. It's in my blood. My grandfather, King Edward, absolutely lived for it. Just before he died he received news that his horse Witch of the Air had won the four-fifteen at Kempton Park. He puffed on a cigar to celebrate and died a happy man.'

He interlaced his fingers with hers. 'Do you know what I've always wanted to do, Lily darling? I've always wanted to ride in steeplechases. I'm light enough – you have to be as light in weight as a professional jockey to be a successful steeplechaser – and I'm not scared of risking a few broken bones. When our time in Paris is over, and we're back in England, it's what I'm going to do.'

Lily didn't at all like the sound of broken bones, but she didn't try to dissuade him. She had learned long ago that when David decided upon something, nothing in the world would make him change his mind.

It was the same when he wanted something – as he wanted her. Ever since their snowy February walk in the Bois de Boulogne their lovemaking had become more and more daring. In the de Valmys' large secluded rear garden was a summerhouse and David had brought cushions and travel rugs from the house for its cane furniture. It had become a secret place of retreat for the two of them – and it was where she had given herself to him as if they were already married.

She'd had no regrets. That they now belonged to each other in the most complete way possible filled her with indescribable happiness. She wasn't frightened of becoming pregnant, because even if she did become pregnant, all it would mean was that they would be married as soon as possible instead of waiting for Christmas, which was when David anticipated their wedding would be.

'My parents were married at St James's Palace, in the Chapel Royal,' he said to her. 'It was where my great-grandmother Queen Victoria was married, and I expect it will be where we will be married.'

'What about your grandfather? Where did King Edward marry Queen Alexandra?'

'They were married in St George's Chapel at Windsor. But they weren't king and queen when they married. Like me, my grandfather was Prince of Wales, and he wasn't that much older than me. Twenty, or twenty-one.'

She didn't say that the big difference between his grandfather's wedding and his would be that his grandfather's bride had been a royal princess.

Whenever the subject of her being non-royal came up, he always said urgently, 'Please don't worry about the King not giving his permission, Lily. When I first broached the subject with him he was utterly unprepared for it, and he would have thought that I was just temporarily infatuated with you. Now, after all this time, he'll know differently. The instant I'm back in England I'll speak to him. If our betrothal is announced straight away it will leave plenty of time for arrangements to be put in place for a Christmas wedding.'

She looked away from him and across the steel-grey river to the Île de la Cité.

Notre-Dame was looking poetically grand, its towers and spire heart-achingly beautiful against the pale spring sky. If they wanted, they could cross the river and explore it, just as they could go, and do, anything else they wanted. Once they returned to England all such freedom would be at an end. David would no longer be the 'Earl of Chester' and would again be locked into his royal role.

His entry to Oxford, in October, would be hanging over him and, while he continued to prepare for it, he would also be continuing with what he always called his 'princeing' life and carrying out whatever public engagements King George required of him.

Much as he would hate once again being on the royal roundabout, he was at least familiar with it. It was a way of life he had been brought up with. It was very different for her and once they were married her life would be as circumscribed as his. She would be constantly in the public eye and even when in relative privacy, at Buckingham Palace or wherever else they might find themselves living, she would still have the eyes of the royal household on her, not to mention being under the terrifying scrutiny of King George and Queen Mary and other royals.

As always, the thought sent a shiver of apprehension down her spine. She said impulsively, trying to banish it, 'Let's walk over the next bridge and have a look inside Notre-Dame. It will make up for not attending the lecture at the Louvre. You can study the cathedral's great medieval rose windows instead. Mr Hansell will be impressed.'

There was loving amusement in her voice, for David's interest in art was slight. She didn't mind. She was going to teach him. Just as, when it came to being royal, he was going to teach her.

\*     \*     \*

Within days of their visit to Notre-Dame, David found his social calendar becoming alarmingly full.

'I want you to meet the most stimulating minds in France,' Guy de Valmy said to him, resplendent in a pearl-grey suit and waistcoat, a white gardenia in his lapel. 'Politicians, artists, writers, financiers.' With a wave of his hand he made a Gallic, all-encompassing gesture. 'Everyone who is anyone in French society. From now on I shall host a weekly lunch party at which you will be the guest of honour – and at which French, of course, will always be spoken.'

'So there it is,' David said later to Lily. 'Every week, two or three hours of absolute torture. What on earth am I going to talk about to these people?'

'Let them talk to you. Whenever the marquis holds a salon, he always invites my mother and stepfather. Knowing his private agenda where you and I are concerned, I'd lay odds that I shall be invited as well.'

She was, and just knowing she was in the same room helped him to conduct himself in what Guy de Valmy later told him was an exceptionally agreeable *belle et franche* manner.

'You have the same great gift of charm as your grandfather, King Edward,' he had said to him, 'and your French is nearly as good as his was.'

'Which is utter bosh,' David said later to Lily, 'because my grandfather spoke French like a Frenchman, and I'm never going to be able to do that. Do you know what the next stunt is that's been dreamed up for me? I'm to spend a week with the French Mediterranean fleet off the Côte d'Azur. And not even Guy is going to be able to arrange for you to be with me aboard a French battleship!'

The person who went aboard with him was Luc, who treated him with easy familiarity.

'Tell me, David,' he said in English that was much better

than David's French, 'what ees eet like to be 'eir to a throne? What ees eet a king does all day?'

They were leaning on the rails of the French flagship as, at the front of the fleet, it steamed its way from Marseilles in the direction of Toulon.

David took a deep drag of his cigarette. 'What my father does is read and sign endless state papers that arrive in a constant flow of red despatch boxes. He spends time with his secretaries and other officials. He receives ministers and ambassadors and visiting heads of state. He appoints bishops and archbishops. He conducts investitures. He launches ships and opens buildings. He lays foundation stones. He presides at state banquets. He holds a weekly audience with the Prime Minister.'

'Eet sounds very boring.'

David tossed the butt of his cigarette into the sea. 'It is,' he said. 'So is princeing.'

'Princeing?' Luc looked across at him quizzically.

David ran a hand through his hair. 'Princeing is my department. It means a lot of artificial nonsense. Being dressed up in all kinds of fanciful medieval costumes and enduring banquets that go on for hours and never being able to choose what to do, but always being told – even being told who I will marry.'

'*Merde!*' Luc was horror-struck. 'No one would tell me who I was to marry!'

'No one is going to tell me either.' David's almost effeminately handsome face was grim. 'When I'm king, I won't do things the same way my father has always done them. I shall be far more modern and up to date. My father's social circle is very restricted and he simply accepts whatever he's told about things.'

He turned around, resting his elbows on the deck rails, his back to the sea. 'Take the suffragettes for instance. No one is allowed to speak the word suffragette in the King's presence. It's a subject he won't even discuss. Which means he's never heard their side of things. If he had, he might not be so opposed to them.'

Luc grinned. 'And you, David? Do you sympathize with these wild, wild women who chain themselves to the railings of Ten Downing Street?'

He knew Luc expected him to grin back in amusement, but he didn't. Instead he said with feeling, 'Lily's eldest sister is a suffragette and I admire her enormously. The wild, wild women, as you call them, are fighting a war for justice. I'm on their side, Luc. Whatever kind of king I turn out to be, I won't be a king in the same Victorian-style mould as my father. My father has never stepped out of line, but I think it's safe to say I shall. Some courtiers – the fuddy-duddies who now serve my father – won't like it, but whatever the opposition I'm determined that, as king, I shall be my own man.'

'Will you also be your own man as Prince of Wales?'

This time it was David who grinned. 'I already am. As a lot of people at court are about to find out.'


Shortly after his return from the Mediterranean the marquis and marquise de Valmy held a ball at their mansion in the avenue du Bois de Boulogne. Compared to the ballrooms David was accustomed to, at Buckingham Palace and at Windsor, the de Valmy ballroom was small. Mirror-lined and flower-filled, it was also very beautiful.

Minutes before the first guests arrived Guy de Valmy very respectfully reminded him that his first dance must be with his hostess and that his next dance should be with Lady Bertie, the wife of the British Ambassador.

'Although I know you will want very much to dance with Lily, comment would be caused if you did so before dancing with the other ladies in the order demanded by protocol. It is necessary, for instance, that before dancing with Lily, you dance with her mother.'

David took the reminder in good part, well aware that in his eagerness to dance with Lily in public, he might well have thrown to the winds the etiquette he was steeped in.

In white tie and tails, his hair the colour of pale barley beneath the light of magnificent chandeliers, he stood next to his host and hostess at the head of their grand staircase as they received their guests.

With his Earl of Chester incognito now completely blown, he accepted endless bows and curtseys. When the marquis and marquise de Villoutrey and Miss Lily Houghton were announced, a smile twitched at the corner of his mouth. His relationship with Lily had been such that at their first meeting curtseying had never occurred to her and afterwards it had been something he hadn't wanted, not from her or from anyone else at Snowberry.

This, however, was the very first time she had come into his company in a formal and public situation. Etiquette was etiquette and her curtseying to him was going to be a novel experience for both of them.

As she began walking up the curving sweep of the staircase in the wake of her mother and stepfather his heart slammed hard against his ribs. He had never seen her in an evening gown before and she looked so beautiful he could hardly breathe. Her gown was a dusky shade of pink that perfectly complemented her night-black hair and violet-dark eyes. The narrow chiffon skirt fell to her ankles in rivulets of tiny, floating pleats and she was wearing long glittering earrings and a matching bracelet that he suspected had been lent to her by her mother.

Her stepfather made his bow. Her mother – in a haze of Guerlain's L'Heure Bleue perfume and wearing a sizzling Poiret gown of black and gold, diamonds dancing against her neck – dipped an elegant curtsey.

Then Lily was standing before him.

Her eyes met his, bright with amusement, and then she sank into a curtsey that couldn't have been deeper if she had been curtseying to his father.

His face was as expressionless as he could make it, but there was laughter bubbling in his throat as he inclined his head. After that, as she shook hands with the de Valmys and then followed her mother and Henri into the ballroom, he continued greeting the guests, impatient to have the task over and done with.

He had never before been so keen to enter a ballroom. He waltzed with the marquise de Valmy. He waltzed with Lady Bertie. He waltzed with countless other ladies of mature age who would have felt themselves snubbed if he had not. Then at last, ignoring the scores of debutante-aged French girls all desperate to catch his eyes, he danced with Lily.

She stepped into the circle of his arms, knowing that she belonged there, looking every inch the princess he was determined she soon would be.

The orchestra launched into the opening strains of 'The Blue Danube'. From now on he knew that Strauss would always be his favourite composer, 'The Blue Danube' his favourite waltz.

'I love you,' he said as he swept her out into the middle of the floor.

'I know.' Her lips curved in a deep smile of contentment. 'I love you too. Isn't it wonderful? Isn't it just too magical for words?'

The blatant love in his eyes was her answer and as they whirled round and round the room she knew that no matter how old they became the evening was one neither of them would forget; it was a treasured memory that would last for ever.

# THIRTY-THREE

King George stomped down a Buckingham Palace red-carpeted corridor, heading towards his library. David had arrived back from France late the previous evening and the King had requested an early-morning meeting with him in order to review the months David had spent as a guest of the marquis de Valmy and to inform him of how he would be spending the next few months.

He rounded a corner, bypassed a giant marble statue by Canova and saw with satisfaction that David was already approaching the library from the opposite direction.

'Nice to have you home, my boy,' he said as David walked up to him and gave him the bow all his children gave when meeting with him.

'It's nice to be home, sir.' It wasn't true. What David wanted, more than anything else in the world, was to be back in Paris with Lily.

Scarlet-liveried footmen with powdered hair and white-gloved hands closed the library's double doors behind them. David licked dry lips, his heart pumping like a piston. All his life he had lived in fear of his father's one-to-one interviews and this interview, when he was determined that the subject of his marriage to Lily was going to be settled once and for all, was going to need all the stamina he could muster.

King George settled himself behind his massive Biedermeier desk.

David stood in front of it, legs apart midshipman fashion, just as he had done ever since he was thirteen years old and had first gone to naval college.

The King came straight to the point. 'It would seem you made a very good impression in France, David. Guy de Valmy tells me you impressed everyone you met.'

'That was very kind of him, sir.'

'And Mr Hansell tells me you've learned quite a lot about French history and French political structure.'

'Yes, sir. Though Mr Hansell didn't take me in those subjects himself, sir. Monsieur Escoffier supervised my education in French history and politics.'

'Yes, indeed. I have his report here.' The King drew a folder from the middle desk drawer. Inside it were several letters. Looking at the top letter, he said, 'Monsieur Escoffier has reported that your progress in all things French has been truly amazing.'

David had the grace to blush, well aware that in saying so the kindly Monsieur Escoffier had been exceedingly generous.

The blush went unnoticed by his father who was already referring to a second letter. 'The British Ambassador, Sir Francis Bertie, has written that nothing could have been more self-possessed and tactful than your manner when, in his company, you visited the studio of the painter Monsieur Gillot. He says that in conversation with Monsieur Gillot, you did not hesitate at all in your French.'

He looked up from the letter. 'By that, David, I take it to mean that you have finally lost your John Bull accent?'

'Yes, sir. I think so, sir.'

King George, whose own French was execrable, didn't try to test him.

'Then that is all very satisfactory, David. So now we come to the plans made for you in the interim before you go to Oxford.'

'Sir, if I could just interrupt you for a moment. There's something very urgent I must—'

'Germany,' King George said as if David hadn't spoken. 'Your German is very good, of course. Far better than your French ever was, but there is always room for improvement. On this trip abroad you will be staying with relations. First at the Württemberg court with King Wilhelm and Queen Charlotte and then at Neustrelitz with the Dowager Grand Duchess of Mecklenburg-Strelitz.'

David gritted his teeth. Württemberg, with Uncle Willie and Aunt Charlotte wouldn't be too much of an ordeal, but Neustrelitz, with his mother's aunt Augusta and her son, Grand Duke Adolph Friedrich, would be deathly boring.

The arrangements had, however, been put in place and so there was no point in protesting about them, especially not when he wanted to keep his father in a good mood.

'Captain Cullen will not accompany you. He has proved an excellent equerry, but it is time he now gave his attention to his army career. Several names are under consideration as to your future equerry.'

If David hadn't been about to bring Lily's name into the conversation he would have felt vast relief at the thought of never again having to endure Piers Cullen's humourless company. As it was, struggling to keep his voice steady, he said, 'You may remember, Papa, that last summer I expressed the wish to become betrothed to the dearest girl in the whole world—'

King George's rare good humour vanished. He jumped to his feet, his froglike eyes bulging. 'Not another word!' There was spittle at the corners of his mouth. 'You're going to marry who I damn well say you're going to marry! And you'll marry when I say so, and not a day before!'

David flinched, but stood his ground. 'With all due respect, sir, I am not going to marry Grand Duchess Olga. I'm going to marry a girl of my own choosing. A girl I love with all my heart.'

His father picked up a paperweight and hurled it in the direction of David's head.

Sheet-white, David ducked.

The paperweight smashed into the wall.

'You won't be marrying Olga, because the offer that you do so has been rejected!' That it had been – on the grounds that Olga was still too young for such a decision to be taken – was only compounding King George's current fury. 'What you will be doing, David, is spending the summer in Germany and then the next three years at Oxford. While you are there you will form no unsavoury relationships with housemaids, waitresses or any other kind of scheming adventuress.'

Hearing his father describe the girl he loved so dearly as an adventuress was more than David could bear. 'Lily is neither a housemaid, a waitress, nor an adventuress,' he said tightly. 'She is the daughter of the late Viscount Houghton and the granddaughter of the Earl of May. As far as I am concerned that makes her quite well born enough to be my wife.'

'You're an insolent, stupid young fool!' The veins at King George's temples stood out ugly and purple. 'You are heir to the greatest throne in the world. The girl you marry *has* to be royal. Surely you have the sense to see that?'

'I see that it's why you're sending me to Germany. You're hoping I'll find a German princess who takes my fancy. Well, it's never going to happen. I love Lily. *Really* love her. If you'd only meet her—'

373

'I shan't be meeting her, but Lord Esher will be meeting with Lord May. That, David, will put an end to this stupidity. You're dismissed. By the time we next talk, I pray to God you will have returned to your senses!'

There was nothing for it but for David to leave the room. In the corridor he leaned against the wall to steady his breathing. Nothing had gone as he had hoped it would. All that had been achieved was that his father now knew Lily's identity. He'd lost a battle – a battle he'd thought he would win – but he hadn't yet lost the war. He still had the morganatic card up his sleeve. If Emperor Franz-Josef's heir had married morganatically, he could see no reason why he shouldn't be able to. A morganatic marriage might well suit Lily very well, for she wouldn't then be in the limelight all the time – something he knew she wasn't looking forward to.

King George took far longer to get his breath back than David. For a good half-hour he remained in the library and then, the veins at his temples still throbbing, he went in search of his wife.

She was sitting with a lady-in-waiting in the small sitting room adjacent to her bedroom. There was a fire in the hearth and a small table was set for morning coffee. Both of them were sewing.

The minute he entered the room they both rose hastily to their feet. Queen Mary, realizing instantly how agitated he was, swiftly dismissed her lady-in-waiting and when the door had closed she said in concern, 'George, what is it? What has happened?'

'In my first interview with David since he returned from France he's had the nerve – the unmitigated gall – to tell me he still wants to marry a girl of his own choice. Does the boy have no idea of the responsibilities attendant on his

374

position as heir to the throne? Where is his sense of vocation? His sense of duty? Has Hansell taught him nothing about the history and tradition of the British monarchy?'

As he was speaking he was striding up and down the room, every line of his body taut with frustration and a fury he couldn't curb. 'It turns out the girl in question is the daughter of the late Viscount Houghton. Whenever has a British heir to the throne married the daughter of a viscount? It's ridiculous. Totally unthinkable.'

He came to a halt in his pacing. 'As he won't listen to me, you must speak to him, May.'

Queen Mary froze. She never spoke to her children – or anyone else – about anything other than superficial matters. But as she never disobeyed George, it meant she was now between the rocks and a hard place.

'I'll get Esher to speak to him as well, and the Prime Minister and the Archbishop of Canterbury. David has to be brought to an understanding of how gravely inappropriate his liaison with this young woman is. If he's acting like this at seventeen, how is he going to be acting in another ten years? It doesn't bear thinking about.'

An hour later, fortified by a glass of sherry, Queen Mary made her way to David's suite of rooms. When she entered his private sitting room it was to find him at his bureau, writing a letter. She wondered to whom he was writing and whether it was to the girl he was so infuriatingly besotted with.

'Mama!' He sprang to his feet. His mother had never before visited him unannounced. In fact, he could never remember her ever visiting him in his private rooms. Even when he was a small child, confined with Bertie to the nursery, her visits had been few and far between. It was he and Bertie who, shepherded by Lala Bill, had been taken to visit her.

'It's . . . it's nice to see you, Mama.'

Queen Mary inclined her head, grateful that for the moment David was without his equerry and that Finch was nowhere in sight.

'Please sit down, Mama.' There could be only one reason for his mother's unexpected visit. The King had spoken to her about Lily. He felt a flare of panic at the thought, and then relief. When he mentioned the word morganatic to her, she was bound to be sympathetic. How, with her family history, could she be anything else?

'For what I have to say David, I would prefer to stand.'

'Have you come to talk to me about Lily, Mama? Because if you have, I'm so glad. I've wanted to talk to you about her for a long time and—'

His mother raised a heavily beringed hand to silence him. Lily. So that was the girl's name. It was a very common name, more suitable for a housemaid than for someone well born.

'It won't do, David. When you marry, you will marry suitably.'

'Lily is suitable, Mama.' His eyes, the same midsummer blue as her own, pleaded with her for understanding. 'She's the dearest girl imaginable, and she is wonderfully good for me. She not only makes me happier than I've been before in my life, she gives me confidence to do all the things I find so difficult.'

'What things?' Queen Mary was finding the interview stressful. 'You are not making sense, David.'

'Being on show at ceremonial occasions. She helped me enormously when it came to the coronation and my investiture and I know that if I only have her by my side I won't mind being Prince of Wales. She always encourages me so, you see.'

Queen Mary stared at him, appalled. That he had even

discussed the coronation and his investiture with anyone outside the family was inconceivable to her. As to him implying that he *minded* being Prince of Wales . . . words failed her and she felt very much in need of a large brandy.

Without betraying by a flicker how hard she was finding it to maintain her composure, she said stiffly, 'Brides for future Kings of England have always been royal. Only someone brought up to be royal could possibly cope with the stresses and strains of the exalted position marriage to a Prince of Wales gives.'

He ran a hand nervously over his golden hair. 'Elsewhere, in other countries, accommodations have been made, Mama.'

This time her stare wasn't appalled. It was bewildered.

'Emperor Franz Josef's heir married a non-royal, Mama, and morganatically. I don't think Lily would mind such an arrangement. She's marrying me because she loves me, not because she wants to become a princess. So the title of countess, which is Franz Josef's wife's title, wouldn't matter to her. The thing is, we would still be married and—'

'A morganatic marriage?' Queen Mary felt as if she were about to faint. How did David know about such a thing? He couldn't, of course, know about her own morganatic family background. None of their relations, not even the crassly insensitive Kaiser, would have talked of such a thing in front of him. She put a hand out to a nearby chair in order to steady herself. 'England is not Austria–Hungary. In England there is no precedent for a morganatic marriage.'

'But if Lily and I are happy to abide by the rules of a morganatic marriage – if we are happy that it would be Bertie's children, not ours, that stood in the line of succession to the throne – why would it matter? It would be a solution to the problem, just as it was a solution for your grandfather when he married a non-royal Hungarian countess.'

Queen Mary's knuckles were bloodless as she gripped the back of the chair. She wanted to express to David the humiliation her grandfather's children and grandchildren had suffered as a result of that monumentally selfish marriage. She wanted to portray to him the agony she had undergone as a young girl, a lone serene highness among royal highnesses; the bitterness she still felt at having been perceived as someone not quite royal enough.

Try as she might, she couldn't do so. She was simply too inhibited. When it came to verbal communications of an intimate nature, she simply couldn't bring herself to say the words. Even on her honeymoon with George she had had to resort to pen and paper in order to express her feelings for him.

She did what she always did in such situations. She abruptly terminated the conversation. 'Your father and I expect you to dine with us this evening. I believe Lord Esher will be joining us.'

'Yes, Mama,' he said, equally tersely, knowing very well why Esher had been invited that evening. It was so that Esher, too, could impress on him where his duty lay.

The door had closed behind her and, ignoring the letter he had been writing to Bertie, he walked across to the deep window that looked out over the front courtyard of the palace. Once again, nothing had gone as he had expected. His mother had not been sympathetic when he had suggested the possibility of his marrying Lily morganatically. At his mention of her grandfather's morganatic marriage, she had simply brought the conversation to a swift end.

He put a hand high on the window and leaned his head against his arm, looking down at the great marble edifice that was a memorial to Queen Victoria. He had been so sure that the morganatic card was the one that would solve all his and Lily's problems. Now he could sense from his mother's reaction to the word that his assumption had been very, very wrong.

Things were escalating fast.

But all in the wrong direction.

'Then it got worse,' he said despairingly to Lily.

It was shortly after ten o'clock the next day and they were sitting on a wooden seat overlooking Snowberry's lake.

'Worse? How?' He had told her he was to leave for Germany the next morning; he had told her about the interview with his father and had just finished telling her about the interview with his mother. Lily's face was distraught. 'How could things possibly have got worse, David?'

His arm was around her and he hugged her tightly. 'When I went in to dinner I found myself facing not only Lord Esher, but the Prime Minister and the Archbishop of Canterbury. Asquith told me it was my duty to put my country before everything else, and Archbishop Davidson lectured me on how I must devote my life to the exalted, predestined role I will one day have to play.'

His eyes glinted fiercely. 'But I don't have to play that role, Lily. It isn't inescapable. There are options open to me.'

'I'm sorry, sweetheart. I don't understand.' Tears stung the backs of her eyes as she thought of the way the five people at that dinner table – King George, Queen Mary, Prime Minister Asquith, Archbishop Davidson and Lord Esher – had, together, crushed all their dearest hopes.

He hooked a finger under her chin, tilting her head to his. 'No one can force me to become king, Lily. If it is a choice between one day becoming King Edward VIII, or marrying you, then there is no choice at all.'

'But how . . .? Who . . .?' She couldn't understand what he was telling her.

'Bertie will have to pick up the reins,' he said. 'It won't

379

be easy for him, not with his speech impediment, but he's got a dogged, determined nature. He won't be the same kind of king that I would be, but he'll do all right. I'll be quite happy to put princeing behind me, dearest Lily. All I want is to have a life of my own, and a life lived with you.'

# THIRTY-FOUR

Long after David had returned to London, Lily remained in a state of heartsick, numbed disbelief. When they were in Paris together, David had been so certain that King George would view the idea of their marriage very differently now that they had proved their love by being constant to each other for nearly a year, that she, too, had been equally confident.

Now she saw with sickening clarity just how misplaced that confidence had been. David wasn't just any prince. He was the Prince of Wales. The heir to the throne. The powers that be weren't going to allow him to marry a plain Miss Lily Houghton. Only a princess – or the equivalent of a princess – was going to be acceptable to them.

Because the King, the Prime Minister and the Archbishop of Canterbury were united and adamant in their demand that the future Queen of England should be a queen with royal blood, David was going to walk away from his destiny by not acquiescing to their demands, but by marrying her anyway.

Their marriage would mean he would never be Edward VIII; would never be crowned in Westminster Abbey; would never live up to the duties and responsibilities of the life he had been born into. The people's much-loved golden prince would never be a much-loved great king.

Instead, Bertie would be king. Shy, stammering, introverted Bertie, who didn't have a scrap of David's handsome looks, glamour and charisma, and who was highly unlikely to ever be the modernizing, radical kind of king that she knew David had determined on being.

Sitting up in her eyrie, finished and half-finished paintings scattered around her, her bust of David taking pride of place, she knew it was a sacrifice David couldn't be allowed to make.

At the thought of how strong she was going to have to be, pain knifed through her. She tried to breathe deeply and steadily, but it was as if the walls of her studio were closing in on her.

Abruptly she rose to her feet. If she was to think clearly about what she had to do next, she had to have fresh air. She hurried downstairs, snatched a jacket from a hook in the lobby and, with Fizz and Florin at her heels, set off for a long trudge in the woods.

Rose hadn't been back to Snowberry in over three weeks and as she stepped off the train and walked towards the lone taxi that served the station, she was deep in unhappy thought. Though she'd tried her best to continue taking briefs from Hal and generally behave towards him as if he didn't set her blood racing and her pulse pounding, it was proving to be impossible. There was only one answer as far as she could see, and that was to stop taking briefs from him and to stop writing articles for the *Daily Despatch*.

It was a hard decision to have to come to and not only emotionally, for in writing, and then seeing what she had written published in a national newspaper to be read by hundreds of thousands of people, she had experienced a fulfilment she knew no other kind of work would ever give her. Finding another Fleet Street editor who would give her a chance as Hal had done would not be easy and might well prove impossible.

When she stepped out of the taxi at Snowberry her grandfather walked out of the house to meet her, a small rifle under his arm, Homer at his heels.

'Hello, my pet.' He kissed her on the cheek. 'Are you staying for a while?'

'Not for long, Grandfather. I'm leaving for Southampton on Thursday night to be given a press tour of the *Titanic*.'

'Well, that will be a grand experience for you, but make sure you have a word with Iris before you leave. She's at Sissbury all the time now and she has some very special news for you.'

One look at her grandfather's highly satisfied face and Rose knew at once what Iris's news was.

'She's having a baby?'

He nodded happily. 'It's due in early September. Don't go haring up to the studio in search of Lily. She went out about an hour ago with the dogs.'

'Which direction?'

'The woods. I'm not going in the same direction. I'm heading for the hill.'

'To shoot rabbits?'

He said defensively, 'Wild rabbits aren't tame rabbits, Rose. They have to be kept under control.'

It was an argument she'd heard before and didn't agree with, but she'd no intention of getting into a discussion about it now. 'I'll go and meet up with Lily,' she said and, hoping he would be unsuccessful once he reached the hill, she set off towards the woods.

When after a fifteen-minute walk she saw Lily approaching

from the opposite direction, she came to an abrupt halt. Lily's head was bowed, her shoulders hunched and though Rose couldn't be sure she was almost certain Lily was crying.

'Lily!' she called out, beginning to walk again, this time very fast. 'Lily! What's the matter? Are you all right?'

Lily lifted her head and Rose saw she wasn't merely distressed, but grief-stricken.

Appalled, she ran up to her, saying urgently as she came to a breathless halt and put her arms comfortingly around her, 'Lily love, whatever has happened?'

'David and I are not going to be able to marry.' Lily's voice was raw with pain. 'King George won't even consider it, and neither will the Prime Minister nor the Archbishop of Canterbury.'

'Oh sweetheart, I'm so sorry.'

'There's worse, Rose. David won't accept their decision. He says he's going to marry me anyway, even if it means him never becoming king.'

Rose blinked. 'He can't not be the next king, Lily. Not unless he dies before his father.'

'He can if he steps down from the succession in order to marry me. That is what he is going to do, Rose. Not even my refusal to marry him will prevent him from doing what he's set on, because he won't accept such a refusal. He's shatteringly obstinate. Once he's determined on a course of action, nothing in the world will deflect him. The only thing that would is if I were to marry someone else. I would do that, only it isn't an option I have.'

'Of course it is! You could—'

'No, I couldn't, Rose. I'm having a baby.'

Rose opened her mouth to speak, but no words came.

Fizz and Florin skittered around their feet. In one of the nearby trees two rival birds wrangled noisily. A small woodland creature scuttled fast into the undergrowth, evading the dogs.

All Rose could think of was that if things had been different, if King George had given David and Lily his blessing when David had first asked for it, the baby Lily was carrying would be second in line to the throne.

'Oh dear God!' she said at last. 'Oh *dear* God, what on earth are you going to do?'

Lily began walking again, her hands deep in the pockets of her jacket. 'I don't know. I only know I mustn't tell David about the baby. If I do no force on earth will prevent him from announcing himself to be the father and then his reputation will be in tatters, the scandal worldwide. The only way to avoid such a nightmare is for me to go away, which will be relatively easy for me to do, because David is about to leave for Germany in order to perfect his German. Once he realizes what I've done he will, though, race back and try and find me. The only way to prevent him from doing so is for you and Grandfather to convince him that I've married someone else.'

Giddily, Rose tried to think. 'Is David leaving for Germany immediately?' she asked, seizing on the only thing that could possibly give them breathing space in which to act.

'Yes. He leaves for Württemberg tomorrow.'

'Then what you are thinking of doing could be done. But wherever you went Lily, you couldn't go on your own.'

'I was hoping you would come with me.' Her voice was hesitant, as if, with the best will in the world, Rose might not be able to.

'Of course I'll come with you. How could you possibly think for a moment that I wouldn't?'

'I don't know . . . your life in London . . . Christabel . . . the *Daily Despatch*.'

'Christabel can easily do without me, and so can the *Daily*

*Despatch*.' She didn't say a word about Hal – who would probably not even notice her absence – because she couldn't trust herself to say his name without her voice giving her away.

As they stepped out of the woods and began approaching the house, Lily said bleakly, 'How could something so beautiful as David's love for me, and mine for him, turn into a situation so ghastly, Rose?'

Rose had no answer.

She was too busy feverishly trying to work out what to do next.

They entered the house to be met by a harassed-looking William. 'There has been a telephone call for his lordship from Lord Esher, Miss Rose. I told Lord Esher his lordship was out for a morning's shooting and he said not to worry, but that he would be at Snowberry by lunchtime.'

Rose and Lily looked at each other. Lord Esher was not a close friend, or even an acquaintance, of their grandfather. He was, though, known to be a close friend and adviser to King George. Both of them knew what his purpose was in coming to Snowberry.

'I'm going up to the studio.' Lily was so pale she looked ill. 'I need to be on my own for a little while, Rose.'

Rose nodded. In order to get her thoughts in order, she, too, needed to be on her own for a little while. One thing was abundantly clear. Lily's horrendous situation had made her own one relatively simple. She wouldn't now wait until after her tour of the *Titanic* to sever all contact with Hal and the *Daily Despatch*. She would do so immediately. And as for where she and Lily should now go, she would speak to Rory. Even if Iris and Marigold weren't told the entire truth of the situation, Rory would have to be told. She needed someone she could confide in; someone whose advice she could trust.

386

She walked into the drawing room. If she telephoned Rory now, and if he was in London, then it was just possible that if he drove fast, he could be at Snowberry before Lord Esher arrived.

She put her hand out towards the telephone and Fizz and Florin erupted in a storm of barking to tell her that a car was coming down the drive.

She dropped her hand, her heart racing. Was Snowberry's visitor Lord Esher? When he had telephoned Snowberry had he already been nearby and not, as she and Lily had assumed, still in London?

The drawing room didn't look out over the drive. From its French doors and large windows she could only see the vast lawns stretching down to the lake and the hill rising on its far side; the hill where her grandfather, oblivious of Lord Esher's impending arrival, was still happily hunting rabbits.

She heard the front door open. Heard footsteps approaching the drawing room. With her heart feeling as if it was somewhere up in her throat, she smoothed her skirt and faced the door.

Rory, kilt swinging, strode into the room.

'Oh dear God.' Weakly she sank on to a sofa. 'I thought you were Lord Esher.'

'Esher? Why on earth? He's not Marigold's latest conquest, is he?'

'No. Though I wish Marigold was the reason he's coming. As it is, King George now knows Lily's identity and Lord Esher is coming down to speak with Grandfather.'

'I take it King George isn't happy about the prospect of David marrying Lily?'

'No, he isn't. From what Lily has told me the King has reacted exactly as everyone – other than David and Lily – expected him to react.'

Rory sat down on the arm of a nearby chair. 'So this is the end of the fairy-tale?'

'Yes – and the beginning of a nightmare.'

Rose never indulged in unnecessary dramatics and Rory frowned. 'How so? If the King now knows and disapproves, they have to stop seeing each other. That's all there is to it.'

'No, it isn't. Will you pour me a whisky, Rory? You'd better have one, too. A large one.'

He'd never known her to drink spirits; with his frown deepening, he did as she asked. When he was again seated on the arm of the chair and they both had glasses in their hands, he said, 'Come on, Rose. Tell me the worst. It can't be that bad.'

She didn't waste her breath in telling him that it was. She said, 'I know you are on friendly terms with David, having met him so often at Snowberry, but you don't know the real David. The real David is the most obstinate young man alive. When he wants something he won't allow anything to stand in his way – and I really do mean anything.'

She took a swallow of her whisky. 'He has told Lily that even if it means abnegating all his royal responsibilities and Prince Albert stepping into his shoes, he is going to marry her.'

'He can't. The Royal Marriages Act won't allow him to. Ever since seventeen seventy-two no descendant of King George II has been allowed to marry without the monarch's consent. Not if he, or she, is under twenty-five.'

'What happens after they are twenty-five?'

'I'm not sure. I'd have to check. But I think that after they are twenty-five they can marry if they give a year's notice to the King's privy council. Or they can if both Houses of Parliament don't object.'

Rose pushed a straying strand of chestnut hair back into the thick knot in the nape of her neck. 'The Royal Marriages

Act isn't going to prevent David from telling King George that unless he's allowed to marry Lily he's no longer going to carry out any of his duties as Prince of Wales. That is what he's going to do when he comes back from Germany.'

'Germany?'

'As of tomorrow he'll be at the court of Württemberg and he's going to be there for several weeks. Once he's back and has dropped his bombshell, the King, the Prime Minister and the Archbishop of Canterbury are all going to consider him a disgrace to his position. After all, if he isn't putting duty first in this situation, how can he be expected to do so in the future, when he's king? If what you say is true, it will all be for nothing. Because of the Royal Marriages Act he *still* won't be able to marry Lily.'

'You're not taking into account the possibility that faced with such stubbornness on David's part, King George might well change his mind and give his consent after all.'

'I'm not sure he can. There's never been a non-royal Princess of Wales – or not since medieval times. Mr Asquith has spoken to David and has told him it's something the Government couldn't possibly countenance. The Archbishop of Canterbury has told him the same thing. When David comes back from Germany and tells his father what he intends, the almost certain result is that he'll never succeed to the throne.'

'How does Lily feel about that?'

Rose drained her glass. 'She isn't going to allow him to make such a sacrifice.'

'Just how is she going to stop him?' Rory asked with deep interest.

With an unsteady hand Rose set her empty glass down on the coffee table in front of the sofa. 'Lily says that her refusal to marry him wouldn't be enough to prevent him from acting as he intends. She says he would be so certain she would marry him if she could that he'd simply take no notice of her. She says the only thing that will prevent him abandoning all his royal duties is if she marries someone else.'

Rory, who had strong private thoughts on who that someone else should be, swirled the whisky around in his glass and said, not giving his thoughts away, 'That could well be a very good idea.'

'It may be a good idea, but it isn't a feasible one.'

'Why not?'

'Because no one is likely to propose to her. Lily is pregnant, Rory. Seven weeks going on eight.'

The blood drained from Rory's face.

She said tautly, 'What Lily and I have decided is that while David is in Germany she will write to him telling him she has fallen in love elsewhere and has married. She and I are then going to go somewhere she can have the baby and where she can stay long enough so that if David ever does discover she's had a baby, she'll be able to fudge about exactly how old it is.'

The shock he had sustained turned to incredulity. 'Are you telling me David doesn't know about the baby?'

'No. And for obvious reasons he must never know he is the father – and nor must anyone else.'

'Sweet Christ, I should think not!'

At the thought of the scandal and the constitutional repercussions if it ever became known that the seventeen-year-old Prince of Wales had fathered a child Rory's head span.

He put down his glass of whisky and rose to his feet.

Her hand shot out to restrain him. 'Please don't go back to London, Rory! I want you to be here when Lord Esher arrives. I want you to be here when Lily and I tell Grandfather about the baby – and about what Lily has decided to do.'

'I'm not going back to London.' His voice was as grim

as his face. 'I'll be here when Esher arrives. Where is Lily now, Rose? In her studio?'

'Yes, she wanted to be on her own for a little while.'

'I dare say she did, but I'm not going to allow her to be on her own. I'm certainly not going to allow the two of you to go off to God knows where by yourselves.'

With a pulse pounding at his jawline, he strode from the room.

She hesitated for a moment and then sprang to her feet and hurried after him, wanting to know what he intended saying to Lily, but by the time she reached the hall he was already taking the second flight of stairs two at a time.

Rory didn't knock on the studio's door. He simply opened it and walked in.

Lily was seated on the long seat in front of the floor-to-ceiling skylight, her knees pulled up to her chest, her arms around them. Startled, she turned her head towards him, her eyes darkly ringed, her face deathly pale.

'Rose has told me,' he said. 'She's told me everything.'

'About the baby as well?'

He nodded.

'I'm going to go away.' Her voice was hoarse from all the crying she had done. 'It's the only way I can prevent David from ruining his life. You see, Rory, David was pre-destined to be a prince. He's only just begun to carry out public duties, but already when he does so he makes far more impact than King George has ever done. King George is too stern to be charming, but David can't help but be charming. He simply *is*.'

He drew up a battered bentwood chair and sat within touching distance of her.

She said, 'When we were in Paris, because David's visit was a private one, he was there incognito, and for the first few weeks the incognito worked – sort of. After that, if he went to the opera or somewhere similar with the marquis and marquise de Valmy and a party of their friends, photographers sprang out of the woodwork and crowds gathered to cheer him and wish him well. He was *fantastic* with those crowds, Rory. He responded to them in a way that was quite wonderful. Though he doesn't like a lot of what he describes as "princeing", he's very good at it. More than good. He's gifted. That is why he can't possibly abandon the role he was born to fulfil. That is why I'm going to have to lose him – and he's going to have to lose me.'

He took her hand in his. 'You're right to think that only if you marry someone else will he give you up. So what I'm going to ask you, Lily, is this: will you marry me? I know you're not in love with me. You are still in love with David and maybe always will be. That's something I'm prepared to accept. But I'm in love with you, Lily. If it hadn't been for David I would have told you so months ago. I know that you like me an awful lot and that you like being with me and that's a start, isn't it? Who knows, maybe you'll begin to love me a little and one day love me rather a lot.'

Time wavered and halted. As sunlight streamed through the skylight window on his fiery red hair, Lily remembered all the times when she had raced happily to meet him, at Snowberry and at her Great-aunt Sibyl's and at Castle Dounreay. When she had been with Rory she had never been unhappy. He was handsome and honourable and brave and never boring, and she knew that debutantes in their droves would, if he had proposed to them, have accepted instantly.

'I'll leave the Foreign Office,' he said, his eyes holding hers. 'We'll live at Gruinart, which is about as far from Windsor and Buckingham Palace as it is possible to get. At Gruinart you'll be able to paint and sculpt to your heart's content and I'll be far happier managing the family estate instead of leaving things in the hands of an estate manager. It will get you out of the terrible situation you are in – and it will make me very happy. Please say yes, Lily.'

In her present hideous situation she knew that this was a proposal she would be insane to refuse – though she also knew that it was one she would have turned down if it hadn't been Rory proposing to her.

But she wasn't going to refuse Rory's proposal.

He had been part of her life ever since she was born and though she had never thought herself in love with him, she had most certainly always loved him, and he loved her. If she was to save David from regal suicide, it was enough. It was more than enough.

'Yes,' she said. 'But we'll have to marry soon, Rory. Before David returns from Germany.'

'The sooner, the better.' He drew her to her feet, kissing her on the cheek, as he had always kissed her. Passion would come later, when she was over her grief for David. He was too much in love with her – and too desperate for her to be in love with him – to want to spoil things by rushing them.

# THIRTY-FIVE

Rose's reaction, when Rory and Lily had entered the drawing-room hand in hand and had told her they were going to marry, was one of unspeakable relief. Hard on its heels came fresh anxieties.

'Lord Esher must be told *why* Lily is marrying in such haste. He has to be told that David intends abdicating his royal role in order to spend the rest of his life with Lily and that the only way she can prevent him from reneging on his birthright in such a way is by marrying elsewhere. It has to be impressed on him that it will all be for nothing if David is told of the marriage, or of Lily's reasons for entering into it, before it takes place.'

There was something else that she felt was vitally important.

'The only people to know that the baby is David's, and not Rory's, must be the three of us. No one else must know. Not Iris. Especially not Marigold. Not even Grandfather.'

Rory and Lily's agreement was total and then, with that matter settled, Rory said, 'As the wedding needs to take place before David returns from Germany, we have to decide where it is going to happen so that the banns can be called. Is it to be on Islay, or here in Hampshire?'

'Hampshire, I think,' Rose said, as if she, not Lily, was to be the bride. 'The more people who can vouch for the wedding having taken place, the better. I suggest both of you go and speak to the vicar straight away. Banns have to be called on three successive Sundays which will give you a wedding date of somewhere around the end of April.'

Neither Lily nor Rory wanted a fancy wedding and when Rose received an invitation to an afternoon party at Lord Westcliff's, in Hampstead, Lily insisted she return to London in order to attend it.

'There are hardly any wedding arrangements to make and so you may just as well be in London.' Lily sounded almost as practical as Iris. 'I didn't know you knew Lord Westcliff. Is he a friend of Great-aunt Sybil's?'

'No, I don't think so. And I don't know him.'

Lily stared at her, mystified. 'Then why have you received an invitation from him?'

'I don't know.' And then, realizing she needed to do at least a little explaining, she said, 'He owns the *Daily Despatch*, Lily. Perhaps it has been sent to me in error. Or perhaps it isn't a genuine invitation and someone is playing a joke on me.'

'Why don't you ring Mr Green? He'd know if it was a joke or not.'

Rose hadn't rung Hal, but she had rung his secretary.

'Of course it isn't a mistake, Miss Houghton.' Hal's secretary was quite affronted that Rose had thought such a mistake even possible. 'Lord Westcliff is a socialist who behaves very generously to his employees. The party is an annual event.'

'Does everyone go?' she'd asked.

'Absolutely everyone. Even the husbands and wives of employees are invited. Children aren't, of course, but Lord

Westcliff always makes an exception with Mr Green and he always takes Jacinta.'

For a moment Rose wondered if she had heard correctly. She couldn't have. It wasn't possible.

'Jacinta?' she said, waiting for the world to be made right again.

Hal's secretary said helpfully, 'Jacinta is Mr Green's adopted daughter. She's a sweet girl. It's always a pleasure to see her. Do please remember, Miss Houghton, that absolutely *everyone* attends Lord Westcliff's party. To not attend is quite unthinkable.'

The line went dead and Rose, feeling as if the ground was shelving away beneath her feet, clutched the telephone receiver, her knuckles white.

An adopted daughter? Surely only married men had adopted daughters? As she thought of what his behaviour in asking her out to dinner would mean if he was married, she felt physically ill. It would mean he had no respect for her at all. It would mean he wasn't even close to being the kind of man she had believed him to be.

With difficulty she prised her fingers from the telephone. Then she went in search of her grandfather.

'Do you know if Lord Jethney is at home or in London?' she asked.

Her grandfather put down the newspaper he had been reading. 'He's at home, Rose. Why do you want to know?'

'Nothing important. I just wanted to ask him something about an article I'm writing.'

She left him to his paper and ten minutes later was cycling in the direction of Theo's family home.

She had been there before on occasions such as a birthday party for Jerusha, but she had never been there unaccompanied – and had certainly never uninvited.

When the butler opened the door to her she could tell by

the expression on his face that though he recognized her as being one of Lord May's granddaughters, he had no idea which granddaughter she was. Like all good butlers he was imperturbable and though he must have thought her unexpected, windblown arrival most odd, he didn't betray his feelings by a flicker.

Theo wasn't so composed. 'Good heavens, Rose!' he said, striding to meet her as she entered the drawing room. 'Is the telephone line down? Is your grandfather ill?'

'No – and no one is ill. I need to ask you something and speaking on the telephone just didn't seem the right way of going about it.'

'Sit down. Would you like a cup of tea? A sherry?'

She shook her head. 'No thank you, Theo.' She sat down, saying apologetically, 'I'm truly sorry to be troubling you in this way – and when you know what I've come about you're probably going to think me an awful fool . . .'

'I know you too well to ever think that, Rose.'

He seated himself in a nearby armchair.

She clasped her hands tightly in her lap, not knowing how to start.

Seeing her dilemma, he said gently, 'If there's anything I can help you with, Rose, whatever it is, you have only to ask.'

Knowing that she was going to reveal far more about herself than she could possibly feel comfortable with, but knowing she had no option, she said, 'Please believe me when I say I have a very good reason for asking this – that I'm not asking out of prurient interest – but . . . is Hal Green married?'

Amused that that was all she wanted to know and even more amused at what he assumed was her reason for wanting to know it, he said gravely, 'Hal is a bachelor, Rose. And a very eligible one.'

Her relief was vast. If she had been on her own she would probably have burst into tears.

'Am I allowed to ask why it was so important for you to know?' Theo asked, though he was pretty sure he already knew the answer.

'A little time ago he invited me to have dinner with him. I didn't accept the invitation because . . . well, because romantic relationships aren't compatible with being a militant suffragette. Earlier today, though, I received an invitation to a party at Lord Westcliff's. I thought perhaps the invitation was some kind of a joke and rang Hal's secretary, who explained to me that it was an annual event held for all of Lord Westcliff's employees. She said that the husbands and wives of employees went as well, but not children – apart from Hal's adopted daughter, Jacinta.'

'Ah! And so the conclusion that he could very well be married?'

She nodded.

He smiled. 'As you no doubt know by now, Rose, Hal is a very unusual kind of man. Jacinta is Spanish. Her parents were employed by him as a cook and as a chauffeur. Four years ago they were killed in a train accident, and when it was found there was no other family, Hal adopted their orphaned daughter. It was an action entirely typical of him.'

A little while later, as he accompanied her to the door, he said musingly, 'I'm not sure you are right in thinking that romantic relationships are incompatible with being a suffragette, Rose. If two people who love each other espouse the same cause, there is absolutely no telling what they might achieve together.' He smiled at her affectionately. 'And in my book,' he added, 'men like Hal Green don't come along very often.'

She knew very well what he was hinting – and she also knew she was going to disappoint him. Her concern with whether Hal was married or not wasn't because she wanted to become Mrs Hal Green. It was because she hadn't been able to bear the thought that he was dishonourable. She did, though, think there could be a little leeway in her principles. Romance didn't have to lead to the shackles of marriage. If Hal sensed the change in her thinking and made a romantic overture to her again, she was going to accept it. And the very best scenario for such an event to take place was at a party.

On the day before the party she went to a fashion house patronized by her great-aunt and bought herself a ready-made gown of eau-de-nil and a wide-brimmed hat of the same colour, decorated with a white rose.

'I hope you are not thinking of travelling to Lord Westcliff's on public transport,' her great-aunt said to her, very pleased at how elegant Rose looked. 'I shall not be needing the Daimler, and so Surtees will both take you and bring you home.'

Lord Westcliff's London home was in Hampstead. It was a warm day for April and the party was taking place as much in the large garden as it was in the house. A small orchestra was playing within the house. It seemed that everyone, apart from herself, knew someone to whom they could talk. As waiters served flutes of champagne and glasses of orange juice, scores of small groups chatted noisily together with people constantly drifting, glass in hand, from one group to another.

French doors led from the house out on to a terrace and it seemed to her that by standing near to them she could appear to be either on the point of entering the house, or on the point of walking out into the garden, and wouldn't look to be so obviously unaccompanied.

A waiter approached her and she put her empty glass of

orange juice on the tray he proffered. As she was picking up another one Hal entered the crowded room and her heart leaped.

Then she saw that he wasn't alone.

Joy vanished in an instant.

The woman walking closely at his side and laughing at something he had just said was wearing a cornflower-blue silk dress that emphasized her tiny waist and lovely breasts and looked as if it had come from a Parisian fashion house. Instead of a hat, there was a knot of camellias in her hair, which was as pale as summer wheat.

Hal said something else as he smiled down at her. Laughing again, she hugged his arm.

Not wanting to see any more, Rose turned away so quickly orange juice slopped over her gloved hand.

She met the gaze of a young girl aged about twelve.

The girl said, eyeing her with interest, 'You've just spilled orange juice on your glove.'

'Yes, I know.' Rose struggled for composure. 'It was very clumsy of me.'

'I'm always doing things like that. I've just stood on the hem of my dress and torn it. Papa Hal is going to be very irritated.'

She'd known immediately, of course, who the child was, but hearing her speak of Hal in such a way transfixed her.

There was loving indulgence in her voice. It was exactly the way she and Iris, Marigold and Lily often spoke of their grandfather. They did so not because he had done what he felt was right – which was providing them with a roof over their heads – but because he had loved them and cherished them and had never treated them with anything but the most exquisite kindness. In a moment of utter certainty Rose knew that Jacinta was as fortunate in Hal as she and her sisters had been in their grandfather. She also knew that Theo had been speaking the literal truth when he had said that men like Hal didn't come along very often.

'That's Papa Hal over there.' Jacinta gestured in Hal's direction. 'Do you know him?'

'A little.'

The blood was drumming in her ears. If she had behaved differently there was every possibility she would now be the young woman holding his arm; the young woman who was absorbing all his attention. She didn't know it was possible to feel such pain; such intense regret: such bitter unhappiness.

Unaware of Rose's distress, Jacinta said disarmingly, 'My name is Jacinta. What is yours?'

'Miss Houghton.'

Panic throbbed high in her throat. She had to leave the party, but she couldn't cross the room. To cross the room would be to risk attracting his attention.

'I'd like to go home without having to weave a way through all these groups of people, Jacinta. Is there a gate in the garden that leads into the street?'

'Yes, but it is right at the bottom of the garden, at the far side of the shrubbery. Would you like me to come with you?'

'No thank you, Jacinta. I'll be able to find it.'

Somehow she managed a goodbye smile and stepped out on to the terrace. It was crowded with people, but no one knew her and no one made any attempt to waylay her in conversation. Swiftly she walked down the steps and on to the lawn. Here, too, there were several groups of people, because although it was still only April, the sun was as warm as if it was May.

With tears burning the backs of her eyes she wove a path between Lord Westcliff's guests.

In the house, Jacinta edged her way towards Hal.

'You're going to be very cross with me,' she said when she

reached his side, knowing that he wouldn't be, because he never was. 'I've trodden on the hem of my dress and torn it.'

Hal made a facial expression of exasperation that made her laugh.

'I've just been talking to ever such a nice lady,' she said, glad that the blonde lady was no longer hanging on to his arm and that she had him to herself. 'Her name is Miss Houghton. I would have liked to talk to her some more, but she said she wanted to go home. She asked if there was a gate in the garden that led into the street. I told her there was and she walked off so quickly I didn't have time to say anything else.'

Partygoers hadn't ventured into the lower part of the garden and as Rose reached it she walked as quickly as her high heels would allow, desperate to be back in her bedroom at her great-aunt's where, with the door locked, she could give way to her unhappiness.

The shrubbery slowed her down, for the path between the high banks of laurels and rhododendrons was narrow and twisting. Suddenly, with the gate not yet in sight, she realized someone was running after her – and that the running footsteps were far too heavy to be Jacinta's.

Alarmed, she spun round just as Hal rounded the last corner of the path.

He came to a halt a yard or so in front of her, saying a trifle breathlessly as he pushed an unruly lock of hair back from his forehead: 'Jacinta insisted I came after you. Though to be honest, she didn't have to insist very much. She's my adopted daughter, but I know she will have explained that. It's the first thing she tells anyone. What I want to know is, why are you leaving the party before it has scarcely begun? I promised Gerald I'd introduce you to him and he's on the terrace, waiting for me to do so.'

'Gerald?' She hadn't a clue who he was talking about – and didn't care. All that mattered was that he was behaving towards her as he had always done and that – the blonde notwithstanding – there was a glimmer of hope their relationship was again on its old footing.

'Gerald,' he repeated with exaggerated patience. 'Lord Westcliff. Your host. My uncle.' A thought suddenly occurred to him and his eyes darkened in concern. 'You're not ill or anything, are you, Rose?'

'No.' As it was impossible to tell him the truth – though she rather thought she would one day – she said, 'There was no one I knew and I felt out of place.'

Amusement replaced his concern. 'Hard-nosed journalists don't care if they know no one. And – trust me, Rose – they never feel out of place.'

She shot him a wobbly smile. 'I'll try and remember.'

His answering smile melted her bones. 'Come back to the house. Jacinta wants to talk with you some more and my uncle – who is not accustomed to waiting for people – is still waiting for the two of us to put in an appearance.'

He crooked his arm in order that she could slip her hand through it.

She did so, as if it was the most natural thing in the world.

It was on the tip of her tongue to ask about his blonde companion, and then instinct told her that whoever the young woman was, she no longer mattered. Only the new relationship she and Hal were forming mattered.

As they walked together back to the house she knew that from now on things were going to be all right between them. That they were going to be more than all right. That for her and Hal Green, things were going to be wonderful.

# THIRTY-SIX

Marigold was in a depression so deep she didn't know how she was ever going to claw her way out of it. For everyone else, life was roaring along full of interest and excitement, and in her life, all interest and excitement had come to a grinding, stultifying halt.

She was in a cinematograph theatre that had been commandeered by Sibyl in order that one of her guests, Mr Zac Zimmerman, an American director with the American Mutoscope and Biograph Company, could give her and her other guests a private showing of his latest film. Everyone gathered there, apart from Marigold, was in a state of excited anticipation.

Marigold felt more like slitting her throat than joining in the general chatter. Alone of all her sisters, her life had become as flat as a pancake. Iris had the baby to look forward to and (though it was hard to understand why) she was also blissfully happy living at Sissbury with the chinless Toby, who had recently bought himself out of the Guards.

Rose was in the throes of a love affair with Hal Green – and having met Hal, Marigold was, for the first time in her life, envious of her blue-stocking sister.

As for Lily . . . When it came to Lily, words failed her. Because King George wouldn't give his consent for her and David to marry, and because David had vowed to marry her even if it meant renouncing his succession to the throne, Lily had decided to marry Rory.

'She's doing it to prevent David from denying his destiny,' Rose had said to her.

Rory hadn't denied Lily's motive, but he'd added that though Lily didn't realize it yet, he was going to be far better for her than David ever would be.

All Marigold knew was that all her hopes of becoming sister-in-law to the Prince of Wales, and one day sister-in-law to the King, were in ruins.

With Snowberry now a house full of wedding plans, she had put a temporary end to visits there – especially after her last visit, when Piers Cullen had unexpectedly turned up, demanding to see Lily.

Mercifully, Lily had been at Sissbury, discussing with Iris the small reception that was to be held at Snowberry after her and Rory's wedding.

'Lily isn't here,' Marigold had said to him and then, thinking herself rather clever, had added, 'She's visiting relatives on the Isle of Islay.'

'You're a bloody liar!'

He had been so furious she had thought he was going to hit her. Instead, white-lipped and cobra-eyed, he had stormed back to his car and roared off down the drive, missing Homer by inches.

'The star of the movie is Mary Pickford,' Zac Zimmerman was saying to those about to watch it. 'She's a great gal. Every nickelodeon in the country is showing a one-reeler or a two-reeler that I've featured her in. Give it another year and she'll be as famous as blueberry pie.'

Marigold was listening to him with only half an ear. If all

her sisters' love lives were going great guns, hers certainly wasn't. Making that fact even worse was all the fuss *Tatler* was making about Maxim's forthcoming wedding to Anne Greveney. A leading article had been gushing.

It is rumoured the bride will be wearing the pearl-encrusted gown Prince Yurenev's mother wore at her wedding. Her fifteen-foot point de Flanders lace veil will be held in place by a tiara containing over three hundred brilliants, the centrepiece being a white sapphire of thirty-seven carats. Wedding gifts already on display at the Yurenev palace in St Petersburg include a ruby and diamond parure, a gift from the Tsar and Tsarina, and a parure of diamonds and pearls from the groom's parents to the bride.

When she first read the article Marigold had wondered what had been included in the parures. Usually such a large set of jewellery included a diadem, a necklace, drop earrings and stud earrings, a brooch, a bracelet. Sometimes it even included a waist-clasp and hair combs.

Even worse than the thought of all the jewels that could have been hers, and now never would be, was the way she was being cold-shouldered by people she had assumed were her friends. Without casting a poor reflection on himself, Maxim had spread enough salacious rumours about her to ensure she now rarely received invitations to parties or weekends in the country. If it weren't for Sibyl, who was unconventional enough to stand by her, her social life would have been zilch.

The lights were lowered, the jerky movie began, and for a brief half-hour Marigold forgot all about Maxim and Anne Greveney. She wanted to be Mary Pickford. She wanted to be up there on the screen, one minute in the arms of a dashing hero, next minute struggling against the lecherous hold of a wicked villain. She wanted to be tied to a railway track and rescued seconds before a train thundered down on her. She wanted to be seen and adored by thousands and thousands of cinemagoers. In a moment of shattering revelation she knew what she wanted to be. She wanted to be a movie star.

That evening, when the guests who had attended the private viewing were seated around Sibyl's mammoth dinner table, the talk was all about Hollywood and the movies.

'But what about New York?' Ivor Conisborough asked Zac Zimmerman, bemused. 'Are you telling me films aren't being made there any more?'

'Of course they are. It's where Biograph is still based. But in the little village of Hollywood, movie-makers don't have to pay the fees demanded by Thomas Edison. He's the guy who owns the patent on the movie-making process. Also, the mild weather and the reliable sunlight make it possible to film movies outdoors all year round. Hollywood is already home to over a dozen film companies – and larger studios are becoming the norm.'

He leaned back in his chair, a big burly man with a shock of silver hair and a luxuriant moustache and beard.

Marigold made no attempt to take part in the conversation. When she spoke to Mr Zimmerman, it would be when he was on his own.

One of Sibyl's closest friends, Delia Conisborough, rested her chin on the back of her hand and said, intrigued, 'Are films going to become longer, Mr Zimmerman?'

'Heck, yes. Over here, in Britain, Will Barker of Barker Motion Photography has just finished making a full-length feature film about King Henry VIII, and he intends to make a film about Queen Victoria and another about one of Edward IV's mistresses, Jane Shore. Or is it Jane Shire?'

'Shore,' Delia Conisborough said, amused.

'I'm going to do the same kind of thing, Lady Conisborough. I'm going to be making historical epics. Biblical epics.'

Lord Stamfordham, who was seated next to Sibyl, said drily, 'Big would seem to be in fashion. A fellow countryman of yours, Colonel John Jacob Astor, tells me he is leaving for New York tomorrow aboard the *Titanic*.'

Zac Zimmerman grinned at him. He liked trumping the British. 'And so', he said with great satisfaction, 'am I.'

The conversation turned from movie-making to what Lord Stamfordham declared was one of the greatest works of man: the *Titanic*.

Marigold, thanks to Rose's first-hand descriptions, knew a great deal about the liner. She knew that the first-class dining room simulated the decorations of Hatfield House, the Jacobean mansion that was home to the Marquess of Salisbury, and that the dining room's annexe was covered with Aubusson tapestries.

'The first-class lounge is decorated and furnished in the style of Versailles,' Rose had said to her when she had returned from being shown around the ship on its press day. 'The palm court is in the style of Louis XVI – Mother would feel very at home in it – and the state rooms are Italian Renaissance gone mad.'

Rose was far too aware of working-class poverty to have drooled over such excessive luxury, but Marigold would have liked the opportunity to have drooled. An Italian Renaissance state room would, she felt, suit her very well.

When dinner was over, and when the men had finished their port and cigars and had rejoined the ladies in the drawing room, Marigold chose her moment and, excusing herself from the people she had been speaking with, sashayed across the room to waylay Zac Zimmerman.

Her Titian hair was piled high on her head in a way that looked as if the slightest movement would send it tumbling down to her waist in a torrent of waves and curls. Her gown was sizzling turquoise and designed by Poiret. The neckline plunged front and back, revealing porcelain-white skin. The skirt was slashed to the knee and her arms were bare except for a thick silver bracelet clamped above one elbow.

Zac Zimmerman watched her approach with appreciation, hypnotized by the way her body moved beneath the clinging fabric.

As when she had first met Strickland, Marigold knew exactly what it was she wanted, and when she came to a halt in front of him, she didn't waste time in small talk.

'When we were at the theatre I heard you describe Mary Pickford as "the Girl With the Golden Curls" and "the Nation's Sweetheart", Mr Zimmerman.'

He nodded. 'I sure did. Because that is what she is.'

'Yet at the dinner table you said you wanted to make epics. Biblical epics.'

Her voice had a sexy, throaty catch to it. He found it as bewitching as her face.

Entranced, he wondered if she was wearing anything beneath her seductive gown and, doubting it, said, 'I did – and I meant it.'

In the background someone had begun to play the piano. Both of them ignored it.

'What kind of Bible stories were you thinking of making into epics, Mr Zimmerman?'

Her manner was amused and teasing, as if she knew his answer would make a fool of him and as if that was what she wanted. Not seeing how a straight answer could give her her wish, he said, 'Judith and Holofernes. Samson and Delilah. Salome and John the Baptist.'

Marigold tilted her head a little to one side. 'What did Judith do to Holofernes, Mr Zimmerman?'

'She cut off his head while he was asleep.'

'What did Delilah do to Samson?'

'She cut off his hair to destroy his strength in order that he would be captured by his enemies.'

'What did they do when they caught him?'

'They put red-hot pokers in his eyes to blind him.'

Marigold smiled seraphically. 'What did Salome do to John the Baptist?'

'She caused him to have his head chopped off.'

Marigold's smile deepened. 'Do you really think, Mr Zimmerman, that Mary Pickford, with her demure little face and golden curls, could ever play the part of any one of those women?'

Zac stared at her, and then said slowly, 'No. I guess I don't.'

'I could. I could act Mary Pickford off the screen.'

Looking at her, he found it quite easy to believe. 'So what is it you want, Miss Houghton?'

It was an unnecessary question and both of them knew it.

'It's Marigold. I want you to take me with you when you return to Hollywood.'

'I guess you missed what I said at the dinner table, Marigold. I sail on the *Titanic* tomorrow.'

'I know.'

Something stirred in him that hadn't stirred for a long time. She had no ticket and it would be a devil of a job squaring things with the purser. He could do it, though. By God he could.

Over her shoulder he could see her great-aunt approaching them. 'Be in Southampton, at the dockside, for ten o'clock tomorrow morning. She sails at midday.' Then, to Sibyl, he said, 'Your titled guests seem to have enjoyed my picture show, Lady Harland. It's been very gratifying.'

410

Marigold didn't stay to hear any more. She had a lot of decisions to make. It was already eleven o'clock at night, far too late to travel down to Snowberry and then, in the morning, leave Snowberry for Southampton. Nor, if she had to be at the dockside for ten o'clock, was there enough time in the morning to make a detour to Snowberry. Which meant she was going to be leaving the country without saying goodbye to anyone.

She didn't think it mattered too much about Iris. Iris was too absorbed in her new role in life as a wife and expectant mother to be too concerned if Marigold left for a long stay in America. Sailing tomorrow would mean missing Lily's wedding to Rory, but as Lily was going to be living on Islay after the wedding and Marigold would then see her only rarely anyway, she didn't think not being able to tell Lily mattered much either. Rose and her grandfather were, however, a little different.

Not in a million years would Rose approve of her sailing to America at a moment's notice, and especially not in the company of a man twice her age whom she had only just met. The row between them would be terrific, which meant it would be far more sensible to simply write a letter to Rose that she would receive after the *Titanic* had sailed.

That left only her grandfather. Her grandfather would be devastated at her leaving without even saying goodbye to him. Thinking of how great his distress would be, she thought of alternatives. Perhaps she could sail at a later date, on a different ship? But who, then, would pay for her passage? In sailing on the *Titanic*, unsaid, but taken for granted, was the agreement that Zac Zimmerman would pay.

Also, in sailing on another ship she would miss the experience of travelling in decadent luxury.

She would write her grandfather a very loving letter, and when he saw her on the silver screen, her dream fulfilled, he would be so proud of her that he would forgive her the manner in which she'd left England. Where Sibyl was concerned she would also write a letter, and not leave it, but post it. When she left in the morning she would tell Sibyl she was returning to Snowberry. That way the alarm couldn't be given and no one would be sent after her to drag her from the ship.

There was, however, one person she would say goodbye to, and that was Strickland. Strickland was totally unshockable and it was highly likely that he would, like her, regard Hollywood as being her destiny.

It was after midnight and Strickland put down his paintbrush and palette and looked at her as if she had taken leave of her senses. 'Hollywood? Do you know where Hollywood is, Marigold? It's in California. You do you know where California is, don't you? It's on the very far side of the United States, two thousand, perhaps nearly three thousand miles distant from New York.'

'The further it is, the better. I don't want to be on this side of the Atlantic Ocean when Maxim marries Anne Greveney. It is already being trumpeted as the wedding of the year and I just don't want to know about it. Neither do I want to continue living as I am, not being invited anywhere. I might as well be a leper for all the invitations I receive.'

Without removing the cigarette that was plastered to his lower lip, Strickland said, 'What does your family think?'

'Nothing as yet. There's no time to go down to Snowberry and tell them, and so I'm going to write letters once I'm aboard the ship.'

'That's a coward's way of doing things, Marigold. I never took you for a coward.'

'Because I'm not. I'm doing it because it's after midnight now and I have to be at the dockside by ten o'clock tomorrow morning. So before you tell me I could telephone Snowberry,

412

I think breaking such news on the telephone would be far more distressing for everyone concerned than doing it the way I'm going to do it.'

She looked around the studio. 'I'm going to miss you, Strickland. Life won't be quite the same without you.'

'Ditto,' Strickland said feelingly.

'And Persephone? Where is she? I thought I might take her with me. I think that one look at it might be enough to persuade Mr Zimmerman she'd be a good subject for a movie.'

Strickland removed the cigarette from his mouth and a fleck of tobacco from his tongue. He'd never told her that it was Lord Jethney who had bought the painting from Maxim. He'd simply told her she needn't worry about it any more; that it was no longer in Maxim Yurenev's possession. On reflection, he still thought it was better for her not to know the truth.

'She's safely under wraps – and too valuable to manhandle all the way across an ocean and a continent. Listen to me one last time, Marigold. Going off in this manner is going to devastate your family. You don't know the kind of man Zimmerman is. You don't know a single person in America. It is the craziest, most reckless scheme I've ever heard of. Think about it sensibly and don't go to Southampton tomorrow. Please.'

She kissed him on the cheek. 'You're growing into an old fusspot, Strickland. Now I must go. I came here in a hansom and it's outside, waiting to take me back to St James's Street.'

He walked out of the house with her and her last words to him, as the horse trotted away down the street and she leaned out of the hansom's window, were: 'Isn't it wonderful, Strickland? Next time you see me I'll be on the silver screen!'

He stomped back into the house, not thinking it wonderful

at all. There was an endearing warmth to Marigold's allure that he was going to miss. He was also going to miss her volatility and sheer exuberance. He had become fonder of her than he was of any other human being and he was convinced she was heading for disaster. He'd done his best to make her see how dangerously reckless she was being and, as usual, she'd taken not the slightest notice. Who, then, would she take notice of?

The answer came to him with the same certainty it had when he had been pondering how to persuade Maxim Yurenev into parting with Persephone.

Lord Jethney.

He could hardly ring Lord Jethney up at one-thirty in the morning, though. Or could he? He decided he couldn't.

Marigold had told him the *Titanic* sailed at midday. If he spoke to Jethney first thing in the morning Jethney would have time to travel by rail down to Southampton. With a good chauffeur, he would even have time to be driven there.

He went to bed to dream of white slave-traders called Zimmerman and of Marigold being tied to a railway track where, when the train bore down on her, no rescuer appeared.

'Lord Jethney is not at home,' a butler said when, at seven o'clock, he telephoned Lord Jethney's home in Hampshire.

'Where will I be able to contact him? It's a matter of urgency.'

'I'm not at liberty to say, sir.'

It was the exact same stuffy response he'd received when trying to track Prince Yurenev down. Damning all butlers to hell, he forced himself to think. If Jethney wasn't at his home in Hampshire then he must be at his London home. Other than knowing it would be within handy reach of the Houses of Parliament, Strickland didn't have a clue as to where it was. He certainly had no London telephone number for Jethney.

Looking at the clock, realizing that time was fast running out, he crammed a wide black-brimmed hat on his head, swirled a black cape around his shoulders, and, looking like a Transylvanian vampire unhappily abroad in daylight, he set off for the House of Lords.

No one was willing to help him. Lord Jethney was expected at the House for ten o'clock when he had an important government meeting. And his lordship would certainly not be able to see anyone until afterwards, and not even then unless they had an appointment with him.

Ten o'clock would, he knew, be far too late. It simply wouldn't give Jethney enough time to make up his mind to go to Southampton, and to get there before midday. He wondered if the *Titanic* was calling in at any other port before heading out across the North Atlantic for New York. Many trans-Atlantic liners called at Cherbourg, in France, to pick up continental passengers. Nearly all of them also called in at Queenstown in Ireland, to collect Irish emigrants travelling steerage.

He strode out into Parliament Square wondering where he could get the information he needed; wondering where the nearest shipping office was.

A familiar, top-hatted figure, dressed appropriately for the House of Lords in a frock coat, was striding down towards him, a briefcase in one hand, a walking cane in the other.

'Jethney!' he cried. 'Thank God! Jethney, you have to give me five minutes of your time! It's about Marigold!'

Theo came to an abrupt halt.

'She's sailing on the *Titanic* in just over three hours' time with an American by the name of Zimmerman. She only met him yesterday. He's told her he's going to make her into a movie star. I've done my best to dissuade her, but she thinks it's all going to be a marvellous adventure and—'

Theo was no longer listening to him. Big Ben was showing 8.45 and the only boat train to Southampton left Waterloo at nine o'clock. If he missed it, he didn't have a hope in hell of boarding the *Titanic* before she sailed.

Without another word he stepped out into the street to flag down a taxi. 'Waterloo,' Strickland heard him bark at the driver. 'I'm a government minister and the matter is urgent!'

Once in the cab Theo marshalled his thoughts. Where Marigold was concerned he'd been going to make no approach to her until after Jerusha had been dead for a year. When her affair with Prince Yurenev had come to such an abrupt and ugly end, he had been tempted not to wait so long; but in the end he had decided that it was best for both his reputation and Marigold's that he kept to his first decision. Now he absolutely could no longer do so. He couldn't allow her to sail to America. If she did, she would in all likelihood be lost to him for ever – and he couldn't allow that. Not when he loved her as much as he'd ever done.

At Waterloo he found God was being good to him: the boat train was still in the station. As a government minister he didn't waste time buying a ticket. He sprinted down the platform, stepping breathlessly into a first-class carriage. He would buy a ticket off the guard. For the moment he would simply get his breath back.

It was only as he did so that he remembered he was supposed to be chairing a government meeting at ten o'clock. There was nothing that could be done about it. Someone else would have to chair it. He would apologize profusely when he was back in London, explaining he had been faced with a life and death situation – and he would do so feeling he was speaking the truth.

416

The journey gave him time to reflect on the two possible outcomes of what he was doing. Either Marigold would listen to sense, or she wouldn't. He had a dreadful feeling that when it came to the choice of being made into a movie star, or becoming the second Lady Jethney, Marigold was going to plump for being made into a movie star. Whichever choice she made, one thing he was going to do was tell her that Persephone was in his possession, not Strickland's.

Marigold was in her element. Wearing a chinchilla fur that had been one of her first presents from Maxim, she was leaning over one of the first-class deck rails, Zac Zimmerman at her side. On either side of them were scores of other first-class passengers, all determined to enjoy the moment of departure to the full. The ship's orchestra was playing on deck, while on the dockside a brass band was entertaining the vast crowd waiting to see a moment of history being made: the moment when the biggest ship in the world slid from its berth and out to sea.

There were so many last-minute passengers hurrying up the gangplank and so many relatives of those who were travelling on the liner scurrying down again after saying their goodbyes, that Marigold didn't see Theo board; nor did she see him having a swift urgent word with the ship's officer whose task it was to welcome passengers.

Once on the first-class deck and with only minutes to go before the ship sailed, Theo spotted her and began barrelling his way through the crowd towards her.

'Marigold!' he shouted, but it was pointless. Everyone was shouting. Those on deck were calling goodbyes to friends and relatives on the dockside; friends and relatives were responding in kind. All were trying to make their voices heard over the sound of the brass band and the ship's orchestra.

Only when he laid a hand on her arm, and she turned to

see who was being so impertinently familiar, did she realize he was on board.

'Theo!' The shock was so great that she put a hand over her heart.

'Now what the hell . . .' Zac began proprietorially, but then, seeing that the thick-set, grim-faced intruder was known to Marigold – and remembering the circumstances under which Marigold was with him – he thought better of what he'd been going to say and fell silent, watching Theo with narrowed eyes.

No other visitors were now scurrying down the gangplank. Ropes were being cast off. The deck beneath their feet was throbbing as the ship prepared to get under way. Knowing he had only three or four minutes at the most before the gangplank was raised, Theo said urgently, 'Forget America, Marigold. I love you and I want you to marry me. We only have seconds, darling. What is your answer going to be? Yes or no?'

The drama of the moment was meat and drink to Marigold. She could go to Hollywood with Zac, or she could marry Theo who stood every chance of one day becoming prime minister. If she married Theo it didn't have to mean that she'd have to put an end to her dreams of being a movie star. Hadn't Zac said at dinner the previous evening that there was a British Film Company by the name of Barker Motion Photography and that Will Barker had just made a full-length film about Henry VIII and that he was going to make another one about Queen Victoria?

If the idea was put to him, why shouldn't Barker make a film about Henry's daughter Elizabeth, who had become just as great a queen – if not greater – than Queen Victoria? Like Elizabeth, her hair was a blazing, fiery red. As Good Queen Bess she would be sensational. Off screen, she would be Lady Jethney.

When it came to such a choice, the decision was easy.

'Yes!' she shouted above the cacophony of noise being made all around them.

Exultantly Theo grabbed hold of her hand and, ignoring a bewildered Zac Zimmerman, dragged her after him as he fought a way through the crush in the direction of the gangplank.

They reached it without a second to spare. The *Titanic*'s mammoth whistle blew. And blew again. And again.

It was the signal for the moment of departure. As the gangplank juddered and shook, Theo and Marigold hurtled down it, hand in hand.

With the firm ground under their feet, Marigold looked up at the great black sides of the ship to the point on the first-class deck where she had left Zac Zimmerman.

He was waving to her, not angry, but smiling, and as the *Titanic* gathered speed, heading in the direction of the English Channel, those nearest to him heard him shout, 'What a gal! God in heaven! *What a gal!*'

# THIRTY-SEVEN

Five days later the first news of the sinking arrived by wireless at the *Daily Despatch* office. At first the only information was that the *Titanic* had struck an iceberg and had called for aid.

There was no way of double-checking the story and Hal held fire. Then came news that reporters in New York were storming the White Star Line offices at 9 Broadway for further news.

Before he pitched in to what he suspected were going to be the busiest few hours he'd ever experienced Hal telephoned Rose.

'The *Titanic* has hit an iceberg and is in trouble. Get over here fast. I want you working in the office with other reporters. You've been aboard her. They haven't.'

The next wire said that White Star's Vice-President, Philip A. S. Franklin, had made light of the reports that the ship was in trouble. 'Even if the *Titanic* had hit ice, she could float indefinitely,' he was reported as saying. 'We place absolute confidence in the *Titanic*. We believe that the boat is unsinkable.'

Hal was no longer so sure. The silence after the first wire

saying that the ship had called for aid was too long. His fingers itched to be the first British newspaper to publish the banner headline of the year – but he couldn't risk issuing it without confirmation.

'What are the American papers saying?' he demanded of his staff. 'What headline is the New York *Herald* running with?'

By wireless he learned that the *Herald* had run with: 'THE NEW TITANIC STRIKES ICE AND CALLS FOR AID. VESSELS RUSH TO HER SIDE'.

The *Evening Sun* had run with: 'ALL SAVED FROM TITANIC AFTER COLLISION'.

Hal chewed his fingernails, settled Rose at a desk with a typewriter and chanced his arm, deciding on the banner headline: 'TITANIC SINKING. WOMEN AND CHILDREN TAKEN OFF IN LIFEBOATS'.

Hours later, when confirmation came, his headline read: 'LOSS OF LIFE AS TITANIC SINKS'.


A horrified Marigold bought every newspaper she could lay her hands on. One report declared that out of a passenger list of 2,340, 1,500 had drowned. Another that 1,800 had drowned.

'But when are they going to publish a list of names of survivors?' she asked Theo. 'How can we know if Zac Zimmerman has survived?'

'He was a first-class passenger, Marigold. He's bound to have been shepherded into a lifeboat.' Theo didn't at all mind her concern about Zac Zimmerman. If she hadn't been concerned about him, he would have been very disappointed in her.

Rose relayed to them all the up-to-the-minute news. Only 4 first-class women passengers had lost their lives out of a total of 143. In second-class only 15 had survived out of a total of 93.

'What about third-class passengers?' Theo asked Rose. 'How many women in third-class were saved?'

It was a moment when Rose knew why she liked Theo so much. 'You are the only person I know who has shown any interest in those who were travelling steerage. No one knows as yet how many of them drowned, but it's a certainty it will be a far higher proportion than those travelling second-class, or first-class.'

The final published figures proved her right. Only 81 women in third-class were saved out of a total 179.

'God alone knows the number of men in third-class who died,' Rose said bitterly to Theo.

The figures showed that out of a total of 462 men, only 54 had been rescued.

When White Star published the complete list of survivors' names, Zac Zimmerman's was not among them. His name did, however, feature prominently in a survivor's account of the sinking.

Miss Susie Durham had described her experiences to the American press:

The lifeboat I was in was one of the last to leave and because of the steep tilt of the ship it was very hard to get into. Mr Zimmerman helped the crew pass women and children into it. Then a member of the crew said that one of the boys in the boat was too old to be counted as a child. His mother said he was only thirteen, and he looked to be younger, but the crew member said he had to get out of the boat as it was for women and children only. He did, and Mr Zimmerman picked him up and even though the crew member had drawn a pistol and was threatening to shoot him if he did so, he put the boy back in the boat. Then he helped other crewmen lower the boat.

422

If he'd wanted to jump into it, he could have, but he didn't. I think he knew the boat might overturn if too many people were in it. The last I saw of him, he was standing on the deck in his evening clothes, smoking a cigar.

Marigold had cried when she'd read Miss Durham's account.

Theo had done his best to comfort her, putting his arms around her and telling her not to cry for Zac Zimmerman, but instead to be proud of him.

She was – but she knew it would be a long time before she stopped thinking of the moment on the *Titanic* when she had been faced with the choice of sailing on her, or returning to London with Theo. What would have happened to her if she'd stayed? Would she have been one of the survivors, or one of the dead?

Terrible though the *Titanic* disaster was, Iris's thoughts were centred almost entirely on the preparations for Rory and Lily's wedding. The wedding itself was going to take place in the local village church; the reception was going to be held at Snowberry. As Rose was in London, now a full-time member of the staff of the *Daily Despatch*, and as Lily was too distressed that David was still writing to her believing they were going to be together for ever, all the wedding arrangements had fallen on her.

She didn't mind. It was the kind of thing she was good at. She was only a little disappointed that Lily wanted everything to be so starkly simple.

There were to be no bridesmaids. Lily didn't want an extravagant wedding breakfast, either.

'Watercress soup for the first course, then?' Millie had said to her queryingly.

'I think so. Then salmon mayonnaise, followed by fillets of beef with appropriate vegetables.'

'To finish, a mousse of apricots and champagne-primrose jelly,' Millie had said. 'This is a perfect time of year for primrose jelly. Who is going to do the primrose-picking? You or me?'

'I will.'

'How many are we catering for?'

'Twenty-one. When Lily said she wanted the wedding to be small, she really meant it.'

The wedding cake wasn't going to be small. Millie had made two wedding cakes, both for Lily's mother. They had been five-tiered and she wasn't about to settle for anything less when it came to Lily. 'White royal icing with touches of lemon,' she'd said when Iris had asked her about it. 'With a traditional wedding couple on top of the cake, and lots of silver horse-shoes and silver slippers for good luck.'

Though she had had only three weeks in which to do it, everything that had needed to be done had been done. It was the first of May and Lily's wedding morning. Iris had decorated the church with vases of sweet-smelling lilac, and Lily's wedding bouquet of mauve beribboned anemones was on the hall table, just waiting for her to pick it up when she left later for the church.

Their mother, stepfather, their two stepsisters and Great-aunt Sibyl were due to arrive at any moment. Marigold and Theo and Theo's two sons were expected within the hour, as were Rose, Hal Green and his daughter, Jacinta. It would be the first time Iris had met Hal and Jacinta, and it was something she was looking forward to nearly as much as she was looking forward to the wedding.

Other guests, guests who would be going straight to the church, included Toby's parents, Daphne Harbury and the artist

Lawrence Strickland. Toby was best man. The sun was shining. Snowberry was looking its glorious best and Iris was satisfied that everything was going well. Or she was until she walked into the drawing room and found Lily in floods of tears.

Appalled, she crossed the room to her, saying urgently, 'Lily, you can't cry! Think about how red it will make your eyes! You leave for the church in less than an hour!'

Lily, who was already wearing the dress she had chosen to be married in, gave a shuddering sob. There was a letter in her lap and the royal crest on it – David's royal crest – was clearly visible.

'David says how much he is missing me. How he can't wait to take me in his arms again. How he is counting the days until he leaves Neustrelitz.'

She handed Iris the letter, tears still falling down her face. 'How can I give so much pain to someone I love with all my heart? I can't bear the thought of his dear face when he reads the letter I'm going to have to write to him after the wedding. It's killing me, Iris. Truly it is.'

Iris looked down at the letter in her hand.

My own beloved darling girl,

How I've been thinking of you tonight! I'm so longing to see you again, sweetheart. Württemberg was bad enough, but the court here at Neustrelitz is even worse. It's so boring there are times when I quite literally think I'm going to go off my head. All Great-aunt Augusta – I don't know if she is my great-aunt, but she is my mother's aunt and I call her great-aunt – does is go on and on about what a wonderful queen my mother is and what an awful lot I will have to live up to once my father dies and I'm king. How I long to tell her that the chances are it is Bertie who will be the next king! As I can't, I just have to suffer it

I miss you so much, my darling, and just want to have you in my arms again! In another few weeks you will be, and then I'm never going to let you go. Not for anyone! Not for anything! Not ever! I have a calendar by my bed – and a photograph of you holding one of the buns – and I cross the days off every night. When I go to sleep I dream of you and of how happy we are going to be and when I think of doing no more princeing I'm happier than ever!

I'm going to have to finish now as I'm very tired. I've been out shooting all day with my cousin-of-a-kind Grand Duke Adolph. Don't get upset, sweetheart. I didn't want to go and I tried very hard not to hit anything! And this is one more day gone until we are together again – never again to be parted.

Goodnight, my own sweet darling,

Your own very loving and adoring David

Sombre-faced, Iris handed her the letter back. She knew the last three weeks had been excruciating for Lily, who had not only been receiving such letters on a nearly daily basis, but had also had to reply to them in a way that wouldn't alarm David or make him suspicious.

She said quietly and with certainty, 'You've been amazingly strong up to now, Lily, and for Rory's sake you have to continue to be strong. David's birthright is to be a Prince of Wales the country can look up to and see as a figurehead. He may think it is a role he can choose to abandon, but it isn't. Think of all the people he would be letting down: a whole country. And not just this country, either, but Canada, Australia, New Zealand, South Africa and India and goodness only knows where else. In marrying Rory before David tells the King he's going to abdicate his rights to the succession, you are doing the right thing.'

There came the distant sound of cars coming down the drive.

She put a hand under Lily's arm, drawing her to her feet. 'Come along, sweetheart. People are arriving. Go upstairs and wash your face. For Rory's sake you must look a happy bride.'

The cars were nearer now – almost at the door.

Ashen-faced, Lily nodded, and holding the letter close to her breast she walked from the room.

She went to her bedroom and carefully put David's letter in the box that held all his other letters, and then she went to the top of the house, to her studio. There was something she had to do before she left for the church. One final act before the life she had lived up to now – the life that had included David – was over, and her new life with Rory began.

The studio was full of sunlight. It fell in strong shafts over the bust she had sculpted nearly a year ago, when she had fallen so headlong in love with David and when everything – even becoming Princess of Wales one day – had seemed possible.

She stood in front of it and then, with her fingertips, she traced the contours of his dearly beloved face. It was the goodbye that she would never give him in the flesh. The goodbye that was being given because she loved him so very, very much.

She wondered how he would manage without her, and prayed that he would do so well. Then she removed a sheet that was covering a stack of prepared canvases and gently placed it over the sculpture she had so lovingly and skilfully crafted.

Some day, far in the future, when her pain had eased, she would unveil it and it would take pride of place in one of her sisters' homes – perhaps even in her and Rory's home. For now, though, she had to turn her thoughts to Rory. To the life they were going to build together on Islay. She thought of the way the baby she and David had created would never have to live within a prison-house of formality and pomposity and rigid etiquette as David had always done – and always would do.

Instead he, or she, would have the most beautiful Hebridean island of all for a playground. She would have her freedom, too. The freedom to paint and sculpt. The freedom to go where she wanted, when she wanted. The freedom of not being watched by a royal household of censorious eyes. She would have the greatest blessing of all, for unlike David she would never be lonely. Rory had always been in her life and now would be there for ever.

After the wedding reception she and Rory were travelling straight to Islay. She wouldn't be in the studio again for a long time. Looking around, she silently said goodbye to it and then turned and began making her way down to the drawing room where her family were fast assembling.

She paused at the foot of the stairs, listening to the chatter that was coming from the drawing room. She could hear her mother saying bewilderedly, 'But why wasn't I asked to help arrange the wedding, Iris? Why is it so small and informal?'

She didn't hear Iris's reply because Fizz and Florin rushed past her, barking excitedly to welcome Rose, who entered the house accompanied by a startlingly handsome man. Marigold had already described Hal for her. 'He's all dark and damn-your-eyes,' she had said graphically, and for once Lily had to admit that Marigold hadn't been exaggerating.

'Hal, Lily,' Rose said, introducing them. 'Lily, Hal . . . and Jacinta, Hal's daughter.'

'Are you the bride?' Jacinta asked as Lily shook hands with her. 'I do like your dress. I can see it's not really a wedding dress, but it's very pretty.'

'Thank you,' Lily said gravely. Her dress was a very simple one of white voile with a lace fichu collar. It most certainly wasn't a typical wedding dress, but she hadn't wanted to wear one and Rory had told her to wear whatever she felt most comfortable wearing.

'Are Marigold, Theo and the boys here yet?' Rose asked as Lily picked up her bouquet from the hall table.

'I don't know. I haven't been downstairs at all since people began arriving.'

Rose looked at Lily's pale face with disquiet. Hal still didn't know the history behind Lily's wedding to Rory, and she had told her grandfather and Iris and Marigold not to mention it in his presence. Hal was a newspaper editor. When he asked her to marry him – which she was sure he would do – then she would tell him. When he had become family she would be able to rest easy that he wouldn't be tempted to put what he was told into print.

His presence meant she couldn't speak to Lily as she would have liked, but as they reached the drawing room and Hal opened the door for them, she did say in a low, urgent voice, 'If you're having second thoughts, Lily, please tell me.'

'No. I know I'm doing the only thing I possibly can do. Rory will make me happy, Rose. Happiness is something he's very good at it. And I'm going to make him happy too.'

With Jacinta walking behind her as if she were her bridesmaid, Lily entered the room to the acclamation of her family, and fifty minutes later, in a church smelling of lilac and with her mother dabbing at her eyes with a handkerchief, she became Mrs Rory Sinclair.

Rose's sense of relief when the wedding was over was vast. If any of the guests suspected that the bride was nearly three months pregnant, their thoughts hadn't been put into words – and Lily didn't look pregnant. She looked as delicate as a camellia, her blue-black hair caught in a shining coil on the nape of her neck, little ringlets escaping round her temples.

At the wedding breakfast Toby had made a speech in which he managed to be surprisingly funny. Their grandfather had made a speech during which he'd had to blow his nose vigorously in order to disguise the fact that, at the thought of losing Lily to Islay, he was close to tears. Rory, resplendent in a black doublet and kilt, a lace jabot at his throat and lace ruffles at his wrists, had responded with a short speech of thanks on behalf of himself and Lily.

Toasts had been made, champagne had been drunk, and when the wedding party had spilled out on to the terrace and into the garden, Rory and Lily had done so hand in hand.

Rose watched them, her throat tightening.

'They look grand, don't they?' Millie said, coming up to her. 'He'll make her happy. He has the knack. If you have a minute, could you help me move the wedding cake from the wedding-breakfast table to another table where the bottom tier will be easier to slice? I've asked Tilly, but she's too frightened of dropping it.'

Rose walked back into the house with her and, as she did so, the front-door bell clanged. Moments later William came into the dining room saying bewilderedly, 'Captain Cullen has arrived to speak with Miss Lily, Miss Rose.'

Rose was in the process of transferring the wedding cake from what had been the top table to a small lace-covered table that had been prepared especially for it. It was only thanks to Millie that the cake didn't come to grief.

She walked out of the room and down the corridor, her face tense.

Piers Cullen was standing in the middle of the hall, staring down at a trail of wedding rice.

He raised his head, his eyes meeting hers. 'Who's got

married?' he demanded. From her dress it quite obviously wasn't Rose and he added sneeringly, 'Marigold?'

'No.' It wasn't a moment Rose had foreseen, though she realized now that it should have been. There was no point in lying. Even in the hall the sound of the partying on the terrace and on the lawn could be heard, and he would only have to walk through the drawing room to the open French doors to see who the bride was.

'Well who, then?'

'Lily,' she said, and waited for the explosion.

It didn't come. She'd robbed him of the breath to give vent to one. He was so shocked she thought he was going to faint.

At last he said hoarsely, 'Who to?'

'Her cousin Rory. Rory Sinclair.'

'I don't believe you! *I don't believe you!*'

He pushed her so violently out of his way that she went crashing to her knees. As she struggled to her feet, he raced for the drawing-room door. Seizing hold of its handle he slammed it back on its hinges.

With bleeding knees she hurtled after him, terrified of what he was going to do. As William and Millie came running, she yelled at them to keep back, knowing that one blow from Piers could be the end for either of them.

'Piers!' she shouted. '*Piers!*'

Incredibly, once he reached the open French doors he came to a breathless halt, putting a hand to the door-jamb to steady himself.

She came to a halt a little way behind him, certain he had lost his senses, that he was mad – and probably always had been.

Looking past him she could see exactly what he was seeing. The terrace with wedding guests sitting in cane chairs set around white-clothed tables. Her grandfather holding court at one of them, deep in conversation with her stepfather, the step-grandson-in-law he rarely saw. Great-aunt Sibyl was sitting with them, a glass of champagne in her hand. A little way off from them, Marguerite, Camille and Jacinta were playing with Fizz and Florin, trying to teach the dogs tricks, Marguerite and Camille doing so in French, Jacinta showing off by doing so in Spanish.

On the lawn her mother, looking incredibly lovely in rose-pink chiffon and a hat laden with white ostrich feathers, was talking to Strickland and he was looking down his long Roman nose at her in rapt fascination. Hal, hands in his pockets, was talking to Toby. Daphne was walking down to the lakeside with Theo's boys one at either side of her and Theo, Marigold and Iris were standing in a little half-circle around the bride and groom.

Marigold was wearing an emerald-green silk dress and a matching hat laden with yellow roses. It dipped seductively low over her eyes as, with a net-gloved hand tucked into the crook of Theo's arm, she laughed at something Rory was saying.

Rory and Lily were still hand in hand. A slight breeze stirred Lily's voile skirt and lifted the edges of her lace collar.

Though she couldn't see his face, Rose knew Piers's eyes were locked on Lily.

He said in a strangled voice, 'Does Prince Edward know?'

'No. Lily will be writing to him tonight.'

Still looking at Lily, his whole body juddered.

Rose pressed a fist to her mouth, petrified as to what was going to happen next. If he sprinted towards Lily, what would Rory do? What would Toby, Hal, Theo and Strickland do? The whole idyllic scene on the terrace and on the lawn would be reduced to one of ugly violence.

He didn't move forward. He gave a low moan and whipped round to face her.

'Tell her she needn't bother!' he yelled. 'Tell Lily I'll do the job for her!' With a face contorted in pain he strode past her, out of the room, out of the house.

As she heard the sound of his car careering down the drive Rose's knees gave way and she half fell on to the nearest sofa. She was certain of only one thing. If Piers Cullen had had a gun on him, he would have shot Rory between the eyes. She suspected that he would then have turned the gun on himself.

Piers's Lanchester swerved from one side of the drive to the other. Lily may have married Sinclair, she may have become lost to him, but he could still fulfil one obsession. He could give himself the pleasure of telling Edward that she was lost to him, too. As he reached the road his teeth were bared in something between a grimace and a gleeful smile. No longer Edward's equerry, he didn't even have a position to worry about losing. He could take revenge for all the hurts, slights and indignities Edward had dealt him by dealing Edward the blow that would, Piers was sure, absolutely destroy him. Although no longer in royal service, he knew where Edward was. He also knew he could be at Neustrelitz before Lily's letter arrived there.

Lily wasn't going to deliver the fatal blow to Edward.

He was.

The pleasure he was going to derive from doing so would help ease the torture of his own loss – and give him more pleasure than any sexual satisfaction could possibly provide.

# THIRTY-EIGHT

Rose sat alone in the drawing room, her hands clenched tightly in her lap. Her fear and panic had been so great during her nightmare scene with Piers that she hadn't taken literally his demented intention of telling David that Lily had married Rory. For one thing, David was in Germany, so how could he?

But he had.

A private trunk call from Germany to England had been impossible even for David, and when he had phoned her, in a state of hysteria, he had done so from a hotel in Dover.

'Tell me it isn't true!' he'd begged when a series of operators had finally connected him to Snowberry. 'Tell me that bastard Cullen has simply gone off his head!'

The line had been very crackly and there had been sobs in his voice.

'I can't, David,' she'd said. 'Lily married Rory three days ago.'

His response had been frantic. 'But she can't have! She can't! I've only just received a long loving letter from her! Please help me, Rose! I think I'm going mad!'

It was an impossible conversation to conduct over a bad

434

telephone line. 'We need to talk face to face, David.' She tried to keep her voice steady, and couldn't. 'Can you get down to Snowberry?

'I'm coming straight there!'

After that the only sound had been of a dangling telephone receiver and she had known he hadn't even paused long enough to sever the connection, or to put the receiver back on its rest.

That had been an hour and a half ago.

With every minute that went by, her tension mounted. She had sent her grandfather to Sissbury on a spurious errand. Marigold was at Sibyl's. Telling Millie that she wanted the house to herself – and why – she had sent her and Tilly on a chauffeured afternoon trip to Winchester. William she had sent down to the village pub with instructions not to come back until teatime.

If the heir to the throne was going to have a complete nervous breakdown, she didn't want anyone but herself witnessing it.

When the doorbell jangled she took a deep steadying breath.

'I don't believe it!' were his first frenzied words when she opened the door. 'I won't believe it! You're going to have to prove it to me, Rose. Where is Lily? I have to see her! I *must* see her!'

She led the way into the drawing room. 'Lily is in Scotland. She and Rory have decided to live at his family home on the Isle of Islay.'

She crossed to a drinks tray, poured him a large brandy and pressed it into his unresisting hand.

When he had taken a great gulp of it, she said, 'The proof you want is on the small table by the sofa.'

He thrust the glass of brandy back at her and covered the distance to the sofa in two swift strides.

Her heart ached for him as he picked up the wedding certificate, looking at it in dizzying disbelief.

Crushing it into a ball he turned round to her. 'But we love each other,' he said, his face as white as parchment. 'Why has she done this? How can she not love me any more?'

'She does love you, David.' Her voice was full of compassion. He looked so young, so vulnerable, so lost and alone that it was all she could do not to put her arms around him. 'But once you told her that you were going to abandon all your royal duties – that you were going to step down from the line of succession in order to marry her – she knew that she was going to have to be the strong one of the two of you. It's because she loves you that she has done what she has. She wants you to fulfil your birthright – and if you love her, that is exactly what you will do.'

He stared at her in torment, blind, deaf and dumb with pain.

'Rory will make her happy, David. He cares about her very much.'

'But Lily loves *me*, Rose! If my father had given his consent for us to marry, we would have been betrothed now! There would never have been any question of her marrying anyone other than me!'

It was so terribly true, Rose couldn't speak.

He ran his fingers distractedly through his hair. 'And now I'm going to be imprisoned for ever without having anyone at my side that I truly love. How am I to survive without her?'

The cry came from his heart and, to her despair, she had no answer for him.

For a horrendous moment she thought he was going to burst into tears.

She said gently, 'Lily gave me something to give to you, David.'

She held out the letter Lily had written with such anguish.

He took it from her, his hand unsteady. Making no attempt to open it, he said, 'Would you leave me on my own for a little while, Rose?'

'Of course I will. I'll be in the hall.'

When the door had closed behind her he stood for a long time without moving, remembering the first time he had entered Snowberry; remembering the first time he had been in this wonderfully comfortable drawing room where, uniquely, he had been treated as if he was just an ordinary young man.

It was an experience that he would never enjoy again.

He walked to the French doors and as he stepped out on to the terrace he was overcome by a sense of déjà vu. It was a beautiful May morning. Small white clouds were drifting across an azure sky. The air was heavy with fragrance, the scent of carnations as thick as smoke in the sun.

On just such a day, a year ago, he had stood on Dartmouth Naval College's terrace, staring across it to manicured gardens and beyond the gardens to a steeply sloping, tree-studded hillside. He had been intensely unhappy, not knowing that within an hour, his life would change. Not knowing that because of Lily, he would, for a year, be the happiest young man on earth.

As he looked across Snowberry's lawns to the lake and the hillside rising on the far side of it, he knew no such miracle was about to happen now. He had had his slice of happiness and it would not come again.

Rage for the person who had robbed him of it crashed over him in thunderous waves. It was a rage that was going to last a lifetime and the object of it wasn't Rory; it was his father, King George.

His father had denied him Lily as a wife because, even though Lily would have made the most wonderful Princess

437

of Wales Britain had ever had, he had been set on having a foreign princess as a daughter-in-law.

It was a desire David was determined to cheat him of.

They could parade princesses in front of him until they were blue in the face, but he would never marry one of them. As he now couldn't have Lily, he would have no one. When he was crowned as King Edward VIII, he would be crowned without a royal queen consort at his side.

With tears stinging the backs of his eyes he looked down at the letter in his hand and, at long last and with a breaking heart, opened it.

My dearest darling David,

What I have done, I have done because I love you and because I want the very best for you. You were born to a great destiny, my sweetheart, and it is one you must live up to in the very best possible way. Be a magnificent Prince of Wales and when the time comes for you to be king, be the most splendid, most well-loved king that Britain has ever had. I have never been as happy as I have been this last year, beloved. For the rest of my life, no matter how old I may one day become, you will be in my prayers and in my heart.

Your very own, very loving Lily

Nestling in a corner of the envelope was a glossily silky, blue-black curl. Reverently he laid it in the palm of one hand. With the other hand he took out his gold pocket-watch and turning it face downwards clicked the back of it open. Then he laid the curl inside, snapped the watch shut and replaced it in the waistcoat pocket closest to his heart.

From now on, wherever he went, whatever he wore, the curl she had cut from her hair would go with him. It would be with him when he was crowned king. It would be with him when he died.

Inner strength and determination flooded through him.

He couldn't allow Lily's sacrifice of their happiness to be in vain. For her sake he had to become the kind of Prince of Wales – and later king – that she wanted him to be.

For Lily – and for Lily alone – he would become a spectacular Prince of Wales. A golden prince. A prince the world would never forget.

Fiercely resolute, he turned and began walking back towards the house.

Ten minutes later he was at the wheel of his Austro-Daimler, heading once again towards Windsor and the royal life he had been born into.

A royal life that he was now going to live to the very best of his ability.

# What's next?

Tell us the name of an author you love

| Rebecca Dean | **Go** ▶ |

and we'll find your next great book.

# Read on for ...

- Q&A with the author

- An exclusive extract from Rebecca Dean's next novel – *The Shadow Queen* (out July 2011)

Rebecca Dean on

# THE GOLDEN PRINCE

Although *The Golden Prince* is a novel largely based on the story of Edward VIII, you also manage to explore controversial issues relative to the early twentieth century, such as women's rights and female independence. Rose in particular equates marriage with surrendering all independence, a very sceptical and cynical view of the tradition. In your opinion, what are the concerns of the modern-day woman, and how does marriage figure in her life?

The modern woman is much more well-rounded, thank goodness, than the women of a century ago. Then, working-class women lived in a constant sea of poverty and hardship from which there was rarely any escape. For upper-class women, such as Rose and her sisters, there was a prison of a different kind. Financial independence was rare. No matter how intelligent or ambitious they were, careers weren't open to them. Shielded from life's harsh realities by their fathers and then by their husbands, they lived comfortable and, for the most part, purposeless lives. Their common interest being society, and their position in it. Presentation at court and the debutante season that followed was nothing more than a titled husband-hunting fest. Marriage mattered. It was what gave a woman her identity. Modern-day women – financially independent and career-fulfilled – have their own identity. Marriage is something they embark on by choice, not out of social necessity.

Many teenagers would no doubt proclaim the benefits of celebrity and notoriety, as fame-seeking programmes such as *Britain's Got Talent* and *The X-Factor* dominate television viewing. *The Golden Prince* however, offers insight into the restrictions of such a lifestyle, with David referring to his title as a 'straitjacket of burdens and responsibilities'. For David, being a member of the Royal Family isn't at all as glamorous as we would imagine – words like 'etiquette' and 'reputation' seem to follow him around. Could you describe a typical, regimented day in the life of Edward VIII?

In the morning Edward would be woken and attended by his valet, Frederick Finch. Edward liked Finch, but it would have been all the same if he hadn't. Finch hadn't been engaged by him and, if he had taken a personal dislike to him, he would have been unable to dismiss him. All his personal servants and equerries were chosen for him and he had to suffer them, whether he found them agreeable or not. As no one was his social equal his father, King George, decreed that he should allow no one, apart from siblings and cousins, the intimacy of friendship. It made for a lonely private life that no amount of public adulation could make up for. A typical morning would be spent travelling in the company of his equerry to a city where he was to lay a ceremonial cornerstone or plant a tree – a novel event for those attending the occasion, but a far from novel event for Edward. Lunch would be spent in the company of local middle-aged civic worthies and he would have to watch every word he said in order not to let his father down by appearing unsuitably light-minded. In the afternoon there would be a similar event at another venue and then, in the evening, there would either be a formal banquet – where he would again be seated between the middle-aged or elderly – or he would dine in near silence with his uncommunicative parents and the courtiers in attendance on them. Only with the advent of WW1, when he served as an army officer in France and Italy, did Edward begin to earn a reputation for knowing how to enjoy himself when on leave, his constant refrain being that he had to have a part of his life that was his own.

**Commitment to the family and familial obligation are very strong themes in *The Golden Prince* – both David and Rose especially, comment on duties to their family. Would you say that people today are family-centred, or like Rose, do they aspire to be free agents?**

Family is still of prime importance – but no longer to the exclusion of everything else. Until the battles waged – and were finally won – by suffragettes like Rose and those who thought like her, women had very little choice over the way their lives were lived. Now that there is choice, family and familial obligations revolve far more around the enriching word 'love', than that far chillier word 'duty'.

**As a 'pin-up idol', why do you think Edward was so popular?**

Edward became Prince of Wales and heir to the greatest throne in the world in 1911, an era in which pop idols were non-existent and in which the early film industry had not yet produced pin-ups. It was a void Edward, as handsome as a fairy-tale prince and imbued with the glamour of royalty, filled in a way that was, at that time, unique. He possessed the ability to touch people's hearts in the same way his great-niece-by-marriage, Princess Diana, was to do seventy years later. There was nothing cold, or stiff, or formal about him – and because he was a bachelor prince, young women world-wide could daydream of one day becoming his princess.

**Both your previous novels, *Enemies of the Heart* and *Palace Circle*, as well as *The Golden Prince*, explore the drama of high-society living. Will your next novel follow suit, or are you looking to research other areas?**

Though *The Golden Prince* concentrates on only a year in Edward's life it sets the stage for the book I am currently writing, *The Shadow Queen,* in which the main character is Wallis Simpson, the racy American woman who finally and forever won Edward's heart and changed the history of the British Monarchy.

**Who is your favourite author, and what is it that really strikes you about their work?**

Hilary Mantel. Her Man Booker prize-winning novel *Wolf Hall* is one of the most stunning evocations of a historical figure, Thomas Cromwell, and of another age, Tudor England that I have ever read.

Although Blue Ridge Summit nestled high in Monterey County's mountains, on June 19th 1896 no cooling breezes relieved the stifling heat.

In a holiday cabin attached to the small town's Monterey Inn, Alice Warfield was struggling to give birth to her first child. She and her husband, Teackle, were from Baltimore and were on an extended vacation in Blue Ridge Summit because of its reputation as a health spa and because Teackle was a consumptive. The plan had been for their family physician, Dr Neale, to travel out to Blue Ridge Summit in time for the birth. The baby, though, was uncaring of the plans made for it and when Alice had gone into labour seven weeks prematurely, the doctor hurriedly despatched from Baltimore was a newly graduated student of Dr Neale's, Dr Lewis Allen.

'We're nearly there Mrs Warfield!' the young man said now exultantly, sweat beading his forehead. 'Now when I say pant, pant as if your life depends on it.'

Through a sea of unimaginable pain, Alice panted.

'And now push! PUSH!'

Alice pushed and as above the bed the blades of a ceiling

fan creaked and whirred a red-faced squalling baby girl slithered into Dr Allen's hands.

'It's a girl!' His voice was charged with emotion, his relief that there had been no complications, vast.

An exhausted Alice eased herself up against sweat-soaked pillows. 'Oh, let me see her, Doctor Allen! Is she all right? Has she all her fingers and toes?'

As the baby kicked and squirmed in his hands, Dr Allen said in deep sincerity, 'She's perfect in every way, Mrs Warfield. In fact, she's fit for a king!'

'That is what the doctor said to your mama the instant you were born, Bessie Wallis, and as I said seven years ago to your dear-departed daddy, Dr Allen knew what he was talking about, for Warfields and Montague's – your Mama is a Montague – are two of Maryland's oldest most illustrious families and they have connections to British royalty and not many people can claim that distinction in Baltimore!'

Bessie Wallis loved hearing Grandma Warfield talk about how special the Warfields and Montagues were – though she didn't like being called Bessie Wallis and wished her grandmother would begin just calling her Wallis. Wallis had been her father's middle name, which was why she had been given it, and she much preferred it to Bessie.

'Bessie,' she'd said indignantly to her mother when she was five year old, 'is a cow's name.'

'You'd better not let your Aunt Bessie hear you say that,' her mother had said, vastly amused. 'And never say the word cow in front of Grandma Warfield or both of us will be in trouble.'

Her mother often spoke to her as if they were sisters and as if, where Grandma Warfield and Uncle Sol were concerned, they were somehow in secret collusion.

Uncle Sol was her dear-departed-daddy's elder brother. He

was a bachelor and he and Grandma Warfield lived together in a big tall house on East Preston Street. After her daddy had died, she and her mother had gone to live with Grandma Warfield and Uncle Sol and, though Wallis had always been a little afraid of Uncle Sol – and thought that her mother was also – she adored her grandmother.

Her grandmother was over sixty-years-old – so old Bessie Wallis could hardly imagine it. She had very white hair which she wore piled high on top of her head, and she always dressed in black. Bessie Wallis's mother told her this was because her grandmother was a widow and that she had never dressed in anything else ever since Grandpa Warfield had died a long, long time ago.

'Your Grandpa was one of the most illustrious men Baltimore has ever known,' her grandmother would say while, from behind her, Bessie Wallis's mother would roll her eyes to heaven in a way Bessie Wallis knew was very naughty. 'He was a very prominent member of the Maryland legislature and when the horrid Civil War broke out it was your Grandpa who was the first to call for the secession of Maryland from the Union. Never forget that. It is something for you to be proud of until your dying day.'

Bessie Wallis didn't know what a legislature was, or what secession meant, but she'd promised that she would always be very proud of Grandpa Warfield.

'Silly old crow,' her mother would say later when they were on their own. 'Maryland never did secede from the Union and all Grandpa Warfield got as a reward was a long, long time in a Union prison cell.'

That her grandmother and her mother didn't like each other was something Bessie Wallis had known for as long as she could remember. Her grandmother called her widowed mother flighty. Flighty was another word Bessie Wallis didn't understand, but she knew it was something not very nice simply from the way her grandmother said it. As well as sometimes calling Grandma Warfield 'a silly old crow', because of the way she always dressed in black, her mother also sometimes called her a 'pious old bat'. This was because Grandma Warfield insisted on family prayers every morning – prayers that even the household staff – cook, maids, butler, nurse and valet, had to attend.

Bessie Wallis didn't mind being up early for prayers because she liked to have plenty of time in a morning to get ready for school at Miss O'Donnell's in Elliott Street. She liked her hair to be shiny and her nails clean and she liked all the pencils in her pencil-box to have lovely sharp points.

'I've never known a child be so naturally clean and tidy,' her grandmother said often. 'You're a credit to the name of Warfield, Bessie Wallis – and that's because you come from true aristocratic stock.'

When Bessie Wallis was seven, something happened in the house at East Preston Street that she didn't understand. The atmosphere became tense and strange and one night when she was in bed she heard doors slamming and Uncle Sol's angry voice and then, most terrible of all, the sound of her mother crying.

In the morning her mother left Preston Street and, taking Bessie Wallis with her, moved into a residential hotel. Although Bessie Wallis didn't know the reason for the move, she did know that Uncle Sol was the cause of it.

Several months later they moved again, this time to go and live with Aunt Bessie. There was no early morning prayers at Aunt Bessie's and Bessie Wallis could tell that her mother was much happier living with her sister on West Chase Street than she had been at the residential hotel, or at Grandma Warfield's.

Her mother still took her to visit her grandmother, though.

This, she'd overheard her mother saying to Aunt Bessie, was because she had to 'think of Bessie Wallis's financial future' and because 'Bessie Wallis has an inheritance due her and I'm goin' to see that she gets it.'

Bessie Wallis didn't care about the reasons, she was simply glad that she could again sit on her little petit-point stool at the side of her grandmother's velvet padded rocking-chair and listen to stories such as the one about Robert de Warfield who, a long time ago, had been a friend of King Edward III of England and of how Robert had been so chivalrous and faithful in serving him that the King had made him a Knight of the Garter, which was, her grandmother had said, the highest honour in the whole of the kingdom.

Another of her favourite stories was of Pagan de Warfield who had lived even long before Robert de Warfield and who had accompanied William the Conqueror from France and fought beside him in the great Battle of Hastings. 'And just as Robert was rewarded for his chivalry, so was Pagan,' her grandmother had said with pride. 'He was given a grant of land near to Windsor Castle – the castle kings and queens of England still live in – and it was named Warfield's Walk in his honour.'

These stories of her long departed antecedents made Bessie Wallis feel special and different from everybody else and at school she made sure that everyone knew she was special and different.

She dressed as differently as she possibly could, wearing a green pleated skirt when all the other girls were wearing navy or black ones and, because her grandmother had also told her she was descended from the great Indian Chief, King Powhatan, sometimes sticking a feather in the back of her braided hair – a feather she was always asked to remove.

Another way she found of being different was in being cleverer than everyone else. Her homework was always meticulously done. In class, her attention never strayed. She was a star pupil, always the centre of attention, and that was how she intended things to remain.

The day when she was suddenly faced with a rival started out as ordinarily as any other day. She had left for school in Aunt Bessie's horse-drawn black victoria, sitting as her grandmother always sat; so upright her back didn't touch the upholstery.

There had been a chill in the air and as Ludo, Aunt Bessie's dappled-grey mare, trotted along the tree-lined streets, Bessie Wallis was grateful for the smart blue overcoat she was wearing. It had a matching velvet collar and velvet pocket flaps and though all the other girls in her class wore nice clothes – Miss O'Donnell's school was prestigious and expensive and only well-to-do children attended it – Bessie Wallis was certain no one else had a coat quite as nice.

She was still congratulating herself on this when the carriage came to a halt outside 2812 Elliott Street. Holding her schoolbooks and wooden pencil case neatly in the crook of her arm, Bessie Wallis stepped down from the victoria. They were to have an English history lesson that morning and she was looking forward to it. Though it hadn't happened yet, Bessie Wallis was always hoping Miss O'Donnell would one day mention brave and chivalrous Robert de Warfield, or illustrious and gallant Pagan de Warfield.

Five minutes later Miss O'Donnell rang her hand bell and all Bessie Wallis's fellow pupils scrambled into their seats. Bessie Wallis didn't scramble. She smoothed her skirt beneath her bottom before sitting down and then, with her feet neatly together, side-by-side, she waited in happy anticipation for her school day to begin.

'I have some special news this morning.' Miss O'Donnell looked very pleased with herself. There was a touch of colour in her normally pale cheeks; colour Bessie Wallis had never

451

seen there before. 'A new little girl will be joining our class later today. She is English and has only just arrived in America and so we must all try our very hardest to make her welcome.'

There were groans from the boys who felt there were enough girls in the class already.

'Please, Miss. What is her name, Miss?'

The question came from Violet Dix and Bessie Wallis rolled her eyes exactly as her mother often did. The Dix's were one of the city's oldest families, but Violet never could get it into her head that it was vulgar to address Miss O'Donnell merely as 'Miss'.

Miss O'Donnell said, 'The new girl's name is . . .' and paused dramatically.

It was then Bessie Wallis knew that whatever the name, it was the reason Miss O'Donnell was looking so pleased with herself.

'. . . is Lady Pamela Denby,' Miss O'Donnell finished with a flourish.

Clamour broke out as everyone in the class wanted to know why the new girl had such a funny first Christian name.

"Lady' isn't a Christian name,' Miss O'Donnell said when she could be heard. 'It's a title. Lady Pamela's father is an English duke. All little girls whose fathers are dukes are addressed as 'Lady'.'

John Jasper Bachman, who sat at a desk immediately in front of Bessie Wallis's, shot up his hand. 'And is that what we have to call her, Miss O'Donnell?'

Miss O'Donnell shook her head. 'No, John Jasper. Pamela's father has asked that in class and in the playground, Lady Pamela is known simply as Pamela. And now,' she said, 'we will spend a little time on multiplication and division and then, after break, we will have history.'

John Jasper's hand went up again. 'Please, Miss O'Donnell,

452

when will Lady Pamela – who isn't to be known as Lady Pamela but as Pamela – going to be arriving?'

'Sometime later this morning, John Jasper. And now please open your arithmetic books, copy down the sums I am going to write on the blackboard and then fill in the answers.'

For the first time ever Bessie Wallis found it hard to concentrate on what she'd been asked to do. Was the arrival in class of an English duke's daughter going to be an advantage to her, or a disadvantage?

In the break between classes, when Miss O'Donnell briefly left the classroom, everyone zeroed in around her; eager to point out that the new girl came from a far more distinguished background than she did.

'A duke is someone who is royal, or nearly royal,' Mabel Morgan, the class know-all said, happy at a chance to deflate Bessie Wallis's infuriating self importance, 'and that's a lot more than you are, Bessiewallis Warfield.'

By the way Mabel said her name, Bessie Wallis knew Mabel was running her Christian names together in a way she hated and she itched to slap Mabel's gleefully smug face.

'And though you pretend to be nearly royal, you ain't,' Violet Dix put in spitefully, abandoning the careful diction Miss O'Donnell insisted upon and remaining a step or two behind Mabel so that Bessie Wallis wouldn't easily be able to hit her. 'Worse than that, you and your ma ain't even got any money. My ma says the two of you live on rich relatives charity and that you wouldn't even be at Miss O'Donnell's if it wasn't that your Uncle Sol pays the fees.'

Bessie Wallis balled her fists and stepped forward with the intention of pushing Mabel out of the way so that she could get to Violet. Violet gave a scream and was saved as Miss O'Donnell walked in on them to announce that it was time for their history lesson.

Bessie Wallis seethed all the way through the first part

of the lesson, but when Miss O'Donnell asked suddenly, 'Who knows who tried to blow up the Houses of Parliament in London?' her hand went up immediately in order to answer.

Before she had time to do so, John Jasper beat her to it, leaping from his seat and yelling, 'Guy Fawkes!'

Bessie Wallis was so mad at him and her nerves so strained, she seized hold of her pencil-box and smacked him over the head with it.

The result was a half hour punishment of sitting outside the classroom in the corridor. It was a disgrace she had never experienced before, but it gave her time to think.

If Lady Pamela Denby became her friend – and her friend alone – then it would be to her advantage, for then everyone would see that Pamela recognised how well bred she, Bessie Wallis, was. It would be almost as if she was a duke's daughter also.

She chewed the corner of her lip, aware of a problem.

Whenever two girls became each other's best friend, it was always immediately obvious that one was much prettier – and sometimes even cleverer, too – than the other. If, as well as being a duke's daughter, Pamela Denby was pretty and clever, then she, Bessie Wallis, would fall into the category of playing second fiddle. And there was no way she was going to do that.

She thought of the odds of Pamela Denby being prettier and cleverer than she was, and decided they were practically nil. She thought of her chances of making Pamela Denby her best friend before Mabel Morgan, Violet Dix, or anyone else succeeded in doing so, and knew it was something she could accomplish as easily as she accomplished everything else she set her mind to.

The outer door opened and a draught of chilly air blew through the lobby and down the corridor.

Bessie Wallis was too deep in thought to pay any heed to it.

Lady Pamela Denby would be plain and dim. Making her her best friend – and being the dominant partner in the friendship – was going to be as easy as falling off a log.

Footsteps approached and Bessie Wallis turned her head.

'What on earth are you doing outside the classroom, Bessie Wallis?' the school secretary asked as she walked towards her, a girl Bessie Wallis's own age beside her.

Bessie Wallis had no need to ask the girl's identity.

There was only one person it could be.

'I was feeling a little faint.' She had no intention of admitting that she'd been sent out of the classroom in disgrace. 'Miss O'Donnell thought there would be more air out here than in the classroom.'

The amused expression in the girl's eyes – eyes that were a mesmerising sea green – showed that she, at least, didn't believe a word of her explanation and had guessed the real reason she was in the corridor.

Bessie Wallis was overcome by a feeling she'd never experienced before; the feeling that, for the first time ever, she'd met her match.

Though it was intuition that told her Pamela was fiercely bright, she needed no intuition at all to realise that Pamela was also jaw-droppingly beautiful. Her amazing coloured eyes were wide-set and thick-lashed. Her hair, caught at the top of her head in a large lavender bow, cascaded down her back in a river of waves and curls the colour and sheen of spun gold.

Before they had even spoken to each other, Bessie Wallis knew that Pamela Denby was the one person in the world she would never be able to get the better of.

'We're having a history lesson,' she said at last, when she

455

could trust her voice to be steady. 'It's about Guy Fawkes and how he tried to blow up the Houses of Parliament.'

Pamela grinned. 'That's good. Because I'm English I know all about kings and queens.'

What she couldn't know, as the school secretary ushered the two of them into the classroom, was that for as long as she lived her life would be inextricably intertwined with Bessie Wallis's and that though for the most part they would be best friends, they would also sometimes be enemies.

Beyond her imagination was that though both of them would marry kings – only one of them would be a queen.